THE INCREDIBL[E] DOC ATLAS

The Doc Atlas Omnibus

For Lydia —
soon you'll be
signing your book
for me. :)

Michael

THE INCREDIBLE ADVENTURES OF DOC ATLAS

The Doc Atlas Omnibus

By
Michael A. Black
And
Raymond L. Lovato

Cover and Doc Atlas Emblem by Geof Darrow
Illustrations by Tim Faurote and Matthew Lovato

Oak Tree Press   Taylorville, IL

Oak Tree Press

Oak Tree Press books may be purchased for educational, business or sales promotional purposes. Contact Publisher for quantity discounts.

First Edition, October 2011
Cover by Kurt Bredt
Interior Design by Linda Rigsbee
Cover and Doc Atlas Emblem by Geof Darrow
Illustrations by Tim Faurote and Matthew Lovato

ISBN 978-1-61009-025-4
LCCN 2011933060

Dedication

Mike's:
For Tom and Ginger Johnson

Ray's:
For Susan, who never stopped believing.

Foreword

Heroes

SINCE TIME IMMEMORIAL, our world has been filled with the astounding tales of Heroes: from fictional heroes like Hercules, Tarzan, Indiana Jones, and James Bond to real life heroes like Davy Crocket, Elliot Ness, Audie Murphy, and the men of Seal Team 6.

So, who is Doc Atlas?

The simple answer: he is a hero for the ages. Years ago, my best friend Mike Black and I began tossing around ideas about the old pulp magazine characters we came to admire so dearly. We wondered how their great adventures would have played out had they been conceived mixing today's sensibilities with the drama of that era. What resulted was Doc Atlas. He is a fleshed out tribute to those pulp heroes who began in the early 1900's and reached their heyday in the 1940's. Doc Atlas is truly a Hero for his Age. It was as if Scottish essayist Thomas Carlyle was describing Doc Atlas when he wrote, "Heroes are clear-sighted men; their deeds, their words are the best of the period."

Doc Atlas is a hero in the classic mold of the pulp adventurer: scientist, independently wealthy, inventor, surgeon, explorer, a man of action who has dedicated his life to the protection and betterment of mankind. A globe trotter who spends his days locked in battle with the vilest forces of evil ever conceived. In his adventures he is assisted by his two ex-military colleagues; Lieutenant Colonel Thomas "Mad Dog" Deagan and Captain Edward "Ace" Assante. Both were close friends and companions of Doc's father, a scientist-adventurer of the first order in the early years of the 20th century. Also along for the ride is Penelope "Penny" Cartier, a reporter who can hold her own in a scrap and has an eye for our taciturn hero.

The stories are also written with the benefit of historical hindsight that was not available to the original pulp writers. Historical figures and events wind their way through the adventures of Doc Atlas. Doc Atlas also differs from many of the pulp era's archetypal heroes in that his tales are grounded in reality, infused with human emotions, passion and pain. He is the melding of modern day angst with stoic, old fashioned heroics. He is a man aspiring to be the perfect hero in an increasingly complex world. Doc Atlas has dedicated his life striving to stay one step ahead of the modern evils spawned by World War II and the Atomic Age, continuing in a heroic tradition while the world changes so very quickly around him. Trying to be the hero whom Carlyle described as, " ... true to his origin. A Hero can be a Poet, Prophet, King or what you will, according to the world he finds himself born into."

Lastly, where did a hero like Doc Atlas come from?

As with every great and complex man, he is the sum total of his youthful experiences. In Doc's case, he owes a debt of gratitude to Andrew Black, Michael's father and one of the greatest men I have ever known. An inveterate reader, Mr. Black passed down Western, Sci-Fi, Detective, and Ace Pulp reprints to two little boys who have been best friends since they were six-years old. Both being born on Halloween, we began a life-long tradition of trying to outdo each other with unique birthday gifts every year.

One year my gift was the first ever chapter of a Doc Atlas' World War II adventure: *Doc Atlas: His Master's Voice*. Chapter One ended with a cliff-hanger. Mike tore through the wrapping paper searching for what came next, but, alas, no more pages followed! It was a mischievous trick on my part; one of many he has endured in our adventures together. Mike grumbled and complained for 365 days until Chapter Two arrived on the next Halloween.

Of course, this chapter concluded with another cliffhanger. What followed were continuous threats of severe bodily harm made by Mike unless the novella was finished in its totality. So, one year later, the entire *His Master's Voice* was presented on Halloween. But Mike had not been sitting idly by. He had a surprise of his own. That same year he presented me with the complete *Melody of Vengeance*, his own grand tale of Doc Atlas and his comrades.

And a Hero was born.

Several Doc Atlas novellas have appeared in various neo-pulp magazines and anthologies in the intervening years, during which time Mike and I have continued to explore various plots and ideas for the characters. Now, five of these novellas have been collected in this one volume. They exemplify the best of heroic adventure tales for all ages. So sit back and enjoy the adventures of Doc Atlas as he battles to overcome perilous death traps, uses his remarkable skills to save countless lives and vanquish vile villains. I am extremely grateful that, after all these years, I am still able to share in the plotting, research, story ideas, and the unbridled excitement of these breathtaking adventures with my oldest and truest friend.

Welcome to the world of Doc Atlas.

Raymond Lovato
Rancho Mirage, California   2011

Table of Contents

The Riddle of the Sphinx

Special thanks to Arthur C. Sippo, M.D., M.P.H., F.A.C.P.M.
for his assistance

Yucatan peninsula, Mexico, Monday, September 22nd, 1947

ARTHUR GUFFREY SHONE the light from his portable lamp over the inscriptions on the wall once again. He couldn't help giving in to the impulse to rub his fingers slightly over the chiseled hieroglyphics, especially the one that had made his heart leap as soon as he'd seen it. It was amazing that after all these years he had finally found the vindication he'd been searching for— evidence that proved their theory beyond a shadow of a doubt. Now he'd show them. He'd show all of them. Some grit clung to his fingers and he rubbed them together, studying it. Then he heard Audrey's voice call to him from farther up the tunnel.

"Father, are you coming?" she asked. "It's beginning to get dark."

"I'll be along shortly," Guffrey said. "Just want to try to make a few more notes."

"But we'll have the photographs for that."

He noticed the persistence in her voice and thought how much it reminded him of her mother. She never cared about his penchant for poking around in old dank tombs either. But now it had all come full circle.

Now he finally had the indisputable facts. He sighed, regretting that his late wife would not be able to witness his vindication and greatest triumph.

"You go ahead, dear," Guffrey called. "I'll be along in a few minutes. You just take that film to be developed immediately."

He heard her "Oh, Father" exclamation as her footsteps grew fainter. Good, she was gone. He took out his notebook and made some more preliminary sketches in the dim light of the portable lamp. The face of the Sphinx-like figure seemed almost to stare back at him as his gaze rose again to the wall.

"Why have you suddenly appeared, my ancient friend," Guffrey said aloud, "giving me another riddle to solve?" He examined his fingers again, then wiped them on his pants.

He heaved a long, slow sigh and closed his notebook.

Perhaps it was time to go up to the surface, he thought, shining the weakening lamp on his wristwatch. But as he turned, he heard the first sounds of the scraping noises. Stones rubbing against stones, and then he felt the rumble beneath his feet. He held the lamp up at arm's length so it shone directly down the mouth of the tunnel. The light at the end was fading from view, as if someone were drawing a dark curtain across the entranceway. Guffrey felt the surge of panic and he tried to force his obsolescent legs to sprint down the stone pathway. But before he could manage to take one step he felt the hand on his shoulder, and the room was plunged into total blackness.

New York City, early afternoon, three days later

The tall, blond man stood with his hands clasped behind his back as he looked out the bright windows on the 87th floor of the sumptuously furnished library. A folded telegram lay on the polished mahogany table a few feet behind him, and the man turned his tawny colored eyes on it. His face had a chiseled, handsome look to it, although it seemed completely devoid of emotion. The powerful sweep of his shoulders and arms made his physical prowess obvious, even in the expertly tailored brown business suit that he wore. His eyes moved to the door and moments later it opened as three people, two men and a woman entered. The woman, whose dark-hair hung around her shoulders in a soft, curling wave, was strikingly beautiful. Her head tilted slightly back with laughter. The man on her left, was tall and handsome, with carefully combed brown hair and a well-trimmed mustache. Impeccably dressed, he carried a long, finely crafted cane, as he walked with a barely noticeable limp. He looked amazingly like Errol Flynn. He was laughing as well. The other man was shorter and older than either of them, but powerfully built. The sleeves of his garish sport jacket were pulled tight over huge biceps and his large hands protruded from each cuff.

"Very funny, Ace," the shorter man said, wiping at his face with a handkerchief. "Very funny."

"My pleasure," Ace said, nodding to the man by the window. "I was just showing Mad Dog here my new carnation, Doc." He stuck his hand in his pants pocket and suddenly a misty spray shot from the flower on his lapel.

The woman giggled again, and Thomas "Mad Dog" Deagan, the shorter man said, "Aww, come on, Penny. It ain't that funny. What if he'd a done it to you?"

"And ruin my makeup?" Penelope Cartier said. "Ace knows better than that."

"Indeed I do," Ace Assante said, making a show of gallantly pulling a chair out for Penny to sit down. He glanced up and asked, "What's going on, Doc?"

The tall blond man pointed to the folded paper on the table and turned back to the window. Assante glanced quickly at the others and unfolded it and spread the paper out flat on the table top for everyone to read.

TELEGRAM: WESTERN UNION
TO DOC ATLAS, EMPIRE STATE BUILDING, 87th FLOOR, NEW YORK CITY, USA
FROM MISS AUDREY GUFFREY, SANTA MERIDA, MEXICO
NEED HELP STOP CONCERNS RIDDLE OF THE SPHINX STOP FATHER MISSING STOP NO ONE ELSE CAN HELP STOP PLEASE COME IMMEDIATELY STOP

AUDREY

Assante's brow furrowed as he looked at the others who seemed as baffled as he.

"What's this all about, Doc?" he asked. "And I don't understand this reference to the Riddle of the Sphinx."

As Doc Atlas turned toward them, the sunlight streamed in through the windows backlighting his powerful torso. "Professor Arthur Guffrey was a former associate of my father," Doc said. "At one time he was a world-renowned archeologist specializing in Egyptian artifacts and studies."

"I recall reading about him before the war," Assante said. "He was known as a man who was outstanding in his field."

"Yeah, I remember seeing him standing out there, too," said Deagan. "Only I didn't know it was his field."

Penny burst out laughing and smacked Deagan playfully on the shoulder while Assante shot him a scowl.

"Your dad was quite the expert in that stuff, too," Deagan said.

"He was at that, Thomas," Doc said, smiling briefly. "And at one time he and Dr. Guffrey were close friends."

"Is that where this Sphinx business comes in?" Penny asked.

Doc nodded. "I'm sure you all are aware of the Riddle of the Sphinx. What is the only animal who walks on four legs in the morning, two legs at midday, and three legs in the evening?"

Deagan scratched his head. "Don't sound like no animal I ever seen."

"You idiot," Assante said.

Penny laid a hand on Deagan's arm, smiling.

"It's supposed to be a reference to the different ages of man," she said. "A baby, a mature adult, and an older person."

"With a cane," Assante said, holding his up and twisting it to show the razor-sharp blade housed within. "Care for me to sharpen your wits a bit?"

Doc went to the chalkboard on the far wall and began writing.

"As you know, the traditional belief is that the Sphinx, as well as the pyramids, were built around 2520, B.C., during the reign of Khafre, as a self-tribute to the pharaoh. My father went on an expedition to Egypt in 1939. He was accompanied by Professor Guffrey. Together they explored the tomb of King Fhatid. My father and Professor Guffrey were friends at the time."

"At the time?" Ace said, giving Doc a questioning look.

"They had a falling out shortly thereafter," Doc continued. "Upon their return to New York with their artifacts, Guffrey became associated with a certain radical theory espoused by a charlatan named K. C. Edgar."

"I've heard of him," Penny said. "Don't they call him the Sleeping Prophet, or something?"

"The Transcendental Prophet," Doc said. His lips twitched with a hint of a smile. "I believe Edgar's unofficial title was carefully fashioned by him to deflect scrutiny of his theory that the Sphinx was built long before the reign of Khafre." He wrote another date on the board. "In fact, Edgar theorized that its origin predated the construction of the pyramids. In 7000 BC."

"Were the Egyptians that advanced of a civilization then?" Penny asked.

Doc shook his head. "It's dubious, but in Edgar's vision the Sphinx wasn't created by them." He drew a symbol on the chalkboard. It looked like the face of the sphinx with a star-like aura around it. "He credited its creation to the pilgrims from the lost city of Atlantis."

"Huh?" Deagan said.

Assante shook his head. "It's unbelievable that someone would believe that malarkey, much less an educated man like Professor Guffrey."

"Hey, I dunno," Deagan said. "I seen this movie serial once about Atlantis. They was supposed to be pretty far advanced."

"Oh Mad Dog, come on," Penny said.

"As I said," added Assante. "Only a moron would subscribe to such tripe."

"Regardless of the worth of the theory," Doc said, interceding in his group's customary good-natured banter, "it caused the aforementioned rift between Dr. Guffrey and my father. They never spoke again. Guffrey always blamed my father for not supporting him publicly. He lost his affiliation with the museum, and subsequently his job at the university. His wife died soon thereafter, and Guffrey took his young daughter with him searching for proof of the theory."

"Old K.C. Edgar seems to be making a living off it," Deagan said.

"He preys upon the weak minded," Assante said, tilting his cane toward Deagan's head. "Perhaps you'd like to join his flock?"

"Keep that fancy stick away from me or I'll take it and shove it—"

"Thomas," Doc said in a quiet tone. "Will you see to the preparation of the Athena?"

"Sure, Doc."

"And see that it's fully fueled. I've estimated the quickest route will be to fly over the Gulf to the Yucatan peninsula." He looked at Assante. "Ace, can you file the necessary flight plans? I would like to leave this afternoon. We'll probably need to refuel again in Houston."

Assante nodded as he got up.

"I'll need time to pack," Penny said, standing up and grabbing her purse.

"Unfortunately, you won't be accompanying us this time," Doc said.

"What? You can't keep me away from a story like this," she said, placing her hands on her hips.

"There's been an outbreak of smallpox in the area, Penny," Doc said. "It's far too risky for you." He walked over to her.

"But what about you guys?" she said.

"We've all been vaccinated," Doc said. "You have not."

"You weren't vaccinated?" Ace asked.

Penny shook her head quickly. "My parents didn't believe in it."

"Well," said Deagan, slapping his left shoulder. "Our Uncle Sam did, before we went overseas during the war."

Ace raised his eyebrows and affected a sad-looking smile as he nodded.

"Hey I sure hope that Audrey gal doesn't get the pox," Deagan said. "I remember that time I met her back when she was a kid. She was a real sweetie."

"She signed the telegram Audrey," Ace said. "Do you know her well, Doc?"

"We've known each other since childhood," he said, "although she is five years younger than I."

"Bet she had a crush on you, too, huh?" Deagan said, grinning.

Doc said nothing.

"Where can I get vaccinated?" Penny asked, looking worried.

"Come on," said Doc. "Let's go to the laboratory. I've already prepared one for you."

"Then I *can* go with after all?" she asked.

Doc shook his head. "I would want you to stay for at least 72 hours to assure that the vaccination had developed the proper antibodies. I'm afraid we can't afford to wait the necessary time."

"This just isn't fair," Penny said, pouting. "You guys get to have all the fun. Not to mention the great story I'll be missing out on."

"Aww, don't worry none," Deagan said, laying a commiserating palm on her arm. "I'm sure Ace here will take a lot of notes for you so you can still write your article and then one of them pulp novels where you always make me look like the monkey's uncle."

"If anything is written to depict you as closer to your hirsute origins," Ace said caustically, "I'll be glad to assist. Though I'd hardly call it a novel."

Santa Merida, Mexico, Seventeen hours later

Doc and Deagan stood in the hot, dry air and stretched as Ace negotiated with the owner of the small airfield. Displaying a smile interspersed with glints of shiny gold, he gladly agreed to watch Doc's plane for the rather generous offered price. He smiled again as he looked over at the silver metallic body of the big DC-4 gleaming in the early morning sunshine. After having flown all night, Deagan and Assante looked and felt exhausted. Only Doc appeared unaffected, although he'd spent nearly all his time at the controls, spelled only occasionally by Ace.

"Make sure you tell him half now and half when we get back," Deagan said, wiping his face with a handkerchief.

"What kind of fool do you think I am?" Ace shot back.

"I ain't gonna answer that one," Deagan said, grinning broadly. "Let's just say it's a good job for a mouthpiece."

Assante looked at him sternly for a few seconds then turned back to the Mexican and began talking again in rapid Spanish. Doc looked on, monitoring the conversation, but letting Ace do all the talking. Although he was fluent in several languages, including Spanish, it was Doc's customary preference not to demonstrate to others that he could speak and understand their languages.

"He says that won't be a problem," Ace said.

The Mexican's eyes grew large as Doc removed a large roll of Pesos from a brown money-belt and counted out the agreed-upon amount.

"Ask him where we might rent some vehicles to travel to the interior," Doc said.

As Assante began the new inquiries, Doc turned to Deagan.

"Thomas, make sure the Athena is properly secured and bring each of us sidearms," he said.

"Gotcha, Doc," Mad Dog said, ambling toward the plane.

Ace continued his discussion with the other man, who was leaning over his desk drawing a map of sorts.

Assante straightened up and showed the paper to Doc.

"He says we can probably rent some motorcycles at this place," Ace said. "It's doubtful whether we'll be able to find any cars that would make the trip. I asked him about the area near Santa Merida. It's rather mountainous with heavy foliage. There's a macadamized road that goes there, but it's very dangerous."

Doc nodded.

"Tengo cuidado, senor. La caretera es muy peligroso," the man said. "Hay muchos bandidos alla."

Just then Deagan walked up and handed Doc a Colt Government Model forty-five and a holster. The Mexican's eyes widened. "What'd he say, Ace?" Deagan asked.

"He said to watch out for bandits," Ace said with a grin.

Deagan smiled too, as he pulled out the forty-five and chambered a round. "Well, we got plenty of *bandidos* where we come from, too, partner," he said, trying his best to imitate John Wayne. "In fact, a lot of times we eat 'em for breakfast."

* * *

The vehicle shop turned out to be little more than a run-down looking barn composed of rotting wood and ill-fitted corrugated aluminum sheets. The owner spoke, sitting under the shade of an overhang, fanning himself as he continued to sweat profusely. Finally, after several minutes of sometimes heated conversation, Ace turned back to Doc and said, "He says he only has two motorcycles available for rent at this time."

Doc surveyed the area beyond where the man sat, which was littered with automobile parts of all shapes and sizes.

"Very well," Doc said. "Tell him we'll look at them."

With that decided, the man rose ponderously from his chair and motioned for them to follow. He led them through a fenced-in area and through stacks of boxes. At the end of the aisle the man pulled a large canvas tarp that had been spread across two Army model 841 Indian motorcycles, one of which had an attached sidecar. Both of the machines looked to be in good condition.

Deagan let out a low whistle, running his hand over the white star on the gas tank.

"Wow," he said. "This is swell. I ain't had my keister on an Indian since 1939."

The man said something in Spanish to Ace, and grinned.

"What'd he say?" Deagan asked.

"Believe me, you don't want to know," Ace said. He turned to Doc and told him the price. Doc reached in his money belt and removed the roll of bills again.

"Come on, Ace," Deagan said. "What did this guy say about me?"

Assante smiled and shook his head. Doc paid the man and went to the motorcycle with the sidecar.

"It seems two of us will have to use this one," he said.

"Ha," Deagan said. "And I know who it ain't gonna be." He turned his thumb toward his chest.

"Ask him the way to the local constable, Ace," Doc said. "I want to check on the status of Professor Guffrey before we leave."

Ace spoke to the man again as Deagan went over to the other motorcycle and ran his hand over the curve of the gas tank.

"She's a beaut, Doc," he said. "Good condition, too. How about we take her with us when we leave? I'll pay you when we get back to New York."

Doc smiled. "We'll see, Thomas." He punched the kick-starter as Ace came back over to them.

"Okay, I got the directions," he said, then turning to Deagan, added, "You really want me to tell you what that guy said before?"

Deagan nodded.

"He asked if your short legs would reach the pedals," Ace said, grinning.

"What?" Deagan snorted. "Pedals?"

Ace laughed as he held his hands out, palms up. "Hey, Mac, I'm just the messenger."

"Oh yeah?" Deagan said, marching over to the Mexican whose large grin began to fade as he saw the advancing American. The man started a quick trot down the aisle with Deagan in steady pursuit. Doc called out to him, but Deagan continued until Ace shot by him on the motorcycle, waving and laughing. Deagan's lower lip drew up and overlapped his upper, and he removed his hat and threw it on the ground. Doc pulled up next to him on the motorcycle with the sidecar.

"The man really said, 'Looks like your friend likes it,'" Doc said.

"That dirty son of a. . ." Deagan began to say, looking in Assante's direction.

"With Ace's leg the way it is," Doc said, strapping his goggles in place, "it might have been problematic for him to assume the rather cramped position in the sidecar, Thomas." Deagan seemed to consider this for a moment, then nodded, getting into the truncated seat without further comment as he, too, slipped on a pair of goggles.

The town was a ramshackle collection of buildings and houses. Most of them were one story brick stucco with ornately tiled roofs. A few of the more prestigious institutions, like the bank and the jail, were solid brick, but the main road bisecting the small hamlet was unpaved. As they rode down the dusty street, following Ace's clearly visible tracks and residual dust cloud, crowds of small children rushed to look at them and point.

When they got to the constable's office, Ace was already in a heated conversation with two men in uniform. One of them was large and very obese. He had captain's bars on his starched cap, but was wearing a sweat-soaked tee shirt. The other man was smaller and wore a tan shirt. It, too, was soaked through with sweat, and on the sleeves were upside-down sergeant's chevrons. A tag on his shirt above his left pocket said GARCIA. The heavy man sat down in a chair in the shade and began fanning himself with some papers.

Deagan gave Ace a dirty look as he and Doc dismounted, but said nothing. Ace came over to them looking rather drawn.

"I'm afraid I might have rubbed the local constabulary the wrong way," he said pointing to his side. "They took my gun away."

"Leave it to a lawyer," Deagan said.

The obese man glanced at them and said something in a low voice.

"*Senores*," the sergeant said. "*El capitan* requests that you surrender your firearms immediately."

"Listen, bub," Deagan said. "I ain't gonna give up my——"

Doc gently laid a hand on Deagan's shoulder, while at the same time removed his own weapon and handed it toward the policeman.

"I assume we will get receipts to reclaim them upon our return?" he said.

The little sergeant withdrew the sleek black-barreled Colt from the holster and held it up, smiling.

"Ah, it is a beautiful *pistola, senor.* I will be very happy to hold it for you."

"Just don't forget the receipt, pal," Deagan said, handing his gun over as well. The sergeant holstered Doc's weapon and carried them both inside.

"Have you asked about Professor Guffrey?" Doc asked.

"Yes, he has, *senor,*" the large man said. "I am *Capitan* Cruz. The daughter of the *profesor* has already made a report about his absence."

"I see," said Doc. "And has your investigation yielded any more information as to his whereabouts?"

Captain Cruz canted his head and smiled slightly.

"*La senorita* is very worried," he said. "But some of my men went with her to search the ruins and the area. I told her that her father must have wandered off in the jungle."

"La selva es muy peligroso," Sergeant Garcia said, coming back through the door with a paper. "Here is your receipt, *senor.* You may pick up your *pistolas* when you leave Santa Merida."

"Thank you," Doc said. "Has anyone from the camp been in town today?"

"*Si, el profesor egipcio* and his *guia,*" Garcia said, pointing to the building across the street. An open-topped jeep sat in front of the building, which had a peeling yellow sign with black letters that said *TIENDA, MERCADO Y TELEGRAMAS.* A swarthy looking man with dark eyes and hair pulled back into a ponytail sat in the front seat eyeing them. He was carving a piece of wood into some sort of totem with a long, flat knife. Several small children watched in awe as he finished the carving, held it up, and tossed it to them. The children fought over the gift, until one emerged victorious and ran off with the others in hot pursuit. The man spat in the dust and began cleaning his fingernails with the knife.

Doc turned to the Captain and asked, "Do you have any theories on Professor Guffrey's disappearance?"

Cruz licked his lips before he spoke. "You know, like my *sergento* told you, the jungle, it is a very dangerous place." He sighed heavily. "My guess is that he became confused and wandered off. It is my hope that some of the natives found him."

"Natives?" Doc asked.

"*Si.* There are *muchos indios* who live around the ruins," Cruz said. "They are a very secretive people. It is *posible* that they are caring for him in one of their remote camps. My men are checking daily for any news. But," he shrugged and shook his head, "to be quite honest with you, the longer it goes. . ." He left the sentence unfinished.

"I see," Doc said. "Could you please spread the word that I'm offering a substantial reward for any information leading to the safe return of the Professor?"

Cruz raised his eyebrows. "And how much would that be, *senor?*"

"Let's say, fifty thousand pesos."

Garcia let out a low whistle and grinned. "*Senor*, you offer that kind of *dinero*, I will go out looking for the body of Cortez himself."

Doc looked across the street at the shop and saw another man exiting with two locals carrying a large box of provisions. The man was short and heavyset, with a rotund physique, looking rather soft in the middle. He was as darkly complected as the man in the jeep, but he did not have the look of a Mexican. The two local men placed the boxes in the back of the vehicle, and the short man got in. The two men held out their hands as he tossed them a few coins. The swarthy man in the driver's seat said something to them in a low, guttural voice. The dialogue continued, out of earshot of Doc and company. The man in the jeep jammed the knife into a leather sheath on his belt and snarled something at the two men. They both looked across toward the jail, then hurried off.

Doc strode across the street toward the jeep, the man behind the wheel eyeing him carefully. The high cheekbones and obsidian eyes suggested more than just a trace of Indian blood, Doc decided, as did the silver and turquoise-stone necklace the man wore.

"I'm Dr. Michael Atlas and these are my associates, Misters Deagan and Assante," Doc said, holding out his hand. "Are you by chance with the Guffrey expedition?"

The driver ignored Doc's outstretched hand, but the smaller man immediately got out and rushed around to shake it. Doc noticed flecks of gray in the man's black hair and mustache.

"Ah, yes, Dr. Atlas," he said, placing his other hand on top of Doc's as well. "I am Dr. Mohammed Rabbat, Professor's Guffrey's partner. We met some time ago in my country, Egypt. This is our local guide, Carlos. We were just in picking up supplies and checking to see if there'd been any word from you. I'm surprised you were able to get here so quickly."

"Professor Guffrey was a friend of my father," Doc said. "Is Audrey here as well?"

Rabbat steepled his fingers and grunted slightly.

"I am certain that she would have made the trip had she known you were arriving," he said. "But she has seldom left the encampment since her father's disappearance."

"There's been no news?" Doc asked.

Rabbat shook his head sadly. "We've searched the ruins several times, thinking that he possibly got trapped in an unexplored room. But it is as if he simply vanished."

"What about the Captain's theory that he's lost in the jungle?"

Rabbat's breath hissed out in a derisive rush.

"Ah, that man has already made up his mind that the Professor will never be found," he said. "His efforts to assist us have been ludicrously inefficient."

"Well, Doc just sweetened the pie a bit by offering a reward," Deagan said. "Money talks, especially south of the border."

Rabbat looked at him with a grim smile. "I'm afraid, sir, that we have already tried that ourselves. It has met with little success."

"Perhaps it would be beneficial for us to see the area where Professor Guffrey disappeared," Doc said. "Can you show us the way to the camp?"

"Of course," Rabbat said. "If you will follow us?"

He went around and got in the jeep. Doc exchanged glances with the man behind the wheel. Carlos pressed the starter button, and the jeep's engine sputtered to life.

Ace turned quickly to check Deagan's whereabouts, but saw Mad Dog already cramming himself into the sidecar.

"You look good in there," Ace said as he walked to his motorcycle.

"Don't push it," Deagan said. "I'm still taking that thing for a ride before this is through."

"Not if I can help it," Ace said, snapping the starter with his boot.

Rabbat told them the ruins were perhaps 15 kilometers southeast of the town. "The road is passable almost all the way," he said. "We will wait for you at the juncture where the trail to the ruins begins if you wish."

Doc nodded.

"You will perhaps not wish to ride too closely behind us," Rabbat said, smiling and showing a set of small teeth inlaid with gold. "The dust can be very unpleasant."

Doc adjusted his goggles as they watched the jeep pull away. Deagan looked up from the sidecar, "That guy kind of reminds me of a fat Peter Lorre. Professor Rabbat, huh? You ever heard of him?"

"Only by reputation," Doc said, kicking the starter. "But I wasn't aware that he subscribes to the K.C. Edgar theories. Still he's considered one of the preeminent Egyptologists in the world today."

"Another guy who's outstanding in his field, huh?" Deagan said, pulling his goggles down and slapping the top of the sidecar. "Man, this thing was made for a man half my size."

At the outskirts of the town they passed some women squatting by a stream washing clothes. More groups of half-naked children came to watch the progression of vehicles as they passed. Perhaps thirty yards beyond the last buildings the foliage began to swell up with a scattering of dwarf-like trees and rows of cactuses. The farther inland they went, the more verdant the landscape became. Rabbat's jeep was a hundred yards ahead of them leaving a cloudy turbulence in its wake. Doc backed off the accelerator slightly creating more distance and keeping the speed under thirty miles per hour. Ace pulled up along side and shouted at Deagan.

"How you enjoying the trip?" The sandy dust covered the lower portion of his face and his mustache.

"I used to ride sidesaddle when I was in the army," Deagan said. "But it was hard to find a lawyer to do my driving in them days."

Doc smiled at the banter as he scanned the road ahead. The jeep rounded a turn, and suddenly something whipped sinuously across the dusty surface like a big serpent. It took Doc a split second to realize what it was, and he immediately cut the handlebars to the right, steering toward Ace's motorcycle. Deagan looked up as the two vehicles abruptly veered toward a near collision, then he heard Doc yell, "Thomas, duck!" With that said, the golden avenger jumped upward and out of the seat of his motorcycle, traveling over the top of Deagan in the sidecar, and plowing into Assante.

Reacting instinctively to Doc's warning, Deagan hunched forward. Doc simultaneously grabbed Ace, ripping him completely off his bike, then spun in midair so that when they landed on the rough surface seconds later, Ace's thinner form was spared much of the impact. Ace's motorcycle twisted onto its side and began rotating in a circular motion for a few seconds as the rear wheel continued to spin. Doc's motorcycle continued forward, slowing to a stop. Deagan hopped out and began running back toward his two fallen partners when he was abruptly knocked backward with a violent jerk.

"What the?" he started to say as the first shot rang out. Doc was already up on his feet, carrying the unconscious Assante on one shoulder and scrambling towards the now fallen Deagan.

Another shot whizzed past Doc's head and he dipped slightly to his side, brushing the ground with his left hand for balance. He reached Deagan with two more hurried steps and grabbed him by the collar, using his momentum to push all three of them into the thick shrubbery alongside the roadway.

Deagan began scrambling along in a low crouch as Doc released his collar.

"Was that what I think it was?" he asked in a hushed, breathless tone.

"Piano wire," Doc said, not bothering to add that he'd seen the wire rising from the dirt moments after the jeep had passed. They heard voices off to their right.

Deagan accepted Ace's still limp form from Doc and continued thrashing through the underbrush, muttering curses as he was attacked by a myriad of thorns and cactus needles. Doc quickly withdrew two small sphere-like objects from the back of his money belt and angled off to the right. More voices filtered toward them. Doc flattened out as he heard the sounds of at least two men approaching.

"Fueron alla," one of the men said. He held a large revolver with an extended barrel at his side. The other man, who was holding a similar weapon, grunted and began pushing some stray branches out of their way as they moved forward.

Doc twisted the first sphere with a quick, deft motion, then rose to his knees. With a powerful and accurate throw, he sent it hurling toward the two men, clipping the first man between the eyes. The man was obviously stunned, but the second man caught Doc's movement and grinned malevolently as he raised his pistol.

"You throw stones, huh, hombre?" he said. "Now you die."

But before he could fire, a terrific explosion erupted, sending both men flying pell-mell through the sea of undergrowth as a result of the concussive wave. Doc, who had immediately flattened and covered his ears after tossing the miniature grenade, rose quickly and shot forward. Both assailants were dead. He retrieved their weapons and checked the cylinders. One pistol had two rounds expended; the other still had a full load. Placing the fully loaded weapon in his belt, Doc moved forward with the second one held in front of him. Moments later he heard a voice yell in Spanish.

"Manuel, que paso?" the voice said. "Que causa la explosion?"

The third man came through the bushes holding a long barreled pistol in one hand and an army walkie-talkie in the other. His eyes looked sinister under a red bandana that had been tied over the top of his skull.

"Halto," Doc said, leveling his pistol at the man. "Suelte su arma."

But instead of heeding Doc's command to drop his weapon, the man began to raise the pistol and aim it. Doc squeezed off two shots striking him in the chest and the forehead. He was dead before he hit the ground.

* * *

As the cloud of dust from Rabbat's jeep began to dissipate, the five men stood along the side of the road and looked at the three bodies. Doc had placed them in supine positions on the ground.

"When we heard the explosion," Dr. Rabbat said, "we immediately turned around. We never imagined. . ." He let the sentence trail off as Carlos went over to the first body.

"Bandidos," Carlos said, using his boot to raise the limp head of the dead man.

"Allah be praised," Dr. Rabbat said, steepling his fingers. "As I said, we never imagined they would dare attack you, Dr. Atlas. We've gone to and from the town so many times without incident."

"Do they look at all familiar?" Doc asked.

"I saw them back by la tienda," Carlos said. "They must have seen you take the dinero out of your belt."

"Obviously you seen it, too," Deagan said, scowling.

Carlos looked back at Deagan with a vapid expression, his dark eyes shining like obsidian.

"I must say," Dr. Rabbat said. "I find it simply amazing that you were able to subdue your assailants with such aplomb. You must have been in the military, yes?"

Doc nodded.

"And those miniature explosives," Rabbat said. "May I see one?"

Doc glanced at the Egyptian momentarily, then removed one of the two remaining spheres from the special pouch on his belt.

"Amazing, simply amazing," Rabbat said, rolling it in his hand. "And you activate it how?"

"It requires a certain amount of manual dexterity," Doc said, pointing to the clearly marked sections, "but you merely twist the halves in opposite directions. The delay fuse is approximately four seconds."

"Then boom," Deagan said, flipping his huge hands up in an explanatory gesture.

"Ingenious," Rabbat said, carefully handing the sphere back to Doc. "It is little wonder that you were able to prevail."

"We've been in a lot tighter spots than this," Ace said, grinning.

"Whaddya mean 'we?'" Deagan asked. "If it wasn't for me and Doc carrying your limp keister all over these damn woods, you'd a been back there wearing a French necktie."

"A French necktie?" Rabbat asked.

"That's what we used to call 'em in the War," Deagan said.

"The French resistance used to stretch piano wire across the road at throat level to decapitate Nazi motorcyclists," Ace said. "Say, Doc, we'd better report this little encounter to the authorities. Especially since they made such a production out of confiscating our weapons."

"That is not necessary," said Carlos. He spat on the nearest corpse. "As I told you, these men are bandidos. No one cares if they live or die. There is no need to notify la policia."

"Just the same, the incident needs to be reported," Doc said. He turned to Dr. Rabbat. "Would you mind if we used your jeep to transport these men back to town?"

"But of course," Rabbat said. "But I would prefer to deliver the supplies to the camp first." He glanced at Carlos. "They will surely be going nowhere, eh?"

Carlos smiled.

"Very well," Doc said. "We'll proceed to the camp. Then you and Thomas can go back to speak to the authorities, Ace."

Assante nodded. His head swiveled around as Deagan began walking across the road toward the fallen Indian motorcycle.

"Hey, where do you think you're going with that?" Ace said.

"Nowheres," Deagan said, picking up the motorcycle and righting it by using only one arm. He looked at Ace and held his hand out in a magnanimous proffering gesture and grinned. "At least not yet, anyway."

* * *

The road wound sinuously through the ubiquitous forest for a few more miles, at which point the jeep turned left down a secondary dirt road. This road seemed well traveled, but recently cut bushes hung limply on each of the edges. It was as if a caravan of laborers had just finished hacking the path through the dense vegetation. Ahead of them Doc and the others saw a huge pyramid-like structure rising above the canopy of trees in symmetrical fashion. The tapering pattern of the rich brown bricks narrowed to a flat peak, dwarfing the verdant forest. The closer they got, the more immense the structure appeared. Suddenly rows of stone walls sprung up on either side of the road, along with a series of smaller buildings in various stages of dilapidation. Much of the construction had been done with heavy limestones, although the buildings seemed to have been fashioned out of the same brown bricks as the pyramid.

A small encampment of perhaps a dozen tents scattered among the ruins came into view, with several stacks of wooden crates in between them. Two men, obviously both local natives, stood at the edge of the road with rifles. As they saw the jeep they perked up. Doc saw Carlos stop and talk with the men, gesturing and pointing. Then he turned back toward Doc and waved.

As they drove past, the sentries came to attention and saluted, then collapsed into a mocking laughter.

"I'd like to take those rifles away from them and show them what to do with 'em," Deagan muttered from the sidecar.

Doc pulled to a stop beside the jeep and dismounted.

"Is it necessary to have armed guards here?" he asked Dr. Rabbat.

"Ah," the other man said, smiling somewhat sadly. "Unfortunately, there is a contingent of rather unfriendly natives in the region. Mayan descendants. Although they have not caused us any unpleasantness, they hold these ruins to be very sacred. The guards are perhaps our insurance that we will be allowed to complete our excavation unmolested."

"Michael, thank God you've come," Doc heard a female voice say. He turned in time to see Audrey Guffrey running from one of the nearby tents. Her long auburn hair trailed behind her like a reddish flame. She was in her late-twenties and voluptuously built. Deagan gave out a low whistle as she literally threw herself into Doc's arm, pushing her head onto his powerful chest.

"Hey, she makes Rita Hayworth look like your grandmother," he said to Assante.

"Now I'm really getting worried," Ace shot back. "We've found something we agree on."

The Guffrey girl's sobs were quieted by Doc, who ushered her off to one of the tents, keeping his arm around her waist in an avuncular gesture. They went inside the tent, and moments later Doc emerged and went back to Deagan and Assante.

"I need to confer with Audrey at this time," Doc said. "You two go back to town and report the confrontation with the bandits to the police."

"Roger-wilco, Doc," Deagan said. "And this time, I'm taking the Indian."

"Over my dead body," Ace said, smiling.

"Hey, that can be arranged," Deagan shot back with an equally broad grin.

"Ask Dr. Rabbat's man to accompany you," Doc said. "He seems to have a thorough knowledge of the countryside." He pointed to an old army truck with a canopy parked near the adjacent tents. "Perhaps both of you had better ride in that with Carlos. It should offer more ballistic cover than a motorcycle, and it's dusk now. It will surely be dark upon your return." Doc smiled. "And it might be problematic trying to carry three corpses on the motorcycles."

Deagan snorted and the smile faded from Assante's face. But both men trudged wearily over to the truck. Doc went back to the tent and stepped inside. Audrey Guffrey sat on one of the two cots, the mosquito netting pushed to one side, her face in her hands. She looked up at Doc, and he saw the twin trails of tears streaming down from her eyes.

"Oh, Michael," she said. "I'm so afraid for Father. I just know something terrible has happened to him."

Doc sat down on the cot across from her, removing his handkerchief and holding it toward her.

"Please, tell me everything," he said. "Start at the beginning and leave nothing out, no matter how insignificant it may seem."

* * *

Meanwhile, early evening in New York City

The artificial lighting glowed in the morgue office of the New York Times as Penny's nimble fingers sped through the files marked "G, for Guffrey." She had already found numerous articles on the distinguished accomplishments and discoveries of Professor Arthur Guffrey. She'd even found one detailing the famous Egyptian excavation that involved Doc's father, as well as another article describing the bitter feud that had developed shortly thereafter. Neither disturbed her as much as the scrawled handwritten notation at the bottom of the card saying: See society page, 06-10-41. Audrey Guffrey escorted to Radcliff graduation dance by son of Dr. Victor Atlas.

It couldn't be Doc, could it? she wondered, rapidly searching the files for the society section. Not her Doc escorting some other woman to a dance?

Penny reached the end of the files in the folder and tossed it aside, immediately digging into the next one.

Ah, relax, she told herself, trying to conjure up a laugh. She's a bookworm. Some professor's daughter. Majored in anthropology, for crying out loud. Probably looks like Elsa Lanchester in *The Bride of Frankenstein*, only with glasses.

She pursed her lips and blew some errant hairs away from her face. The itching resumed again on the burgeoning scab on her left shoulder, and she rubbed her fingers gingerly over the Band Aid.

Yeah, she thought. Real thick glasses. Doc was probably ordered to do it by his father, and he probably hated every minute of it. I'll bet he was bored out of his mind.

And then she found the file marked SOCIETY, and popped it open. The stunning picture of Doc in a tuxedo, smiling, and the gorgeous creature next to him, her head tilted back in a half-laugh, half-smile, her full lips parted ever-so-slightly, the sensual curving sweep of her breasts beneath the elegant evening gown, made Penny's heart skip a beat.

No, this wasn't fair, she thought. That can't be her. It isn't possible. Her fingernail traced the caption under the photo and she dreaded each word as she read it.

> *Dr. Michael G. Atlas, son of prominent scientist and inventor, Victor Atlas, and Audrey S. Guffrey, daughter of renowned archeologist Arthur Guffrey, seem oblivious to the well-publicized feud between their fathers and they make a great couple at the Radcliff graduation dance. Miss Guffrey plans to begin a course of study to become a physician, just like her escort, Dr. Atlas.*

A great couple, thought Penny. That settles it. I'm going to Mexico if I have to beg, borrow, or steal my way down there.

* * *

Doc placed the last picture down on the cot and was about to speak when he heard the honking. Audrey looked up at him with a perplexed expression.

"It must be my associates returning earlier than expected," Doc said. He stood and flipped open the tent flap in time to see the beat-up old army truck pulling into the encampment. Carlos was at the wheel, but Deagan was leaning over pressing the horn.

Doc strode over to the vehicle as Ace and Mad Dog piled out.

"Hey, Doc, guess what?" Deagan began.

"A problem with habeas corpus," Ace said.

Deagan frowned. "We went back to find them bodies and take 'em to town like you told us—"

"But they were gone," Ace said, finishing the sentence.

Deagan shot him another disparaging look.

"Any idea who might have taken them?" Doc asked, directing his gaze toward Carlos.

The man shrugged slightly and spat in the dirt.

"I don't know," he said. "Maybe it was some of the big jungle cats. Panteras. There are many of them in this area."

"Huh?" Deagan said. "Some cats drag off three bodies?"

Carlos smiled slightly. "Senor, you haff never seen our cats."

Deagan frowned.

"What do you want us to do now, Doc?" he asked.

Doc seemed to consider this for a moment as he looked around. The sky was already beginning to darken.

"What time does the local constabulary's office close?" he asked Carlos.

"We might be able to find them at la taberna local," he said.

Doc looked at him, and then to Ace, who translated, "The local tavern."

"It's getting dark," Doc said. "Perhaps the matter can wait until morning."

"Swell," Deagan said, rubbing his hands together and pointing toward the center of the encampment where a man was placing a pot on a grill over a large campfire. "I don't know about the rest of you, but I'm getting pretty hungry."

"Dangle the thought of a banana in front of a gorilla," Ace said, smiling at Audrey while pointing to Deagan, "and he'll forget the task at hand in favor of satisfying his baser instincts."

"I got some basic instinct for ya," Deagan said, balling up his fist.

"Are you two always like this?" she asked, a faint smile tracing her lips.

"Nah, we're usually a lot worse," Deagan said. "But it's good to see those pretty eyes of yours smiling. You might not remember me, but we met way back when you was just a kid. You see, I've known Doc and his father for a long time."

"I'm sure she remembers her first trip to the zoo," Ace said, stepping up and looping her arm through his. "Come, let us depart to the dining area for some civilized conversation."

"You two get along as well as Fred Allen and Jack Benny," Audrey said, smiling.

As the trio moved away, Doc studied Carlos. The man's eyes followed Audrey momentarily, then snapped back toward Doc, as if some preternatural instinct had told him he was being watched. A hint of smile twitched at his lip.

Doc nodded and began walking toward the campfire.

Deagan was already pointing to the carcass of a bird roasting on a spit. "What is it, bud?" he asked. "A chicken?"

The cook shook his head and furrowed his brow. Ace started to speak, but Audrey said something in fluent Spanish and the Mexican smiled and nodded.

"Pavo salvaje," he said. "Y frijoles."

"Wild turkey and kidney beans," Ace said. "In case you're interested."

"Oh, you speak Spanish, Mr. Assante?" Audrey asked.

"Please, call me Ace," he answered with a dashing smile. "All my friends do."

"And I won't tell you what else we call him," Deagan said with a grin. He clapped his hands together and rubbed them vigorously. "Say, fellas, after we eat, what do you say to a little game of five card stud?"

The group of Mexicans looked perplexed.

"Hey, Ace," Deagan asked. "How do you say poker in Spanish?"

Ace smiled and said, "Mi amigo dice que necesita los articulos de tocador."

The cook, who was standing over the simmering pot, looked at Deagan with a frown and pointed to the edge of the forest.

Deagan's brow furrowed. "Huh? What's over there?"

"I'm afraid that's not an accurate translation, Mr. Deagan," Audrey said, smiling. "Your friend told him you needed to go to visit the latrine."

Deagan scowled at Ace and said, "I shoulda known better. . ."

"Is that what I said?" Ace grinned and shrugged. "My Spanish is a little rusty."

Audrey laughed and quickly added, "But we'll hardly have time for card games, I'm afraid. We'll have to prepare some sleeping quarters for the three of you as soon as possible. You'll need mosquito netting, or you'll literally be eaten alive."

Deagan slapped his forearm.

"Yeah, I did notice them little critters," he said. "Seem to be getting worse now that the sun's going down."

"They can be unbearable," Audrey said. "I have some insect repellent in my tent."

"You don't need to worry about me, none, ma'am," he said. "I spent enough time in the infantry to be able to sleep just about anywheres. And as for mosquitoes, they couldn't be no worse here than they was in the Philippines, right, Doc?"

"Wasn't that where you caught malaria?" Ace asked caustically.

"Well, at least I made it over to both theaters, buster," Deagan said. "Instead of playing Mr. Fancy-pants lawyer in Europe after the dirty work was done."

"Hey, it was my bombing runs that helped end that dirty work, remember?" Assante said.

"Do you have a spare tent we could use?" Doc asked.

Audrey nodded as she turned to Doc. "Michael, you might as well sleep in my tent. Father's bunk is empty and I'd feel safer with you close by."

Doc nodded slightly, showing no emotion.

Deagan shot a quick glance at Ace, then raised his eyebrows.

"Your two friends can stay in that one," she said, pointing to a tent to the left. "The men who were using it left unexpectedly today."

"Oh really?" Ace said. "For what reason?"

"Indios," Carlos said, suddenly stepping over to the stew pot and sipping from the ladle. "They were afraid of los indios after the professor desaparece."

Deagan looked grimly at Ace, and then at Doc. The big Mexican's words needed no translation.

* * *

"So what ever happened to your plans to attend medical school?" Doc asked Audrey as they walked down the pebbled trail toward the large pyramid.

"Well, I finished my nursing courses," she said, turning her face to smile at him. "But I felt compelled to go with Father on an expedition. The next thing I knew, we were traveling to another location. And then another." She looked down. "I'm sorry I wasn't there for you when your father died."

Doc nodded.

"But at least you caught the men responsible, right?" she said. She pointed to the entrance that was only about twenty yards away. "Perhaps it gave a sense of justice or closure?"

Doc shook his head. "Justice is often elusive. Closure perhaps even more so. It's given me some solace to try and continue his work in certain areas."

Audrey led them down the intricate tunnel, her portable lamp bouncing over the rough stone walls as she walked. The passageway was capacious, perhaps measuring seven feet by twelve. Doc was close behind her, his lamp held steady, followed by Deagan, Assante, and Dr. Rabbat. Deagan started to whistle until the dust from the earthen floor rose up to his face. He coughed a few times and stopped.

"Now I finally understand the significance of Buck's *The Good Earth*," Ace said.

Audrey turned to Doc and smiled slightly, but it was a tense smile. "It veers to the left just up ahead," she said. "I was right about here when he called to me."

Doc nodded, his chiseled features seemed unperturbed, but also cognizant of everything. He directed the beam from his lamp toward the ceiling and walls as they walked. The corridor narrowed to about six feet across. Doc and Assante had to stoop a bit as the ceiling slanted downward slightly as it met with solid looking rocks ahead. Audrey turned to the left and as they followed they saw that the corridor had expanded back to its normal spacious width.

"The room is down here," she said. "About thirty more feet."

The beam of her light swept over another set of pillars crossed by a heavy stone lintel. It obviously led to another, larger space.

"Wait until you see it, Dr. Atlas," Rabbat said. "It will convince you beyond a shadow of a doubt."

Doc said nothing, but merely followed behind Audrey, pausing periodically to touch the sides of the corridor.

As they passed between the pillars the passage opened into an enormous room with high ceilings and two enormous segmented support beams in the center. Doc estimated that they were near the center of the pyramid. Audrey shone her light over the walls, which were covered with intricate hieroglyphical markings depicting cryptic figures and symbols.

"There," Professor Rabbat grunted, his light centering on a leonine body with the flaring crown and humanoid face on the opposite wall. The figure was surrounded by a seven-pointed star. "You are familiar with the Pyramid of Khafre, are you not? This carving is virtually a mirror image of the Sphinx. You will notice, too, the crescentic flourishes around the edges of the surrounding star. . . The positioning of this symbol above the others. . . Everything points to its significance." His voice became almost animated with excitement. "It is just as it was described in the prophesies of K.C. Edgar. Professor Guffrey had been very excited about its discovery. He called it the Western Sphinx. It is believed to be the first such hieroglyph of its kind found on this continent."

Doc moved forward to examine the wall. He held his beam near the intricately carved figures.

"Exactly when did you become familiar with this theory, Professor?" Doc asked.

"Several years ago. In my country."

"Is that when you met Dr. Guffrey?"

"Why, no, it is not," Rabbat said. "Actually, we met for the first time here. But we had corresponded previously. I was familiar with his endorsement of the Atlantis theory, and contacted him." Rabbat continued speak in a rapid excited voice.

"It is the theory of K.C. Edgar that the Sphinx is much older than the pyramids themselves, having been built by the original ancestors of the lost continent of Atlantis," he said. He moved over and traced his fingers across some drawings on the adjacent wall. "You see here, this obviously depicts a large body of water, does it not?"

Deagan and Assante moved forward to study the section.

"Looks like it could be just about anything to me," Deagan said.

Professor Rabbat's head jerked as if he'd been slapped. He shone his light over another section. "But, if you please, look here. This is most definitely an homage to Horas, the Serpent King of the monument at Abydos."

Deagan's features scrunched up and he squinted. "I'd say it's a bird. Seen quite a few of 'em on the way here, too."

"I'm starting to get worried again, Doc," Ace said. "Mad Dog and I are agreeing on something again."

Rabbat huffed loudly.

"But the prophecies predicted the discovery that the two cultures would be ultimately linked." Rabbat's hand fluttered as he spoke. "Surely you cannot dismiss all of the theories of a man of such genius," he said. "Why if we had the time, I would gladly give you a lecture on just how many of his prophecies have indeed come to pass."

"Yeah?" Deagan said. "Don't forget the Nazi's were great for quoting that one old French guy that it was prophesized that they were gonna win the War, too. What was that old frog's name, Ace?"

"Nostradamus," Assante replied. "But like most prophets, the accuracy of their predictions is almost always directly proportional to the skill and artistic license of the person who interprets them."

"Leave it to a lawyer to resay in twenty words what I said in ten," Deagan said.

"I've seen enough," Doc said, turning and heading out of the room. "We must get back to camp and get some rest. We'll explore this further tomorrow."

The others glanced at each other briefly, then turned to follow him.

* * *

The hushed tones of the voices carried to him over the incessant chirping of a myriad of insects and Doc immediately snapped awake. He didn't move, but began to soak in the surroundings with all of his senses: Audrey's soft breathing on the cot to his left, the heavy humidity that seemed to encompass everything like an invisible blanket, the ubiquitous insects. . .

And then he heard it again, and the chirping stopped. It was a grunt of pain followed by more hushed tones. Doc's arm swept upward to push away the mosquito netting and he moved his legs cautiously off the cot. He reached for his boots, tapping each one at the heel and turning it upside-down before inserting his foot and lacing it tightly. Deagan had always called it a "scorpion check" when they had been on their special missions in the Philippines.

Doc stood and glanced down at the still slumbering Audrey before refastening the netting around his cot and noiselessly slipping out of the tent. The air was silent, which meant that the insects were still in a heightened state of alert. He proceeded in the direction he'd heard the last noises, moving quietly through the ruins toward the base of the pyramid.

Another muffled grunt of pain floated toward him, followed by the harsh, whispering voices: at least two disparate tones, both of them familiar.

"Do not incapacitate him to the point where he cannot tell us where it's at."

It was Rabbat.

"Shut up. I know what I am doing."

Carlos, Doc thought. Then the same voice continued in a language that was totally foreign, full of harsh sounding clicks and fricatives.

"Ask him," Rabbat said. "Ask him about the idols."

Doc's fingertips gently pushed aside a few leaves so he could survey the three figures without revealing himself. Professor Rabbat stood off to one side while Carlos held a small, slumping figure by the back of the shirt. The third person was slightly built, with long hair braided into a ponytail, and his arms were bound securely to a stick wedged horizontally across his back. His clothes were in tatters, and his bare feet were tied to a hobble fashioned from some rough looking rope. The dark head drooped toward his chest, but shot upward and emitted a sharp cry of pain as Carlos stepped around and hit him in the stomach, saying something in the strange, guttural language.

Doc could see that the captive was young, no more than a boy in his teens. He pushed aside the branches and stepped forward.

"What is going on here?" he asked.

The heads of both Carlos and Rabbat twisted toward him in surprise. Doc held them in a steady gaze.

"Why, Dr. Atlas," Professor Rabbat said nervously. "How did you come upon us?"

Doc did not answer. Rabbat's face jittered slightly before he continued.

"We didn't hear you approach. You startled us."

"Obviously," Doc said. He gestured toward the captive. "Who is he?"

"Un asesino," Carlos said, reaching his right hand down by his belt. "I caught him sneaking around our camp." His right hand came up with his long-bladed knife and he raised it to the boy's throat.

"He is from one of the local Indian tribes," Rabbat said quickly. "We were questioning him about the disappearance of Professor Guffrey. I'm convinced this man knows the whereabouts of our friend."

"Man?" Doc said. "He looks more like a boy. And if he is a criminal, he should be turned over to the authorities, not beaten and tortured."

"But we have no time," Rabbat countered. "The Professor's life is at stake."

"I will make him talk," Carlos said, pressing the sharpened edge of the blade against the flesh. The metal glinted in the moonlight as a few drops of blood seeped over the shiny surface. The boy hissed in pain and terror.

Doc moved forward and seized Carlos's wrist. The muscles of the other man's arm tensed up, but the knife slowly was pulled away from the boy's throat. A thin slash, trickling crimson, was now visible under his Adam's apple.

"Let me go, yanqui, or I will keel you," Carlos spat through clenched jaws, his lips curled back from his teeth in a feral snarl.

"Not with this," Doc said. He extended his thumb up over the back of the other man's right hand and twisted, causing Carlos's fingers to immediately open up. The knife slipped from his grasp. Doc caught it with his free hand, but continued the pressure.

"Release him," Doc said, exerting enough force to put Carlos on his knees. He grunted, but complied, freeing his grip on the boy's torn shirt. Doc held the wrist immobile for a few seconds more. The boy looked at them, his dark eyes darting from figure to figure, then he tried to run for the thicker underbrush at a quick sprint. Doc's boot stomped on the dragging loop of the hobble and tripped the boy before he could get two steps. Rabbat's features distorted into a grimace.

"Atlas, you fool," he said. "You almost let him get away."

Doc released his hold on Carlos and allowed the man to get to his feet.

"Give me back my cuchillo, senor," Carlos said, rubbing his wrist with his left hand.

"I think not," Doc said. He flipped the blade into the air, catching it by the tip. He then turned abruptly and threw the knife with incredible force at a tree several yards away, burying it almost to the hilt. "Perhaps by the time you can work it free, you'll have cooled down."

He looked into Carlos's angry dark eyes momentarily and then turned and picked up the fallen Indian boy. He started back to camp with the boy in tow.

"If we're in danger of attack," he said over his shoulder, "we should post some guards. My associates and I will assist."

* * *

Doc gently shook Deagan awake, and then Ace. Both men had been in the deep sleep that sheer physical exhaustion brought, but did their best to shake off their fatigue. Doc held a finger to his lips to indicate silence, then pointed to the boy.

"Looks like we got company," Deagan whispered.

Doc held up his backpack. He removed one of the pistols that they'd taken from the slain bandits and handed it to Ace. Then he removed his wireless signal transmitter and a small portable generator. They moved with practiced stealth out of the tent and into the bushes.

Doc quickly surveyed the area, then leaned close to his two friends. In hushed tones he explained their objectives.

"Ace, you watch the base. Thomas and I will climb to the top." He indicated the captive. "Keep your eye on him, too. He may know the whereabouts of Professor Guffrey."

Ace doubled the rope of the hobble around his left fist while holding the pistol in his right. They all began a careful and quiet trip toward the pyramid with Doc in the lead. It took them perhaps ten minutes to reach the stone base. Doc paused and held up his fist to indicate a stop. He spoke with subdued deliberation again.

"We can't risk any lights being seen here. Ace, I suggest you take up a position over there." He indicated a dense patch of shrubbery. Ace nodded and moved toward it with the boy. Doc turned to Deagan.

"Thomas, use caution on this ascent," he said. "These steps are particularly hazardous."

"Gotcha, Doc," Mad Dog said. "I'll follow your lead."

Doc adjusted the backpack and began moving up the steps of the pyramid. Each one was about eight inches high, but only five to six inches deep. The slant of the structure made the upward climb possible, but tedious. Doc moved on all fours, and Deagan followed suit, but not at Doc's fast pace. Several times Doc had to slow and wait for the shorter man to catch up to him. Finally, after several minutes of hard work, they reached a flat section on top of the massive, man-made formation.

Doc quickly slipped off the backpack and removed the generator and wireless. He handed the generator to Deagan.

"Give me a minute, will ya, Doc," Deagan said, his breathing coming in gasps. "Too many of those Havana stogies."

Doc nodded and took the generator back. After attaching the wires, he set the transmitter on the surface in front of Deagan and began twisting the handles of the generator himself.

"I'll do this portion, Thomas," he said. "If you'll send the code."

Deagan nodded. "Shoot," he said.

Doc spun the handles around in alternating circles, creating the necessary current to power the transmission. As he did this he dictated the message that he wanted sent. Deagan's nimble finger pecked out the words in Morse code with expert acuity. When they had finished Doc continued to spin for power while they waited for an acknowledgement. When it came moments later, Doc released the handles and let them slow to a stop. He and Deagan sat under the black velvet sky as he repacked the equipment in the backpack.

"Man, this is high," Deagan said. "I'll bet you could see almost to Mexico City in the daytime, huh?"

"Probably not too likely," Doc said.

"Hey, Doc, why do you think they built something like this way out in the middle of nowhere?"

"Most likely as a tribute to some Mayan king," Doc said. "A tomb to house a deity."

"Tomb? You mean there's somebody buried inside this thing?"

Doc nodded, and he heard Deagan's laughter in the darkness.

"Hey, Doc, I just thought of something. Who'd a thought that you and me would be up on top of the world's tallest tombstone in Mexico, sending a message that my girl Polly's gonna read in New York later today?" He laughed again, and said, "It's too bad we'll never be able to thank him for the use of his oversized abode."

Doc allowed himself a rare smile before they began their descent.

As they reached the bottom Doc saw Ace emerge from the brush with the captive Indian in tow.

"Hey, Doc," Deagan asked. "What we gonna do with that guy?"

Doc considered this for a moment, then said, "Ace and I will watch him. He has a wound that needs attention. Thomas, I need you to go guard Audrey's tent, but don't wake her just yet."

New York City, Several hours later

Penny watched as Polly St. Clair, Doc's chief secretary, finished the last of her soup and wiped her lips with the napkin.

"Thanks for taking me to lunch, Penny," Polly said. "I was really famished, and it's been a while since we got to catch up on our girl talk."

"Don't mention it," Penny said, lighting a cigarette and blowing the stream of smoke away from the table. "So have you heard anything from Doc?"

"Yeah. In fact, he sent one of his coded messages last night." She patted her folder.

"Really? Well, what did he say?" Penny asked.

Polly smiled. "You know he doesn't like me to talk about anything, but I guess he wouldn't mind you knowing. He's asked me to check on some Egyptian professor. I've got to finish the research and send him a reply at midnight tonight."

"What?" Penny asked. "You mean he's somewhere close to a telegraph office?"

"No," Polly said, placing her fingers on Penny's arm. "Doc maintains a network of ham radio operators and telegraph offices all over the country. Pays them a stipend to monitor our emergency frequency in case he needs to contact me about something." She picked up her cup and drained the last of her coffee. "Say, that reminds me. I have to send out some checks before the end of the month."

Penny looked at Polly before speaking, then asked, "Did Doc say anything about meeting an Audrey Guffrey down there?"

"Audrey? You know about her?" Polly said, her eyes widening.

"What is it I'm supposed to know?"

"Just that her and Doc were," she paused and shrugged. "Childhood friends, I guess."

Or childhood sweethearts, Penny thought.

Polly stood. "I gotta go powder my nose. You want to come along?"

"Nah," Penny said, picking up her own coffee cup. "Let me finish this first." She took another drag on her cigarette as Polly grabbed her purse and moved away from the table. As soon as she had disappeared, Penny quickly stubbed out her cigarette and flipped open the folder. She paged through several sheets until she found it.

POLLY, NEED YOU TO CHECK ON THE CREDENTIALS AND WHEREABOUTS OF A DR MOHAMMED RABBAT, PROFESSOR OF EGYPTOLOGY FROM THE UNIVERSITY OF CAIRO. WILL MONITOR FREQUENCY FOR A REPLY AT MIDNIGHT TONIGHT. PLEASE EXPEDITE. THOMAS SENDS HIS REGARDS.

DOC

Thomas sends his regards, Penny thought. Isn't that sweet. Wonder why he didn't even tell her to say hello to me? She flipped the folder shut with a slam just as Polly came out of the ladies' room.

Penny stood and took two bits out of her purse, plunking it on the table for the waitress. Polly looked at her as she reached the table.

"Guess lunchtime's over, huh?" she asked.

"Yeah," Penny said, grabbing the check. "I got an appointment with my editor."

* * *

Lou Stoner sat behind his desk with his hands clasped on the crown of his head. The huge cigar in his mouth glowed as he alternated prodigious puffs with equally prodigious draws. He cocked his head and glanced at Penny who was standing in front of him.

"Look, kid," Stoner said. "I can sympathize with you wanting to go down Mexico way to see your boyfriend, Atlas, but every time I go out on a limb for you on one of these wild goose chases, it ends up getting sawed off."

Penny placed both of her hands on his cluttered desktop and leaned forward. His eyebrows perked up at the sight of the lacy edges of her brassiere, which was suddenly visible due to the top two buttons of her blouse being undone. Penny acted as if she hadn't noticed it.

"I mean," Stoner said, "I'm all for romance, but. . ."

"Look, boss, romance has nothing to do with it," she said. "There's a story here, chief. I can smell it."

"Ah, I dunno," Stoner said, releasing his hands from his head and swiveling forward in his chair. He looked away and puffed on his cigar.

"This has something to do with the disappearance of this guy Dr. Guffrey," Penny said. "And some Egyptian professor named Rabbat. I got that much."

Stoner tapped some ash into the tray, and glanced at her again. She leaned forward some more, causing the loop of her blouse to droop considerably.

"Anyway," she continued, "Doc wouldn't have sent a secret message to his headquarters in the middle of the night unless something big was brewing. If you let me look into this, we can scoop every paper in town."

"I dunno," Stoner said, his gaze narrowing on the lacy edges and spilling cleavage before him.

Penny's gaze seemed to follow his, then she quickly straightened up, placing her palms over her breasts and opening her mouth in a look of total shock and embarrassment.

"Mr. Stoner!" she said, quickly fiddling with her buttons. "Why didn't you tell me my blouse was undone?"

She turned around, hoping that something akin to a crimson blush would creep up her neck.

"I . . . ah, I'm sorry," Stoner sputtered. His cigar sent a spray of ashes into the air in front of him as he reached for a pad of papers inside his desk drawer and quickly signed one. "Here," he said. "There's your damn travel voucher. Go down to payroll and get the advance money you need. Then go ahead and take off to pack."

"I already am packed," Penny said, snaring the voucher as she still fiddled with the last button. She smiled and said, "Thanks, Boss."

Worked like a charm, she thought on her way out.

The Yucatan, mid-morning

The eastern sun crept upward in the sky, casting the section of the ruins in shadow. Audrey watched as Doc carefully removed the bandage and examined the wound on the boy's throat while Deagan held the Indian's arms. They had untied his upper body earlier, but he still wore the hobble. Doc reached into his backpack and removed a tube, squeezing some cream onto his fingertips and applying it to the wound-site.

"It's a good thing he doesn't need stitches," Audrey said. "In this primitive wilderness, there'd be no one to remove them."

"This anti-bacterial ointment should prevent infection," Doc said.

"But Doc has these neat disposable stitches he uses, too," Deagan said. "They just disappear on their own. Used 'em on me a couple times."

"That's hardly a ringing endorsement," Ace said with a grin.

Deagan frowned. "Actually, Doc has all kinds of inventions. A camera that develops the picture by itself, a small radio receiver we can wear on our belts, special goggles so you can see in total darkness. . . All kinds of stuff. Ace gets patents on all of them for him."

"If Doc wasn't already rich," Assante said, "he would be."

Audrey smiled and looked up at Doc.

"Have you retained your nurse's training?" Doc asked.

"As many times as I've been in the field?" she said. "You bet."

"Then could you apply the bandage, please? I want to repack my kit." He stooped and began replacing his equipment.

Audrey moved forward and cut a swath of gauze.

"I didn't know you was a nurse, Audrey," Deagan said.

"Actually, at one time I was planning to go on to medical school," she said, and affixing the gauze with tape to the boy's neck.

"Why didn't you?" Deagan asked.

She smiled winsomely. "Too many trips around the world with my father, I suppose." Her gaze shifted to the ground. "If only I knew what happened to him. Where he was. . ."

"You think this guy knows something?" Deagan asked, applying a bit of pressure to the Indian's arms.

The boy grimaced.

"Thomas," Doc said. "You can release him now."

Deagan looked surprised, but complied. The boy jumped away and stared at them with a wary expression, his dark eyes finally centering on Doc.

"Do you speak any of the Mayan dialects?" Doc asked Audrey.

"Only a few words," she said. "My father taught me some. But Carlos does. Should I find him?"

Doc shook his head. "I don't completely trust Carlos." He removed his knife from its sheath, and knelt, cutting the rope restricting the Indian's feet. The dark eyes flashed in amazement, but instead of fleeing, he merely nodded and began working the knots around his ankles loose.

"Do you know the word for 'father'?" Doc asked.

Audrey shook her head "I'm not sure I could pronounce it even if I did."

"Perhaps you have a picture of your father then?" Doc asked.

Audrey reached inside her heavy khaki blouse and removed a small locket that was suspended around her neck by a delicate gold chain. She popped open the clasp and held it up displaying facial photos of a man and a woman. "My parents," she said.

Doc took the chain from her neck and held the locket toward the Indian boy.

"We are looking for this man," he said, pointing to the picture of Professor Guffrey. "Have you seen him?"

The Indian looked at the picture, but gave no indication that he understood. Doc pointed again, then gestured at the surrounding jungle questioningly.

The Indian appeared contemplative for a moment, then stood up, dropping the unknotted ropes. He looked again at Doc, who made a gesture indicating the boy was free to leave.

"We letting him go, Doc?" Deagan asked.

Doc nodded.

The boy started to run, then stopped, looking to see if they were pursuing him. When he saw they weren't, he stopped and looked at them again. Finally, he pointed to his neck, and gestured for them to follow. They followed him to the base of the pyramid entrance.

"We going inside, Doc?" Deagan asked.

Doc halted and looked around. There was no sign of Carlos, Rabbat, or any of the other men.

"We may have prying eyes," Doc said. "You and Ace stay here by the entrance." He took a thin, but extremely powerful flashlight out of his utility belt. The Indian boy went inside and Doc and Audrey followed. The boy led them down the same pathway to the room with the high ceiling.

He began gesticulating and speaking Mayan. Doc swept the beam of his flashlight over the walls, but could make little sense of the boy's words. He shook his head.

"If only we knew what he was trying to tell us," Audrey said.

Doc moved forward and pointed to the Sphinx-like figure.

The Indian stared at it intently, then his lips curled back in and he said something. He motioned for them to follow, and left the decorated room. Instead of heading in the same direction they'd come, he turned and proceeded down a passageway that went deeper into the pyramid.

"When did your father become associated with Professor Rabbat?" Doc asked.

"He contacted us about three months ago in New York," she said. "He was familiar with my father's series of articles, and mentioned the discovery down here that seemed to tie them together. We came almost immediately."

The boy paused in front of them and spoke quickly. He pointed toward the wall, and then past them in the direction they'd just come. Doc and Audrey looked behind them as a grinding rumble enveloped them. Doc brought his flashlight up in time to let the bean sweep up over a slab of stone that was moving out in perpendicular fashion from the wall, blocking the passage.

"Oh, my God, Michael," Audrey said. "What's happening?"

"Obviously this section of stone was fitted into the wall to provide some sort of closure," Doc said. He shone his flashlight toward the Indian, who was pressing on a flat portion of rock near the base of the wall. The boy rose and gestured to them again. The area before them had opened up displaying a previously secret darkened hallway.

"Have you ever gone down this one before?" Doc asked, following the Indian through the opening.

"No," said Audrey. "We didn't even know it existed."

The passageway was very narrow, and full of cobwebs and dust. The walls felt cool and gritty to their touch, and the air seemed to have taken on a heavier consistency. Doc had to turn sideways several times because it wouldn't accommodate the width of his shoulders. The ceiling sloped downward as well, causing them to go on all fours.

"Michael, I'm not sure we should be doing this," Audrey said. "What if he's leading us into a trap?" The strain in her voice was evident.

Doc considered this for a moment, but he did not slow down. He had switched off his light to save the battery just in case they did find themselves lost, but he felt comfortable that he could negotiate the return should it become necessary.

"Let's keep going," he said.

The passage narrowed further and angled downward, forcing them to crawl. The Indian was squirming ahead of them, and Doc suddenly wondered if perhaps the space would become too small for his massive physique.

"Audrey, are you all right?" he asked over his shoulder.

"Yes," she said, coughing slightly. "But this is terrible."

Doc had completely lost sight of the Indian boy. He thought about pausing to try and pull out his flashlight again, but realized the light would destroy whatever visual purple his eyes had developed up to this point. Plus, stopping might alarm Audrey.

He pressed on, using his elbows to propel him. The area ahead was totally black now, yet a sudden coolness teased his face. The tunnel ended and a new passageway abruptly opened up, allowing him to stand. He heard Audrey's labored breathing, removed his flashlight again, and shone it down at the hole, stooping to help her through the opening and to her feet.

"Oh, thank heavens we're out of there," she said, brushing some of her long auburn tresses away from her face. "I must look a sight."

"We both do," Doc said, smiling as he looked at her dirt streaked face and clothes.

Blinking to adjust his eyes, Doc saw the Indian boy standing a few yards away. The cavern was immense. Enormous tapering stalactites hung suspended above them, met with corresponding mirror images extending upward from the floor, and the air was musty smelling.

"Is this another part of the pyramid?" Audrey asked. "I've never been in here before."

"We're below ground here," Doc said. "It must be some underground cave, probably caused by a subterranean river."

They began following the Indian boy again down another huge corridor that made several sinuous twists and turns. The sandy bottom seemed to bear out that the path had been forged by rushing water, and was now a dry basin. But several times they passed through shallow pools of standing water. Finally the Indian stopped, said something in Mayan, and pointed. Doc looked at the stone wall in front of them. It felt solidly in place, and he doubted that any system of fulcrum and balances, no matter how sophisticated, could move it. The breeze licked at their faces again, and the boy smiled. Doc looked upward and saw the cuts in the limestone that formed a primitive ladder.

The Indian boy scurried up first, followed by Audrey, who was boosted up by Doc. He then brought up the rear. The wall canted slightly allowing them to climb upward without much effort. A perpendicular juncture was at the top, and they had to crawl once more, but this time a small square of light was visible at the far end, holding the promise of sunlight and an exit to the outside.

* * *

Assante was looking at his watch again when Deagan tapped him on the shoulder and said, "We got company."

Ace looked up and saw Dr. Rabbat, Carlos, and several of their men heading toward the pyramid entrance. They were a rough-looking bunch and a couple of them carried rifles.

"Good morning, gentlemen," Rabbat said. "We wanted to speak with Dr. Atlas."

"Him and Audrey went into this stack of stones," Deagan said, gesturing with his thumb. "They ain't come out yet."

"Ah, yes," Rabbat said. "Do you perhaps know the whereabouts of the suspected killer?"

"Killer?" Ace said. "And who might that be?"

"That Indian youth," Rabbat said.

"He's in there with Doc," Deagan said.

"Then there is great danger." Rabbat placed a hand on his forehead. "Carlos is convinced that he was not only here last night to do us harm, but that he was also behind the attacks against you on the road."

Deagan and Assante exchanged glances.

"It had to be los indios," Carlos said. "No one else could have taken the dead bandidos."

"I thought you said it was jungle cats?" Ace asked.

Carlos shrugged. "I thought it might be at first. But mis hermanos just got back from there. They found no tracks de los gatos grandes."

"Don't you see," Rabbat said. "The Indians regard this place as sacred ground, much as my own people once regarded the great pyramids as sacrosanct. It makes perfect sense that they would want to strike back at Professor Guffrey for violating their sanctity." He steepled his fingers. "Please, we must try to find Dr. Atlas and Audrey before some harm befalls them."

Deagan puckered his lower lip.

"I don't guess it'd do any harm for us to mosey on in there," he said. "How about it, Ace?"

Assante shook his head. "I have an aversion to dark places," he said, taking out his cigarette case. "I'll wait here if you don't mind."

"As you wish," Rabbat said. He handed Deagan one of the portable lamps and they went inside the structure. Ace offered a cigarette to Carlos who grunted gracias, and accepted Ace's lighter. Assante knew Deagan was more than capable of handling Rabbat, should the occasion arise, and the solidness of the pistol stuck in his belt gave him a sense of reassurance as well. The feeling vanished, however, when Deagan hurried out several minutes later with a worried look on his face.

"Ace," Mad Dog said, "Doc ain't anywhere to be found in there."

* * *

Beams of sunlight streamed into the front of the cave through the hanging tendrils of roots from a denuded tree. The Indian boy pushed them aside and scrambled down the slanting embankment with a practiced ease. Doc studied the terrain as he helped Audrey negotiate the earthen slope down to the basin floor. They appeared to be in some sort of large sinkhole that was perhaps fifty feet across and thirty feet deep. Pools of standing water were at various places in the large depression.

"What is this place, Michael?" Audrey asked.

"The ground beneath us was eroded away by the underground river long ago," Doc said. "This portion collapsed down to the limestone base, unlike the cave from which we just emerged."

"Ohhhh, that water looks so clear," Audrey said. "What I wouldn't give to be able to take a quick bath, or even just wash my face." She smiled self-effacingly. "I must look a fright."

Doc smiled. "No amount of surface dirt could deter your natural beauty."

The Indian boy was perhaps twenty yards ahead of them now. He turned and waited, pointing at the opposite embankment. Two other Indians, dressed in more traditional native wear, stood there holding long spears. Several more came up to the edge and stood looking down at them. Doc felt Audrey's hand grip his.

"Don't be afraid," he said. "I have a weapon, but I don't believe they intend to harm us."

As they walked farther the top line of the embankment began to fill with more figures, men, women, and children, all pointing and talking in their strange clicking tongue. Audrey's other hand touched Doc's arm, but she said nothing. The Indian boy had reached the other side of the hole and began climbing the lattice-like network of exposed tree roots. As he neared the top, some of the natives reached down to help him over the cusp. He spoke to them, gesturing back at Audrey and Doc, then motioned for them to join him.

Doc boosted Audrey up on the tangled skein of roots and followed closely behind her. Outstretched hands helped her as she climbed to the top, and Doc quickened his pace and swung his legs over the embankment at the same time as Audrey. It was clear to all that he needed no assistance.

The forest, although still densely vegetated, opened into a small clearing. Several sets of primitive-looking huts with straw roofs were visible, as was a smoldering campfire. The crowd began opening as the Indian boy moved toward the camp with Doc and Audrey following. More natives, mostly women in brightly colored skirts carrying infants, were standing by the huts, their dark eyes staring intently at the new visitors. A bare-chested man with high cheekbones and a regal look emerged from a hut and looked startled at the intrusion until he saw the boy. He hurried forth and smiled, stopping to hug the youth with both of his arms.

They spoke in the harsh sounding language again, with the boy gesturing and pointing to his throat. The other man stared at Doc and continued to listen. Doc surveyed the surroundings, taking in everything from the dimensions of the settlement to the approximate number of people present. Suddenly he saw a pale figure with gold spectacles rise from a log in front of a far hut. He touched Audrey's arm gently and pointed. She looked and gasped, the tears already starting to stream down her dust covered cheeks.

"Oh, my God," she said. "It's Father!"

Doc watched as she ran forward, meeting Professor Arthur Guffrey in the center of the camp. They embraced and Doc saw that the old man was crying as well.

A fortuitous reunion, he thought.

He walked up to them and placed his hand on the professor's shoulder. "We're glad that you're all right, Dr. Guffrey," he said.

The old man looked up at him and smiled.

"Michael," he said, "thank God you're here. I kept praying that somehow you'd come. When the Mayans told me of a tall man with Herculean proportions at the pyramid, I knew that Audrey must have contacted you."

"Father, we've been so worried. Where have you been these past few days? What happened?"

Professor Guffrey patted his daughter's arm and gestured toward the boy. "Balam approached me that day inside the pyramid, when I was alone, and brought me here. This man is Balam's father, the chieftain, Ahaw Sahal. But there's no time to explain that now." They were joined by the boy and the older man, who said something to the professor. Guffrey turned to Doc. "Michael, come with me. There's a great need for your abilities and very little time."

Doc's brow furrowed slightly, but he let the old man lead him to the entranceway of the closest hut. Doc peered inside. In the cool darkness a small boy of perhaps five or six lay shivering on a straw mat, seeming to float in and out of consciousness. Beside him were a woman and an old man, his hair hanging in long gray braids down in front of his shoulders.

"That's Saknik, the spiritual leader of the tribe," Professor Guffrey said. "A shaman, or holy man. His grandson is very ill. I've tried my best to comfort him, but I'm afraid he needs someone with more medical expertise than I have."

Doc went in and knelt beside the boy, placing the back of his hand on the child's forehead. He probed various parts of the boy's body with his fingers, centering on the right side, which when touched elicited a moaning cry. Standing, Doc went back to the doorway.

"Are you fluent in their language?" he asked.

"Hardly," Professor Guffrey said. "I mean, I can communicate in the basic sense, and a few of them speak some Spanish." He smiled weakly. "I have learned quite a bit during the last few days, but it's been anything but fluent."

"The boy has acute appendicitis," Doc said. "He needs immediate surgery. There's a significant chance his vermiform appendix will rupture, in which case the resulting peritonitis will surely be fatal."

"Oh no," Audrey said. "But you can't possibly do anything here. It's so primitive."

"If only I had my medical kit," Doc said. He glanced back inside the hut. "He won't survive unless we act now."

"They were telling me of a legend," Professor Guffrey said. "It came from a vision of the holy man. It said a tall stranger from the north, adorned with gold, shall arrive and perform a miracle." His fingers touched his gold-rimmed spectacles. "I think they saw my glasses and assumed it was me. That's why they abducted me that day in the pyramid."

Doc's amber colored eyes were already surveying the camp. He went over and grabbed some metallic pots that had been stacked alongside one of the huts. "Have someone fill these with water," he said. "I'll need more. Start heating them immediately." With that said, Doc went to the edge of the camp and squatted down to examine some vegetation. After a few minutes of searching, he uprooted several plants and brought back an assortment of digitate leaves to the hut. "If they will grind these into paste, and mix it with water, it should serve as an anesthesia." He went to one of the women and eyed the hem of her long dress.

"Professor, can you ask them about the needles they use to sew their dresses?

Guffrey came over and spoke a few words, gesturing emphatically. At first the woman's face showed no sign of comprehension, but then she smiled and nodded. She went to a hut across the encampment and returned moments later with several needles and some dark thread. The professor took it and hurriedly showed it to Doc.

"Will this do?" he asked.

"It may suffice for the exterior stitches," Doc said, taking the needles and examining them. He went to the fire and held each into the flames briefly, then bent them into circular curves by using the wooden spools of thread. He looked around. "We'll need something less coarse for the internal stitches. Something fine."

"What about my hair?" Audrey asked.

Doc shook his head. "Human hair is too brittle."

"They have some long horse hair wound around one of their spools," the professor said. "I saw it earlier."

"Get it at once. We'll have to boil the hair to sterilize it," Doc said. He looked at Audrey. "Do you feel able to assist me?"

"Michael, you can't be serious," she said, drawing her hands to her mouth. "This is insane. To attempt surgery under such conditions. . . How can you possibly succeed?"

Doc placed both of his hands on her shoulders and looked into her eyes.

"There's a slim possibility we can make a small incision and remove the infected appendage and stitch up the organ," he said. "The surgical site will have to be closed in at least two layers, deep inside and then closer to the skin. I'll need your to help staunch the flow of blood among other things. Do you remember your surgical training?"

"It's been so long," she said. "Since college."

"Audrey," Professor Guffrey said, "you used to be very good at fixing injuries during our expeditions."

"But this is so different," she said. "I don't know, Michael. I just don't know."

"Come, let's wash ourselves and prepare," Doc said. He removed his knife from its sheath and handed it to the professor. "Please see that this, as well as the needles and hair, are sterilized."

Audrey stood immobile, her gaze fixed on the boy in the hut. Doc reached out and took her hand gently in his. Her eyes turned toward him and he pulled her close.

"We're that boy's only chance," he said. "We must make the attempt. And I believe in you."

* * *

Deagan tossed down Doc's backpack and placed his hands on his hips. "Dammit, Ace," he said. "If we only knew where Doc went to."

Assante brought his cigarette to his lips and nodded. He'd been watching the activity by Professor Rabbat's tent. Carlos and several of his men were loading their rifles and talking among themselves.

"What they been saying?" Deagan asked, following Ace's gaze.

"They're forming a search party to go look for Doc and Audrey."

"Well, we can't afford not to go along, can we?"

"They're talking about raiding the Indian village."

"So the question is, do we lick 'em or join 'em, huh?" Deagan did a quick head count. "Too many of 'em to try and lick here. What we got between us, ten rounds of ammunition?"

"Eight." Assante grinned. "This weapon had four rounds expended, remember?"

"Well, I don't think Doc would approve of us tagging along with 'em while they massacre indigenous personnel," Deagan said. "Even if we were trying to rescue him."

"Plus, it'll be getting dark soon," he said, "and I don't know about you, but traipsing around in the jungle at night with those guys doesn't seem too prudent."

Deagan scratched his jaw and nodded to Carlos as he looked up. The big Mexican nodded back, then said something in Spanish to his associates.

"We may not have to after all," Ace said. "It sounds like they're not sure exactly where the village is at. Maybe we can forestall any searching tonight by telling them we'll help them in the morning."

"You got something there, Ace. Besides, I'm thinking if Doc was in real trouble, he'd have activated his emergency beacon." He picked up the backpack again and removed a black directional finder about the size of a camera. It had a compass attached. "But just the same, you and me better take turns sleeping tonight."

"And keep an extra eye on our friends there, too," Ace said. He blew out a cloud of smoke and began stripping the butt of his cigarette.

Somewhere just outside of Mexico City

Penny watched the sun disappearing beyond the distant trees of the horizon as the train rumbled forward at what seemed like an interminably slow pace. The car was full of people, all chatting in Spanish and pleasantly ignoring her. Her suitcase sat between her knees, and she felt the slow trickle of a drop of sweat roll down the back of her neck as more hot air blew in through the open windows.

If this damn train would pick up some speed, she thought, maybe it would cool us off. I'm going to need a bath and a clean dress before I go looking for Doc, too.

The train seemed to slow somehow, and more unpleasant smells from a passing farm wafted in mixing with the pervasive scent of human body odor that seemed to be hanging inside the packed train car.

Penny licked her lips and thought she'd give anything for a drink of cold New York water. A man sitting across the aisle unscrewed the cap of a hip flask and took a slow pull. Upon seeing her watching him, he smiled, showing a gap of several missing teeth, and held the flask out toward her.

Penny shook her head and turned away.

Oh swell, she thought. A Mexican masher and I can't even tell him to go jump in the lake because he wouldn't understand me.

The train jerked abruptly a few times, then slowed to a stop, its wheels making a screeching sound against the metallic rails. The conductor came to the end of the car and called something out in Spanish. Some people across from her got up, and Penny did also, figuring she'd at least move to another car, away from the masher. As she neared the door, lugging her suitcase in front of her and bumping into people standing and sitting in the aisle, she looked back to see a mix of people scrambling into her seat. More people got on and began showing their tickets to the conductor, who chatted with them rapidly.

"Excuse me," Penny said, trying to look over the man's shoulder into the next car for an open seat. She saw none. "How far is it to Santa Merida?"

The conductor repeated Santa Merida and several people standing in the area between the two doors laughed. He was a rather short, heavyset man, with a drooping black mustache.

"Lo siento, senoritia," he said. "But that is a very long, long way to go yet."

"That man back there was bothering me," Penny said, cocking her head in the direction of the car.

The conductor nodded, and held up his hand. "I will try to find you a seat in another car after the next stop. Pero, it will take most of the night before we reach el estacion del cambio."

"Is that where Santa Merida is?" Penny asked.

"No, senorita," the conductor said, smiling again. "That is where you must change trains."

* * *

Doc and Audrey emerged from the hut as darkness had begun to descend upon the village. Professor Guffrey followed them and gave his daughter a hug. Then he turned to Doc. His hands and arms were covered with bloodstains, and his face was dappled with speckles of crimson.

"Michael, that was the most amazing piece of surgery I've ever seen," Guffrey said. "I would have never believed it possible."

Doc smiled. "Your assistance was invaluable, Professor, but I must commend Audrey. Without her I would never have been able to do it."

The old shaman, Saknik, came over and placed his hand on Doc's arm in an obvious gesture of gratitude. The old man smiled, showing the gaps in his teeth, and then faded away into the darkness.

"He is pretty amazing, isn't he, Father?" Audrey said. She kept staring at Doc. She was almost as bloodstained as he.

"How on earth did you learn such unorthodox techniques?" the Professor asked.

"Because of my medical knowledge, and my other skills," Doc said. "I was placed with a special insertion team in the military. Our experience in the Philippines was under the worst conditions. Unfortunately, I learned a lot about battlefield surgery techniques with minimal equipment."

Professor Guffrey placed his hand on Doc's shoulder and shook his head. "You're an extraordinary man."

"We'd better wash up," Doc said, moving toward the pots hanging over the campfire.

"What I really need is a bath," Audrey said. "But I guess that's out of the question here."

"Not necessarily," Professor Guffrey said. "There are several pools in the basin that the natives use for bathing purposes. They're spring-fed and actually quite nice, but the largest one is about twelve feet deep."

"Oh, then I can go for a swim," Audrey said.

"That would not be advisable," Doc said. "Remember that Carlos spoke of large feral cats in the area."

"They howl at night sometimes," Professor Guffrey agreed. "But mostly they go after these large rat-like animals called esquintla. Besides, once my daughter has her mind made up about something. . ." He smiled as he let the sentence trail off. "She reminds me so much of her mother."

"Fiddlesticks," said Audrey. "I'll be fine. And if you're so worried, Michael, perhaps you could come along to guard me. You have a pistol there, don't you?"

Doc said nothing for a moment, then began heading through the camp. "Very well," he said over his shoulder. "I'll grab us a torch to light the way."

After planting the burning torch securely in the earth at the edge of the edge of the sinkhole, Doc helped Audrey descend the tangle of dried roots.

"It's almost like a ladder," she joked as they climbed down. Once on solid ground, Doc removed his small flashlight and shone it around. The batteries were almost used up since they had continuously focused it on the surgical area once the natural light had begun to fade. He pointed to the largest of the three pools.

"That must be the deep one your father spoke about."

"Let's go then," Audrey said, snatching his flashlight and beginning to run. He caught up to her almost immediately, but purposely stayed a few steps behind. At the edge of the water she stopped abruptly and they almost collided.

"Here's your flashlight, Michael. Now I'll thank you to turn around."

Doc's brow furrowed.

"Unless you're going to watch me get undressed, that is," she added.

Doc immediately turned around and replaced his flashlight in its holder.

"Mmmm, the water's delicious," Audrey said.

Doc began to turn. "Don't drink any," he said, then heard her soft laugh.

"After all the countless expeditions to some of the most primitive countries on earth," she said, "do you really think I'd take the chance on catching typhoid fever drinking some unpurified water?"

"There's a danger of hepatitis, too," he said.

He suddenly felt a splash of cold water sprinkle over his back.

"Okay, I'm in," Audrey said. "You can turn around now. Or better yet, why don't you join me?"

Doc considered this for a moment, then began unbuttoning his shirt. He removed his boots and socks next, followed by his utility belt. After emptying all his pants pockets, he stood and walked to the edge of the pool, stepping over the tangled heap of her clothes.

"You can undress all the way, Michael," Audrey said. "I promise not to look."

Doc smiled. The pale light of the full moon shone down through the void in the trees, lighting the outline of her body in the clear water.

"These pants will dry quickly," he said, wading waist-deep into the water. He immediately began to scrub at his hands and face. Audrey kicked her way into the center of the pool, using an even breaststroke. Doc admonished her not to go too far.

"Swim to me, Michael," she said.

Doc stood and watched her body gracefully cut through the water. He raised his arms and dove under the surface, propelling himself with powerful strokes, until he surfaced and swam near her. She splashed some water at him again. Doc turned over on his back and swam around her, circling her form.

"How deep do you think it is here?" she asked breathlessly.

"Deep enough that we should return to shallower water," he said, and began swimming back toward the edge. He stopped where the water was waist-deep again, and listened to make sure he could hear her smooth kicks behind him. But he heard nothing. Doc turned, and saw only the ripples from his body breaking the smooth surface of the water.

"Audrey," he called. And then she surfaced behind him, her arms encircling his waist, her smooth body pressing against his back.

"Don't move, Michael," she said. "I just want to hold you like this for a minute."

He could feel her breasts pushing against him as the rapidity of her breathing began to lessen.

"That was so wonderful, what you did, saving that boy's life," she said. "And to think I was actually part of it."

"You did well," Doc said, suddenly thankful that he was waist-deep in cold water. "But the danger's far from over for him. He still has to make it through the night."

He felt her arms squeeze him tighter.

"So do we, Michael," she said. "So do we."

* * *

Deagan snapped awake at the first sound of the buzzing. The first thing he did was to immediately raise his pistol and survey the area. But only the bright glints of sunlight cresting over the eastern top of the pyramid and the ubiquitous chirping of the insects greeted him. He glanced over at Assante who was still sound asleep, and then toward the tents that housed Carlos and Rabbat. The flaps of their tents were closed, but several of their men lounged around in haphazard fashion, snoring, probably from the vast quantities of tequila they had consumed after the agreement to postpone any search for Doc and Audrey.

The proposed search party had been put off until morning principally because Ace and Deagan had explained that Doc possessed a special miniature beacon that, once activated, would lead them to his position. "Alls he has to do is trigger the switch," Deagan had told them, holding up Doc's backpack, "and this will show us which direction to go in."

And now the alarm on the directional finder was buzzing.

Deagan quickly turned off the audible part of the alarm and gently shook Ace awake, holding his finger to his lips to indicate silence. Assante blinked twice, then sat up, staring intently at the backpack. Deagan nodded and they both began a quiet extrication from the tent.

"Which way?" Ace whispered.

Deagan looked at the compass and pointed. They headed through the lower ruins and into the forest. Assante glanced behind them, but it appeared as if Carlos and his bunch had not stirred. He held a thumbs-up to Deagan, who grinned.

"So far, so good," he said in a low voice.

* * *

Doc checked the boy's pulse and respiration rate. The color had come back to his face and torso, and he appeared to be sleeping comfortably. Audrey stood by his side watching, her hands roaming up his arm. The old Indian holy man stood on Doc's other flank, his dark eyes peering down at the boy. The old man said something in Mayan and patted Doc's shoulder.

"Do you think you'll be able to remove these stitches after ten to twelve days?" Doc asked.

"I'm certain I can," Audrey said. "You've already done all the hard work."

Doc nodded. "You'll also need to apply some special topical ointment to prevent any inflection to the subcutaneous tissue."

"Special ointment?" she asked.

"My associates should be here shortly," he said. "They'll be bringing my backpack with my medical supplies."

"But how will they know where to find us?" Audrey asked.

"My dear," Professor Guffrey said. "Haven't you realized by now that Michael here has the situation well in hand?" He reached out and slapped Doc on the back. "Your father must have been very proud of you, son."

Doc made one last examination of his patient, and straightened up.

"When Thomas and Ace get here, I believe I also have some herbal tea in my pack. Perhaps we can begin to boil some water."

"That will be a welcome treat," Professor Guffrey said. He walked toward the campfire and said something to one of the women. She jumped up and grabbed an old, blackened metallic pot and began filling it with water from a nearby barrel-like container.

"Professor," Doc asked, "I need to ask you about your findings here in Mexico."

The professor's mouth stretched downward at the corners.

"What is it you need to know?" he said. "How much of a fool I've been?"

"Father!" Audrey said with a gasp.

Guffrey sighed heavily, and licked his lips. His gaze was fixed on the ground.

"When did you realize that the carving of the Sphinx enclosed in the star and crescents was a fake?" Doc asked.

"It was obvious from the beginning," Guffrey said. "Or at least it should have been." He sighed again. "I was simply too stubborn to admit to myself what I should have known all along. The day Balam took me from the pyramid. . ." He looked up at Audrey, "when you called out to me, that's when I finally realized it. I'd just reached up and touched it. . ."

"And that's when you discovered the graphite on your fingertips?" Doc asked.

Guffrey nodded.

"Someone had smeared the carving with it to give the illusion that it had been there as long as the other hieroglyphics," Guffrey said. "I suppose I hadn't noticed it before because I was so eager to believe that I'd finally found the proof I'd been searching for. That, and I believed the assurances of Professor Rabbat."

"You mean he lied to us?" Audrey asked. "But why?"

"I suspect it had something to do with obtaining your father's funding and reputation to get this expedition started," Doc said. "Had you met him before? In Egypt perhaps?"

"No. We'd corresponded," Guffrey said. "I was actually very flattered that a man of his rather distinguished reputation would agree to join me in this venture."

"I'm afraid all is not as it seems with him, too," Doc said. "I have reason to suspect that he is not actually the real Professor Rabbat."

Guffrey's jaw seemed to visibly drop.

"I became suspicious when after our initial meeting in town," Doc said. "He mentioned that he'd met you before in the Middle East on an expedition. Then he insisted that we follow him at a distance to the camp, ostensibly to avoid the dust of the road. The bandits who subsequently attacked us had been lying in wait, and I have no doubt the passing of Rabbat's jeep was some sort of pre-arranged signal. Otherwise, they would not have known we be passing along that road at that particular time. He also changed his story after we arrived in camp, denying that you'd ever met. Then I caught him and Carlos torturing that boy as to the whereabouts of some idols."

"Yes," Guffrey said. "The Mayans do have a treasured shrine. They've kept it within a series of caves near here for thousands of years. It's been passed from generation to generation. It's a closely guarded secret. A legend of sorts, but I've been privileged enough to see it."

"You have?" Audrey asked. "What does it look like?"

"It's beautiful," Guffrey said. "Two magnificent jade totems with jeweled eyes on a base of gold. Well, not exactly—"

His description was cut short by an explosion of ascending birds from the tree-line surrounding the village, followed by Deagan's loud, whooping yell from across the campground. He and Assante had emerged from the forested area near the far side of the large sinkhole and had begun to traverse the rough shrubbery. Doc waved over to them and smiled.

"I believe the infantry has arrived," he said.

The villagers came forward, some carrying spears, bows and arrows. A few had ancient looking rifles. Doc rushed forward and greeted Deagan and Ace more profusely than was his custom.

"Jeeze, what a reception committee," Deagan said, looking at the array of heavily armed Indians.

"I would have thought you'd be used to dodging the slings and arrows of outrageous fortune by now," Ace said. The tension in his voice was obvious.

Audrey and Professor Guffrey approached Doc, and Audrey smiled at Deagan.

"I hope you gentlemen brought Michael's medical kit," she said.

Deagan held up the backpack and then grinned.

"Hi, Audrey. Don't tell me this is your dad?"

"It most certainly is," she said. "Father, may I introduce you to two of the finest gentlemen I've ever met."

"At least one of the finest," Ace said, reaching across Deagan's chest to shake hands with the professor.

The Chief, Ahaw Sahal and Balam came forward and Doc asked Professor Guffrey to complete the introductions. Doc took the backpack from Deagan and headed back to the hut, motioning for Saknik, the shaman, to accompany him.

* * *

"So old Peter Lorre's a phony, huh?" Deagan said as they sat around the campfire drinking the tea Audrey had prepared. "I never did trust that guy. Too creepy looking."

"What's our next move, Doc?" Ace asked. "I'm certain they didn't follow us here."

"He's certain," Deagan said, cocking his thumb toward Assante. "Only because I kept insistin' that we circle back and wait, then erase our trail."

"If you'd been alone," Ace said, "it probably would have been easier for you to swing from tree to tree."

Before Deagan could reply, Doc spoke.

"Professor Guffrey, we need to warn these people of the imminent danger," he said. "I'm certain now that their primary intention all along was to gain possession of those idols you spoke of."

The professor considered this for a moment and nodded.

"They probably are worth a lot of money to some," he said. "But the Mayans have been dealing with people who have tried to steal from them for centuries." He raised his eyebrows a bit. "On the other hand, many of the Mayan treasures have been pilfered through the years. . ."

"And from what I saw when Rabbat and Carlos had Balam," Doc said, "they will spare no mercy to obtain what they're after."

The professor rose and set his drinking mug by his feet.

"They've managed to keep the idols safe by moving them to various locations periodically," he said. "The shrine is never left unguarded. Come on, I'll show you where it's at now."

He went to Ahaw Sahal and Balam and spoke haltingly, using extensive gestures. The chief nodded and gestured for Doc and the others to follow. They moved to the edge of the sinkhole and began climbing down, one by one. Doc descended quickly, then waited to assist Audrey and then Ace, although he took pains to not make it obvious. Deagan was able to climb down with little trouble, showing an incredible nimbleness. Professor Guffrey and the shaman were the last to descend.

Balam led them across the basin floor, past the large pools of water, and into the mouth of a small cave. He waited and let the shaman and his father enter first. Professor Guffrey held out his hand and said, "We're probably the first outsiders to have been granted this privilege in quite a while."

As they walked into the cave the air temperature seemed to cool noticeably and the musty smell increased. About one hundred yards ahead light flickered from a pair of burning torches. A man stood near the torches armed with a large club. He did a ritualistic salute when Ahaw Sahal and Saknik approached and then stepped aside. Behind him they could see it in the center of a small enclave perhaps fifteen feet square.

The idols were perhaps two feet tall, their cool, mint green color almost coquettish in its translucence. The two figures were mirror images of each other, except the face of the one of the left was frowning, while its counterpart had what could only be described as a smile of mirth. Both statues held a smaller figure against their torsos, the faces of which corresponded respectively to the expressions of the larger physiognomies. Their greenish glow shimmered in the torchlight, as did the brilliant yellow base upon which they were mounted. The base had a lustrous shimmer, and seemed to be formed from solid cubes of gold.

"Oh, it's so beautiful," Audrey said.

"From what I can gather," Professor Guffrey said, "they're supposed to represent the duality of man. Good and evil. The similarity to the various incarnations of Buddha in the Eastern depictions is startling."

"Much like the collective unconscious that has been discussed in the works of Carl Gustav Jung," Doc said.

"Collective what?" Deagan asked.

"Unconscious," Ace said. "Like we all wish you were most of the time."

"It's a theory based on the similar themes that run through disparate cultures," Audrey said.

"We must take proper precautions," Doc started to say.

But a sudden staccato crack of gunfire echoed through the cave, accompanied by distant screaming.

"What the hell? That sounded like a Thompson," Deagan said, wrinkling his brow as he glanced at the others.

Doc, Assante, and Deagan rushed forward, their guns drawn, only to see Carlos, Rabbat and several others standing near the mouth of the cave holding a group of Mayan women and children at gunpoint.

"Hola," Carlos said, his teeth a flash of white under his dark mustache. "It was nice of you to finally lead us to the right cave, gringos." His smile twisted into a scowl and he raised the military style walkie-talkie to his lips and spoke something in Spanish. Then he turned to Doc and said, "Listen to me. More of my compadres are outside the cave with los ninos y muheres. We haff a machinegun, and we know how to use it." He hung the radio on the handle of his holstered forty-five automatic and grabbed a small child by the hair, pulling the screaming child close. In a silver flash the knife appeared in his hand and he pressed it against the child's throat.

"You are too far away this time to grab me, right, hombre?" he said, looking straight at Doc. "Now, throw me your weapons or I will cut this little latoso's neck like a chicken's."

Doc stood silently, not moving.

"Do it!" Carlos said.

Professor Rabbat walked down next to Carlos and held up his hand.

"My friend is a very ruthless man, Dr. Atlas," Rabbat said. "I fear that you know only too well that he is capable of carrying out what he said." He shrugged and smiled, but Doc could see that Rabbat's face was wet with sweat. "All we wish is for you to comply. We are only after the idols, and once we have them, we shall leave here peacefully. Now tell me, doctor, are they worth this child's life?"

The small boy screamed as Carlos drew the honed metal across a section of his neck, leaving a crimson smear.

"Do I finish the job or not?" his voice rasped.

"We'll comply," Doc said, "but you'll never get out of here alive."

Rabbat smiled.

"We are more than willing to take that chance," he said. "Now toss your weapons over there." He pointed with his pistol to the side wall farthest away from them. "And do not forgot to remove your famous utility belt also, Dr. Atlas."

Doc's nostrils flared. Not trusting Rabbat or Carlos in the least, but knowing not to obey would mean the certain death of the child, he tossed the pistol away, then removed his belt. Deagan and Ace relinquished theirs also.

"Now release the child," Doc said.

Rabbat's low chuckle reverberated in the cave.

"I'm afraid you are in no position to put forth demands," he said. He held up his pistol and pointed it at them. "Nonetheless, I do not wish to shoot you. As I said, our only interest is in obtaining the idols. Now, move back, if you please."

Doc and the others backed up slowly, hands raised. Balam, his father, and Saknik stood at the opening to the treasure room along with the guard. Ahaw Sahal pushed Balam away and centered himself in the doorway, speaking directly to Carlos in Mayan.

Carlos sheathed his knife and, still holding the boy's hair in his left hand, grabbed his pistol with his right. His arm straightened and the corresponding explosion was deafening in the confined space. The guard's hands clutched his chest as he tumbled forward. Carlos grinned, adjusting his aim, and fired two more shots. Ahaw Sahal collapsed next to the guard as the ejected rounds popping back over Carlos's shoulder. Balam rushed forward to his fallen father, tears streaming down his face. Doc quickly moved to assist, pressing his palm against the wound site as the dark blood began seeping through his fingers.

Rabbat brushed past them as Carlos transferred his aim toward the others.

"You dirty son of a . . ." Deagan said. "Shooting an unarmed man like that."

"Maybe I shoot some more, un?" Carlos said. Then to Rabbat, "Hurry up. Traiga los."

"I can't manage it myself," Rabbat called out. There's too much here."

Carlos pointed his gun at Deagan.

"You look very strong, monkey man. You go help my friend move them out here, eh?"

Deagan's lips curled up into a growl, but he moved toward the room. Carlos whistled at Audrey. "Help him, senoritia, or I will shoot su padre next."

Audrey, her face awash with silent tears followed Deagan into the room.

Doc glanced after them and saw Rabbat filling his pockets with the golden cubes. His pant legs bulging grotesquely, he licked his lips and began filling his backpack with more of the lustrous metal. Deagan hoisted the two idols from their base and held them toward Rabbat.

"You carry them over to Carlos and we'll give you the child," Rabbat said. He grabbed Audrey by the arm and pushed her out in front of him. "Do not try to interfere if you value this woman's life."

Audrey stepped cautiously over the splayed legs of the fallen Ahaw Sahal, followed by Deagan.

"Michael, can you save him?" she asked.

Before Doc could answer Carlos smashed Deagan's head with the barrel of his pistol and roughly shoved the child hostage forward. He snatched Audrey's arm, pressing the barrel of the pistol against her temple as the idols fell to the dirt floor. Rabbat stooped and picked them up, carefully brushing them off, before handing them to one of Carlos's men. Rabbat readjusted the heavily laden backpack.

"Now we haff three treasures, eh?" he said, his free arm snaking around to draw her close to his body. "Come on. Let's go." He began pulling Audrey toward the entrance. "She will come with us so you won't shoot in the backs, eh?"

"That's more your style," Ace said, helping Deagan to his feet.

Rabbat rushed to follow, his legs pumping in an almost exaggerated fashion due to the extra weight.

"Carlos, wait," Rabbat said. "Wait for me. Help me carry some of this. We'll be rich men."

Carlos smirked.

"You can carry it yourself," he said. "We haff what we came for, no?"

Doc felt Ahaw Sahal's ragged breathing cease. He glanced to Balam, who knelt beside him in stunned disbelief. Standing, Doc turned and began moving toward Rabbat, who turned and fired his pistol. The round went wild, but it caused Doc and the others to duck. Rabbat fired another round that ricocheted off the walls.

"I advise you not to advance," he said breathlessly. Then he stooped and picked up Doc's utility belt, digging frantically into one of the pouches. "I have something for you, Dr. Atlas."

Doc's face showed alarm as he rose quickly and began pushing the others farther back into the tunnels. Rabbat fired his weapon several more times, the reports sounding more and more distant in the enclosed walls. The shooting ceased and the small sphere came bouncing off the walls, the hollow pocking sound being punctuated four seconds later by the powerful echo of the explosion. Clouds of dust billowed toward them as the sections of walls and roof collapsed. Doc continued to herd the others into the deeper recesses of the cave as the heavy rumbling continued. Unable to breathe, they fell to the ground gasping in the inky blackness, the damp soil offering them no shelter or relief.

* * *

The entrance of the cave had erupted outward with a hoard of frightened bats shooting up into the sky accompanied by the effluvial billows from the preceding explosion. Several of Carlos's henchmen looked shocked and the one holding the Tommygun paused to cross himself. Then they heard coughing, accompanied by voices and Rabbat, Carlos, and Audrey emerged covered with dust. Carlos was practically dragging her, pausing to slap her face at her non-compliance. Two of his men followed, one of whom carried the jade idols.

"You got 'em, huh, boss?" the man with the machinegun asked.

Carlos threw Audrey down to the ground and told them to tie her hands. "She's coming with us," he said.

"We're wasting time taking her," Rabbat said. "We have more than we anticipated, and she will only slow us down. Leave her here."

"Have you forgotten she can identify us?" Carlos said, brushing some of the dust from his shirt.

"Very well," Rabbat said. "Shoot her then. But let's go."

Carlos smirked at him, then looked at Audrey with a sinister hunger in his eyes.

"I've been watching la senorita all these weeks," he said. "Now I do not intend to give her up until I tire of her. Besides, I do not think that the famous Doc Atlas will be following us now."

"And what about the rest of the natives?" Rabbat asked. "We've got a long way back to the camp."

Carlos turned to the man holding the machinegun and said, "Joaquin, fuego la."

Joaquin nodded and raised the Thompson, sending a burst in an arcing motion into the surrounding trees.

"Those hinchapelotas haff never seen a weapon like this one," Carlos said. He glanced down at the two men binding Audrey's hands behind her back. Apparently satisfied that she was sufficiently secured, he looked at the group, then said, "Vaminous, mis hermanos." The man carrying the idols headed into the forest as well as the two pushing Audrey. Carlos dropped back and waited for them to pass him, then he too started walking at a rapid pace. Joaquin, with the machinegun, fell in behind him.

"Wait," Rabbat called. "I need some help with this gold."

"Gold? You can keep that for yourself," Carlos said, his voice lowering into a harsh sneer. "Like I tol' you, I haff what I came for."

* * *

Doc checked each of them after their coughing subsided. The dust had seemed to roll past them, but left a grainy feel to the air. The old shaman spoke in Mayan, and Doc heard Professor Guffrey's voice.

"Michael, he's asking if you have any fire."

"Will this do?" Ace asked, taking out his Zippo Storm King lighter. His thumb rotated the wheel against the flint and the flame illuminated the cavern.

Balam and Saknik looked around and spoke.

"They're trying to figure out where we are," Guffrey said.

"Doc, you think there's a way out of here, or should we start digging?" Deagan asked.

"Let's trust in the judgment of our hosts," Doc said, pointing toward the two Indians.

Balam held out his hand in a manner that requested the lighter. Ace gave it to him. Then the youth started walking down the tunnel. The others followed. After a few minutes they came to a fork in the path. Without hesitation Balam led them down the one to the left. After a few more circuitous turns, they felt a coolness to the air and the passageway opened up into the massive underground cavern that Doc had been through before. Balam went to one wall where a piece of wood lay on a rock. He felt the end, and then held the flame of the lighter to it. It burst into flame and he handed the lighter back to Ace.

Doc reached out and placed a hand on Balam's shoulder.

"Professor," he said. "Tell him that we need to get back to the pyramid as soon as possible."

Guffrey spoke in halting fashion, gesturing copiously as if to compensate for his lack of vocabulary. Finally Balam seemed to understand, and nodded. He pointed to his right and began a quick trot, the fire of the torch whistling in the coolness of the subterranean ambiance.

"Where we headed, Doc?" Ace asked.

"There's a passageway that will take us up through the pyramid," Doc said. "I have no doubt that's where Carlos and Rabbat are going. We might be able to make better time than they, since we're less obstructed down here. If so, we should arrive first and have the element of surprise."

"It's called out flanking 'em," Deagan said. "In case you didn't know, flyboy." He strode past Ace, who hurried to keep up.

* * *

Rabbat had barely been able to keep them in sight as the trek progressed. His pace slowed measurably, and despite his panting and calls for the others to slow down, he kept falling farther and farther behind. Breathing in gasps from the unaccustomed exercise and the heaviness of the load he carried, he paused to wipe his forehead.

A snapping sound came from behind him and he drew his pistol. The heavy drooping vines and scrawny trees were all beginning to look alike to him, but he saw no one. A bird burst from one of the branches and he foolishly fired off a round.

"Carlos," he called. "Where are you?"

No answer.

Rabbat started moving again, but his sense of direction seemed thrown off. Was the camp this way? All at once he wasn't sure. The detritus of the forest crackled loudly under his boots, but he was suddenly certain that he heard someone approaching from his rear. He whirled and fired, seeing nothing but the vast wall of verdancy.

Panting he turned and began to trudge onward again. He paused to loosen Doc's utility belt from around his waist. He still had one of the miniature grenades left. That would be his trump card should he need it. Let those stupid savages come, he thought.

Then the first arrow struck him in the left calf. The pain shot up his leg and he reached down to remove it. But the slightest touch caused him to double over in pain. He twisted to the ground, firing off the remaining rounds in his pistol at the area behind him.

The jungle seemed quiet except for the sound of his own ragged breathing.

Reload, he thought. Must reload.

He turned, fishing in his shirt pocket for more ammunition, but as he turned the light filtering through the trees seemed to darken momentarily. When he looked up the sunlight glinted off the metallic point of the spear.

* * *

Doc watched as Balam gave the torch to Deagan and reached out toward the stone wall. He knelt, feeling his way down, then pressed several of the large blocks. The familiar grinding noises started and the wall in front of them began to move.

"This is the same passage that closed before me the day I was taken," Professor Guffrey said.

"Well I'll be a monkey's uncle," Deagan said.

"Don't belabor the obvious," Ace said, moving by him.

Deagan's lower lip thrust out, but he held his hand out for the others to pass through before him. Doc quickly assumed the lead. The opening of the pyramid was just ahead, the massive stone lintels framing the brightness of the sunlight. At the entrance to the pyramid he paused, edging up to the vertical stone to sneak a look at the campsite. Through the ruins Doc could see Carlos carefully directing his henchmen to wrap the two idols in a large canvas tarp. As they began securing it with ropes, two others stood guard, including the one with the machinegun. Another was holding Audrey, who was still bound, next to the jeep. The military field radio still hung from Carlos's belt.

"There are at least six of them," Doc said, holding his fingers up toward Balam as he spoke. "They're heavily armed, and they still have Audrey. I don't see Rabbat with them."

Professor Guffrey covered his face with his hands.

"Oh, my God, what have I done, bringing her here?" he said.

Balam said something in Mayan and placed a hand on the professor's shoulder. Guffrey straightened up and said, "He says that he's certain his people are on the way."

"If we don't act now, they may not arrive in time," Doc said. "We can't let them leave in those vehicles."

"What's the plan, Doc?" Deagan asked.

"We'll have to move quickly while we still have the element of surprise," Doc said. "We need a diversion."

"Leave that to me and Ace," Deagan said. "Come on, fly-boy. Think you can hot-wire that truck?" He pointed to the old military half-ton that was perhaps fifty feet from where Carlos and the others stood. "We might be able to work our way around this wall to them trees to get to it."

Ace grinned. "Lead on, McDuff."

"That's McDeagan to you," Mad Dog said as they began a crouching trot behind the lower walls ringing the pathway to the pyramid.

"Professor, you and Saknik stay here," Doc said. Doc motioned for Balam to follow him, and moved in the opposite direction from Deagan and Ace. They ran through the scattered ruins, moving between the concentric rings of low walls until they were near the edge of the camp. Doc cautiously peered around the wall toward the closest tent. It was more than thirty feet away. It was certain death if they were seen running toward it. He looked toward the truck. No sign of Deagan or Ace. He debated taking the initiative, but he was still too far from Carlos and his men to have a chance.

Suddenly he heard the sound of gunfire, but at a distance. Carlos appeared startled as well, and he raised his radio and spoke. After listening he yelled, "Tenga prisa. Los indios vienen." The two men holding Audrey placed her in the rear seat of the jeep and began heading for the truck. Carlos pushed the men away from the canvas package and carried it to the jeep himself. He was just placing it the passenger seat next to him when the old half-ton army truck roared to life and began driving toward them. The henchmen rushed the truck, their weapons raised. The truck continued, with no one discernable behind the wheel.

Doc placed a calming hand on Balam's shoulder, then pointed to himself, and then the nearest set of tents. He indicated for the boy to remain there. In an instant, Doc was off, moving so quickly that he reached the tents in a matter of seconds.

Several rounds erupted from the Tommygun, shattering the truck's windshield, but still the vehicle moved forward. The machinegunner continued his spraying, and bullets hit the radiator and blew out the front tires. His compadres yelled at him to stop firing, but he continued until the Thompson ran out of ammo. Two of the other men rushed the vehicle, which had limped to a stop a few feet away from them, and ripped open the door, guns drawn, revealing a drooping group of hastily knitted wires and a large branch wedged between the seat and the gas pedal.

The man at the driver's door turned around with a quizzical look on his face, only to jerk and clutch at the large knife, buried almost to the hilt, suddenly protruding from his chest. The other man whirled as Doc was upon him, hurling one of the sharpened tent stakes. It pierced the shoulder of his gun arm, and he fell forward curling up in pain. Doc reached the man with the Thompson just as he was attempting to lock in a new magazine. He brought the solid wooden butt of the weapon up toward Doc's face in a sweeping arc, but the Golden Avenger dodged it with accomplished ease. His fist slammed into the man's jaw, seeming almost momentarily to separate the henchman's head from his body.

Doc grabbed the machinegun, but a bullet whizzed by his head. He instinctively dropped and continued to try and rearm the weapon.

The two other men who had rushed the truck were firing their handguns at him. One of them smiled and steadied his aim, apparently confident that he had Doc in his sights. But before he could fire Deagan and Ace jumped from the rear bed of the truck. Deagan threw himself forward in a flying tackle, knocking the gunman's arms upward before he was roughly brought to the ground. The second man turned, pointing the long muzzle of his revolver at the now prone Deagan, but a shot rang out the gunman's head exploded in a crimson mist. As he twisted to the ground, Doc saw Assante crouching by the truck with one of the dead henchmen's pistols.

A primal cry sounded from the other side of the compound as the forest seemed to spit forth a hundred Indians brandishing weapons of all sorts. Two of the last of Carlos's bunch ran a few yards in front of them, but they were quickly overtaken. From the screams and the accompanying chopping strikes, Doc knew that these two crooks were no longer a threat.

He turned his view back to the immediate scene in time to see Carlos and his sole remaining confederate, who was trying to scramble into the jeep. Carlos raised his pistol and shot the man in the back of the head, pushing the slumping body out of the way as he got behind the wheel of the jeep and started it up. Doc could see Audrey's face recoil in terror as the jeep bounced over the uneven ground toward the macadamized road.

Balam ran down to join them and the surging crowd of Indians continued forward. As the group came upon Doc and the others, Balam jumped in front of them, yelling in his native tongue. The Indians stopped, looking at Doc and the dead henchmen. Several of them carried items taken from the men already killed, and one held Doc's bloody utility belt.

Doc grabbed the belt and began running toward the center of the camp.

"Thomas, Ace," he yelled. "The motorcycles."

Deagan and Ace ran forward, each trying to get to the Indian first. Deagan managed to outrun Ace's limping pace, but just as he got there, Doc shot past him and jumped on the seat.

"I'll need you two to take the one with the sidecar, Thomas," Doc said. "I'll draw his fire and you get Audrey." His foot kicked down the starter. The motorcycle roared to life and Doc sped forward after the jeep.

Deagan nodded and turned, but as he did so he saw that Assante had assumed the driver's seat in the two-man cycle.

"Let's go," Ace said, grinning as he revved the accelerator.

Deagan quickly sandwiched himself into the sidecar and Ace tore out after Doc.

Doc could barely see in the cloud of dust left in the jeep's wake. Nonetheless, he pressed onward, trying to listen for the other vehicle over the high-pitched whine of the motorcycle's engine. The dust cloud thinned slightly and he caught a glimpse of the jeep. Carlos was leaning back over the seat and a red glow erupted from the gun in his fist.

Doc banked to the side and hoped that Deagan and Ace were not in the bullet's path. Seconds later they appeared beside him, Ace smiling brightly. He'd taken the time to place his goggles on his face, as had

Deagan. Doc indicated that he'd go right and they criss-crossed the gravel road. Twisting the accelerator, Doc shot closer to the jeep as Carlos fired another shot.

Dropping back, Doc zigzagged again, coming up to the left side of the jeep. Carlos twisted, trying to turn, but Doc adroitly steered the motorcycle right again. As Carlos turned to level his weapon at Doc, Ace and

Deagan roared up to the left rear of the jeep. Deagan had wedged his short legs into the top portion of the sidecar, and was stretching the rest of his body outward. Ace veered in closer to the jeep and Deagan snatched Audrey in his powerful arms.

Ace immediately slowed, allowing the jeep to continue hurtling forward. Carlos glanced quickly at them, and then raised his pistol at Doc, who was immediately alongside on the right, and fired just as Doc grabbed the canvas covered idols.

The muzzle flash of the point blank discharge looked like a small explosion to Ace and Mad Dog.

"Did Doc get hit?" Deagan yelled, still holding Audrey across his lap in the sidecar.

Ace's lips pulled into a grim line as he saw Doc's motorcycle careening out of control before him, skidding across the road in a sideways skid, leaving a thick gouge in the surface gravel as it went.

But suddenly Doc seemed to regain control of the machine, his feet splaying outward for stability. In a split-second he stopped the cycle, dropped the canvas covered totems, and ran forward down the road. He was reaching into his utility belt as he ran. The jeep was at least sixty yards away from him now, but Doc's right arm cocked back then shot forward in a flash. The miniature grenade spanned the distance in four seconds and detonated just as Carlos had swiveled in the seat to fire another round.

Everyone stared at the brightness of the blast, then shielded their eyes from subsequent percussive wave. As the cloud of dust rolled past them, Ace, Deagan, and Audrey looked up, searching for any sight of Doc, but couldn't see him. Ace drove forward slowly, while Deagan untied Audrey's hands. The Indian motorcycle lay on its side in the middle of the road.

"Doc," Ace called, coughing slightly. "Where are you? Are you all right?"

"I am," Doc said.

Through the powdery mist they saw him emerging from the side of the road carrying the canvas-wrapped idols.

"That last round was point blank," Deagan said. "Did he hit you?"

Doc held up the canvas to show them the perforation of the bullet hole. He undid the ropes securing the tarp and laid the package on the road and began flipping it over and over. After several rolls the two jade idols were at the end of the canvas trail. The left leg of the frowning idol had been completely shattered just below the hip.

"I'm afraid our dour friend here sustained a rather grievous injury," Doc said. Then he smiled as he looked at Audrey. "But I don't think any emergency surgery will be in order this time.

* * *

Hours later, Deagan and Ace came through the camp with a group of natives following. Doc, Professor Guffrey, and Audrey stood up and waved. As they neared Doc the Indians dropped back, as if in awe. Deagan rested the Thompson on his shoulder and held a black backpack in his other hand.

"This'll make a nice addition to our arsenal, won't it?" he said.

"Any sign of Rabbat?" Audrey asked. "I'd hate to think that he's out there somewhere watching us."

"No need to worry about that," Ace said.

"They led us to his body," added Deagan. "It looks like an old fashioned pin cushion. He ain't gonna be bothering nobody no more."

"We saw to a quick burial," Ace said. "Figured it would save explaining that these people were only defending themselves after being attacked."

"I've buried those killed by the Indians as well," Doc said. "The others we'll notify the local authorities about."

Deagan grunted in approval and held the backpack toward Doc.

"Looks like Rabbat fell behind the others because he was weighted down with this."

Doc opened the pack and took out several of the lustrous yellow cubes.

"The lure of gold," Ace said. "As old as mankind itself."

Doc tested the weight of the metal in his hand, then took out his knife. The sun glistened off the stone as he held one of the cubes up and scraped it with the blade. Deagan's face broke into a wide grin as he saw the yellow flakes. Ace looked questioningly.

"He was actually weighted down with a whole lot of nothin'." Deagan said. "That's fool's gold, ain't it?"

"Also known as pyrite," Doc said. "One of the most common metallic substances found in the earth's crust. With its luster, it's often mistaken for gold, but is significantly less dense and much more brittle."

"It's why the Spaniards left the Mayans," Professor Guffrey said. "They had no gold to steal."

"Add the Egyptians to that list now," Ace said, with a grin.

Several of the natives moved forward now, behind Saknik and Balam. They carried the two idols. Balam spoke to Professor Guffrey and gestured at Doc.

"Michael," Guffrey said. "They want to give you the idols for saving the chief's son and routing Carlos and the others."

"Professor," Doc said, "please tell them I'm very grateful, but I can hardly accept such a gift."

Guffrey leaned closer.

"Remember, son," he said, smiling. "I've spent quite a bit of time with them these past few days. Not to accept their offering would be considered an egregious affront."

Doc was silent for a moment.

"Then I will take this one," he said, reaching out for the broken statue whose twisted frown now looked like a grimace of pain. He held it up and smiled. "It not only saved my life, but perhaps its removal will signal an end to evil in the area. Also tell them that I will make sure that it is kept in a place of honor."

Guffrey did a rough translation and the Indians began a collective cheering. The old shaman placed a hand on Doc's shoulder and smiled.

* * *

The next morning the sun was rising over the village of Santa Merida as Doc and company were unloading a few medical supplies from the plane and placing them into Professor Guffrey's new jeep. Audrey stood by watching with a wistful expression on her face. Doc looked up and saw her, then smiled.

"Are you sure you won't come back with us now?" he asked.

She smiled and shook her head.

"I have to stay just a little bit longer," she said. "To help my father get set up for his new project. Besides, I have some medical work left to do. I'll have to remove that boy's stitches." She smiled as she gestured at the boxes of supplies. "We have a lot of people down here to vaccinate, and the means to do it, now."

"A book on the similarities between the Egyptian and Mayan cultures is a worthwhile undertaking for him," he said. "So when can I tell the medical school to expect you?"

"I'll be home for Christmas," she said, reaching out and taking his hand. "Michael, you've made such difference here. And for me, too. You've made me see that my true calling is medicine. How can I ever thank you?"

"You becoming a good physician will be reward enough," Doc said.

Audrey's hand caressed his face, and she leaned forward to kiss him. Slowly, Doc's arms went around to embrace her.

"Whoever that woman is, who's stolen your heart," Audrey said, her lips whispering close to his ear, "she's a lucky girl."

They continued in their embrace, oblivious to those around them, and to the approach of a slow moving taxicab down the main street of the town. The cab stopped abruptly. Doc and Audrey kissed again as the taxi's door slammed. Then Doc heard Deagan say, "Hey, look who's here."

Doc glanced over Audrey's shoulder to see a dark haired woman, looking rumpled and exhausted, approaching from a distance carrying two large suitcases. As the woman got closer, Deagan slapped Ace on the shoulder and pointed.

"What? Penny?" Ace said. "How the hell did you get all the way down here?"

"It wasn't easy," Penny said, letting her suitcases drop to the ground at the sides. She glared at Doc and Audrey who were about twenty feet away. Doc had not acknowledged her arrival at all.

"Well, ain't you a sight for sore eyes," Deagan said. "We missed ya."

"Yeah, I'll bet," Penny said. "It sure looks that way."

"Aww, don't let that make you jealous," Deagan said. "Her and Doc are old friends."

"From way back," Ace said.

"I know that," Penny said, her face flushing. "And I am not jealous!"

Doc and Audrey were at the jeep now. He helped her into the seat and placed the final box in the back and pulled the canvas tarp tight around the load. She leaned forward and kissed him gently on the cheek.

"I'll call you when I get back to New York," she said.

Doc smiled and nodded. "I'll be looking forward to seeing you there." He waved as the Professor put the jeep in gear and drove off. Then he turned and strolled over to Penny, his expression somewhat stern.

"Penelope," he said, "I believe I forbad you to come down here."

"And I can see why, too," she said, looking at the departing jeep.

Doc reached out for her arm.

"Let me check your vaccination," he said, but she immediately pulled away.

"Don't touch me," she said.

Doc stared at her for a moment, then turned away. "Very well. Thomas, could you see that her baggage is properly placed in the Athena. Ace, let's get the plane prepared. We have a long flight."

"Okay, Doc," Assante said. He started to move forward, but Penny ran up to him.

"Ace," Penny said, reaching out and touching his arm. "Do you remember when we first met, you invited me to the opera?"

"Yes, but that was a while ago," he said. "Before—"

"Well, is the offer still good?"

Ace looked to Doc, who said nothing.

"Well, is it?" Penny asked.

"I . . . I'll have to check my social calendar," Ace said rather evasively.

"Good," said Penny. Then, turning to Doc, added, "And why don't we make it a double date? You can ask Audrey?"

"Perhaps I shall," Doc said, walking toward the plane.

"Whooeee," said Deagan, lighting up one of his cigars and blowing out a prodigious smoke ring. "Better make sure that plane's A-okay, guys. I think I see a storm a coming."

THE END

Desert Shadows II

July 7th, 1947
THE SKIES OVER
SOUTHERN NEW MEXICO
NEAR A TOWN
CALLED ROSWELL

ROBERT FIELDING ADJUSTED the fuel mixture on his North American T-6 Texan single engine plane as he began the gradual slanting descent that would bring him down near the landing strip on his ranch. Being near the Roswell Army Air Field, he radioed the tower that he'd be descending from 4,000 feet and that his banking turn would take him close to their air space. Since he'd gotten the T-6 for a nominal sum from military surplus, he didn't want it mistaken for one of the military's planes.

"Roger, T-6," the voice said over the radio. We show you on screen. All looks clear for your descent. Over."

"Roger that, Roswell Tower," Fielding said into his own mike. "Thanks for the—"

He never finished the transmission. Something seemed to whiz by the front of his plane leaving a discernible wake. He grabbed the yoke with both hands to guide the small plane through the turbulence. The unexpected roughness didn't bother him as much as the tower having told him he was clear. After all, he was a former Army Air Corp flier himself, and hated the thought of another serviceman being remiss in his duties. If an air traffic controller would have broadcast erroneous information like that when he'd been on active duty, the guy would have found himself standing before a review board in a hurry.

"Roswell Tower," said Fielding, "you guys aren't flying any of those new fangled jet fighters up this way, are you?"

"Negative, T-6," the radio replied. "I say again, our screen shows you on a clear descent. Over."

Another wave of turbulence shook the small plane and Fielding grabbed the yoke once more. Something was causing the disturbance. Something like a plane traveling at a hell of a speed. He reached for the mike again.

"Roswell from T-6 Texan, I'm experiencing some high turbulence up here. Are you sure you guys don't show any other crafts in the area? Over."

"Negative, T.6. Do you need to set down on our field? Over."

Fielding was considering taking them up on their offer. The Air Base was closer than his ranch by several miles, and there damn sure was something causing these sheers. The question was what? Then he saw a shining glint of something hovering in the sky to his left. Huge. . . Circular. . .

What the hell is that? he asked himself.

All at once he heard a strange whining sound. Like the whistle of an approaching artillery shell. It seemed to grow louder. Fielding glanced around the cockpit. No other aircraft in sight. The turbulence started again, but this time much stronger. He had to keep both hands on the yoke to maintain control, but even so he could feel the plane jumping and lurching like a yo-yo. Still he did not lose control, nor did he panic. After all, he'd flown 25 missions over Germany in worse situations than this. And he'd been copilot to the best. Fielding grabbed for the mike.

"Roswell Tower, this is T-6. Mayday! Mayday! I'm losing cont—"

But before he could finish the cockpit glass exploded sending a burst of a thousand needle-like shards over him. Wind seared his bloodied face. Trying to shield his eyes with one hand, he pulled back on the yoke with his other. Maybe if he could get above it. . . Suddenly he heard the sputtering of the engine as it faded out, and the howling noise increased, seeming to rupture his eardrums. Blood burst from his nose, then his mouth. Unable to breathe, Fielding tried to pull the nose of the plane up, but the noise continued to increase. He felt something pop in each ear, then the thundering roar of the plane as it spun into an almost vertical dive drowning out everything. Even the sound of his screams.

* * *

The cab pulled up the busy sidewalk in front of the Empire State Building at 34th and 5th. The man inside got out slowly, extending his long legs first, then bracing himself on the door and gaining purchase with a long, wooden cane. The cane had an ornately formed handle that seemed to fit easily into the man's powerful hand. As he stood and reached for his wallet, people passing by were taken by his startling handsomeness. He was a dead ringer for Errol Flynn.

As the cab pulled away, the man moved with slow deliberation toward the main entrance of the tallest of buildings. The doorman, a big dough-faced Irishman, touched the brim of his cap and said, "Good afternoon to you, Mr. Assante."

Edward "Ace" Assante merely nodded, which was a surprise to O'Bannion, the doorman. Assante was usually the cheerful picture of style and grace. But today he looked fatigued and saddened.

"Would everything be all right with you, sir?" O'Bannion asked. His permanent duty station as the doorman, and his assistance to Doc Atlas and his crew on several occasions, had given him something of a familiarity with the famous group.

Ace showed him a weary smile, then shook his head.

"I've had better days," he said, then proceeded toward the express elevator that would take him up to the floor of the headquarters of Doc Atlas. Slipping his special key in the slot, Ace twisted it and waited for the express elevator to begin its quick ascent. He glanced up at the video monitor in case Doc or Polly, Doc's chief secretary, were watching to see who was inside. A special alarm sounded inside Doc's quarters whenever anyone used the express. The regular elevators did not stop at Doc's floors.

The doors whooshed open a few seconds later and Ace stepped into the hallway that led to Doc's main office. The heels of his shoes echoed against the highly polished marble. After pushing through the doors, Ace saw a pretty redhead sitting behind the large desk busily typing. She looked up and smiled brightly as Assante entered.

"Hi, Ace," she said. "They're in the gymnasium."Ace nodded and proceeded onward.

"Gosh, are you all right?" Polly asked.

Ace merely shook his head and continued through the door to the left, which he knew led to Doc's living quarters. Beyond that were his laboratory, equipment rooms, and gym. Doc's headquarters was so large that they took up the entire floor as well as the ones above and below. One of the floors contained a massive main-frame computer, the first of its kind, along with an entire staff of office workers. It was their job to feed information into the computer so that Doc could run projections for virtually any subject of which he had interest or concern. Often times the Government would contact him for assistance due to his incredible abilities and intelligence.

Assante continued down the hallway and through the doors that opened into the gymnasium. It was a long room with heavy mats lining the walls. Several rows of weightlifting equipment were stacked against one wall, and high jumping, pole vaulting, and parallel bars sat within an extended oblong track. Tables containing stacks of such eclectic items as bowling pins, baseballs, archery equipment, and fencing swords lay in organized groups. Twin ropes, thick as huge cables, were attached to a bare steel girder along the ceiling. And at the far end of the gym Ace could see two men near a maze of boxing equipment. One of the men, the shorter of the two, was holding a heavy bag that was attached to a metallic frame. Each blow caused the thick corded muscles of his arms to fan outward in bas-relief displaying a sense of power. The other man was a tawny haired Adonis. He was six-foot one and the muscles of his perfectly proportioned body seemed to bulge on his frame like bundled piano wire. Each blow that he sent whistling into the heavy bag practically lifted the shorter man off his feet. And Ace knew that Doc was holding back with his punches.

Stopping a few yards from them, Assante felt in his pocket for his cigarettes and withdrew one from a fancy silver case. Taking his lighter, he flipped back the tip, but before he could flick the wheel to strike the flint, the shorter man yelled at him.

"Hey, Ace, what the hell you doing? You know that Doc don't allow no smoking here in the gym. Especially when he's working out. And you're wearing dress shoes, too, you knucklehead."

Assante merely held the lighter out and stared at it.

"You deaf, shyster?" the shorter man, Thomas "Mad Dog" Deagan yelled again. "I told ya no smoking."

"Thomas," Doc Atlas said, pausing from his punching drill. "Ace seems a bit preoccupied."

"When ain't he preoccupied?" Deagan said. He waited for the customary caustic, but friendly reply that usually continued into an ongoing banter between the two old friends. But none came.

"Doc, if you have a minute, I'd like to speak to you," Assante said. He still held the lighter in his fist.

"Certainly," Doc said.

"We still got another round to go," Deagan said.

"I'll wait for you in the library then?" Assante asked.

Doc nodded and resumed punching the bag.

Ace walked back across the polished wood floor and through the set of doors that led to the conference room. Inside, he removed his hat and sat at a table near the entrance. Grabbing an ashtray, he lighted his cigarette, pausing to watch the flame, then clipping down the lid. He read the inscription on the side of the Zippo as the tears welled up in his eyes.

TO ACE—
MAY GOD ALWAYS BE YOUR CO-PILOT
BOB FIELDING.

Assante was staring wistfully at the writing when the door burst open and a startlingly attractive woman came in. She had raven-black hair that hung about her shoulders, and features that were at once beautiful and symmetrically perfect. Her light blue suit showed the exquisite curves of her elegant figure, and she had begun unfastening the buttons of the jacket as she walked. Flinging the coat onto the tabletop, she set down the sheaf of papers she had and reached in her purse.

"Hi, Ace," she said."Where's Doc?"

It took Penelope Cartier, top reporter for the *New York Times,* only half a heartbeat to tune in on Assante's melancholy mood.

"Ace, what's wrong?" she asked, moving over to him and placing a hand on his shoulder with the familiarity of a close friend, or an old lover. "You look terrible."

"A buddy of mine was killed," Assante said. "We served together in the War."

"Oh, that's terrible. I'm so sorry."

Assante's thumb closed over the lighter and he put it in his pocket. Penny's hand lightly moved toward his neck.

"He was my co-pilot," Assante said. "We flew 25 missions together, before I got hit. He managed to get the B-17 back to England, as chewed up as she was, and radioed for an ambulance as we were setting down. Probably saved my leg and my life."

Penny leaned her hip against him as he brought both hands to cover his face. Reaching down, she quickly plucked the smoldering cigarette from between his fingers and brought it to her own lips. Just then the door opened quickly and Deagan entered, wiping his face with a sodden towel.

"Man, if I coulda punched half as hard as Doc, I woulda been able to take on Joe Louis," he said. He glanced over at Assante and added, "What's the matter, shyster? Lose a big case, or something?"

"Mad Dog, leave him alone," Penny said. She exhaled a smoky breath and shot him a reproachful glance. "He just lost a friend."

"Oh yeah?" Deagan said, giving his face a few more ineffectual wipes. "Anybody I'd know?"

"I doubt it," Assante said. "He was from my old bombardier unit."

Deagan grunted. As a retired military man, he'd lost plenty of buddies himself, and knew the bond men shared after serving together. "Sorry to hear that, Ace," he said.

Assante nodded an acknowledgment.

"His wife called me this morning," he said. "Wanted to know if I'd come out to the funeral. Be one of the pall bearers. I figured it's the least I could do. He practically saved my life once."

"Where's the funeral at?" Deagan asked.

"New Mexico," Assante said. "A little place called Roswell. But he crashed near an Army Air Base and the military's holding his body as well as the wreckage." Assante's brow furrowed as he looked at Deagan. "The family can't even cut through all the red tape to make the necessary funeral arrangements. I thought if you or Doc could make a few phone calls it might break the log jam."

"Sure, I'll do what I can," Deagan said. "You know the name of the base commander?"

Assante shook his bead.

"My secretary's been trying to get me reservations on a flight to Santa Fe or Albuquerque, but it seems that everything's booked up."

The door opened again and Doc Atlas strode in. Despite the towel around his neck, his body still gleamed with a fine sheen of perspiration that seemed to accentuate the powerful symmetry of his chiseled musculature.

"It won't be necessary for you to fly commercially, Ace," Doc said. "I've just called the maintenance crew at the airfield to prepare the Pegasus. We can fly directly there."

As soon as Doc Atlas entered the room, Penny quickly stubbed out the cigarette and discreetly removed her hand from Ace's shoulder.

"Doc," Assante said, looking up at the Golden Avenger. "I certainly appreciate it, but I couldn't ask you to drop all your own personal business."

"Actually, it will serve a double purpose," Doc said. "I've been asked by Washington to proceed out to Roswell Army Air Field to take part in an informal investigation. I was going to ask you to accompany me anyway."

"Investigation?" said Assante. "What kind?"

"I'll brief you all on the plane," Doc said. "I must shower and prepare for the trip." He turned and abruptly pushed through the door to his living quarters.

Used to Docs tacit announcements, the others were not surprised by this. But as Deagan scratched his jaw, and Assante continued to look perplexed, Penny grabbed the newspaper she'd been holding and spread it out on the table top in front of them.

"Hey, guys, what do you want to bet it has to do with something about this?" she said, smiling triumphantly. The two men stared down at the block letters of the headline, and then back to one another. It read:

FLYING SAUCER CRASHES NEAR AIR BASE ARMY TO HOLD BRIEFING WITH DETAILS

Deagan emitted a low whistle. "No wonder there ain't no room on any of the planes flying west, " he said.

* * *

The Pegasus was a Cessna UC-78 Bobcat Light Personnel Transport plane that Doc usually used for quick jaunts. His crew at the air-field had it fueled and set up for him upon arrival. Since Penny insisted on coming along due to the burgeoning UFO stories emanating from the area, Doc elected to delay the take-off until she had packed enough clothes for several days. Doc and Ace did the customary pre-flight inspection themselves while the crew fueled the plane. With Ace in the co-pilot's seat, and Doc at the controls, the Pegasus taxied to the runway and took off flawlessly into the strong northern wind. Once airborne Doc radioed ahead with his flight plan, which was practically pre-approved due to Doc's prominence.

After setting down in Chicago and Joplin, for refueling, Doc again took off toward New Mexico. Somewhere over Kansas he noticed Ace's eyes starting to droop.

"Ace, are you tired?" Doc asked.

Assante snapped awake.

"No. Why? Did I miss something?"

"Perhaps some adequate rest," Doc said with a rare smile. "Why don't you go in back and take a nap."

Ace yawned.

"Yeah, I guess I'm not doing much good up here, am I?" he said. "Maybe I'll go back and test some of that awful coffee Mad Dog always brings along in his old thermos."

Ace left the cockpit and went back into the plane. Doc continued flying, his amber eyes scanning the horizon tirelessly. Presently Penny came forward holding a cup of steaming black coffee in both hands. Cautiously, she released her grip with one of her hands and gently touched Doc's shoulder.

"I thought you might like some of this, darling," she said.

"Thank you," said Doc.

Penny moved into the seat next to him and gazed through the glass windshield at the darkening sky.

"Oh my God, it's so beautiful up here," she said. "Look, those clouds are all in a row."

"They always are. It's just the curve of the horizon that makes them appear on different levels from the ground."

"Really?" she said. "Just perception, or I guess people's misperceptions." She glanced back into the plane and smiled. "The two of them are back there chatting like long-lost school chums instead of arguing like they usually do. Ace is talking about all the missions he flew with that Fielding fellow."

"Beneath the surface of their bickering," Doc said, "lies a deep friendship between them."

"There certainly does," she said. Her dark eyes slowly took in the powerful symmetry of Doc's well-proportioned, but powerful body. "So, have you seen any suspicious unidentified flying objects?"

"None," Doc said.

"What do you think about all this brouhaha in New Mexico? Do you think it could be true?"

"I have yet to form an opinion," Doc said. "But it might not be prudent to subscribe to this current wave of hysteria too quickly."

"I suppose not. But the paper's printed a three thousand dollar reward for anyone who can find proof that a flying saucer really did crash there." She looked at him and sighed. "Do you think there actually are crafts and creatures from other worlds?"

Doc didn't answer, as was his custom with most hypothetical questions. Used to this, Penny continued.

"The first half of the century's almost over, and just look at how far we've come," she said. "Buck Rogers doesn't seem so far fetched anymore. We'll probably send a man to the moon by the end of the century, don't you think?"

"Perhaps," Doc said. "Perhaps sooner."

Upon landing at Roswell Army Air Field and securing the Pegasus in a section reserved for aircraft storage west of the main hanger, Doc, Ace, Deagan and Penny moved away from the airstrip. Although they had flown straight through two time zones, and it was only beginning to get dark here, their fatigue from the long flight was evident on all except Doc. He seemed tireless. An army sergeant with an MP brassard on his arm pulled up for them in a jeep. He glanced at Penny with a startled look and then smiled sheepishly.

"Sorry, ma'am," he said. "I wasn't told you'd be coming along. My orders just specified picking up the gents."

"That's okay, soldier," Penny said, hiking up her skirt so she could step into the back of the jeep. "it won't be the first time I hitched a ride where I had to sit on the back fender. Just get this crate moving so we can cool off."

The sergeant's eyes were glued on her shapely legs.

Ace slipped in next, followed by Deagan, who lowered the seat behind him. Doc got in the front passenger side and turned to the sergeant.

"If you would be so kind as to drop Miss Cartier off by the officer's club, then take us to see the base commander," Doc said.

"Yes, sir."

The jeep took off with a start, spinning away from the parallel twin airstrips and heading toward the cluster of Quonset huts and buildings.

Ace, Deagan, and Doc were ushered into a Spartan looking office with a large gunmetal gray desk opposite the door. Three chairs had been set up in front, and the blades of a large fan blew through a metallic cage circulating the hot air. Both Deagan and Ace had removed their suit jackets and loosened their ties. Doc had worn his usual tan utility shirt and dark pants, but even he seemed to be feeling the effects of the hot, dry desert heat.

"Quite a change from July in New York, eh?" Colonel William Blanchard said as he and another man walked into the room. The other man was tall and dark. His uniform shirt seemed to hang loosely on his lanky frame. Blanchard sat in the chair behind the desk and grinned broadly at Deagan. "It's been a long time, Mad Dog."

Deagan rose and shook Blanchard's extended hand.

"You're right about that, Butch," Deagan said. "What you been doing since the end of the War?"

"Keeping the peace," the Colonel said. "Hell, it's been a while hasn't it?"

"A while since we were young?" Deagan said with a grin. Blanchard's eyebrows lifted, then he shook his head.

"Yes, I think so," he said. "This is Captain Rod Seals with MCI. Military Counter-Intelligence."

Seals moved forward and shook hands with Doc, Ace, and Deagan. His dark eyes seemed to linger on Doc longer than usual, as if he were sizing up the Golden Avenger.

"I just got off the phone with Secretary Forestall," Blanchard said. He took out a handkerchief and wiped his forehead and upper lip. "He explained that he wanted you out here as part of an informal investigative committee."

"That is what he expressed to me also," Doc said. "What can you tell me of this crash incident?"

"Not much," Seals said. He had been standing near the Colonel. Seals removed a pack of cigarettes and said, "Colonel, may I?" Blanchard nodded and handed him an ashtray. Seal first offered the pack around, but no one took any. After extracting one and placing it between his lips, Seals said, "This whole thing's been blown totally out of proportion.

"How's that?" Deagan asked.

Seals lighted his cigarette, shook out the match, and dropped it in the ashtray.

"There never was any flying saucer wreckage recovered," he said. "The press grabbed an unsubstantiated rumor and ran it like it was fact."

"Well, if it wasn't a flying saucer, what was it?" Ace asked. He was leaning forward, both hands resting on the top of his cane.

"Simply put, gentlemen," Seals said, "it was a weather balloon."

"Huh? A balloon?" Deagan said. "But didn't you guys already say it was some kind of alien craft?"

Colonel Blanchard cleared his throat.

"This whole matter has been one confusing SNAFU after another," he said. "Captain."

"The actual crash that the papers are raving about now happened last month sometime," Seals said.

"Last month?" Ace said.

"Right," said Seals. "One of our local ranchers, a Mr. Mac Brazel, noticed some sort of strange wreckage out on the range on June 14th about 85 miles north of here." He went to a section of maps along the far wall. "The wreckage was strewn over about two hundred yards along here. Brazel didn't think much of it until the newspapers started running stories about all these supposed UFO sightings."

"UFO?" Deagan asked.

"Unidentified Flying Objects," Seals said. "Little more than people seeing lights in the sky. We surmise that somehow Brazel got wind of some radio or newspaper offering a reward to anyone who found a flying saucer, as they've been calling them, and he saw a chance to get rich quickly."

Seals took a long drag on the cigarette and let the smoke envelope him as he lifted a large leather briefcase onto the desk.

"On July 7th Brazel dropped off some of the wrecked stuff he'd found at the local sheriffs office. The next day the *Roswell Daily Record* printed this." Seals reached into the briefcase and withdrew a folded newspaper. Holding it in both hands, he spread it out in front of them. The headline stood out in bold lettering:

RAAF Captures Flying Saucer On Ranch in Roswell Region

Seals folded the paper and replaced it in the case. The tip of his cigarette turned to crimson ash.

"This debris, I might add," Seals said, "weighed about five pounds and was composed of wood, tinfoil, and metal. It was the remnants of a high altitude weather balloon. Unfortunately, when one of our overzealous officers in Intelligence recovered the material from the sheriff, he made some outlandish statement about the wreckage being from a flying saucer." Seals frowned.

"Major Marcel is being dealt with appropriately," Colonel Blanchard said.

"Marcel was the man who received the material from Sheriff Wilcox," Seals added. "Apparently he convinced our press officer to go along with his wild theory."

"Where is this wreckage?" Doc asked. All eyes turned to him. "I should like a chance to examine it myself," he said.

"Why, I'm afraid that isn't possible, *Major* Atlas," Colonel Blanchard said quickly, stressing Doc's former military rank. "Everything was transferred to Brigade HQ in Ft. Worth. By order of the General."

Doc turned to Deagan.

"Thomas, tomorrow make the call to General Ramey," Doc said.

Deagan smirked and nodded. Blanchard's lips seemed to stretch into a thin line.

"We also have another matter to attend to," Doc said, turning back to the

Colonel. "I believe that you are holding the remains of a crashed civilian airplane along with the pilot?"

"You're talking about Robert Fielding?" Seals asked, the ash of his cigarette turning bright orange again. "How the hell did you hear about him?"

"He and I flew 25 missions together during the War," Ace said. "His widow called me."

Colonel Blanchard exhaled slowly.

"Yes, regrettably we are holding his remains," he said. "Our base doctor wanted someone to assist him with the autopsy due to some. . . irregularities he noticed. We didn't feel comfortable releasing him or the wreckage until we'd had a chance to go over everything with a fine-tooth comb. Then this flying saucer thing hit the papers and everything got fouled up."

"Sir," Assante said, "do you have any idea how stress-filled this has been for his family?"

"Indeed I do, Captain Assante," Blanchard said, showing that he'd also taken the time to research Ace's former military rank. "Believe me, I wrote plenty of condolence letters home during the War, so I know all about a family's grief."

"With all due respect, sir," Assante said, "we are not at war now."

"Perhaps," Doc said, "if I may be allowed to examine the body, and the wreckage, I could expedite the matter."

"Why, that would certainly help, Major Atlas," Captain Seals said. He'd taken out another cigarette and was flicking open his Zippo. "But like we told you, we're waiting on the arrival of another qualified physician."

"You can call him Doc," Deagan said, popping a large wooden kitchen match with his thumbnail and holding it in front of the Captain's nose. Seals shifted his eyes to Deagan, then flipped the cap to his lighter closed.

* * *

Penny draped her coat over the rear of the bar stool and took a small sip of her martini. A bit too heavy on the vermouth for her tastes, but it was cold and at this point that's all that counted for her. She closed her eyes and leaned her head back, feeling the warmth of the liquor trickle down the inside of her throat. Two large fans, each encased in a crisscross of steel wires, stood at either end of the bar blowing a cooling breeze across the room. After the ubiquitous heat of the desert tarmac, this felt pretty close to heaven. A jukebox at the far end of the room played something slow and soft, and the muted conversations of the groups of uniformed men and women in civilian and nurses attire played an almost whispering accompaniment. Several tables were composed of men in suits and ties, reporters from the look of them, but Penny had no desire to go over and break the ice with any of them. If there was a story here, she'd nose it out herself. Reaching inside her purse for her cigarettes, she'd just removed one from the silver case when a large hand appeared in front of her. It held a silver lighter.

"Allow me," a burly looking man with a short gray beard said. His thumb snapped over the wheel igniting the wick. Penny nodded a thank you as she leaned toward the flame. Tossing her head back to free her hair from her shoulders, she looked at the man more closely.

"Say, aren't you?" she started to ask.

"D. Phillip Stringer, at your service, ma'am," the man said, sliding into the stool next to her and lighting his own cigarette. "And you are, I must say, the closest thing to a breath of fresh air since these two fans got here, Miss Cartier." Stringer grinned, showing her a row of straight, but somewhat discolored teeth.

"You know who I am?" Penny asked.

Stringer held up two fingers to the bartender who immediately brought him a shot glass and a beer.

"Of course I know who you are," Stringer said, emitting a low chuckle. His thick fingers gripped the shot glass and he downed the whiskey in one gulp. "Ahhhhhh. Nothing like that first shot after a long, hard day in front of the typewriter. Right?"

"I agree," Penny said. "But you still haven't answered my question."

"Question?" Stringer said, picking up the stein and taking a copious sip. The foam covered his mustache. "What question was that, my dear?"

"How you knew who I was."

"Oh, that." He took one last pull on his cigarette and stubbed it out. "Why wouldn't I recognize the most famous reporter of the *New York Times*? I read your by-line, even out in these parts. I even enjoy it sometimes."

"But my picture isn't with my by-line."

"True, true," he said, bringing the glass to his lips again. "But then again, it's not every day that the world renown Doc Atlas arrives in some fly-on-the-map little air base like this one, either."

"Oh, so that's it," Penny said. She blew out a cloudy breath. "I should have known."

Stringer grinned at her sardonically.

"So, you could at least return my compliment by saying that you liked my books," he said.

"Was that a compliment?" she asked. She set her cigarette in the ashtray between them and picked up her martini with both hands. After she took another sip, she turned to look at him. "But actually, I did enjoy *A Feast of Fools.*"

"I'll bet you did," Stringer said, draining his stein. "It's a love story. All women like those." He held up two fingers again and the bartender brought him another pair of drinks.

"So what brings a world famous author like you to this little fly-on-the-map air base?" Penny asked.

"The same as you," he said after downing the whiskey. "The possibility of beings from another world."

"And what conclusions have you drawn?" she asked.

"Conclusions?" Stringer said, slamming the shot glass down on the bar. "The damn army's being so close-mouthed about everything that we might as well be back at the front reading censored dispatches. But it's a might more interesting now that you're here." He grinned again and dropped his hand onto Penny's thigh. "Right!" He gave her leg a quick squeeze.

"Wrong" Penny said, tilting her glass so that the clear liquid poured out onto the front of Stringer's pants. He leapt up swearing and waving his arms. "You're lucky I didn't order hot coffee," she said.

Before Stringer could say anything else, he felt a strong set of fingers grab his shoulder.

"Trouble, Penny?" Assante asked, his hand still on the author's upper arm. Deagan's large hand curled around Stringer's other arm, letting him feel the slumbering power in the grip. Captain Rod Seals stood behind them looking somewhat concerned.

"Nothing I couldn't handle, Ace," Penny said. "Do you need me to introduce Misters Assante and Deagan, Mr. Stringer? And who's your handsome friend in uniform?"

Captain Seals stepped forward and introduced himself to Penny.

Stringer's lips curled back into a wicked looking smile and he extended his open palm toward Assante. Ace shook it.

"Dammit. You guys got grips of iron," Stringer said. "Let me buy you both a drink."

"You're *the* D. Phillip Stringer?" Deagan asked. "I used to read your stuff in The *Stars and Stripes*.

"Mr. Stringer is one of the few civilians we allow to have an almost free run of the base," Captain Seals said. "He occasionally obliges our base newspaper, the *Atomic Blast,* with an article or story."

"I remember *Dispatches from the Front* from the War," Assante said. "Good stuff. But I preferred *Blood on the Rose.* Your novel about the fall of Madrid. Were you really there for it?"

Stringer exhaled deeply. "Yeah, I'm a sucker for lost causes, I guess. Got shot up so bad they wouldn't even look at me for any active duty once America got involved."

"Hey, we was never involved in that one, pal," Deagan said. "If memory serves me correctly, Spain remained neutral, but old Franco was still playing footsie with Hitler after he kicked out all the Reds of Madrid. I didn't see nobody coming to help us out."

"Deagan," Stringer said. "You're an Irishman, huh? Maybe you should look at your own Emerald Isle before you go criticizing the Spanish Republicans."

"The only Emerald Isle that I come from is Brooklyn," Deagan said. " And don't you forget it."

Stringer looked at Mad Dog's expression, then blew out a boozy laugh. "Yep, Irish all the way. Put 'er there, pal," he said extending his hand again. "You're all right in my book."

But after Deagan grasped Stringer's hand, it suddenly became apparent that the author was trying to demonstrate that he, too, had a powerful grip. Deagan merely gritted his teeth and squeezed back. Seconds later Stringer's mouth snapped open and he was squealing loudly.

"Okay, okay, you've proved your point," the author said. As Deagan released him Stringer flexed his hand several times. "Hey, I make a living with these, you know."

"Then I'd watch where you put 'em," Deagan said, cocking his head toward Penny.

"Message received. Now, let me buy you guys those drinks, all right?" He motioned to the bartender and said, "Set 'em up for my friends, Fred. Anything they want."

Stringer's gesture was so expansive that he nearly fell over. Captain Seals had disappeared during the posturing, but now he re-entered the club with a small dark complected man wearing a tan chauffeur's uniform. They spoke in whispered tones from the doorway, then Seals left. The other man approached them and spoke in rapid Spanish to Stringer, who replied with equal, but somewhat slurred fluency.

"I guess it's time to go," Stringer said, his bulky form practically collapsing the small man. "But you're all invited out to my place. Not too far from here. It's called The Desert Shadows Ranch. Ask anybody where it's at. We'll have a party. A big party. Maybe you and I can go a few rounds with the gloves on." Just as Deagan and Assante were about to step in and help the small chauffeur, he yelled out, "Gordo!" A huge mustachioed man wearing a serape and a big sombrero moved with astonishing speed through the doorway of the club and grabbed Stringer's now slumping form.

"My apologies, *senores,*" the small chauffeur said, allowing the large man to carry Stringer toward the door.

"*De nada,*" Assante said. When the chauffeur looked surprised, Ace began chatting with him in flawless Spanish.

"Your Spanish is *muy excellente,* senor. I hope that we will meet again before you leave," the chauffeur said, coming to attention and snapping a sharp salute. After executing a precise about-face, he followed Stringer and the giant out of the club.

"Damn, did you see the size of that guy?" Deagan asked, picking up the stein of frosty beer that Stringer had ordered for him. "Musta been seven feet if he was an inch."

"What did the little guy say?" Penny asked Ace.

"His name is Hector," Ace said. "We just talked about how *baracho,* or drunk, his esteemed employer was. Apparently he gets like this often. Has a standing order for his two *empleos* to ferry him home every time he comes on base. He called the big lug *Gordo,* which means large or fat," Assante said

"That guy didn't look so fat to me," Deagan said.

"No, he didn't, did he?" Ace said. He hadn't touched the beer that the bartender had set on the bar in front of him. "You know, there was something funny about the way that guy talked."

"Yeah, he was drunk," Deagan said. He pointed to the frothy stein in front of Ace. "You gonna drink that one?"

Assante frowned and said, "I was referring to the chauffeur. His Spanish was . . ."

"Ace, the beer," Deagan said. "You gonna drink it?"

Assante shoved the stein toward Mad Dog and said, "Be my guest."

"Isn't that what the famous D. Phillip Stringer wanted us to be?" Penny asked, taking out her cigarette case and offering one to Ace. "His guests?"

"Precisely why I prefer to buy my own drink," Assante said, extracting one of her cigarettes and taking out his lighter.

* * *

In the basement of the base hospital army doctor Roland Vincent pulled open the steel drawer that housed the refrigerated body. Doc stood on the other side of the platform in the small, but densely built morgue. The refrigerated units covered virtually the entire wall, like a rectangular grid in a desk. Two other men, both in laboratory coats, stood next to Doc. Both men were substantially older than he and dwarfed by his Herculean proportions.

"All the drawers but two are empty, thank God," Vincent said, peeling back the sheet. Blood had seeped through the white material in several places.

Doc stared down at the twisted body, his amber eyes taking in the various injuries.

One of the men standing next to him, a short plump man with a fuzzy gray beard and hardly any hair on his head, spoke first. His accent was heavily laced with Eastern European inflections.

"Well, Doctor Atlas, what do you make of it?"

When Doc didn't answer the other man in the lab coat chuckled slightly and placed a hand on the bearded man's shoulder.

"Dr. Zimmermann," he said. "I'm afraid our esteemed colleague from New York is well known for being rather taciturn. Among other things."

Zimmermann raised his eyebrows as he watched Doc's silent examination. "But Dr. Vogel, he does speak, does he not?"

"May I see your scope," Doc asked. Vincent handed it to him and Doc peered into each of the dead man's ears, then did the same to the eyes. He stood and felt along the chest cavity down to the lower extremities, taking special notice of the pattern of lividity and bruises. When he had concluded this, he fixed Dr. Vincent with a stern gaze.

"You mentioned another body in storage," Doc said. "Whom might that be?"

"It's one of our pilots, John McGreggor. He crashed his P-51 the day before this man." Vincent pointed to Fielding's corpse.

"I wish to examine his body also," Doc said, slipping off his sport coat and hanging it on the coat rack by the desk. He began rolling up his sleeves. "Do you have a room available for an autopsy?"

"We've already done one on McGreggor," Vincent said. "These two gentlemen assisted me."

Doc looked at the two scientists.

"In the interest of saving you some time, Dr. Atlas," Zimmermann said, "you may read our official report if you wish."

"Thank you, but I prefer to conduct my own examination," Doc said. Then, turning back to Vincent, "Do you have a spare surgical gown that I might borrow, doctor?"

Vincent looked at Doc's massive proportions and shrugged. "We might have to sew two of them together, but I'll see what I can do."

"Let me save you some time, doctor," Vogel said. "We can tell you that the eardrums on McGreggor, the pilot, were ruptured just as Mr. Fielding's were. Each man apparently suffered massive internal hemorrhaging, but considering the tremendous impact of the crash, that is hardly surprising, is it not?"

"Did he have any subdural hematomas in the scalera?" Doc asked.

Vogel and Zimmermann exchanged glances.

"Yes," Vogel said. "Just as Mr. Fielding had."

"Not a pretty thing, to see a body crushed by such impact with the ground," Zimmermann said. "But at least death must have been instantaneous."

"This man was in all probability, dead before he hit the ground," Doc said.

"What?" Zimmermann said. "Why do you think that?"

Doc didn't answer. He just turned and accepted a large surgical gown from Vincent as he reentered the room. But before Doc could slip it on, a distant, but persistent wailing sound began.

"Oh no," said Dr. Vincent. "The sirens. . . The base is on alert."

* * *

"ALL CIVILIAN AND UNAUTHORIZED PERSONNEL WILL REPORT TO THE MAIN GATE AREA IMMEDIATELY," the loud speakers repeated. The base had become alive with uniformed men running between buildings and Military Police jeeps driving about in the lighted darkness. Ace, Deagan, and Penny all went outside and took in the activity.

"Unauthorized personnel," Deagan said. "1 guess that means us too."

"What's going on?" Penny asked as a soldier jostled by her slipping on a flight suit.

"Can't say, ma'am," he said and hurried off in the direction of the airfield.

"They're scrambling fighters," Ace said, pointing.

"Yeah," Deagan added. "And look over there."

His big finger pointed to a row of distant mountains. Strange glowing lights seemed to light up the sky to the west with bright flashes against the dark horizon.

"What on earth is that?" Penny asked, her eyes widening in amazement. Several of the photographers who had been drinking in the press section of the club began snapping photographs. But the snapping flashbulbs attracted a big MP sergeant who meandered over with two equally huge MP's behind him.

"Okay, I'll take the film from them cameras now, gents," the sergeant said.

"Hey, ain't you ever heard of freedom of the press?" one of the reporters yelled.

"Yeah, but right now we're under base alert, so all of youse are subject to my authority," the sergeant said. He snapped his fingers and the two MP's began collecting the cameras.

"Damn, I'd kill for one of those photos to send to New York," Penny said.

"You and the rest of these guys," Deagan said. "Hey, look, there's Doc."

Backlit by the illumination of the airfield and the fighter planes taking off, the powerful figure of Doc Atlas strode across the street toward them. The MP's had finished collecting all the cameras and were ushering the protesting group of reporters toward the main gate. One pressed his lateral baton onto Deagan's shoulder and told him to move.

"Hey, I'm a Lieutenant Colonel, dog face," Deagan said.

"Yeah, and I'm Charlie McCarthy," said the MP.

"Relax, soldier," Penny interjected. "We're just waiting for Doc Atlas. He's coming now."

The MP glanced over his shoulder at the approaching figure and steered quickly around Deagan, Ace, and Penny. As Doc joined them Penny asked if he knew anything about the incident.

"They're sending some fighter planes up to check the area," Doc said. "They feel the strange lights to the west may be cause for alarm."

"What do you think, Doc?" Deagan asked.

Doc didn't answer. His amber eyes scanned the horizon, as he reached into his pocket and withdrew a small, but extremely powerful telescope that was no bigger than a fountain pen. He studied the lights for more than a minute then replaced the telescope in his pocket. He turned back to his group.

"Colonel Blanchard has been kind enough to give us the loan of a military sedan," he said. "I suggest we make use of it now to secure proper lodging in town."

"But, Doc, what about them flying saucers?" Deagan asked. "Ain't we gonna go after 'em?"

"In good time, Thomas, we will get to the bottom of this," Doc said. He pointed the way to the Motor Pool. A worried looking PFC had the black Ford coupe waiting for them with their luggage already stowed in the trunk. After thanking the young soldier the four companions entered the sedan. Doc drove toward the Main Gate area where a long line of autos containing reporters and other civilians was being directed out through the raised barrier by two MPs. Penny and Ace were in the back seat looking through the windows as another pair of fighter planes screamed upward from the runways.

"Those are P-51's," Ace said. "Mustangs. What I wouldn't give to be going up in one of them right now."

The scream of the twin propellers of the P-51 was suddenly drowned out by a new syncopated beating.

"What's that?" Penny asked, straining to lean across Ace to look out the window.

"It's one of those new Sikorsky's," Ace said. "A helicopter. Doc, Mad Dog, and I ran across one of them at the tail-end of the War when we tackled that Von Strohm thing. Remember?"

"I remember you thinking you knew how to fly it," Deagan said with a chuckle. "St. Christopher, be my guide."

"I'm better now," Ace said.

"It's good to see you two getting back to normal," Penny said.

Doc had scarcely gotten on the road to town when he heard a new wailing sound. Seconds later he glanced in the rear vision mirror and saw the red lights of a Military Police jeep fast approaching. As he pulled to the right, Doc noticed another pair of red lights trailing the jeep. An ambulance shot around them going at a high rate of speed. He pulled out his pocket telescope again and surveyed the area.

"It appears that there's been another crash," he said, jamming the Ford into gear and peeling away from the gravel shoulder. Doc followed the fast movements of the ambulance in and around the line of traffic. At times the speedometer reached such a high reading that the needle was beyond the imprinted scale. But Doc hung behind the ambulance, leaving the other traffic trailing far behind. The military vehicles slowed and made a left turn at a juncture heading north. The road was reddish dirt and seemed to travel farther out into the desert. Doc slowed the Ford somewhat due to the dust being stirred up by the preceding vehicles. Then twin columns of black smoke became visible against the velvet sky.

Doc slowed appreciably and veered to the right, away from the crash sight.

"Doc, where are you going?" Ace asked. "It looks like they went down over there."

"The ambulance is en route to assist them, Ace," Doc said. "I thought I caught a glimpse of something over here."

Doc steered off the gravel road and onto the bumpy desert floor. Except for tough shrubbery, cactus, and an occasional areas of brush, the going wasn't too bad. The others strained their eyes to try and see where Doc was heading, but only the expansive desert landscape seemed to loom in front of them. Then suddenly the front of the vehicle bounced over a dip in the earth and headed down an old dry arroyo. Ahead, to their right, a craggy expanse of rock jutted upward. The headlights shone on something white.

"There," Doc said, pointing to the fluttering silk of a parachute tangled at the top of the jagged cliff on some protruding rocks. Beneath the tattered chute a man in an olive drab flight suit dangled from the taut strings perhaps thirty feet above the ground. The outcropping of rocks seemed to be poised around him like deadly talons.

Doc pulled the sedan close to the bottom and they all piled out. The pilot appeared to be unconscious, his arms and legs twisting slowly. Bloody trails dripped from his face, and his left leg appeared to be twisted at an unnatural angle.

Without speaking Doc ran to the base of the rocks and sprang upward, catching one of the jutting stones. Using the momentum of his swing the Golden Avenger seemed to scale the outcropping with amazing agility and speed. In scant seconds

he was edging toward the top next to the injured airman. Gripping the harness of the parachute in one hand, Doc raised the unconscious body as easily as if he were lifting a sack of groceries.

"His left leg is possibly fractured," Doc called out. "And he may have internal injuries as well."

"You want to let him down, Doc, Ace and me will catch him," Deagan yelled.

But Doc was already reaching into another

pocket of his shirt. He withdrew a small folding knife. Looping the para-chute strings into a makeshift clove-hitch knot, Doc let the injured man dangle freely. Using the knife to sever sections of the upper portion of the parachute, Doc quickly twisted the collection of nylon cords into one thick cable and secured them with a second knot. Tightening his grip on the end of the twisted cords with his right hand, Doc braced his powerful legs against the rocks.

"Here he comes, brothers," he said, slowly lowering the pilot with a deft hand-over-hand motion. "Watch his left leg in particular."

"Gotcha covered, Doc," Deagan said as he and Ace reached upward to gently but firmly take hold.

After seeing that the pilot was safely placed on the ground, Doc descended just as rapidly as he had gone up. He immediately knelt next to the injured man and began examining him.

"We'll need something to immobilize his leg," Doc said. "The lid of one of Penelope's suitcases should do." Deagan immediately began moving toward the car. "Thomas, use one of our halo flares to summon assistance also."

"Roger, wilco, Doc," Deagan said, reaching in his coat pocket for one of the compact, but powerful flares that Doc and his assistants always carried when on missions. Pointing the end skyward, Deagan punched the trigger which sent a small missile-like projectile streaking upward. The subsequent explosion flooded the area with an eerie white light, followed by the slow, patagial-like descent of a greenish luminescent spot.

Penny sat down and cradled the unconscious man's head in her lap.

Suddenly his eyes opened and he stared up at her face groggily.

"What? An angel," he said. "Am I in heaven?"

Penny smiled. "No, fly boy, you're still here on good old mother earth, but you're in the best of hands right now." She looked over at Doc.

* * *

Over breakfast the next morning in the hotel dining room, Doc detailed assignments for Penny and Deagan that revolved interviewing the local witnesses of the recent Unidentified Flying Objects sightings. Penny winced as Deagan clapped his hands together and said, "Lemme at them Martians." He spoke loud enough to elicit a round of muffled laughs from the other patrons, many of whom were reporters who were trying to grab something to eat while waiting for a free phone to call in their stories on the crash. Penny had already phoned her editor in New York about their rescue of the downed flier. She took a sip from her coffee as she perused the morning edition of the *Roswell Daily Record*.

Looks like this UFO thing isn't going to go quietly into the night," she said, spreading out the paper to display the headline: *Gen. Ramey Empties Roswell Saucer.* "They're even reporting seeing them in Iran."

"They got a lot of desert over there, too," Deagan said. "Think there's any correlation?"

"Only if you correlate all the sand between your ears," Assante said.

"Aww, you just don't know how to put two and two together unless you got some list of case laws to tell you how to think," Deagan said.

Ace turned to Doc. "So what do you make of last night's crash?"

"At this point I don't have enough information to render an informed opinion," Doc answered. "The pilot stated that after the glass in his cockpit shattered, he was somehow thrown from the plane moments before it began its descent. He remembered hearing and seeing strange noises and lights immediately prior to the explosion."

"But if he'd been hit by some kind of round wouldn't we have heard the report?" Ace asked. "And what kind of gun could bring down a P-51 at night with one shot?"

"Want to know what I think?" Deagan asked, sopping up the yolks of his eggs with a triangle of toasted bread. "I think this whole thing's starting to smell funny."

"What, your eggs?" Assante said, smirking.

"Naw, this whole flying saucer thing," Deagan answered. "Like maybe Old Butch knows more than he told us."

"That's a distinct possibility," Doc said.

"So where do we go from here then?" Penny asked. She took out a cigarette but didn't light it. "And how's interviewing these local yokels going to put us any closer to the truth if it's the military that's stalling?"

"It's my hope that I'll be able to reason with Colonel Blanchard myself this morning," Doc said. "But in the meantime, we can't depend totally on his version of the events. We need to corroborate the events ourselves."

"And that's where Mad Dog and I come in?" Penny said. She began fishing for her lighter, but Ace reached out with his and lighted her cigarette. He then took out one of his own and did the same.

"What would you like me to do, Doc?" he asked.

"I've taken the liberty of contacting the local mortician, Ace," Doc said. "He'll accompany us to the base where we'll secure your friend's body. It's time his family had some closure on that part of this."

"Thanks, Doc," Ace said.

"Take the time you need to assist Mrs. Fielding in making the funeral arrangements. I have some other business that may take me out of the area today, but I expect to meet back here tonight at 1800 hours. We'll designate this to be our temporary headquarters."

Penny glanced up through the smoke at Doc, who was now rising.

"Thomas, if you will take care of the bill with our expense money," he said as he strode toward the door.

* * *

"Major Atlas, I just wanted to thank you personally for all you and your associates did last night," Colonel Blanchard said, leaning across his desk to extend his open palm toward Doc. They were alone in the Colonel's office. "If you weren't so observant, that man probably would have perished before any search party could have found him."

"We were glad to help, Colonel," Doc said, shaking the older man's hand. "And my appreciation as well for your assistance this morning in seeing to the release of Mr. Fielding's body. My friend Ace Assante was particularly grateful."

Blanchard nodded and sat back in his chair.

"But perhaps you could do me another favor," Doc said. "I'm concerned about the entirety of the incident."

"You and me both, Major," Blanchard said. "I've lost three planes in the past two weeks, not to mention that civilian crash. My pilots are beginning to get afraid to take off."

"And what was your opinion of those mysterious lights in the sky?"

Blanchard pursed his lips before answering.

"Why, nothing more than heat lightning," he said. "We've been having a lot of storms sweeping the region lately."

Doc's amber eyes stared straight at the man. Blanchard looked away.

"I'd be curious to know why the base went on alert status last night," Doc said. "That seems an extreme measure for heat lightning."

"Dammit, man," Blanchard said, banging his fist on the desktop. But when he saw his show of belligerence had no effect on Doc, the Colonel sighed.

"All right," he said. "I'll lay my cards on the table. I received a call from Secretary Forestall this morning and he wants this matter of this UFO crash put to rest as soon as possible. Thus, I've been authorized to offer you a plane to fly to 8th Army Headquarters in Fort Worth. General Ramey held a press conference there last night displaying the recovered wreckage. The Secretary thought that a subsequent statement from you might put the whole damn affair to rest once and for all."

Doc nodded, but said nothing. It was his custom to let others speak while he observed and evaluated them.

"In the meantime, he also gave me the go-ahead to bring you up to speed," Blanchard continued. "It's no secret lately that a wave of hysteria has been sweeping the country over these damn flying saucer reports. While the Army Air Corps doesn't put much credence in most of them, there's always the concern that the Russians might use this as an opportunity to launch a surprise attack."

"Do you think that's feasible?" Doc asked.

"Who knows? But we didn't expect Pearl Harbor either, did we?" The Colonel flipped open a folder on his desk and handed the top sheet across to Doc. "This is a top secret authorization I'm showing you, Major. It deals with Project Mogel. I verified your security clearance this morning also."

Doc studied the paper then looked back to the Colonel.

"So you're saying that the wreckage recovered by Mr. Brazel was not a weather balloon after all?" Doc asked.

"That's correct. It was a high altitude research balloon that we've been testing. These balloons have special acoustical equipment designed to monitor Soviet nuclear tests. The special reflective material makes them less visible to radar waves."

"Interesting," Doc said.

"It's no secret that there was a rat at Los Alamos," Blanchard said. "Gave away the secret of the bomb to the damn Russians. Stalin wasn't even surprised when the President told him we'd split the atom. "He snorted. "We figure it's only a matter of time before they explode their own device."

"Probably inevitable," Doc said.

"Plus the area they captured in Germany there at the end of the war contained all the Nazi's latest research on experimental weapons and their V-6 rocket program. Who knows what kind of stuff they found there. But as it stands now, we're still the only ones with the A-bomb. And the 509th is the only base in the world with active atomic weapons." Blanchard's eyes narrowed as he stared across at Doc. "Now, sir, do you see why we go on alert at the drop of a hat?"

Doc nodded. "That is indeed an awesome responsibility, Colonel."

"So you can understand why we've got to work together to put this flying saucer crash rumor to rest? If the news got out that we were worried the Communists might have the bomb, it could be devastating for the country."

"But a campaign of erroneous information may backfire," Doc said.

"Then you won't help?"

Doc considered this for a moment.

"I wish to examine this wreckage myself," he said, standing. "After which I'll speak with General Ramey. And I'll be taking my own plane, the Pegasus, to Fort Worth."

* * *

The Sheriff of Chaves County, George Wilcox, was polite and cooperative to Penny and Deagan. But his account of the material recovered from farmer Mac Brazel two days ago shed little light on the incident. The sheriff leaned back in his chair with a cup of coffee as he spoke. "Mac whispered kinda confidential-like that he might have found one of them flying disks," he said. "I called Roswell Army Air Base figuring that they were a lot better equipped to deal with something like that than I was." The sheriff chuckled quietly. "I've got enough to do with just dealing with problems caused by folks 'round these parts without worrying about something from outer space."

"So whom did you speak to when you called?" Penny asked.

"I got ahold of Major Marcel. He was attached to group intelligence." The sheriff took a long sip from the cup. "Him and another guy came right out. Was real excited, and all. Took the stuff off my hands and, frankly, I was glad to get rid of it."

"What did it look like?" Deagan asked. "Like something from outta this world?"

"Some metal struts," Wilcox said. "And some kinda shiny stuff. As best as I can recollect."

"Aww come on, Sheriff" Penny chided. "Are you telling me that somebody brought you the wreckage of a flying saucer and you didn't take the time to examine it closely?"

Wilcox laughed again, louder this time.

"Well, like I said, Miss Cartier, I'm a bit more concerned with the things happening in Chaves County. And besides, we're used to the local folk telling strange tales around here. Just like the legend of Cactus Jack."

"Cactus Jack?" Deagan said. "Who's that?"

Wilcox chuckled again. "Old Jack Persard. One of our local ranchers. Disappeared way back in the 30's after the bank foreclosed on his place. Went off into the desert with a team of wild mustangs. Every once in a while something somewhere will come up missing and somebody'll claim it was taken by old Jack."

"But this wreckage was something tangible, wasn't it?" Penny said. "Did it look authentic?"

"Authentic," Wilcox said with a snort. "Miss, now how the hell would I know what something from a flying saucer was supposed to look like?"

Deagan and Penny considered the sheriff's question as they tried to trace down Mac Brazel. Unable to find the farmer, who was out attending to his large herd of sheep, they sought out a married couple in Roswell named Wilmot, who had reported seeing a strange oval-shaped object over the western skies a few days prior. But other than saying that the object looked like two saucers turned upside down, Penny and Deagan got little from them.

Sheriff Wilcox had also mentioned a young man named Virgil Horn as another of the local residents claiming to have seen a flying disk recently, more than a month ago. He had made one of the first reports. Horn was stacking boxes in the rear of the local drugstore.

After going in and purchasing a map of the area, Penny smiled alluringly at the proprietor and asked if they might speak to the young stock boy for a moment. The druggist shrugged and said, "I don't expect it would hurt anything. But only for a few minutes. He's got work to do."

At first glance Virgil Horn appeared to be a handsome young man with oily reddish hair and a thin, wiry build. But as he leaned back against a stack of boxes and wiped his forehead with a red bandana, his smile seemed somehow a bit pretentious. As Penny and Deagan began questioning him, the venal side of his nature quickly became apparent.

"Am I gonna be paid for what I seen?" Horn asked.

"I work for the *New York Times*," Penny said. "We don't pay people for interviews. We're the biggest newspaper in the world, and a lot of very important people will be reading about you."

Horn seemed to consider this for a moment. "No money, then, huh?" Penny shook her head. "Well, I suppose I can tell you a little of what I seen," he said. "Maybe that way somebody will want to pay me later."

"Sure," Penny said, but she suspected that it was dubious.

"Me and my best gal Sally was up in the hills about a month ago," Horn said. "Had us a nice little campsite set up with a tent and all. Only her folks didn't know that she wasn't staying at her girlfriend's. She was just here in Roswell visiting. We was just kind of sitting there around the campfire, when all of a sudden we heard this loud noise. Like a bomb going off." Horn made a circular gesture with his hands. "At first I thought it was a lightning bolt, 'cause we been getting a lot of sudden storms this summer. But the sky was clear, except for this real strange glow coming from the south."

He paused and grabbed a bottle of pop from one of the wooden crates. Wedging the cap against the side of the crate, he smacked downward on the bottle to pop it open.

"So me and Sally hopped in my truck and started driving toward the light," Horn said, pausing to take a drink. We must've drove for a couple of miles, then we seen 'em."

"Who?" Penny asked.

"Martians," Horn said. "Little green men all laying around this silver disk and these colored light beams up in the air. Looked like they was hurt, too."

"How far away were you?" Deagan asked.

"Unnn, close enough to see they wasn't human," Horn said. He leaned away from the wall and gestured expansively. "They had these big long heads with white faces, and wore these dark green uniforms."

"They were hurt you say?" Deagan asked. "Did you try to help them?"

"Nope. We just hightailed it outta there. Sounded like a heavy truck was coming down the road, so we figured it was the Army."

"Horn!" a gruff voice yelled from the front of the store. "You telling that damn flying saucer yarn again? I hope to hell you got those boxes all stacked."

Horn took another quick swig from the bottle of pop and set it down.

"That's my boss," he said. "Gotta get back to work." He grabbed a box and moved over toward the stack by the far wall. "So when am I gonna be in your paper, Miss?"

"As soon as we can corroborate your story," Penny said. "Where can we find Sally?"

"Sally?" he said with a frown. "Why she went back to Albuquerque with her folks. Like I said, she was just here visiting."

"Could you show us where it was you saw this?" Penny asked, pulling out her map and spreading it out on the box in front of him.

Horn licked his lips quickly, then squinted at the map. He ran his finger along one of the lines. "If this here's the main highway, then it would have had to be along here somewheres." His fingers traced a section to the southwest of the Army Air Field.

As they left, Penny asked Deagan what he thought.

"Ah, I don't know," Deagan said. "The kid sounded like he was telling the truth, but I don't know. Near that area that he pointed to was White Sands Missile Base. He coulda seen anything and just thought it was a flying saucer."

"My sentiments exactly," Penny said. "And I'm not about to use it without a second source. Not for something as outlandish as a flying saucer report."

Deagan looked at his watch and said, "What you say we grab some lunch? This Martian hunting has made me hungry."

"Is there anything that doesn't?" Penny said with a smile.

* * *

Ace Assante drove the military sedan along the main highway from the Fielding ranch. He lighted a cigarette and blew some smoke out the open window as he ruminated about the morning. His old friend's widow, Mary, had been grateful for Ace's help in securing her husband's body and helping with the funeral arrangements. And Ace was grateful that she'd been pretty much under control. She'd only broken down once, toward the end, when Ace had mentioned how her husband had saved him on that mission.

"He always said you were the bravest out of all of them," she said. "Wealthy enough that you could have gotten out of the dangerous fighting, but you were always right in the worst of it. He loved you like a brother."

The wake would be tomorrow, with the funeral to take place the day after. Hopefully, he could persuade Doc and Deagan to be pall bearers also. He was sure they would agree. Ace was also anxious to tell Doc about the widow's statements about seeing "lights in the sky all around Roswell the last few weeks." Although he wasn't sure if it was factual or just some sort of general hysteria. After all, he thought, this flying saucer craze seems to be sweeping the nation. But he was sure that Doc would find it interesting.

His ruminations were snapped as a truck came barreling up behind him. It was a large vehicle with a heavy canvas tarp securely fastened over the bed. As the truck drew along side of him Ace noticed two swarthy faces behind the windshield. One of them was the large man called Gordo.

Ace nodded as the truck passed. The giant's face showed surprise as he returned the greeting, and the larger vehicle shot around Ace's sedan. The rear end of the truck was also covered with the folds of the heavy tarp, and Ace wondered what it was they would be carrying in it that merited such secrecy. As the larger vehicle swerved in front of him. Ace caught a glimpse of Stringer's chauffeur, Hector, in the side-vision mirror.

There was something that bothered Ace about the man's Spanish. It had been very rapid, the words almost running together instead of separately enunciated. Certainly not at all like the classical lisping of Spain. South American maybe?

His curiosity piqued by the sight of the truck, Ace began to accelerate slightly, keeping it in sight. This continued for several miles, but finally the other vehicle slowed and executed a left turn onto a gravel road perpendicular to the highway. Ace slowed as he passed the point at which the truck had turned and saw a sign posted at the juncture.

DESERT SHADOWS RANCH
ABSOLUTELY NO TRESPASSING
* * *

"Shall I tell you my theory about all this?" D. Phillip Stringer said, setting down his coffee cup and leaning forward.

"I'm sure you will regardless," Penny said, dumping a teaspoon of sugar into her coffee.

Deagan grinned slightly at the drollery of Penny's quip.

"Something went down over the desert out here," Stringer said. "Something from up there." He pointed his thick finger skyward.

"Yeah," Deagan said. "We all know that."

"Please, sir," Dr. Zimmermann said. "Let Mr. Stringer elaborate."

Deagan grunted and shoved his empty plate forward so he could lean his elbows on the table. To hell with manners, he thought. And to hell with D. Phillip Stringer.

Upon entering the diner, Penny and Deagan had barely sat down and ordered when Stringer walked in with the two scientists, Zimmermann and Vogel, in tow. The writer immediately invited himself and his party to eat with Deagan and Penny, and the after dinner talk had gradually shifted to the subject on everyone's mind: Unidentified Flying Objects.

"Yes, Mr. Deagan," said Professor Vogel. "Let the man speak."

With an acknowledging grin, Stringer continued, using his big hands for expansive gestures.

"Let's just say, for argument's sake, that some craft from outer space did crash in the desert out here. It goes without saying that such a craft would probably have been occupied, does it not?"

"Not really," said Deagan. "The Gerries were sending a lot of drones over to England there at the end, remember?"

"Ah, spoken like a true military man," Stringer said.

"Always see every overture as an attack. But what if the occupants of such a craft had peaceful intentions?"

"Then why would it land out here in the middle of nowhere, instead of New York or Washington D.C.?" Penny asked.

"Another skeptic," said Stringer. "And such a comely one at that." He grinned and patted her arm condescendingly. "But your question has merit. Why indeed? Professors?"

"Yes," Zimmermann said.

Vogel said nothing. He merely squinted from behind his thick spectacles. "You were both part of that momentous project that started several hundred miles north of here at Los Alamos, and culminated in Alamogordo, correct?"

Zimmerman's eyebrows raised, but he gave no answer. The burly author removed a thick cigar from his pocket and continued.

"I'm referring to what was known as The Manhattan Project," he said. He withdrew a silver lighter and popped back the lid. His thumb flicked the wheel, striking the flint and igniting the wick. "So why indeed, Miss Cartier? Why indeed?"

"So you're saying that all these strange reports have something to do with the atomic bomb?" Penny said.

Stringer rotated the end of the cigar in the yellow flame, puffing copiously as he spoke.

"Fat Man and Little Boy," he said. "The prototype was first exploded out here. What if this attracted the attention of another world? One much more advanced than ours. Perhaps they would decide to send out an exploratory craft to gauge the degree of our civilization."

He blew out a prodigious cloud of smoke.

"Mind if l use your lighter, bud?" Deagan asked, taking out one of his own cigars.

"Certainly," said Stringer, handing it to Mad Dog.

Deagan quickly snapped a light for himself, then closed the lid with his thumb. He paused, as if admiring the lighter, and looked closely at the inscription. "What the hell kind of writing is this?" he asked.

"Just a gift from my time with the Spanish Loyalists," Stringer said. He plucked the lighter from Deagan's fingers.

"You make these flying saucer sightings sound like something from that old Orson Welles radio show," Penny said.

"Actually, his theory has merit," Zimmermann said. "We know that the residual radioactivity from the explosion will have a long, detectable afterlife."

"Which is an unfortunate and deadly by-product of the weapon," Vogel said. "I sometimes wonder if we made the right decision even exploding it."

"What the hell you talking about?" Deagan said. "Would you rather have seen thousands of GI's killed trying to invade Japan?"

Vogel looked at him with moist eyes.

"No, Mr. Deagan," he said. "But it's just that, I sometimes fear for our future now that we have unleashed this terrible power."

"Listen, buster," Deagan said, gesturing with his fore and middle fingers. The big cigar was between them and spraying ashes over the top of the table. Penny quickly covered her coffee. "Just be glad we got to the finish line first. If the Japs or the Gerries woulda got the A-bomb first, they woulda used it against us in a heartbeat. And I'll bet they wouldn't have stopped, either."

"Hot damn," said Stringer. "I'm beginning to like your attitude more and more, Mr. Deagan. The flag, apple pie, and Doc Atlas."

"You're damn right," Deagan said. "And I'll tell you something else. Whatever it is that's going on out here in the desert, Doc'll get to the bottom of it. You can take that to the bank."

Deagan was about to say more when he suddenly straightened up and felt his side. Penny looked at him expectantly as he reached down and removed a small black metal device from a clip on his belt. The device vibrated in his hand, and a small red light flashed on top.

"What on earth is that?" Stringer asked.

"A special radio transmitter," Deagan said. "We all carry 'em for when Doc wants to get ahold of us." He got up from the table. "Excuse me. I gotta make a call."

As he was leaving the waitress came and brought them more coffee. "How does he know where to call?" Stringer asked, dumping sugar into his cup.

"It's pre-arranged," Penny said. "By the number of flashes. That particular one directed him to call the hotel, which was designated our temporary headquarters." She withdrew a cigarette and held it up. "Doc thinks of everything. He always covers all the angles."

Stringer immediately took out his lighter.

"An amazing man," he said, holding the flame over toward Penny. "And a very formidable foe, I would imagine."

"I certainly wouldn't want to go against him," she said, exhaling a cloud of smoke.

"Nor would I," Zimmermann said. "The man's mind is ingenious. Tell me, Miss. Did Dr. Atlas invent that little radio receiver?"

Penny nodded.

"But it's so small," said Vogel. "How did he do it?"

"Hendrick," said Zimmerman, "remember at Los Alamos when we were having problems trying to figure out how to scale down the compression trigger, and Oppie called someone for consultation?"

The other man nodded, then suddenly looked surprised.

"But I thought Dr. Atlas spent the war on the front lines?" he said. "I read about his exploits in the newspapers."

"Doc was on the front," Deagan said, coming back to the table and resuming his seat. "In both theaters. He figured he could best serve out there where the action was."

"But he was constantly being called for other things, too," Penny said. Then, turning to Deagan, she asked, "What's up?"

"It was Ace at the hotel," Deagan said. "Doc left a message for us. He had to fly to Ft. Worth, but he wants you, me, and Ace to meet him on the base at twenty-hundred. He should be coming in about that time in the Pegasus."

"That sounds important," Stringer said, pocketing his lighter again.

"Where Doc's concerned," Deagan said, drawing heavily on his cigar, "it usually is."

*   *   *

The special press conference and meeting with General Roger Ramey at 8th Air Force Headquarters in Fort Worth, Texas had taken longer than Doc had anticipated. Now it was growing dark and he automatically switched to instrument guidance to maintain his heading back to Roswell. The edge of the sun was descending below the distant mountains on the horizon and Doc ruminated about the events of earlier that afternoon.

Ramey had taken particular care to explain to all the reporters present that the items recovered from the Roswell area crash were from a high-altitude weather balloon, not a flying saucer. The items were spread out on a carpeted floor, and Ramey and Colonel Thomas Dubose held up the shiny foil and metallic struts. "Sticks and tinfoil," he explained, used to track the balloon by radar. He then permitted some photographers to snap a few pictures. Ramey was grateful that Doc had agreed to stand silently off to the side to tacitly endorse the General's statements.

Ramey also went on radio to emphatically deny that the wreckage was from outer space. He stated that the previous report issued by the public relations officer at Roswell had been erroneous. All seemed to be going as planned until some of the photographers complained that they weren't allowed to get close enough. A second press conference was hastily scheduled, at which time some of the reporters claimed that something was amiss.

"Hey, this ain't the same stuff we saw yesterday," one of them said. "It's the old switcheroo."

Ramey denied any switching had occurred. The reporters began to ask Doc for a comment.

"Obviously, this material is from some sort of balloon," Doc said. "Other than that, I have no comment at this time."

Grumbling about an army cover-up, the men from the various newspapers began to make their trek back to their hotels to work on their stories before phoning them in. One of them grumbled that after today the story would probably fade. But Doc was sure that the current wave of hysteria would be further exacerbated by this governmental conspiracy theory that some of the reporters had espoused. But he expected no less, and told the general so.

"Misleading the press was not prudent," he said.

"Well, dammit, Major, I can't very well say the wreckage was from a spying instrument that we're going to use to monitor the Soviets, can I?" Ramey said.

"My only point, General," Doc had answered calmly, "is that a deliberate campaign of misinformation can, and usually does, backfire eventually."

"Well, as long as it holds together long enough for us to fashion this new bomb, I'll be satisfied," Ramey said. "We're racing the Russians on this one, believe me. That's why this Project Mogel is so damn important. We know they're working hard on producing an atomic bomb. There'll be no stopping Stalin if he succeeds. Who knows where he'll pop up."

"Ironic that only a few years ago we considered him our ally," Doc said.

"War makes strange bedfellows, doesn't it?" the General said, smiling. "I've no doubt that as we speak, he's trying to come up with ways to steal our designs and material. And with Oppenheimer backing out of working on the superbomb, we're at the mercy of eccentrics like Zimmerman and Vogel. You worked with them at Los Alamos, didn't you?"

"Not directly," Doc said. "I spent most of my time overseas."

"I know that," Ramey said. "I remember you dropping behind enemy lines and delivering back tremendous amounts of intelligence. I don't know how you were able to do it."

"My fluency in German helped," Doc said. "And my knowledge of the European Continent. I'd traveled extensively there before the war."

The General straightened in his chair and looked Doc straight in the eye. "Major, I know what kind of man you are, and I know I couldn't be talking to a greater American," he said. "But understand this. We have to safeguard our atomic secrets at all costs. It's imperative. And I don't trust those scientific types. Not after Los Alamos. That espionage there was never cleared up to my satisfaction."

General Ramey's words kept ringing in Doc's memory as he scanned the darkened horizon. If, as the General suggested, the wreckage was nothing more than a high-altitude balloon, albeit an experimental model from Project Mogel, where did the hysteria about lights in the sky come from? And what was causing so many planes to go down? Something was definitely amiss. And before he and his companions left New Mexico, he would have to find out what it was.

Glancing at his instrument panel, Doc picked up his radio mike and began transmitting.

"Calling Roswell Army Airfield," he said. "This is Pegasus One, over." An indistinct, static laden reply came back over the radio.

Doc estimated that he was just out of radio range. He waited another few minutes, then rebroadcast. This time the reply was perfectly audible.

"Come in, Pegasus," the air traffic controller said. "We read you loud and clear. Over."

"I am approximately ninety kilometers south, southeast of your location," Doc said, giving his heading. "My estimated time of arrival is approximately twenty-minutes. Over."

"Roger, Pegasus," the base said. "Do you have further orders? Over."

"Negative," Doc said. "I'll advise prior to final approach. Over."

As Doc replaced the mike he saw something flicker in the distance. A bright flash of luminescence appeared to the northwest, and then it was gone. His eyes continued to scan the velvet sky. Had he imagined it? Perhaps it was a reflection of some sort. The hazy cloud cover could create conditions ripe for that. But these explanations evaporated when the eerie light appeared again, longer this time, before vanishing. Doc adjusted his course slightly, heading for the area of the light. His strong fingers grasped the mike once again.

"Roswell tower, this is Pegasus, over."

"Pegasus, this is Roswell. Over."

"Do you show any other aircraft in the vicinity?" Doc asked. He gave his coordinates.

"Negative, Pegasus. Over." The controller's voice sounded tight and brittle.

"I'm seeing something directly ahead," Doc said. "I've adjusted my heading to try and intercept. Over."

"Roger, Pegasus. Can you identify the other craft? Over."

"At this time it appears only as a bright yellow light in the sky," Doc said. But before he could elaborate further, he heard his starboard engine begin to miss its cycling. Doc quickly glanced out the right window. The engine began to sputter and go out. Suddenly the port side engine quit too. With both engines out Doc gripped the yoke and tried to glide into the wind. But a horrible humming sound, like the scream of a banshee, seemed to whip through the cockpit.

"Roswell, this is Pegasus," Doc said, wrapping his arm around his head to shield his ears. "I'm in trouble. Both engines out. Some sort of—"

Before he could finish the glass surrounding the cockpit shattered smacking Doc's face with the impact of a sledgehammer. Reeling from the impact, Doc lowered his arm, suddenly feeling an enormous pressure engulfing his head. Placing both hands over his ears, Doc unhooked his safety harness and stumbled back into the plane. The howling pain continued, seeming to increase with each passing second. Away from the now open cockpit, the sound lessened somewhat, but Doc fell forward as the floor seemed to slant abruptly into a downward sloping angle. The fuselage began a slow roll over, and Doc suddenly knew the plane was going into a spin. A "deadman's spin" they called it. A spin from which it was non-recoverable.

The plane rolled over again, almost lazily this time, but Doc was thrown violently around like a buoy caught in an unruly surf. Grasping the seats, Doc's mighty arms pulled him upward toward the closed compartments where the emergency parachutes were stored. If he could only get one on in time, he might be able to bail out.

The plane rolled again, just as Doc grasped the storage locker handle. Ripping the metal door open, Doc thrust his hand inside and felt for the heavy canvas container. He found one.

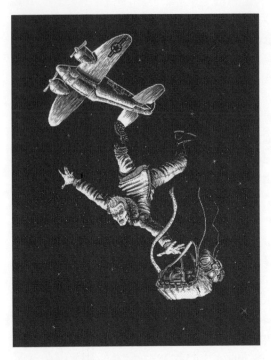

The plane rotated again, quicker this time and Doc knew now that the centrifugal force would be tremendous. Slipping his right arm through the loop of the parachute, Doc went hand-over-hand toward the exit door. The plane's descent steepened. Bracing his powerful legs against the seats, Doc strained upward to open the door. He estimated that he had less than ninety seconds before he would hit the ground. For what seemed like an eternity the hatch would not budge. Then suddenly the door popped open, caught in the vortex and was ripped from its hinges.

The momentum violently tore Doc out of the plane, his hands reaching, searching for the straps of the parachute as the spinning fuselage suddenly began to whirl toward him from out of the darkness.

* * *

Penny, Deagan, and Ace sat at a table in the Officer's Club, but instead of drinks, only three empty cups of coffee sat in front of them. Deagan was drumming his fingers on the table and Penny looked up at him.

"What time is he supposed to get here?" she asked.

"The message said by twenty-hundred," Deagan said, glancing down at his watch. "Or twenty minutes ago."

"I was told that Doc and Ramey hosted another press conference, then they had a meeting afterward," Ace said. He forced a smile as he touched Penny's hand. "Try not to worry. Doc could make a flight like that one in his sleep."

Just as she was about to answer, the post siren began an ominous wail.

Uniformed pilots began getting up immediately and hurriedly rushing out of the building.

"Sounds like another alert," Deagan said.

"Maybe we'd better go check this one out," Ace said, his smile fading.

The lights near the twin airstrips were lighted, and they saw several P-51's positioning for takeoff. An ambulance and two MP jeeps also began zooming toward the from gate. Deagan grabbed a soldier who was running toward one of the massive hangers.

"Hey, what's going on?" he asked the soldier.

"A plane went down southeast of here," the soldier said.

"What plane?" Penny asked. "Was it Doc's?"

The soldier stared at her momentarily, then tried to pull away from Deagan's powerful grasp.

"I dunno," the young soldier said. "Honest. Now, please, sir, let go of my arm."

Deagan released him and exchanged glances with Ace.

"Come on," Assante said. "Blanchard's billets are over there."

Finding no response at the Post Commander's Quarters, the three of them moved to the Orderly Room. A worried looking Lieutenant Colonel sat behind a large desk and spoke in hushed tones on the phone. Deagan pushed past an MP guarding the door and stopped just short of the officer's desk.

"We need some answers, bud," he said. "Where's Butchie?"

The Lt. Colonel hung up the phone and eyed Deagan nervously. "Colonel Blanchard is not currently available," he said. "I'm Lt. Colonel Hopkins. May I help you?"

"That ain't what I asked," said Deagan.

"The Colonel's on leave. I'm the Operations Officer."

"We heard a plane went down," Ace said, stepping forward. "We're friends and associates of Doc Atlas."

"Was it his plane?" Penny asked.

The Lt. Colonel's mouth opened slightly, but no sound came out. Finally, he spoke. "I'm told that it was. We have a search and rescue team headed to the area at this very moment."

Deagan and Ace exchanged glances.

"Where's it at?" Ace asked. "Was there any communication from Doc?"

"He radioed that he was in trouble," Col. Hopkins said, licking his lips. "Then his transmission was cut off."

"We need a plane," Ace said calmly,

"Are you crazy?" Hopkins said. "I can't spare any planes right now. There's a storm front moving in, and we're expecting a plane load of VIP's later on tonight."

"The man asked you for a plane, bud," Deagan said. "And he was a lot more polite than I'm gonna be."

"You can't threaten me."

"I ain't," Deagan said. He quickly smacked his large right fist into his open left palm. "I'm promising you."

"Look, give us anything," Ace said. "But let us go assist with the search." The Lt. Colonel lowered his eyes.

"I can't," he said. "We've got. . ." His voice trailed off. "We're doing everything we can at the moment."

"Please, Colonel," Penny said. "Doc could be out there. . . hurt."

Ace had strolled over by the window and looked out. The airfield activity seemed to have slowed somewhat. "Give us one of those Sikorsky's," he said. "They're just sitting over there. No one's using them."

"You can fly a helicopter?" Hopkins asked.

"This guy can fly anything," Deagan said.

"This is highly irregular," the Lt. Colonel said slowly.

"Desperate times call for desperate measures, Colonel," said Ace. He picked up the phone on the desk and held it out toward the other man. "Make the authorizing call, sir."

The Lt Colonel hesitated slightly, then took the phone from Ace. "This is Colonel Hopkins. Get the Sikorsky ready for take off."

* * *

Penny stood next to the oval section of asphalt as the large rotors of the helicopter began whirling. Through the glass windshield she saw Ace pulling back on the stick, causing the Sikorsky to rise up almost vertically. He smiled and gave her a "thumbs-up" sign, but it did little to ease her racing heart.

What if Doc's hurt? she wondered. Or even worse. No, she thought. She would not allow herself to even consider that. But the thoughts kept worming their way into her consciousness like stubborn parasites. What if. . .

What if he's dead? she thought, allowing herself to ask the question. *And I've never even told him how I feel about him.*

An MP jeep coasted by her and the soldier yelled for her to get off the airfield. Turning away, she began strolling absently toward the hangar area.

The wind had begun to pick up, and a crooked streak of lightning exploded across the western sky. The storm they'd been talking about was coming. Penny hoped that it would not hamper the rescue search. The heel of her shoe twisted in a slight pockmark in the cement and she stumbled slightly. Catching herself, Penny felt a sudden pain shoot through her ankle and went to lean against the ribbed wall of one of the large hangars in front of her. The numerals 51 were painted in black over an adjacent door. Removing her shoe, she rubbed her ankle, thinking how nice it would be for women to be able to wear comfortable shoes.

But I'll only wish for one miracle at a time, she thought. And this one's that Doc is okay.

The voices coming from the window distracted her from her reverie. The words came quickly, a mixture of soft sibilant sounds. What was it? She moved closer to the slightly open window. Inside she could see the beams of flashlights as forms moved stealthily in the darkness. Moving to the door, Penny's hand grasped the knob and twisted. It was not locked.

Slipping through a sliver of an opening, Penny positioned herself behind a row of lockers and removed both her high-heeled shoes. The rough cement felt cold against the soles of her feet, but she ignored it and crept forward. The flashlight beams seemed to be bouncing upward near a large military truck. She heard a grunting effort, then her eyes adjusted enough to the darkness that she could see a large box being lifted onto the rear bed of the truck. The man lifting it was the huge servant who'd helped Stringer out of the bar. Gordo, she thought, remembering the name.

"Now you're certain this will fulfill our bargain," a voice said in English. Accented English. Penny peered around a large wooden box and saw two men standing in the shadows near the truck.

"But of course, *herr doctor*," the second man said. "I assure you it will."

She recognized this man's voice without having to see his face. She'd heard it often enough pontificating in the last two days. It was D. Phillip Stringer.

"My family," the other man said. "When can I expect them?"

"Dr. Vogel," Stringer said. "We have not yet accomplished our task here. You must have patience."

"Patience," Vogel said. "You hold my loved ones hostage and you speak of patience. I despise you, and all you stand for."

"Yes," Stringer said, watching the giant's progress as he worked the heavy metallic box back farther into the truck. "Sometimes I despise myself."

"You speak of your family being held hostage, senor," another man said, appearing from the side of the vehicle. "Yet my *pais* has been under the tyrannical rule of the imperialist Americans for almost half a century."

Penny saw Hector, the small chauffeur, step into sight. He was dressed in military fatigues and seemed to be holding something long and tubular in front of him.

"And now, Dr. Vogel," Stringer said. "It's time for our departure. And yours as well. Get in the truck, old man."

"What? I cannot leave," Vogel said. "My involvement in this will be found out. You guaranteed secrecy."

Stringer's head lolled backward in a subdued, but still braying laugh.

"I lied," he said. "Now get in there, dammit, or I'll have Gordo break your legs and carry you in."

Hector moved forward and whipped the long tubular object across the scientist's temple. Vogel collapsed to his knees. Hector hit him again and Vogel fell the rest of the way.

"Careful," Stringer said. "Don't leave any bloodstains."

Hector replied with something in Spanish.

Penny whirled around, trying to get back toward to the door. Something was terribly wrong here, and she knew she'd have to flag down the first MP she saw. But as she began to run she dropped one of her high-heeled shoes which she'd been carrying. It skittered across the floor and she was sure they'd heard her. Increasing her pace into an all-out run, Penny dashed forward. The door to the hangar was only a few feet away now, but she could hear voices and movements behind her. With three more steps she made it to the door and pushed it open. Just as she did this she ran into someone. The impact knocked both of them back, and she saw it was Captain Seals, the MCI officer.

"What? Miss Cartier," Seals said, looking at her.

"Oh, thank God," she said, regaining her balance and pointing to the hangar. "There's some spies in there."

"Spies? What are you talking about?"

"Come on, I'll explain later. We've got to get out of here now. We need the MPs."

"I think not," Seals said. He quickly swung his arm in a looping, overhead movement. A heavy leather sap grazed Penny's temple, but it was still enough to send her down in a heap on the sidewalk. Seals glanced around quickly, then stooped and picked up her unconscious form. A breathless D. Phillip Stringer appeared in the doorway moments later and stopped.

"Hold that damn door open for me," Seals said, grunting as he carried Penny inside. "Get her damn shoes."

Stringer smiled as they went past, looking down at Penny's firm neck and long, dark tresses hanging downward.

"Now that's no way to treat a lady," he said.

                                    * * *

Doc wasn't sure where he was when he regained consciousness, or how long he'd been out. Because of this, he was careful not to move or show any other, outward signs that he was awake. Instead, he kept his eyes closed and let his other senses provide input. He knew he was lying on a hard surface. The ground, probably. A few feet away he heard stirring movements and someone whistling a song. A western song that he'd heard in an old Gene Autry movie: *Don't Fence Me In.* The whistler stopped and swore. Doc's nostrils detected something burning, and on his skin he could feel the heat from what he inferred was a bonfire. His wrists and ankles felt free and unbound. With slow and cautious deliberation he opened his eyes.

The yellow whirl of a campfire licked at a bloody carcass of some small animal on a rotating spit. An ancient looking metal coffee pot sat at the base of the fire on two sticks over some glowing embers. An equally ancient looking man, replete with whitish hair that had been looped back into a ponytail, hunched over the fire. When Doc sat up the old man glanced over and the light played over a set of craggy features and an enormous gray mustache.

"I was wondering ifn' you was gonna wake up sooner rather than later," the old man said. "Never thought you'd make it after the way you fell outta the sky like that, but you must be made of cast iron."

Doc said nothing. The old man shrugged and went back to his cooking tasks. Perhaps twenty feet away several horses tied to a long piece of wood weighted by several stones, snorted and stamped.

"What's your name, young fella?" the old codger asked. "You do speak English, don't ya?"

"Michael G. Atlas."

The old man seemed to consider this for a moment, but if he recognized Doc's last name, he didn't show it.

"Jack Persard," he said. "But folks 'round these parts just call me Cactus Jack. Them that knows me, that is, and they ain't but a few, You with the army or something?"

"I was during the War," Doc said, flexing his fingers and busily checking himself for injuries and possible broken bones. He remembered nothing of his freefall after exiting the Pegasus. "What happened to my airplane?"

"That was yours?" Cactus Jack shook his head. "Looked to be a damn fine plane at one time. Not much left of it now, though."

"How far are we from the crash site?"

"Oh, probably 'bout ten, twelve miles. Me and old Apache Joe found you out in the desert. Saw you coming down. Joe thought you was a spirit or something." He chuckled softly. "We used a lean-to to bring you here. Your head was banged up some."

Doc's fingers were already tracing an expanse of cloth that had been wound around his temples.

"Old Joe's all excited about that fancy piece of cloth you floated down to earth in," Cactus Jack said. "Says it'll make a swell tepee. He took it to the reservation. Hope that's all right with you. Thing feels like it was made out of silk."

"It is," Doc said. "And he's welcome to keep it." He stretched his arms, then his legs. Nothing felt broken or sprained, but he did have a variety of contusions and lacerations. They ranged in severity from minor to severe, but Doc didn't think that any required immediate medical attention.

"That's mighty generous of you," Cactus Jack said, grabbing a pair of old metal cups and handing one to Doc. "Here, have some of this." He poured a stream of dark liquid into Doc's cup, and the odor of strong coffee assailed his nostrils.

"Thank you," Doc said, letting the coffee cool before trying a sip. "I have some friends who will probably be worried about me. Where's the nearest telephone?"

The old man laughed as he brought his own steaming cup to his lips.

"Where'd you say you was from? New York City?"

Doc nodded, even though he hadn't mentioned his origin.

"Ain't no phones out this way, that's for sure," Cactus Jack said. He eyed Doc with an appraising squint. "You must be pretty rich to have had your own airplane. You ain't connected with any of them dadburned banks, are ya?"

"No."

"That's good," Cactus Jack said with a resounding nod of his head. "Damn bankers foreclosed on my ranch back in the Depression when times was hard. I lost everything. Settled out here in the high desert, just me, a few remaining Indians, and a couple of herds of wild mustangs." He took another sip from his cup and looked wistfully out over the bleak terrain. "I ain't complaining though. Not like I didn't see it coming."

Doc tried a small sip from his cup. The bitter liquid burned his tongue, but he showed no reaction.

"Like it?" Cactus Jack asked.

Doc made no comment, but took another drink. The old man grunted.

"We must be close to the air base," Doc said, looking at the sky.

"Not too far. Is that where you'll be wanting to go once we've ate?"

Again Doc did not reply. Instead he asked, "You've lived out here for a long time? Tell me, Mr. Persard, have you noticed any strange lights in the sky recently?"

"You're dern tootin' I have," Cactus Jack said taking a more copious swig of his dark brew. "Let me tell you, I seen some things out here lately that would curl the toes off a goat. Especially by my old spread."

"I would appreciate hearing about them," Doc said, allowing himself a rare smile. "And I will have some more of your coffee, please, sir."

* * *

Penny awoke to more voices. Her head felt like it had twin sledgehammers inside it banging away, and she was suddenly conscious that her hands were tied behind her back. Blinking her eyes to try and focus them, she saw Professor Vogel lying a few feet away from her. He was also bound, and a streak of dried blood had wormed its way down the center of his forehead. They were outside, but under some sort of porch roof. Penny could see a lighted ranch-style house a few hundred feet away on a macadamized road. The structure above them seemed to be connected to a larger, barn-like building. The sky was a myriad of bright stars sprinkled over black velvet.

Penny tried to rouse Vogel by wiggling closer to him and nudging the unconscious scientist with her shoeless foot. But all this elicited was a few faint moans.

They must have really clocked him good, she thought.

Turning her attention to the immediate area around her, she began looking for something she could use to free herself. The sharp edge of a broken bottle, or perhaps a loose nail. That was what they always used in the movies, wasn't it? she thought. But nothing was available. Her thoughts suddenly turned to Doc and she wondered if Deagan and Ace had found him.

Oh, God, I hope so, she thought. At least please let him be alive and safe.

"No, I'll take my share now," a voice said from inside the barn.

Another voice spoke up. Penny couldn't quite understand the words, but she was sure it belonged to Stringer.

"Look, comrade." the first man said. The words were redolent of contempt. "I've fulfilled more than my part of the bargain. And after helping you sneak the box off the base tonight, there's no way I can possibly go back. So if you don't mind, I'll take my money and be off to Mexico." She recognized the speaker now. It was Captain Rod Seals, from MCI. The creep who'd belted her with that blackjack.

"Spoken like a true capitalist," Stringer said. "What did you say your job was in the War? A rear echelon file clerk?"

"Ask your Red friends. That's where they recruited me."

Stringer laughed. "A small price to pay, I suppose. All right, you'll get your money tonight, but only after we load the U-235 and tie up a few loose ends."

U-235 Uranium! thought Penny. That was the stuff they'd used to build the atomic bomb. And Seals had called Stringer "comrade." Suddenly it all made sense. Stringer writing about fighting with the Loyalists during the Spanish Civil War. The Loyalists had received help from the Soviet Union. She remembered Deagan questioning the inscription on Stringer's Zippo lighter. At the time it had looked familiar to her, but she couldn't place it. But now she'd bet that it was written in Russian.

"Senor Stringer," a new voice said. "We have little time to position the *macqina.*"

It sounded like the diminutive chauffeur.

Stringer replied in Spanish.

"Speak in English," Seals said. "So I know what you're saying." Stringer laughed again.

"And you're planning on retiring to Mexico?" he said. He spoke again in Spanish to Hector.

"What was that?" Seals asked.

"He said you are a typical capitalist opportunist," Hector said in his heavily accented English. "A man who betrays his country for thirty pieces of silver."

"Oh yeah," said Seals. "Well if I'm a Judas, what does that make you? Aren't you selling out too?"

"I am a Puerto Ricano," Hector shouted back. 'My country will soon be free of your Yankee imperialism. With the help of others, who are the true enemies of fascism, we will strike the fascists of your government until you give us our freedom. *Libertad o muerte.*"

"You're living in a fool's paradise, greaseball, if you think the Soviets give a damn about your tiny little island in the sun," Seals said. "This was all about what's in that lead box. Now give me that briefcase you showed me earlier."

"You think you can insult me and get away with it, gringo?" Hector yelled. "Gordo!"

Penny closed her eyes and wished that she could close out the terrible screams that filtered out of the window from the barn. Then suddenly, the noises stopped after a hideous sounding crack.

"I wish he hadn't done that yet," Stringer said. "Having a front page murder of a military officer is going to attract attention."

"As if the theft of the uranium will not?" Hector said. "Come, *mi compadre*. We will bury him out on the *deseirto* once we have shot down the plane carrying the American Generales and el Secretario."

"Have Gordo load the uranium onto the plane, and tell your men to turn on the runway lights as soon as I give the signal," Stringer said. "I want Dimitri to be able to take off in our plane as soon as they scramble their Mustangs. One plane among many. It will be the perfect subterfuge for us."

Shoot down? Penny thought. She renewed her efforts to free herself, working her wrists raw straining against the fight ropes.

Vogel groaned again. His head moved slightly. He seemed to he waking up. After trying unsuccessfully to get up, Penny spoke gently to him, explaining that they were both being held captive.

"Where are we?" he asked weakly.

"I'm not sure," she said. "It seems to he someplace away from the base. Stringer seems to be setting up some sort of gun to shoot down a plane."

"Oh no, we are at his ranch," Vogel said. "Secretary Forestall and a group of generals were due to arrive tonight. He's going to use the vortex cannon. They are probably already tracking them on Stringer's radar device."

"They've got radar here?" Penny asked. "And what's that other thing you mentioned?"

Vogel grimaced in pain as be attempted to roll on his side to look at her. "It's a weapon devised by the Nazis," he said. "The Soviets recovered it from the German vortex technology research facility at the end of the War. It shoots concentrated sound waves capable of shattering glass and stopping engines. That's what they've been using to shoot down all the planes. It has some kind of high intensity light ray attached to it that acts as a long range sighting device. The light is filtered and reflects off the low altitude clouds causing the bright flashes that everyone's been seeing."

"You knew all about this?" she said. "And you didn say anything?"

"I know you must think me terrible," he said. "But you must understand. They're holding my family hostage. They told me if I helped them obtain enough enriched uranium to develop the plutonium necessary to build their own bomb. . ."

"They'd release your family" Penny said. "But does that justify the deaths of all those innocent pilots?"

"Actually, you might try thinking of it in more metaphorical terms," D. Phillip Stringer said, rounding the corner. "You can't make an omelet without breaking a few eggs, can you?"

Penny scowled at the braying laugh that followed.

"Professor," Stringer continued, squatting down next to the bound scientist and checking his ropes. "There's been a change in plans. The good part is that you're going to see your loved ones a bit sooner than you anticipated." He grinned sardonically. "But you're going to have to take a long plane ride with us first."

Vogel began a series of low sounding sobs.

"What about me?" Penny asked.

Stringer clucked, feigning sympathy.

"You present something of a problem, my dear," he said, swinging over to test the knots on the ropes securing her also. "Your knowledge of nuclear physics is probably a bit lacking for you to accompany us, and I've no real need for a barefoot contessa. But, Hector will tell Gordo to make it quicker for you than he did with our late Captain. And very pretty wildflowers do tend to grow on unmarked graves out here."

"So you used that vortex ray thing to shoot down Doc's plane?" she said. It was more of an accusation than a question.

"I couldn't afford to have your meddlesome hero blundering about now, could I?" Stringer said. "Even though I'm sure he would have gotten nowhere."

Penny swore at him as he walked away. If only Doc were here, she thought. But she wasn't even sure if Doc was alive.

"Professor, we have to try to get loose," she said in a low voice. "Is there anything around you that we can use?"

"It's hopeless," Vogel said. "Do you hear that?" The sound of a heavy truck pulling something equally heavy became audible. "That's the vortex cannon. They're setting it up. They've won. There's nothing we can do now."

Penny swung her leg over and kicked him.

"Look for something sharp, dammit," she said. "Wait, what about your glasses?"

"My glasses? They must have taken them from me," Vogel said. "But wait, I may have a spare pair in my pocket."

Penny wiggled over next to him then rolled onto her side so her hands could explore his coat. The ropes had been tied so tightly that her hands felt numb. But still she worked to feel the scientist's coat. Her fingers traced over something oval. With quiet desperation Penny tore at Vogel's lapels, reaching and straining until finally she felt the smoothness of the glass between her fingertips. Withdrawing the spectacles carefully, she clutched them under her and rolled over them several times. Finally, through tedious positioning and pressing, she managed to cause one of the lenses to break. Gripping the shards she went to work on the ropes. The broken glass cut into her flesh and soon the fragment of glass was slipping from between her blood-covered digits. Several times she thought about stopping, but she considered the alternative and kept going.

"How are your hands, Miss?" Vogel asked quietly.

"I'm not so sure I'll be able to type out this story," Penny said between grunts of effort. "But I think I may be getting somewhere."

With a few more attempts, Penny sawed through the rope. Suddenly the drone of a large airplane became faintly audible.

"That must be the plane with the generals and the Secretary," Vogel said. "They were flying up from Fort Worth. You've got to get behind shelter. Even on the ground, being too close to the ray without protective equipment will incapacitate you."

"Incapacitate? How?"

"Nausea, vertigo. . . Prolonged exposure causes rupture of the small blood vessels and organs. Eventually heart failure and death."

"Swell," Penny said. "Come on, professor, roll over and I'll cut you loose."

"It's too late for me now, Miss. Save yourself. Go. Run. Hide in the desert."

Realizing that Vogel was a lost cause, Penny got to her feet and ran around the corner. A large open barn door yawned before her like the maw of a huge inert creature. The barn was massive, extending at least fifty feet. Above her dim lights burned from a series of suspended lightbulbs, washing over a horribly broken and twisted body. It was Captain Seals.

Putting her horror aside, Penny knelt by the body to see if he had a weapon or perhaps some car keys. The dead man's eyes seemed to stare up at her from his head's unnaturally twisted position. Trying to put the stinging from her lacerated fingers aside, Penny quickly went about her task, finding what appeared to feel like a set of keys in his right front pants pocket. Struggling to force her hand inside, she felt the ragged ends of her fingers brush the flat metal. Working her hand in deeper, she was finally able to snare the keys and pull them out. But just as she did so, an engine at the far end of the barn seemed to rumble to life. Twin beams of headlights switched on, and the lights enveloped her. Standing quickly, Penny turned to run into the fading shadows, but she smacked into someone. Two gloved hands grabbed her wrists, and as she glanced up she saw a long, white slate of a face with two large, dark oval eyes glaring down at her. Some kind of strange looking metallic helmet flared out from the strange head, and secured into a metallic collar set over a dark green suit. She fought unsuccessfully to free herself of the thing's grasp, when suddenly the entire area was illuminated by a powerful burst of white light.

* * *

For the third time Deagan and Assante picked through the wreckage of the Pegasus. The plane had hit the desert floor with tremendous force, breaking apart like a shattered bottle and scattering debris over several hundred yards. With so little left of the fuselage, they felt certain that had Doc survived he would have been in the vicinity. They hurried back to the helicopter and got inside. Both men had grim expressions on their faces as the large overhead rotor began its initial twirling.

"Dammit, where could he be?" Deagan said as the copter began to lift off.

"I think we have enough fuel to circle the area a few more times," Ace said. "Perhaps he was thrown clear or he wandered off."

"I don't know, Ace," Deagan said, his eyes welling with tears. "I think if Doc was alive, he woulda found some way to signal us already."

"Still we're not giving up until we're sure," said Ace.

"You're damn right," Deagan said, surreptitiously wiping at his cheeks. Then, as he looked in the distance his eyes popped open. Quickly grabbing Assante's arm in an iron grip with his left hand, he pointed with the other. "Ace look over there. Is that what I think it is?"

Ace's eyes scanned the darkened horizon and saw the bright star-like light slowly floating downward and he grinned broadly.

"Looks like a halo flare to me," he said.

* * *

The big truck began rolling forward toward Penny and her captor. As she struggled she saw another long, white slated face with slanted oval eyes through the windshield. The gloved hands that gripped her wrists felt like rubber, and she was able to pull one of her wrists, now slick with blood, free. Lashing out with her foot, she aimed a kick at the man's shins but her toes glanced off. She suddenly felt herself being twisted down into the dirt as the front bumper of the truck continued to come at her. The tires stopped about three feet from her and the driver got out. His hands went to his face and began a twisting motion. Suddenly the white face rotated to the side and snapped off like a diver's helmet. The man said something foreign sounding and the one standing over her lifted his arms in a shrug. Reaching back inside the truck, the driver's gloved hand reappeared holding a large barreled revolver. He stepped down from and walked over to Penny.

The man spoke again, and this time Penny recognized it as Spanish. Very rapid Spanish.

"Who are you?" she asked.

The two men exchanged glances and the one holding the pistol shrugged again. He gripped the weapon with both hands and pointed it directly at Penny's face. Her hands covered her eyes. There was no mistaking the intention that was evident on the man's dark visage.

Suddenly the man's evil smile turned into a grimace as the point of a projectile pushed out the front of his rubberized suit. Seconds later Penny heard a clopping sound that sounded like horse's hooves. The man holding the pistol slumped forward and the second man bent quickly to retrieve the gun. But as he did so Penny saw a sight that she would never forget. Two men on horseback riding flat-out toward the barn. One was an old cowboy and the other was Doc. He was holding a long bow beside the horse's flaring nostrils.

The pistol in the cowboy's hand flashed and the second man lurched back against the truck's front bumper, a bloody hole in the side of the green suit. He straightened slightly and began reaching for his comrade's

pistol, but Penny pushed his arm away. The man smacked her with his gloved fist, splitting her lip open. The horses reigned in about twenty feet away and the gun in the old cowboy's hand flashed again.

"Hey, varment," he said. "Looks like you could use a lesson in manners."

Doc leaped from his horse and ran forward, sweeping Penny up in his arms. Tears streamed down her face as she felt his embrace.

"Oh, darling you're alive," she said.

"Yes," Doc said. "Thanks to Cactus Jack. And you? Are you injured?"

"I'll survive," Penny said. "But you've got to stop them. Stringer's a Communist spy and they've got stolen uranium. And there's some kind of sound cannon that they're going to use to shoot down a military plane."

Doc nodded as she spoke and turned to the old cowboy.

"Jack, watch our flank," he said.

The old man dismounted and nodded.

"It'll be a pleasure, pardner."

Doc pried the pistol from the dead man's fingers and immediately checked its cylinder. He then handed the weapon to Cactus Jack and withdrew another arrow from the leather quiver.

"He's damn good with that thing," Cactus Jack said. "Must have some Injun blood in him somewheres."

Penny couldn't help but smile, despite the dire circumstances. She watched as Doc crept around to the side of the barn and fitted the arrow in the bow.

"Please be careful," she said, but doubted that Doc heard her. She felt the old cowboy pulling her toward the shadows of the building.

Doc saw a group of four men loading something into a twin engine Cessna approximately fifty yards to the south on what appeared to be a small dirt airstrip. One of the men appeared to be a giant. The pilot was out rotating the propellers as the other three lifted the box inside. Perhaps thirty feet to his right Doc saw three other men sitting around a large truck. A huge cone-shaped device protruded from the bed of the vehicle. The cone was aimed skyward and seemed to be glowing with some sort of eerie red light. A fourth man sat behind a metallic shield as he looked up through some sort of viewfinder. His gloved left hand was on a throttle and his right was wrapped around a trigger assembly. A beam shot skyward and the cone began an incremental thrumming sound. Doc ran back to the fallen men in the green suit and ripped the helmet off the ground. Slipping it on he ran around the side of the barn and pulled back the bow string.

The first arrow flew straight into the right side of the man holding the trigger. He lurched backward in an arc, screaming silently inside his oversized helmet. One of the men on the ground looked up as the gunner fell, then glanced over to see Doc running toward them. This second man reached immediately to signal the others, and then hopped up to man the vortex cannon.

Still on the run, Doc strung another arrow and fired. This arrow met its mark too, striking the second would-be gunner squarely in the chest. He slumped to the ground and before the others could react, Doc was upon them. Lashing up with a tremendous kick, Doc felled one of the remaining men, then whirled striking the other with a powerful backhand. Both men crumbled like clay pigeons and Doc hopped up to the controls of the sonic weapon. Suddenly he heard the sounds of gunfire behind him, coming from the barn. It only took Doc a few scant seconds to locate and set the safety on the weapon. Then he turned his attention back to Penny and Cactus Jack. A group of four men were advancing on the barn firing rifles as they went. Doc jumped from his position, pulled out three arrows and jammed them into the red dirt. He twisted off the helmet and tossed it down. He nocked the first arrow, raised the bow and fired. It soared, striking one of the riflemen in the neck. The man dropped instantly. Doc reached down and grabbed a second arrow, but before he could string it he was hit across the back with what felt like a two-by-four.

Rolling forward to minimize the impact, Doc swiftly regained his footing. But just as he did so, the huge Gordo swung the thick board again, striking Doc's left shoulder. Once more Doc rolled with the blow as the white hot searing pain shot through his arm. Gordo swung a foot up with surprising agility for a man of his size. But Doc twisted slightly causing the kick to miss its mark. Snaring the giant's leg, Doc raised up from his crouch and pushed.

Gordo lurched backward, but recovered immediately with an almost ursine grace. He grunted and gripped the board with both of his ham-sized hands, as if he were holding a baseball bat.

The two combatants circled each other warily. Doc held his arms slightly elevated, ready to ward off another blow. Gordo's eyes flashed moments before he lashed out allowing Doc to avoid the crushing swing by a fraction of an inch. As the board sailed past, Doc encircled the giant's forearms with his right arm.

Pivoting, Doc attempted to shift his weight to his left, but he realized too late that he'd underestimated Gordo's substantial mass. The bigger man stamped down with his right foot, negating Doc's attempted throw. Rearing backwards, Gordo whipped Doc's body into the side of the truck with a resounding thump. The impact was cushioned by the iron musculature of Doc's mighty back, but he was still momentarily stunned. The Golden Avenger felt his grip on the giant's forearm slipping. Reaching out, Doc managed to grab the end of the board, but Gordo transferred his pull downward and snapped the board loose. Doc felt the sting of slivers of wood embedding themselves deeply into his palm.

Raising the board above his head, Gordo lurched forward delivering a forceful stroke, but Doc swiftly leaped to the side. The board struck the metal fender of the truck and bounced upward. Seizing this opportunity, Doc brought his right foot up with stunning force striking the giant's chest. He then moved to the big man's left and delivered a combination of powerful punches. Gordo seemed unaffected, and he tried to swing the board around at Doc's head. Doc leaned back, away from the arc of the swing, then stepped forward again, smashing a powerful left into the giant's face.

The end of the board skittered across the red dirt as Doc followed up with another series of incredibly rapid punches to Gordo's head.

Dropping the board, Gordo lurched forward and wrapped his arms around Doc, sealing him in a powerful bearhug. Leaning backward, Gordo attempted to apply bone shattering pressure, but Doc shoved with his feet sending them both down in a heap.

As they struck the ground, Gordo's hold was momentarily broken and Doc quickly tried to regain his footing, knowing that the giant outweighed him by at least a hundred pounds. But as he rose, the huge hands snared his head and neck. Gordo grunted attempting to apply the same death lock he'd used earlier to break the neck of the army officer.

Doc's powerful hands grasped the giant's wrists. Twisting, both men struggled on their knees, their breaths coming in rasping gasps, each knowing that the battle was nearing its climax.

Doc grimaced as he braced his powerful neck, staving off the fatal twisting motion that the giant sought to apply. Slowly, inexorably, Doc managed to pull Gordo's huge right hand away. Still gripping the other wrist, Doc managed to pry that one from around his neck. Rising, Doc held the bigger man's arms outstretched. The gleam in Gordo's eyes foretold defeat as Doc twisted the bigger man to the ground and managed to encircle his neck. But the giant made one last ditch effort to throw Doc down. The twisting motion was almost successful, but the Golden Avenger swung his legs in front of Gordo and, still maintaining the iron grip on the big man's neck, flipped him over on his back. Gordo fell with an enormous plopping sound. He attempted to get to his feet, but saw only stars as Doc's fist smashed into his jaw.

Glancing upward, Doc looked in horror as the remaining riflemen were closing in on the barn. A burst of flame shot from one of the barrels into the open doorway. Doc looked quickly for his bow, but saw that it had been crushed during his battle with the giant. Then, just as he was contemplating a suicide charge, he heard the syncopated rhythm of a helicopter approaching. He reached in his pocket for his final halo flare and fired it in a trajectory over the barn. After the initial brightness faded, the slow parachuted descent of the illumination lit up the area. Doc heard a loud whooping yell, followed by the staccato burst of machine gun fire. Seconds later the Sikorsky helicopter swooped in a downward arc, with Ace Assante at the controls and Mad Dog Deagan hanging out the other side of the chopper firing a Thompson submachine gun. Doc felt a surge of relief as the remaining riflemen advancing on the barn fell. He waved at his passing friends but was doubtful that they even saw him.

Suddenly the helicopter's rotors were replaced by another sound. Twin propellers. Doc remembered the Cessna and Penelope's statement that Stringer had stolen some enriched uranium. Glancing to his right, Doc saw the Cessna already beginning its takeoff down the red dirt airstrip.

Picking up the discarded helmet, Doc slipped it on as he leaped aboard the truck. Doc swivelled the base of the vortex cannon toward the direction of the ascending plane. The cannon vibrated beneath him. Gripping the throttle, he adjusted it to a low frequency setting, sighted through the viewfinder, and gripped the trigger. A pinpoint of brightly colored red light seemed to dot the Cessna's starboard wing. Doc squeezed the trigger and the plane's engine immediately sputtered and faded. This occurred just as the Cessna was lifting off into the wind, and the small plane canted downward, the wingtip brushing the ground, sending off a burst of sparks. The wing tore away from the fuselage with savage force, sending the plane into a pell-mell rotation, bouncing on the ground twice before bursting into a flaming inferno.

The Sikorsky helicopter swung over the burning wreckage, Deagan still hanging halfway out of the glass enclosure. It hovered about fifty feet in the air.

Stripping off the helmet, Doc glanced back to see Penny and Cactus Jack emerging from the barn. The old cowboy methodically went over to each of the fallen riflemen and kicked them. Penny rushed to Doc and he put one arm around her.

"Thank God you're safe," she said.

Doc squeezed her gently, his right palm leaving a bloody imprint on her arm.

"Was Stringer in that plane?" Penny asked.

"I assume he was," Doc said. "I saw him loading a metal box on it earlier."

"That must have been the uranium," she said. "At least we won't have to worry about that madman Stalin getting the Bomb."

"For now," Doc said. "But I fear it's only a matter of time now that the atomic genie has been let out of the bottle."

"All of them sidewinders is down for the count," Cactus Jack said, coming up to them. "Say, you look like you been wrestling with a mountain lion yourself."

"Perhaps a grizzly bear would be a more appropriate metaphor," Doc said, nodding his head over toward the fallen giant.

"You guys arrived just like the Lone Ranger and Tonto," Penny said. "But how did you know where to find us?"

"All the credit goes to Mr. Persard," Doc said. "He was aware of the strange goings on here, and told me. I realized that it was most probably connected to the sabotage of the planes, especially after they shot down the Pegasus."

"Yes siree," the old cowboy said. "This here spread used to be mine, Miss. And I guess I never did lose my knack for hiding out in them fading shadows 'round here. Saw that old bearded guy Stringer bringing in all kinds of equipment and illegal aliens. Figured he was up to something."

"Well, you certainly saved my bacon, pardner," Penny said, extending her hand toward Cactus Jack.

The old cowboy grinned as they shook.

"Well, shucks, it was my pleasure, ma'am."

"I guess I'm supposed to say, 'smile when you say that,' right?" Penny asked.

* * *

As the big military DC-9 transport plane taxied to the end of Roswell Army Air Field in preparation for takeoff, Doc and Company fastened their seat belts. Penny twisted around slightly so she could look out the window.

"I don't know about the rest of you, but I'm sure not going to miss this place," she said.

"Oh, I don't know," Deagan said. "It brought back a lot of old memories, right Ace?"

"Yes, and not all of them good, either," Assante said. He leaned forward resting his hands on his cane as his eyes swept around the massive fuselage compartment. "You know, Doc, this is almost as roomy as the old B-19's I used to fly. We ought to consider getting one of these to replace the Pegasus. We could go anywhere in the world then."

"It's something that I've been contemplating for some time, Ace," Doc said. "We'll have to look into it when we get back to New York."

"Hey, Doc," Deagan said. "Do you think old Cactus Jack will take you up on your offer to buy back his ranch for him?"

Penny glanced at Doc.

"You offered to do that for him?" she asked.

"Yes," Doc said. "After all, he did save my life, and yours as well."

"Hey, I'm not arguing," she said. "It's just that he seemed like such a strange character."

"Just like some of them in your books, huh?" Deagan said.

"Actually, he already declined my offer," Doc said. "He told me that the life he's established out on the plains suits him at this particular time. But he is interested in opening a dude ranch in the area and might be in need of some financing. He intends to call it the Desert Shadows Rancho Mirage. I told him the offer stands indefinitely."

"Cactus Jack," Deagan said. "What a guy. As eccentric as they come."

"Actually, he reminds me of you," Ace said. "Too long under the hot sun to think straight."

"Oh yeah, wise guy?" Deagan shot back. "Well, just whose idea was it to commandeer that helicopter that saved the day?"

"Why, I believe it was mine," Ace answered.

"Yours! We'd still be debating with that blown up butterbean officer if it wasn't for me." He smacked his huge right fist into his open left palm. "And if I hadn't had the presence of mind to grab that Tommy gun. . ."

Before the exchange could continue, the propellers increased their speed and the plane began to taxi down the runway.

"See, even the pilots are anxious to get us back to New York," Penny said. "They're probably afraid they'll have to listen to you two argue all the way there." She turned to Doc. "Darling, do you think we've heard the last of this Roswell flying saucer business at least?"

Doc considered the question for a moment as they all felt the plane rising from the runway.

"Sometimes legends take a long time to die," he said with a smile. "And I have a hunch that this particular one will persist for a long time to come."

THE END

Killer Gorilla

III

September 19th, 1948
Death Row, Sing Sing Prison, Ossining, NY

"DEARLY BELOVED," THE prison chaplain began. "We are gathered here today, in the presence of God to join this man and this woman in the bonds of holy matrimony." As the quavering voice continued, Thomas "Mad Dog" Deagan looked on in amazement. He'd thought that he had seen it all in his twenty-plus years as a lieutenant colonel in the U.S. Army, and during his fantastic adventures with Doc Atlas. But this, he reflected, had to take the cake as one of the strangest. The bride was clad in a mid-length light blue dress with an artful bow tied at the back. Her white gloved fingers clutched a drooping bouquet, and her nervous smile, what he could see of it anyway, flickered like a fading bulb at a carnival sideshow. At least she'd been demure enough to wear a veil, he thought, as he glanced at her unnaturally bright red hair and the severity of her heavily applied makeup. But despite her attractiveness, there seemed to be a lingering coarseness about her features. And then there was the groom, who looked painfully wan and drab in his gray and white striped pants and shirt, as he continued to stare defiantly. An odd couple, that was for sure, Deagan reflected.

The walls of the small, windowless, 8 x 12 cell were solid brick, the floor a rough concrete. A cot had been attached to the left wall, and a metal toilet and sink sat in the opposite corner. From the ceiling, encased in a metal cage, a garish overhead light shone down, causing the sweat to glisten on the groom's recently shaved head. A uniformed guard stood to the rear of Deagan, outside of the bars, along with the warden, a grim looking man in a gray, double breasted suit. On the other side of the room, also outside the bars, a dapperly dressed man with salt and pepper hair and a Clark Gable mustache looked on attentively, holding several white envelopes in his hand.

". . .then let him speak now, or forever hold his peace," the chaplain continued. Deagan smirked as he locked eyes with Edward "Ace" Assante, renowned lawyer and another of Atlas's fellow sidekicks. Ace, who was a dead-ringer for a younger version of Errol Flynn, merely smiled slightly as he returned the shorter Deagan's stare. Whereas Assante was tall, dark and extremely handsome, Deagan was short, with bristly reddish hair and features that had been somewhat reshaped in the boxing ring. But despite his short stature, Deagan's broad powerful build suggested a wellspring of strength and power. Between them stood a stunningly beautiful raven-haired woman with the svelte figure of an actress or fashion model. A single tear wound its way down her cheek, toward full red lips and a sharp chin. Despite the slight running of her mascara, her features could only be described as flawless.

"Penny," Mad Dog whispered leaning toward her. "What's wrong? Why you crying?"

"Women always cry at weddings, you idiot," Ace Assante whispered back.

Penelope Cartier quickly dabbed at her eyes with her handkerchief and shook her head slightly.

"Ahem," the chaplain said gravely, as if clearing his throat, his piercing gaze settled harshly on Deagan, who blushed visibly. "I now pronounce you man and wife. You may kiss the bride," he concluded.

Johnny "Spades" Apollo exhaled sharply, his breath sounding almost like a snort. His face was handsome, in a rugged sort of way, with a prominent Roman nose and high cheek bones. But the scowl that twisted his features turned his visage into the portrait of a monster. Barely waiting for his bride to slightly lift her heavy veil, Apollo reached forward and crushed her to him, planting a kiss on her lips. When he was finished he looked over at Assante, Deagan, and Penny and said insolently, "You got enough for my obituary now?"

"Hey, mac," Deagan said, his jaw jutting forward, "you asked us up here, remember?"

The look in Apollo's eyes didn't change, but he seemed to deflate slightly. "I just wanted some formal witnesses that me and Zelda officially tied the knot." He turned to Penny, who was wiping her eyes. "How about you, Cartier? You're gonna mention this in that rag you write for, ain't ya?"

Penny seemed to compose herself almost immediately.

"I'll certainly do my best, Mr. Apollo," she said. "Now," she paused to bring up her pen and steno pad, "although this is a momentous occasion, you are on the brink of your execution."

She spoke carefully as her dark eyes probed his face. "Do you have any last statements to make?"

The searing insolence quickly returned to Apollo's expression.

"Yeah, I got plenty to say," he sneered. "But I ain't gonna say it to you. Just tell your boyfriend Atlas that he ain't heard the last of Johnny Apollo."

"Come on, Penny," Ace said, tugging at her arm, and leaning on his ebony cane. His right knee had been severely damaged during one of his last bombing missions over Berlin. "Let's leave the bride and groom to enjoy their nuptials in private."

"I ain't forgot about you refusing to take my case neither, Assante," Apollo said.

A dazzling smile graced Ace's lips. "Please, Spades, I'm wounded. I thought I explained to you at the time that Judge Becker was a personal friend of mine. It wouldn't have been ethical for me to take your case. Besides, you were excellently represented by Mr. Sorakas." He glanced at the dapper man, who nodded gracefully.

"Since when do you lawyers care about ethics?" Apollo said, his mouth turning downward into a malevolent scowl.

"Since he don't defend scum," Deagan said, stepping up and meeting Apollo's gaze. "Like you."

"For a plug nickel I'd slit your damn throat," Apollo growled.

Deagan balled up his fists, which were about the size of a grapefruits. "Come on and try it."

"Gentlemen, please," the warden said, moving forward. "Johnny, you've got less than forty-five minutes. Don't you want to spend what time's left to you with your bride?"

Apollo seemed to freeze, then said, "Yeah, warden, you're right. I want to be alone with my wife and friends. The rest of you can get the hell out."

"You're sure you won't change your mind about that last meal?" the warden asked.

"I should," Apollo said. "Just to give your boys a little more to clean up after me." He laughed bitterly. "Naw, I don't want no more of your lousy prison chow. Just send in Silky and the doc."

The warden nodded grimly, and held out his arm for Deagan, Penny, and Ace to exit via the single door at the end of the hall. The chaplain followed, saying that he'd return at the end of the visitation period. Apollo watched them go, then, as they were just opening the door to leave, he called out.

"Hey, here's a quote for your damn paper, Cartier, and for the rest of you too. I'm going out tonight just like Two-Gun Crowley. Proud and defiant. But all of youse, keep remembering that maybe, just maybe, you ain't seen the last of Johnny Apollo."

Deagan started to say something in return, but he felt Ace's hand on his sleeve. Assante shook his head slightly and both men went out the door, followed by Penny and the warden. The guard closed the door and stationed himself impassively beside it. Apollo went to Sorakas and leaned close to the lawyer's face.

"You sure you got everything set up?" he asked in a harsh whisper. "Just like I told ya?"

"Yes, John," Sorakas said, holding up the two envelopes. "Everything's in place. The writ's been served allowing us to take charge of your body immediately following . . . the event."

"Aww, can't you damn lawyers ever stop being so mealy mouthed?" Apollo said. "Alls I want to know is if the professor's instructions are being followed to the letter."

"I can assure you that they are," Sorakas said.

The door at the end of the hall opened and three men stepped through. One was a huge, rough looking man with large hands and a face that looked like a catcher's mitt. The other man was shorter, but equally hard looking. He wore a white silk ascot around his neck, which contrasted sharply with his dark blue suit jacket. The third man was much smaller than the others, and had a set of wire-rim glasses perched carefully on an aquiline nose. His hair was white, and a fuzzy beard and mustache surrounded his lips. The eyes behind the glasses shone with an almost demented light. He moved quickly down the hall to the cell and peered in at Apollo, then moved forward.

"You are exciting yourself, no?" he said, with a distinctly European accent. "Zat is not goot."

"Yeah, yeah, I know," Apollo said. He moved to sit down on the cot.

Zelda stepped over to rub her hand over his shiny scalp, and said, "Don't worry, darling. It'll all be okay."

He pushed her away viciously. "Get away from me. Ya think I'm one of them goons who used to go to you in the circus to have his fortune read?"

"Hey, Boss," the man with the silk ascot said quickly. "The professor said not to get worked up, right?"

"Yeah, yeah, Silky, I know," Apollo said. "But there's just so much that can go wrong."

"Johnny," Sorakas said. "We've got everything taken care of. The writ to allow the professor to proceed as planned, the marriage license that will leave Zelda in charge of all your finances so there will be no probate of your holdings. So Silky and Lucas here can keep on running things. And the specially equipped ambulance is already standing by." He smiled benevolently.

"Zis is true," the professor said, moving forward and shining a small pen light into Apollo's eyes. His head bobbed up and down slightly as he spoke. "Now, you must relax. Don't over exert yourself. Save your strength." He leaned over so that his lips were close to Apollo's ear. "And vhen you next avake, you will have zee strength of ten men."

* * *

Penny sat at the desk in the small office, busily writing on her story, her cigarette burning untouched in the ashtray. Assante and Deagan both slumped in chairs on either side of another ash tray. A huge Cuban cigar smoldered between Deagan's fingers, while Assante smoked a Lucky Strike. The warden came to the door and smiled wearily as he extended his open hand toward Assante. Ace tapped Mad Dog on the shoulder and motioned to Penny.

"I think it's time," said Ace. He crushed his cigarette into the ashtray.

"If you would care to move to the viewing room at this time," the warden said, "we should be ready to proceed shortly."

"Thanks, Warden," Deagan said, stubbing out his cigar. Then, turning to Penny, added, "Are you sure you want to see this?"

"It's part of the story," she said. "Besides, I cut my teeth on this one. I was just a stringer when Hirum Heath took me under his wing and let me help him set up the columns that broke the story."

"What ever happened to old Hirum?" the warden asked, walking ahead of them down the hallway, which was a long series of single office doors, facing each other over a highly buffed tile floor. "I heard he just sort of dropped out of sight a year or so ago."

"He wanted it that way," Penny said. "But he did tell me to give you his regards."

The warden nodded. "And Dr. Atlas?"

"Doc's over in Sweden accepting some kind of scientific award," Deagan said. "For his work in discovering something or other. He's a real wizard with that kind of stuff."

"Yes," the warden said. "He expressed interest in examining Apollo's brain after the execution. But with that special writ that Sorakas obtained, I'll have to release the body immediately after the doctor pronounces him dead."

"Any idea what that's about?" Ace asked.

The warden shook his head. Their heels made a clicking sound on the hard, highly polished surface.

"Don't you feel it's strange that Apollo dropped his appeals so abruptly?" Penny said."I mean, he could have easily drawn things out for some time."

"He'd just be postponing the inevitable," Ace said. "A person doesn't orchestrate the assassination of a prominent judge and leave your trademark ace-of-spades playing card in the judge's left hand. You just don't get away with something that bold."

"Unless you got a top-flight shyster like you defending him," Deagan said, his face cracking into a wry grin. Penny smiled too at the constant, but ultimately good-natured, banter between the two men.

"Precisely why I refused to take the case," Assante said. "But what exactly did that writ say?"

"That Apollo's body was to be released to his personal physician, a Doctor Essence, immediately after the execution," the warden said. "I think he convinced Apollo that he could be somehow resuscitated. They even went so far as to have their own private ambulance standing by."

"Huh?" Deagan said. "I mean, they can't do it, can they?"

"Hey," Assante said with a laugh. "Maybe that quack doctor has a new customer here."

"Not hardly," Deagan said. "I was just asking, that's all."

"Dr. Essence?" Penny said. "Is that who that Bela Lugosi character was in the visitor's room?"

"Yes," said the warden, turning the corner and coming to a halt. They were at another door. After a weary sigh, the warden put his hand on the knob and continued. "The. . . doctor has been a frequent visitor to Apollo for the past few months. This is the viewing room. The other guests have already arrived. If you'll excuse me, I have some other tasks that I have to attend to." He opened the door and Penny, Ace, and Deagan went inside.

The room was moderately large, with rows of folding chairs that had been set up in front of a wall with several large windows in it. Numerous people had already taken their places in the section near the windows, but three chairs were conspicuously empty in the front row. Penny, Deagan, and Ace took their seats, nodding a hello to several familiar faces, among them Congressman Roscoe Kelly, District Attorney Stephen Bainbridge, Judge Lorne Taylor, police detective Paul Wilson, and Penny's editor Lou Stoner. Each, in some way, had been connected to the Apollo case. Several other reporters and state officials made up the rest of the small group.

Open Venetian blinds hung suspended on the other side of the glass allowing a view through the windows into the adjacent room of the single, sinister looking chair that sat in the middle of the floor. It had two legs in back and a single, heavier leg in front, replete with two metal footholders. All three legs were bolted to the floor. Large oversized arms stood perpendicular to the sturdy looking backplate, and thick leather straps dangled open and ready to accept each appendage. The floor area at the bottom was covered with rubber matting and thick wires ran to a metal plate on the wall. The execution room itself, like the viewing room, had been painted a pale green color, although the floors were dark tile.

Penny stared at the starkness of the room on the other side of the glass and quickly began jotting down notes on her steno pad. Deagan sat impassively on the left side of her, his big hands resting on his knees. Ace sat to her right, legs crossed, and hands resting on the ornately carved handle of his cane.

Presently the procession entered the other room: Apollo, clopping along in open-toed sandals, the warden still looking grim and solemn, the chaplain reading softly from his open Bible, and the three uniformed guards flanking them. Apollo paused and glanced through the glass windows at the audience. His face twisted into a mixture of defiance and malevolence again, and he spat at the window, then turned to the warden and said, "Let's get it done." He sat in the chair without protestation, and kicked off his sandals. The warden moved forward and began to close the blinds while the condemned man was being strapped in, but Apollo said, "Leave 'em open. Give 'em the show they came to see."

He continued to stare defiantly as the guards began to tighten the straps around his arms, legs, and chest. After wetting his head with a sponge, they began to lower the leather hood over his face. Penny suddenly caught a glimpse of his unyielding stare, the rivulets of water and sweat cascading down his cheeks. Bucking his head suddenly, he tossed off the hands with the hood long enough to yell, "You ain't heard the last of Johnny Apollo! You ain't heard the last of me!" The guard resumed fastening the hood and quickly had it in place. He stepped back and signaled to the warden, who went to a small podium with a telephone on it. Picking up the phone, the warden spoke softly into it, waited, then nodded. After setting the phone back down in the cradle, the warden's mouth drew into a thin line.

"Will the lights really dim?" Penny asked in a hushed whisper, leaning to her left.

"Naw," Deagan said. "The chair's hooked up to a separate power source. That flickering light stuff's only in the movies."

Suddenly Apollo's body began to lurch upward, straining against the straps, a slightly visible tremor seeming to vibrate through his limbs. The leather-encased head jammed back against the heavy chair and a moist gurgling sound could be heard. After perhaps a minute, that seemed like an eternity, the current was reduced from 2000 volts to the continuous 500 voltage flow. The body seemed to relax slightly, the head lolling forward, only to arch backward once more as the voltage was again brought back up to 2000. A dark liquid squirted out from Apollo's open pant legs, and formed a puddle on the rubber matting, while a frothy band of white foam began to seep out from under the leather hood. Penny turned her face away and leaned against Ace's shoulder. He put his arm around her, and she kept her eyes closed for the rest of the final minutes. She opened them when Ace squeezed her arm and said, "Okay, it's over." But she didn't move from his embrace.

For several moments everyone sat in a stunned silence. The only signs of movement were the quick flicking of lighters accompanied by the suddenly redolent smell of burning tobacco. Penny felt Ace's hand move under the lapel of his jacket and withdraw his pack of Luckies. He shook one loose and offered it to her, then grabbing one himself, took out his own lighter. As she sat up she heard Deagan explaining how it wasn't the voltage that was deadly, but the amperage.

"I'll bet I could take 2000 volts and live," he said, "but a rate of only five amps will kill you deader than a mackerel."

"He deserved every amp he got," Detective Paul Wilson said, blowing a stream of smoke toward the ceiling. He was a short, squat looking man with a massive head covered with a shaggy mane of brown hair. "He was nothing more than a coldblooded killer."

"Just the same, Paul," an older, bespectacled, white-haired gentleman said, "he was still a human being."

"Aww, come on, judge," Wilson said. "How can you feel sorry for scum like Apollo?"

The judge smiled benignly and took out a long-stemmed pipe.

"I was wondering the same thing, your honor," Lou Stoner said. Stoner was a heavyset man with thick looking arms and a perpetually quizzical expression. He had only a fringe of brown hair above his ears, and the knot in his neck tie hung loosely under the slack underpinning of his jutting chin.

"After all, judge," District Attorney Bainbridge said, "you were the one who sentenced him to death." Bainbridge was a rather tall, sophisticated looking man in his late forties.

"Which under the circumstances," the judge said, continuing to pack his pipe with tobacco, "I felt was appropriate. But I still can't help recalling that old quote, 'There, but for the grace of God, go I.'"

"How can you be such a bleeding heart?" Deagan said, moving into the conversation. "A guy like Apollo got what he deserved."

"My friend here would have probably preferred to have led a firing squad," Assante said, stepping forward and shaking hands with the judge and the two other men. "How are you, your honor?" Ace turned to Mad Dog and pointed. "And may I present my associate, Lt. Colonel, retired, Thomas E. Deagan."

"Another one of Doc Atlas's crew?" a big, ruggedly handsome man with shortly cropped blonde hair said, stepping up to shake hands with Deagan and Ace."A pleasure to meet you both. I'm Congressman Roscoe J. Kelly. You may have heard of me. I ran on a platform stressing how evil criminals like Apollo should be done away with without the slightest compunction. I used to work with Mayor O'Dwyer back when he was known as Bill-O."

Assante nodded politely, but Deagan shook the congressman's hand vigorously.

"You'll have to excuse my pal here," he said, cocking his head toward Ace. "Ever since he graduated from law school he has trouble recognizing a sensible idea when he hears one. And this is—"He looked around for Penny to introduce her, but suddenly noticed that she wasn't at their sides as usual. Deagan scanned the room and saw her, standing in the corner, near the set of oversized windows, watching as the guards removed the straps from the lifeless body of the executed man.

Ace walked over and placed a hand on her arm.

"Are you all right?" he asked.

"Yes," she said, closing her eyes and glancing away as Apollo's lifeless fingers brushed the floor after falling from the stretcher. "I've just never seen anyone. . . die like that before. It was so. . . brutal."

Ace nodded. "A brutal end for a brutal man," he said.

* * *

Crescent half moons lit by soft-glowing bulbs lined the walls, and slowly revolving ceiling fans spun silently up above. The area behind the orchestra was a huge backdrop made up in a magnificent sidereal display, in which a dark blue screen, oscillating slightly, allowed its myriad of star-shaped perforations to show glimpses of a silvery-white background. A corpulent little man in a black tuxedo mopped his face with his handkerchief as he climbed the stairs to the stage and went to the microphone. The lights in the massive dining hall dimmed slightly, and a hush fell over the crowd. Moments later the bright beam of a spotlight enveloped him and made his shiny face gleam. He gripped the metal stand and spoke directly into the mike.

"Ladies and Gentlemen," he said, his voice booming out through the amplifiers, "welcome to the Annual Fiorello H. La Guardia Memorial All Hallows Eve Charity Ball. On behalf of our current mayor, the honorable William O'Dwyer, let me welcome you all here tonight. In addition to hizzoner and the various political dignitaries, we have many celebrities in attendance, including Mr. Frank Sinatra, who has graciously agreed to accompany the orchestra for our opening dance number."

The applause was deafening, and when it subsided, the lanky singer could be seen making his way up to the stage. Couples immediately began applauding again, then, as the music began to play, they migrated to the dance floor.

Seated at one of the front tables, Deagan's face furrowed into a heavy frown at the enthusiastic applause exhibited by his date of the evening, and regular girlfriend, Polly St. Clair. She was a rather buxom, red-haired lass with a spray of freckles, who was the supervisor of the large contingent of secretaries that Doc employed at his headquarters in the Empire State Building. Across from them sat Ace Assante who was seated beside one of the many dark-haired, sultry beauties that he'd been seen with recently. And at the end of the table, next to Penny, sat Doc Atlas. Even clad in formal evening wear, Doc's magnificent proportions were evident. His tawny hair was combed back majestically from his forehead, giving his handsome features an almost regal cast. Seemingly impassive, his amber-colored eyes moved effortlessly to take in all movement around him.

"What's the matter, Tom?" Polly asked."Don't you like Frank Sinatra?"

"Aww, I got no use for any slacker," Deagan said.

"Give the man a break," Ace said. "He's got a tremendous voice, great timing, and his own distinctive style. Just because he didn't serve is no reason not to appreciate excellent singing when you hear it."

"Besides," Penny said, "you know they wouldn't have put anybody as famous as him in harm's way. He would've probably just been touring with the USO like Glenn Miller."

"Well, maybe if he woulda, I'd have some respect for him," Deagan said. "And not all them movie stars shirked their duty, Penny. Look at Gene Autry and Jimmy Stewart."

"Jimmy Stewart," Polly said, canting her head and rolling her eyes. "Tom always says he flew almost as many combat missions over Germany as you did, Ace."

"He does?" Assante said, leaning forward with a surprised grin.

"I mighta said that once or twice," Deagan muttered quickly. He grabbed his glass and asked if anyone needed a refill.

"Not me," Penny said. The music started to well up from the band shell, and Sinatra began crooning *You'll Never Know*. Standing quickly, Penny took Doc's hand and pulled him gently, but firmly to his feet. "Come on, darling," she said. "How many chances does a girl get to dance while Sinatra's singing?"

As they moved out to the dancing area, all eyes were on them.

"They really make a swell couple, don't they?" Polly said.

"Stunning," Assante answered.

Penny was wearing a white satin gown that left her neck and shoulders bare, and a dark profusion of curls crested each of her well-formed limbs. She placed her hand in Doc's, and, as his arm swept around her waist, they seemed to glide in among the other dancers. Doc delivered each step with a flawless, almost technical preciseness.

"Isn't this nice?" she said.

He merely smiled at her, saying nothing.

"Tell the truth," she continued. "Aren't you glad that I talked you into coming? After all, it is your birthday."

As was his custom when being prodded with questions that he considered unnecessary, Doc still remained silent.

"Well?" she said.

Doc turned. "Actually, it has proved rather expeditious."

"It has?" She smiled. "Really?"

"Certainly. Although it obligated me to go to one of these political functions, of which I'm not fond, it did spare me having to endure one of those surprise parties that you and Polly seem so intent on carrying out each year."

Penny frowned. "Do you realize that this is the first chance we've had to be alone together all evening?" she said, leaning in close to him and pressing her cheek on his chest.

"I'd hardly say we were alone," he said finally.

"Mmmm," she said. "We are as far as I'm concerned." Keeping her face pressed against him, their bodies moved in a seemingly effortless rhythm. Sinatra's mellifluous voice continued to croon out the song, and Penny began to softly hum the melody. Suddenly Doc felt someone tap him on the shoulder and they abruptly stopped dancing. It was Deagan.

"Aaaah, sorry, Doc," he said, holding his hands palms-up by his sides in an apologetic gesture. "But the mayor's over there with the cops, and they said they need to see ya. An emergency, or something."

Doc glanced over to the area near the door and saw the short, squat form of Mayor O'Dwyer standing next to a tall, barrel-chested uniformed police officer. Doc smiled and gently released Penny from his embrace. She sighed, frowned, and then grabbed Deagan's hand.

"No you don't," she said. "Nobody, not even the mayor himself, is going to cheat me out of a dance when Sinatra's singing. Come on, Mad Dog. I'm sure Polly won't mind."

"Aww, Penny, I can't dance," Deagan muttered quickly, trying to get away. But Penny held him tightly and moved in fast, intentionally stepping down hard on his toe.

"Owww," he said.

"Shut up," she said. "I'll teach you."

As Doc approached the mayor and the officer, he extended his hand. The mayor took it in both of his and offered profuse apologies for disturbing him. Doc noticed that the lines around the mayor's eyes seemed to have deepened.

"But Commander Sheridan has informed me that there's been a terrible tragedy," the mayor said, the slight Irish brogue tincturing his words. His mouth drew into a tense line, and he licked his lips. "Judge Taylor's been horribly murdered."

If Doc was surprised by the news, he showed no noticeable effect. Commander Sheridan spoke next.

"There are certain . . . irregularities at the crime scene, Dr. Atlas," he said. "The commissioner thought it would be wise to notify you."

Doc nodded. Glancing back at Deagan and Penny struggling on the dance floor, he said, "Just let me make the appropriate arrangements and I'll be right with you."

Doc strode across the dance floor and stopped next to Deagan and Penny.

"I'll resume now, Thomas," he said.

A look of relief flooded Deagan's face as he quickly stepped back and released Penny.

"Thanks for filling in, Mad Dog," Penny said, easily slipping back into Doc's arms. "And you were swell. I'll bet you could give Fred Astaire a run for his money."

"Yeah, sure," Deagan said bashfully. "Maybe next time you'll let me lead."

Penny giggled as she and Doc began dancing again. But she quickly felt the tenseness in his back and shoulders and looked up at his handsome, yet always enigmatic, face.

"What's wrong, darling?" she asked.

"I'm afraid I'll have to leave after this dance," he said. "There's been a murder."

"Oh?" she asked coyly. "And is it anyone newsworthy?"

"Judge Taylor," Doc said. "The police are requesting my assistance."

Penny stiffened at the news.

"Oh my God," she said. "I just saw him last month at that execution. He seemed like such a gentle soul."

Sinatra was putting his customary stylish finish on the song, leaning in close to the huge, bulbous microphone. When the dancers stopped they immediately broke into a spontaneous and hearty applause. Suddenly another couple bumped into Doc and Penny. The woman was a pretty blonde, and the man was tall and rawboned.

"Well, Miss Cartier, this is a surprise," the big man said. Penny stared for a moment, not recognizing him, but the man went on. "And this must be Dr. Atlas. I'm Congressman Roscoe Kelly. It's a pleasure to meet you."

Doc accepted the congressman's outstretched hand.

"I met Miss Cartier at the Apollo execution," Kelly said. "I was wondering if I'd run into you two tonight. I saw your names on the guest list."

"You're a friend of the mayor?" Penny managed to ask, thinking that there was something oddly familiar about Kelly's companion too.

"Why yes," he said. "We used to work together in the district attorney's office. I served with Bill-O during the war, too."

The orchestra began playing another song and Sinatra was leaning in close to the microphone again.

"Miss Cartier, may I have the honor of this next dance?" Kelly said. He held out his partner's hand toward Doc. "I'm sure this young lady here would love to dance with the famous Doc Atlas." The woman looked coolly at Doc, and slowly wet her upper lip.

"Regrettably I have to leave on an emergency," Doc said.

"And I have to go with him," added Penny.

"Well," Kelly said with a slow grin, "perhaps we'll see each other another time then."

* * *

Judge Taylor's home was located outside the city on a rolling estate of several acres. The house, a huge Georgian colonial-style mansion, was set back from the highway and surrounded by a high wall made of jutting flagstones. The front gates, two harp-shaped wrought iron barriers, stood open. A state police car sat parked in one lane of the entrance. Doc pulled his bronze Cadillac up next to the patrol car and rolled down the window. Still in her evening dress, Penny sat next to him looking radiant.

"I'm sorry," the uniformed state trooper said as he ambled forward waving his hand back and forth. "No entry."

"Good evening, officer," Doc said. He needed no further introduction. The trooper immediately came to attention.

"Oh my gosh, sir," he said quickly. "If I woulda known it was you."

"That's perfectly all right," Doc said, and drove through the open gates. As they made up the winding road toward the house, Penny glanced back at the trooper and smiled.

"Is there any place that your good looks and fabulous reputation can't get you into?" she asked.

Doc said nothing. He was busy scanning the area ahead. Several police cars were parked on the circular drive in front of the large two story brick house. Long white pillars extended downward from a balcony, and a lighted fountain gurgled lugubriously in the center of the drive. The police cars, both marked and unmarked, were parked in haphazard fashion around the front entrance.

"Do you think they'll mind that I called for a photographer?" Penny asked as Doc held open the door for her.

Again, as was his custom, he ignored the question. Their feet made crunching sounds as they walked over the gravel. A second trooper who had been standing at the front door immediately came to attention when he saw Doc approaching and rapped on the wooden door hard with his knuckles. The door opened and Doc and Penny went inside. They were immediately met by a lieutenant from the state police and District Attorney Stephen Bainbridge, who extended his hand.

"Ah, Dr. Atlas," he said, smiling grimly. "Sorry to disturb your Friday night on the town." Then, nodding, he added, "Miss Cartier."

"Where's the body at?" Doc asked.

"The second floor study," Bainbridge said, pointing to a full staircase against the far wall. "Miss Cartier, perhaps it would be better if you waited down here."

"Not on your life, buster," Penny said keeping in step with Doc. "The least you can do after ruining my evening is to let me get a scoop. I've got a photographer on the way."

"That wasn't such a good idea," Bainbridge said.

"Aren't you a little out of your jurisdiction, Mr. D.A.?" Penny said, moving toward the stairway with Doc. Bainbridge merely frowned emphatically.

"Judge Taylor was a personal friend of mine," he said. He went to a nearby sofa and sat down, placing his head in his hands. Penny grimaced shamefully.

"Now that I've managed to be really rude to him, I might as well go with you, darling," Penny whispered as they moved up the stairs. They were met by another uniformed officer who was stationed on the upper landing outside a set of double doors. He glanced from Doc to Penny, then back at Doc again.

"Perhaps you'd better wait out here for the time being," Doc said. "At least until the crime scene has been processed."

Penny nodded and reached in her purse for her cigarettes. The cop quickly fumbled through his pockets and withdrew a book of matches. He struck one on the side of the box and held it out for Penny. She smiled as she leaned forward to place the end of the cigarette into the yellow flame.

"Why, thank you, officer," Penny said, showing one of her most alluring smiles. Blowing out a cloud of smoke, she glanced down at the young cop's name tag. "So tell me, Officer Raymond, what preliminaries can you tell me?" she asked, taking out her notebook and pen.

Doc pushed open the door and went in. The windows near the French doors had been shattered, and the remnants of the wispy curtains hung like torn sails. The couch had been overturned, and a desk lay crushed and broken near the opposite wall. A large sitting chair was on its back, and numerous bookcases also lay in disarray, their contents scattered about the room. Several men stood huddled over a twisted corpse in the center of the floor. The pungent odor of eviscerated organs was ubiquitous. Blood stains dappled the light wallpaper, and low hanging chandelier had been pulled from the ceiling. One of the men in a trench coat, a heavyset, dark complexioned guy in his mid-thirties, looked over and grinned as Doc entered. He tapped a second man who was squatting next to the corpse, and they both stood up.

"How are ya, Atlas?" he said.

"Detective Roland," Doc answered.

"This is my partner, Paul Wilson," Roland said, pointing toward the shorter man next to him.

As was his custom, Doc made no effort to shake hands. He merely strode over to the corpse and glanced down at it.

"Ever seen anything like this?" Hal Roland asked.

Doc didn't answer, but his amber eyes continued to sweep over the battered, broken body.

"Obviously a crime of unbridled fury," Doc said finally. "I trust you're here in an advisory capacity?"

"Yeah," Roland said. "The state boys called down to the precinct for their most experienced crime scene people. That was me and Paul. Especially after they seen what was in the judge's left hand."

Doc's eyes narrowed quizzically. The hand was now empty.

"See for yourself," Roland said. He whistled toward the three technicians engaged in various tasks of photography, measurement, and fingerprint dusting. One of them looked up and Roland said, "Show Atlas here what was in the judge's left hand." The technician stepped carefully away from the body, went over to a white envelope next to an open briefcase, and gingerly opened the envelope. He tilted it so that the contents fell out into his gloved hand. It was a playing card. The ace of spades. A fourth man, who wore the uniform and insignias of a State Police Captain, walked over and extended his hand.

"Dr. Atlas, this is a distinct honor," he said. "I'm Captain Faraday."

Before Doc could answer, the doors opened again and the uniformed officer stuck his head inside.

"Hey, Cap," he said. "Miss Cartier wants to know how long before she'll be able to come in and take a look at things."

Faraday looked perplexed, but Roland said, "Cartier? That's your girlfriend reporter, ain't it?"

Doc ignored him.

Roland turned toward the uniformed officer at the door and said, "Well, hell, no need to keep the lady waiting. Send her in. Just tell her not to touch anything." Wilson smirked at him.

The door swung open and Penny came sauntering in, her eyes sweeping over the disorderly room.

"Thanks, boys," she said. "I really appreciate it."

"Don't mention it," said Roland, who stepped aside and swung his arm out toward the crumpled body on the floor. "This what you came to see?"

Penny stopped suddenly and stared at the twisted broken form that had once been Judge Taylor. The overpowering stench of the mangled body assailed her nostrils. Her breath caught in her throat, and a swarm of black dots seemed to coalesce in front of her eyes all at once. Doc moved with preternatural speed to catch her before she collapsed to the floor.

* * *

The headlights of the dark green Packard swirled in the fog a moment before they were switched off. The car pulled to a stop on the circular drive in front of the large, Victorian-style house. As the two men got out and walked to the front doors, their feet made crunching sounds on the fine gravel. One of the men was short, with an elegant tan overcoat, fine hat, and shoes that were highly polished. The man who followed along behind him was large and somewhat ungainly. His hat and overcoat hung loosely on his oversized form, his hands dangling loosely, but ready at his sides. The tall man bounded up a set of steps and ran the doorbell. A slot in the door opened, closed, then the door swung inward.

"Vito," Silky McCay said, stepping back and holding out his hand. His white silk ascot had been neatly knotted and tucked into place around the collar of his pale blue shirt.

Vito ignored Silky's outstretched hand and brusquely sauntered by.

"I don't shake hands with the hired help," Vito "The Oyster" Geretti said. His bodyguard, Tony Laprey, flashed a smirk at Silky as they strolled by.

"Everybody's waiting in the library," Silky said, trailing them.

"Let 'em wait then," Vito said. "Where's the can at in this damn place?"

Silky pointed toward a hallway and Vito strode away, the hulking Tony following along behind him. As Vito went in the water closet and closed the door, Laprey turned and held up his extended fingers toward Silky in a triggerman's salute. Silky stood staring down at the carpet, his hands in his pockets. After a few minutes he heard a flushing sound and Vito reappeared. He handed his overcoat to Tony and walked back down the hallway.

"Where they at?" he said.

"Follow me," Silky said.

He lead them through a sumptuously furnished living room to another hallway. The library was situated at the end of it. Silky opened twin doors and stepped aside. The room was moderately large, with well-stocked oak bookcases inlaid into the walls. Heavy drapes had been drawn across each of the windows, and a huge, floor-to-ceiling curtain hung across the center, obscuring the north wall. Fifteen men sat in the room in straight-backed chairs that had been arranged facing the curtain on the other side of the room. Numerous heads turned as Vito, Tony, and Silky entered, and greetings were exchanged.

"Can it," Vito said gruffly. "This ain't no social visit. We come to divide things up, didn't we?"

"Let's not be too hasty now," Silky said, stepping up in front of the group.

"Listen, you damn mick," Vito said, his index finger jabbing out in front of him like a probing bayonet. "Like I told you, I don't talk to the hired help. Johnny's dead, and we're here to take over his stock. You better not be planning to try and give us no problems."

The other men in the room stared from one man to the other in silence. Silky smiled and tugged gently at the corners of his white ascot.

"Vito, Vito, Vito," he said. "I asked all of you here for a purpose. Now sit down. Relax. Hear me out." Silky stared at Vito's still angry features, then at the rest of the questioning faces.

Vito snorted and took out a cigar. After lighting it, he muttered, "Okay, but make it quick," and slumped down into a near-by chair.

"First of all, let me introduce Mrs. Johnny Apollo," Silky said, holding out his outstretched palm as Zelda moved from behind the curtain and stood in front of the group. She was clad in a form-fitting, lavender evening gown with a rather plunging neckline. Her substantial figure filled out the curves nicely. A pearl necklace glimmered around her slender neck. "I'm happy to say that her and Johnny were married at Sing Sing right before the execution."

"Don't think that I'm taking orders from some broad neither," Vito said, puffing on the cigar copiously.

Silky smiled and shook his head.

"Zelda and Johnny had been together a long time," he said. "Not only did he feel it was an honorable thing to do, but he was concerned about just this sort of thing happening. He kinda thought that some of you would be greedier than others, and he couldn't bear the thought of any of youse fighting over his portion of the pie." Silky paused and smiled again.

"I'm getting real tired of listening to ya," Vito said. "When I'm finished with my cigar, you ain't gonna have nothing more to say. So you'd better get to the point." Laprey grinned.

"That's exactly what I plan on doin', Vito," Silky said. "Now as I was telling youse, Johnny didn't want some power struggle starting between the other members of the commission ruining things. Breaking up what he worked so hard to build up. That woulda torn him apart. So he thought about it, and decided that he wasn't really gonna leave us."

Vito jerked forward in his chair, twin plums of smoke shooting from his nostrils.

"What the hell you talkin' about?" he said. "Johnny's dead. It was in the papers."

Silky smiled, then waved his hands. Zelda stood up and straightened her dress. She moved slowly to the wall where she snapped off two of the electrical switches, causing the overhead lights to dim substantially. A murmur of voices sounded throughout the room.

"Hey, what you trying to pull, Silky? Laprey's gruff voice asked.

"Sit down and relax," Silky said. Zelda did a slinky walk toward the long opaque curtain from whence she came. Then, grabbing it, she slowly walked across the room, pulling the white cloth with her. Johnny Apollo's huge bodyguard, Lucas, stood holding a Thompson submachine gun. His face was covered with a crafty grin. But before the shocked hoodlums could react, Silky called out for nobody to move.

"We ain't gonna shoot nobody unless they try something stupid," he yelled. "We got more for you to see. Lot's more."

He nodded and Zelda continued her wiggling walk, pulling the curtain with her as she went. Then suddenly a collective gasp could be heard from the seated gangsters, because seated next to Lucas, on a hospital bed, was a huge African mountain gorilla. A bag of clear liquid hung suspended from a metal rail attached to the headboard of the bed, and an intravenous cord down to a needle stuck in the gorilla's left arm. The ape's head was encased in a shiny metallic frame that the sides of its head from a thick chrome rose up along with a corresponding band around the forehead, making it resemble a crown of sorts. Zelda walked over to the bed, sat down next to the monstrous ape, and placed her arm over its shoulder. The fingers of the gorilla's huge dark right hand moved through her reddish hair.

"What kind of sick stunt is this?" Vito said.

"Gentleman, just keep your pants on," Silky said, an almost maniacal grin spreading over his face. "Before I say any more, I want you to listen to somebody." He snapped his fingers and said, "Professor."

A small man with a white beard and a matching lab coat shuffled to the center of the room carrying several posters under his arm. He paused in front of the group, but out of the line of fire of the Thompson that Lucas was still holding, and pushed his wire rimmed glasses up on his nose before starting to speak.

"Hello," the little man said. "I am Dr. Essence." he made a quick bow. Expressions on the gangster's faces ranged from fear to total and complete perplexity. "*Zhortly* before he *vas* to be executed, Johnny Apollo had his associate, Mr. Zilky McCay contact me. *Dey* had heard of my experiments."

"What the hell's he talkin' about?" Vito asked.

Silky held his index finger to his lips.

"*Zince ve vere vurking* under such a strict time limit," Dr. Essence continued, "I *feld* it prudent to be as expedient as possible. Not knowing if I *vould h*af the time to properly prepare a human substitute, I *vent* instead with one more. . . malleable."

"Will you put a lid on this fruit cake and tell us what the hell's goin' on," Vito said angrily. His cigar smoldered untouched between his fingers.

"In plain and simple terms," Silky said, "we took Johnny's body from the prison in a special ambulance as soon as he was electrocuted. The professor was standing by with us. We managed to keep a supply of oxygen pumping through his body, and there was some kind of electronic gizmo attached to his chest."

"What you trying to say?" one of the gangsters asked.

Silky smiled. Zelda leaned forward, her substantial cleavage practically falling out of her low-cut gown. She picked up a small chalk board off the floor and handed it and a piece of chalk to the huge gorilla. The ape placed the board on his lap and began to scribble on it. The professor began a long-winded explanation full of strange sounding scientific terms about a complete blood transfusion, tissue adjustments, and an eventual brain transplantation. He held up various posters as he spoke, showing diagrams of a human male's cranium and brain along side that of a gorilla's.

"This is nuts!" Vito yelled, standing up. "I ain't buying it for a minute. Are you trying to tell me that Johnny's brain was put into some monkey?"

The professor, who had been muttering something about the delicate transplantation of the optic nerves causing a sensitivity to light, stopped suddenly and stared at the standing man. Then he spoke slowly, looking over the top of his glasses: "Sir, monkeys *haf* tails." He pointed to the hulking figure reposing on the bed."*Dis is one of zee* great apes. A mountain gorilla, to be *ezact. Von of our closest anceztors."*

"Maybe one a yours," Vito muttered. There was a smattering of laughter in the background. "Come on, Tony, let's get outta here." He glanced to assure that his bodyguard was standing to join him, then, as he looked back, he became cognizant of the dark pair of eyes in the huge, hairy head glaring at him. The dark fingers set down the chalk, wiped the slate clean with the sheet that covered his legs, and then scrawled five words on the chalk board:

SORRY TO HEAR THAT VITO.

Vito blinked incredulously as his eyes scanned the words. Then he saw Silky removing a large forty-five automatic from under his coat. With a deft gesture, he snapped back the slide, chambering a round. But instead of pointing it Vito's direction, Silky held it by the barrel and extended the weapon toward Zelda. It was then that Vito noticed the trigger-guard had been filed off. Zelda accepted the gun and handed it to the huge, dark palm that had been caressing her head moments before. She stood and moved to the foot of the bed as the gorilla extended the pistol straight out in front of him, its bore perhaps ten feet from the startled gangster.

The explosion of the round was deafening.

* * *

Polly yawned slightly, covering her mouth as she placed the key into the special portal that sent Doc's private express elevator up to his office headquarters on the 86th floor of the Empire State Building. She'd stayed out longer than she'd anticipated with Deagan the night before and was regretting it now. She should have known better, since she had to start at seven o'clock to get everything set-up for the rest of the girls. The elevator rushed upward, causing her knees to bend slightly and a smile to spread over her face. It was almost like taking a Coney Island ride every day to get to work, she thought.

The elevator slowed to a stop and the doors opened. Taking out her keys, Polly moved to the office doors, but was surprised to find them unlocked. Perplexed, she went into the vast office and immediately heard the sound of someone typing.

"Hello?" she called out. "Doc?"

"It's me, Polly," Penny answered. "I hope you don't mind me using one of your typewriters. Doc opened the office up for me so I could finish my story."

Polly saw her sitting at one of the desks near the east windows. Sunlight was streaming in, making Penny's luxurious dark black hair look almost brownish. Polly's heels made an echoing sound as she walked across the room toward Penny. Doc employed over twenty girls as secretaries to handle the tremendous amount of information that was constantly being fed into his huge, prototypical mainframe computer which took up almost the entire remainder of the floor. As, she drew closer, Polly noticed that Penny still had on the same dress that she'd worn to the ball the night before.

"I already started some coffee," Penny said, nodding toward the large, cylindrical pot on a long table.

"Looks like you and Doc got to spend some time together after all, huh?" Polly said, smiling somewhat suggestively.

"Hardly," Penny said, pausing to proof her typed page as she spoke. "When we got here from the crime scene he ended up working in the lab almost all night. I got so tired that I fell asleep on the sofa. He woke me up this morning. That's about as romantic as it got."

"Oh, too bad," Polly said. "Where's Doc now?"

"He had to get his exercise period in," Penny said. "I came down here to finish my story on Judge Taylor's murder."

"Is that where you two ran off to last night?"

"Yeah," Penny said, rolling the paper out of the typewriter and standing up. "It was pretty gruesome. He was literally torn limb from limb. I've never seen anything like it."

"Sounds horrible," Polly said, filling her special cup with some steaming coffee from the large pot.

"It was," she said suppressing a shudder. "Did you and Tom have a good time after we left?" Penny asked, picking up one of the phones and putting her index finger into the dialing-ring.

"Oh, it was wonderful," Polly said. "We even danced a little."

"How about Ace?" Penny said. Then holding up her hand, she spoke into the phone, "Riley, did Lou get in yet? Okay, let me speak to him." She looked back to Polly. "Who was that girl he was with? He never got around to introducing us."

"Oh, her name was Lola," Polly said, taking a tentative sip from her cup. "Ace said she's a singer. But who can keep up with his social life. He probably has to have a special secretary just to handle all his girlfriends. She seemed nice though."

Penny nodded, then spoke into the phone.

"Lou, it's me. I've been up all night working on a scoop," she said. "Guess who got murdered last night?" She paused, listening. "Well, no, that wasn't who I was talking about, but that's very interesting. What? You're kidding... Okay, I have to stop home to change and I'll get right on it. Oh, by the way, Judge Taylor was killed, too, and I've already got the story done on that one." She smiled as she listened, then said, "Yeah, just give me a raise instead," and hung up.

"Guess what," she said, looking at Polly.

"What?"

"They found a playing card in Judge Taylor's left hand last night," Penny said. "The ace-of-spades. Now this morning the cops found the bodies of mobster Vito Geretti and his bodyguard lying in an alley in the Bronx, and what do you think they were holding?"

Polly's eyes widened. "Don't tell me . . ."

"Yeah," Penny said. "And do you know whose trademark that was?"

Polly shook her head.

"Johnny Apollo. He always left that same card in the left hand of all the people he had murdered."

"Oh my God," Polly said. "You don't think he's come back from the dead, do you?"

"Not unless he's disguised as Boris Karloff," Penny said, picking up the phone again. "I'm calling a cab. Tell Doc I had to go. This one is starting to heat up."

* * *

Detective Paul Wilson sat in quasi-slumber outside the autopsy room letting his cigarette languish in the ashtray. His open notebook lay across his lap. The clicking of Penny's high heels on the tile floor brought him snapping awake. He looked up in time to see her smiling wickedly.

"Well, hello, Detective," Penny said. "We meet again."

Wilson nodded and went back to his notes.

"So what can you tell me about Vito Geretti's demise?" Penny asked.

"Not much," was Wilson's curt reply.

"Aww, come on," she said. "I'd level with you. Besides, the way you were dozing, I could've taken off my shoes and snuck over here and stolen your notebook if I'd wanted to be mean."

"You wouldn't have been able to read it anyway," Wilson said. He flipped the notebook closed and stood up. "I'd ask you to stay for the autopsies, but I got a bad back and didn't want to risk picking you up if you fainted again."

"That's not fair," Penny said defensively. "I've seen plenty of things like that."

"I'll bet you have," Wilson said, grinning. "But for now, you'll just have to ask your boyfriend Atlas about old Vito." He cocked his head toward the entrance and Penny turned to see Doc striding down the hall. Doc was dressed in a brown suit and tie. He seldom wore a hat. He stopped next to them and gazed down at Penny.

"If I'd known you were en route over here we could have shared a cab from headquarters," he said.

"I left word with Polly," Penny said.

Doc turned to Wilson, who was taking a final drag on his cigarette.

"The commissioner called me," Doc said. "He mentioned certain similarities in the crime scenes."

"Just one," Wilson said. "An ace-of-spades in the victim's left hands. Other than that, they was both shot in the chest."

"Where are the cards?" Doc asked. "I would like to examine them for fingerprints."

"I figured as much," Wilson said, holding up two white envelopes. "And since my boss keeps sending me on cases that ain't even mine when I'm already up to my elbows in work, I figured I might as well wait around and give 'em to ya personally. Just sign this evidence log sheet."

Doc accepted both items, then returned the sheet to Wilson.

"Thank you, Detective," Doc said.

"My pleasure," said Wilson, picking up his hat. "Anyway, it was kinda nice to see old Vito with a big hole where his heart was supposed to be."

"Well at least tell us if you have any leads," Penny said.

Wilson smirked.

"These mob cases can be tough nuts to crack," he said. "Nobody wants to say nothing." He crammed his hat on his head and started to stroll down the hall. "So if you'll excuse me, I gotta go start rounding up the usual suspects. Call me if you pull one of your scientific miracles out of a hat, Atlas."

Penny and Doc exchanged looks.

* * *

Lou Stoner took a final swig from his hip flask as he headed for the stairs. He'd sent a newsboy down to get a cab for him ten minutes ago. More than ten minutes, he reflected. Tomorrow he'd have to fire that damn kid. But it had been one hell of an afternoon, though. The kind that a true newspaper man dreamt of. First a prominent judge gets murdered. And not just murdered, torn apart, literally. Then, less than twelve hours later, a high ranking mobster and his bodyguard get whacked. And to top it off, both of them have an ace-of-spades in their hands.

One of the typesetters was leaning against the wall on the first floor landing smoking a cigarette as Stoner walked by, nodding a weary hello.

"Working late tonight, huh, boss?" the typesetter said, his ink-stained fingers clasping the cigarette.

"Yeah," Stoner answered. "Almost had to say 'Stop the presses twice.'" He chuckled a phlegmy, heavy-sounding laugh as he moved across the lobby. Just then the main doors opened and he saw Jimmy quickly heading inside. Stoner's brow furrowed as he waved imperatively.

"Whatcha been doing?" he growled. "Where the hell's my cab?"

"There was one waiting for you out front, sir," the kid said. "It was just sitting by the curb, said it was reserved for ya."

"And what you been doing in the meantime," Stoner said, giving the kid a cuff on the ear. "You shoulda come up and told me. Whatta ya been doing, sneakin' a smoke down here?"

"The cabbie give me one, that's all," the boy said defensively, holding his ear.

"Go on, get outta here, ya little louse," Stoner said. He was going to tell him he was fired, but then again, the little punk kinda reminded him of himself when he first started. Watching the kid scurry off, he took out his hip flask again, but realized it was empty. Shrugging, he replaced the flask in his hip pocket and began fumbling for his cigarettes as he walked out the revolving doors. A yellow cab sat idling by the curb basking in the soft glow of the overhead streetlights. Stoner made his way across the now deserted sidewalk and pulled open the door.

As he flopped into the back seat the driver of the hack reached an arm over and held out a lighter. "Here you go, mac," the driver said.

Stoner nodded a thanks and leaned with his cigarette toward the flame. He mumbled his address to the driver and the cab took off. Stoner glanced to watch the newspaper truck pulling into the mouth of the alley to get loaded up for tomorrow's edition. Today's actually, he reflected, looking at his watch. It was well after midnight. A satisfied smile came over his face and he heard the driver say something.

"What was that?" Stoner asked.

"I said, 'It looks like it was a big news day'."

Stoner noticed for the first time what a big guy the driver was. His head, shoulders, and hands were all that were visible from the back seat, but if the rest of him matched those, this guy was a monster. Blinking, Stoner glanced out the window for a familiar landmark to gauge how long it would be before he got to his apartment. A street sign flashed by. It was then he saw that they were going in the opposite direction. The dirty rat was trying to take a circuitous route to jack up the fare!

"Hey, whatta ya think you're doing?" Stoner yelled. "This ain't the right way."

"Sure it is, Lou," the driver said. "Don't worry about it."

"Stop this damn cab," Stoner said. "I'll catch another one."

"Whatever you say, mac," said the driver. With an abrupt turn of the wheel, he pulled into an alley.

Headlights bounced in the cab's interior from the rear, and Stoner glanced over his shoulder in time to see the two lamps of some kind of truck following them into the alley. The cab continued forward at a rather substantial speed, then the lights suddenly shone on a solid brick wall directly ahead of them.

"You dummy," Stoner said. "It's a dead end."

"You're right about that, Lou," the driver said, stopping the cab and leaning over the back seat. Stoner noticed two things: the guys face was long and ugly, and he was holding a big pistol. "Get outta the cab."

Stoner pulled up on the door handle and stepped out into the darkened alley. The truck had stopped about twenty-five feet behind them, its lights still blazing between the darkened walls.

"What is this? A shakedown?" Stoner asked, half smirking to cover his fear. The big guy was still in the car, the gun resting on the door-frame. He grinned and said, "You'll see."

Stoner thought about running. If he could get between the wall of the alley and the side of the truck he might be able to get away. He ambled over to the wall farthest from the driver's side of the taxi and shot a quick look toward the street. But then he heard something strange. Very strange. A snarling sound, coupled with some heavy breathing and a foul odor. His eyes fixed on the source of the sound, and what he saw froze him in his tracks.

Around from the rear of the truck he saw a pair of enormous arms, so long that they reached all the way to the ground. The arms were black and hairy and attached to the biggest pair of shoulders and chest that Stoner had ever seen. But it was the thing's head that shocked him the most. It was the size of a bushel basket, with a bestial face, flat nose, and lips snarling back from a prognathous mouth full of large fang-like teeth and a black tongue. And the head encased in a metal crown of some sort.

It was a gorilla. A very huge gorilla. The kind he'd seen pictures of at the Bronx Zoo. He heard another sound just them. Something like a high-pitched whine of a dentist's drill, then the metal crown seemed to momentarily glow with a slightly bluish light. Or was it just a reflection of the ambient lighting?

He didn't have time to wonder about it for very long, because at that moment the monstrous beast lurched forward, its legs swinging nimbly through the outstretched arms. Stoner was frozen to the spot, feeling his bladder and bowels release in terror. And in another second the huge arms were reaching out for him.

* * *

The dark Cadillac pulled up at the mouth of the alley next to the marked squad cars. Doc Atlas got out of the passenger side and Mad Dog Deagan emerged from the driver's door. They walked over to the uniformed police officer standing next to the wall.

"We were called by Detective Wilson," Doc said.

The uniformed copper nodded and called down to a group of men standing about thirty feet away. One of them turned and began ambling down toward the entrance.

"Morning, Atlas," Wilson said. He hadn't shaved and his clothes looked like he'd slept in them. "We found another body with an ace of spades. The commish said to give you a call. If this keeps up, pretty soon we'll have enough to make a full deck." He waved for them to follow him and turned back down the alley. Slanting rays of sunlight were already beginning to cut into the dank shadows. Wilson sauntered up to the group of men and said, "Hey, move aside. Doc Atlas wants to take a look at things."

The men parted. Doc's expression showed no emotion as he saw the mangled corpse. A photographer was aiming his camera at a twisted arm. Between the fingers the flat, black design of the playing card seemed to stare up at them. The flashbulb popped.

"Some wino was crawling in here looking for a comfortable spot to get some sleep," Wilson said. "He saw what he thought was somebody else sleeping there. Then when he got up closer. . ."Wilson chuckled as he took out a cigarette and lit it. "Like to have sobered him up in a hurry."

Deagan smirked.

"I ain't seen nothing this bad since the war," he said.

"Yeah," Wilson said. "At first we thought it was a jumper, or something."

"Have you identified the body yet?" Doc asked.

"Yeah," said Wilson, taking out his notebook. "It's none other than Lou Stoner, editor for the same paper your girlfriend works for."

"No kidding?" Deagan said, straining to catch a glimpse of the face of the corpse.

"This playing card thing is what links all these recent killings together," Wilson said, exhaling some smoke out his nostrils. "What I want to know is, you found any classifiable prints on the other three?"

"None that I'd like to speak about," Doc said. "But I should like to examine this one also."

"Sure thing," Wilson said. "Lord knows we can use all the help we can get on this one."

* * *

The secretary showed both Ace and Penny into the office and Richard Sorakas moved forward to shake Ace's hand, the well-trimmed gray mustache curling over his standard smile.

"Ace, so good to see you and Miss Cartier again," he said. "Please, sit down." He indicated two leather upholstered chairs in front of his large mahogany desk. After taking his place behind it, he glanced at them and flashed another of his patented smiles.

"Now, to what do I owe the pleasure of this visit?"

"There's been another murder," Ace said.

"Oh?" said Sorakas. "Who?"

"My editor, Lou Stoner," Penny said. "He was found this morning in an alley in Manhattan."

"I'm terribly sorry to hear that," Sorakas said.

"Richard," Ace said, smiling disarmingly. "Perhaps I can be a bit blunt." Sorakas nodded.

"We have reason to believe that these recent murders are somehow connected," Ace continued. "Do you know what was found in Lou Stoner's left hand?"

"Why . . . I haven't the vaguest idea," Sorakas said.

Ace smiled again. Sorakas seemed to take umbrage. "Now see here," he said. "You can't possibly be suggesting that I have any sort of knowledge of these terrible crimes, can you?"

"Mr. Sorakas, you are aware that it was the trademark of your late client, Johnny Apollo, to leave the ace of spades in the hands of his victims, aren't you?" Penny said. She stared right at him, watching his eyes.

"Why. . . that's what makes this whole accusatory tone of yours so preposterous," Sorakas said. "You both were present when Johnny was executed."

"Very true," said Ace. "Which makes this present turn of events even more perplexing, don't you think?"

Sorakas said nothing.

Penny said, "What made Apollo drop all his pending appeals so abruptly?"

"I'm afraid I can't answer that," Sorakas said. "Client-attorney confidentiality."

"Even when your client is dead?" she said.

"How about that Dr. Essence character?" asked Ace. "Where did he come from?"

"I really can't say," Sorakas said, reaching inside his coat pocket for a silver cigarette case. "He seemed to be able to keep Johnny calm during the last few weeks, which was all that mattered from my standpoint."

"How so?" asked Ace.

"Oh come now," Sorakas said, holding the flame of his lighter to the cigarette. "I was merely trying to look out for the best interests of my client. He was on death row, facing execution. We all knew he didn't have a chance in hell to get off."

"Can you think of any of Apollo's underlings who would want to exact a campaign of revenge against people he might have held a grudge against?" Penny asked.

Sorakas considered this for a moment, then shook his head dubiously. "Not off hand. But if I do think of anyone I'll get in contact with you. Now, if you'll excuse me, I am a very busy man." He pressed a button on his intercom and moments later, the secretary who had ushered them in, appeared at the door. "Mr. Assante and Miss Cartier were just leaving," Sorakas said.

Both Ace and Penny stood and moved toward the door. Then Assante paused and turned back to Sorakas.

"Richard," he said. "Just one more item. Doc Atlas has become personally involved in this investigation, and I think you know that when that happens, he always gets to the bottom of things." He punctuated his sentence with a handsome smile, then made a chivalrous gesture for Penny to exit the room first. When they'd gone Sorakas stared after them, blowing a cloud of smoke up toward the ceiling. Then he stubbed out his cigarette and picked up the phone.

* * *

Hints of darkness were just beginning to replace the bright sunshine outside the high windows of the 86th floor of the Empire State Building. In his ultra modern laboratory, Doc Atlas leaned back from the microscope after examining the last slide of the material taken from under Lou Stoner's fingernails. He'd painstakingly analyzed the material, checking its cell make-up through various biological tests. Doc knew immediately that it was not human tissue, but suspected it was from the family *Hominidae.* It took him less than an hour to trace down the exact classification- Family: *Pongidae,* Order: Primates, Class: *Mammalia.* The identification of the species was unmistakable: *Gorilla gorilla.*

Doc had found traces of blood on the shattered French doors at Judge

Martin's home, and matching hair from both locations. And the "finger-prints" that he'd discovered on all of the ace-of-spades playing cards had been distinctly non-human. Two men dead from terrible beatings admin-istered by an extremely powerful and savage foe. The third one shot in the chest. A judge, a newspaper editor and a mobster. Strange bedfellows, that was for sure. But there was no denying the common denominators: all were found with the playing cards in their left hands, and each was, in some way, connected to the late Johnny Apollo.

But the gorilla connection puzzled him. While one of the mature primates was certainly physically capable of wreaking the extensive physical carnage that was present at two of the crime scenes, everything Doc knew about gorillas suggested that they were generally peaceful herbivores, mostly preyed upon by bands of marauding natives. And what could one possibly be doing running around loose in New York?

The buzzer sounded and Doc reached forward and pressed the intercom button.

"Yes?" he said.

"Sorry to disturb you, Doc," Mad Dog Deagan's voice said, "but Penny and Ace are back and you said you wanted to have a meeting at six-thirty."

"I'll be right out," Doc said. "Have everyone assemble in the library."

A few minutes later Doc strolled into the meeting room of his headquarters. It was a sumptuously furnished room with scores of thick books, mostly scientific journals, encased in heavy leather binders, on shelves that ran from the floor to the ceiling. At one end was a huge brightly colored globe of the earth, next to a large blackboard. Several rolled up maps hung above the blackboard. Penny, Ace, and Deagan sat at the head of a large oak table in the room's center. Without pausing, Doc went to the front of the room and stopped.

"Was your interview of Sorakas helpful?" he asked.

"Hardly," said Ace.

"Did you think it would be?" Deagan said, then quickly added, "He's a lawyer, ain't he?"

As Ace scowled, Penny said, "He was very evasive."

Doc considered this momentarily.

"That may say something in itself," he said. "Any other ideas?"

"Obviously there's a strong possibility that someone is enacting a series of revenge killings for Johnny Apollo," Ace said. "Why else would each victim have an ace-of-spades in his hand?"

"Or somebody wants to make it look that way," Deagan countered. "Any other connections between the murders, Doc?"

Doc ignored the question.

"I'd like to go talk to old Hirum Heath," Penny said. "If anyone knew those mobsters it was him. He was the one who got that mobster Bobby Grell to spill the beans on Apollo."

"Perhaps that would be a good idea," Doc said. "But given the recent events I'd like Ace to accompany you."

"Okay," Penny said, her eyes quickly darting toward Ace.

"Thomas, if you can remain here, I have another assignment in mind for you," Doc said. Deagan nodded.

"Should we meet back here later then?" asked Penny.

"Doc, I'm sorry, but I've got some plans," Ace said. "I've got a date for the opera."

Deagan snorted, suppressing a laugh.

"That's all right, Ace," Doc said. Then, turning to Penny, "I'm afraid the assignment for Thomas and myself has no predictable time parameters."

"That's okay," Penny said, sighing. "With all these murders going on, all I want to do is curl up in bed with a good book and a thirty-eight tucked under my pillow."

"Before you leave can you call your paper and arrange for Polly to scan the morgue for some items?" Doc said. Penny smiled and went to the phone. Ace stood up, leaning heavily on his cane.

They went through the office area and into the foyer by the elevators. Ace pressed the button and the doors to the waiting car opened. Penny smiled briefly at Doc and stepped inside. As Ace went to follow, Doc placed his hand on Ace's sleeve and handed him the keys to the Cadillac.

"This is parked in front in my reserved parking space," Doc said. "Why don't you use it for your trip to the opera tonight. Don't worry about returning it until tomorrow."

"Thanks, Doc," Ace said, shooting a triumphant smirk at Deagan. "This will go a long way toward making what I hope will be an extremely enjoyable evening."

Deagan and Doc watched him step into the elevator. Penny made a small wave to them as the doors closed. Doc turned and handed Deagan an envelope.

"Thomas, if you could go downstairs and take Polly to the newspaper office, I'll need her to look up the information on the enclosed list," he said. As Deagan took the envelope, Doc added, "There's also expense money in there for you to take her to dinner afterward."

Deagan's face cracked into a wide grin. "Gee, that's swell, Doc," he said. "Ahhh, can I borrow the Packard?"

"Regrettably not," Doc said. "And I'll need you to return no later than 2300 hours. We shall most probably have information to check out."

"Sure thing, Doc," Deagan said, as he stuck the envelope inside his pocket and headed for the stairwell. After he had gone, Doc went back into his office, sat at his desk, and picked up the phone. He dialed swiftly, then waited until the party at the other end answered.

"This is Michael Atlas," Doc said. "I need to speak to our mutual friend on a matter of the utmost importance."

"Very well," the other party said. "Give me a number where you can be reached."

Doc gave his office number and hung up. Steepling his long fingers in front of his face, Doc pondered the various, seemingly disparate facts that he'd amassed thus far. He stayed in this position until the phone rang approximately ten minutes later. Doc let out a slow breath, dropped his hands, and reached for the phone. Picking it up he said hello.

"What do you want, Atlas?" the gruff voice at the other end of the line asked.

* * *

Ace drove the long, dark Cadillac through the city streets with trepidation, grateful that its automatic transmission made it easier to operate than one of Doc's other, manual transmission cars. With Ace's leg still feeling the effects of his war wounds, the driving duties were normally relegated to Deagan. But Doc had promised him that one day he would be as good as new, and Ace believed him. He had tremendous faith in Doc's world-renowned surgical skills. Penny had been giving Ace directions on where to go, which street to take, and so forth. She was one of only a handful of people who knew where the old, retired reporter lived. As they crossed the George Washington Bridge and headed into Queens, Penny took out a cigarette, lighted it, and blew a cloud of smoke at Ace.

"Say, light one of those for me, would you?" he said.

"Sure," she said, taking another cigarette out of her case, placing it between her lips, and flicking her lighter again. After popping the lid closed, she stuck the lighter back into her purse and reached over, placing the smoldering cigarette between Ace's lips.

"So what opera are you going to see tonight?" she asked.

"Wagner's 'Lohengrin,' Ace said. "There's something so romantic about seeing the knight make that heroic entrance on a boat shaped like a swan." He smiled.

"So. . . who are you taking?" Penny asked.

"Lola," he said. "The girl who was with me at the charity ball."

"Where did you meet her?" Penny asked. Then added, "Turn right up here."

Ace negotiated the turn, then glanced over at her.

"What's with the twenty questions?" he said with a grin.

"Oh, nothing," Penny said. But in her mind she couldn't help but remember the time that she and Ace had gone to the Metropolitan Opera when they'd been seeing each other. But that had been before she'd become involved with Doc, and now that seemed a lifetime ago. Ace began whistling a Wagnerian tune, and Penny gave him a quick, sideways glance before directing him to make another turn.

"Polly said she's some kind of singer," Penny said, matter-of-factly.

"Who?"

"Your girlfriend," she said. "What's her name? Lola?"

"Oh, yes, she is," Ace said, somewhat perplexed.

"So how long have you known her?" Penny asked.

"Long enough to take her to the opera," he said, shooting her a quick look. "But not long enough to consider her 'my girlfriend'."

"I was just curious, that's all," Penny said, blowing a cloud of smoke toward the windshield. "There's no need for you to get so sassy."

"I wasn't."

"It's just that when I saw her at the ball, she didn't seem like your type." She glanced down at her nails.

"What's the matter with you today?" Ace said, glancing at her again. "If I didn't know better, I'd think . . ."

"Think what?"

"Never mind."

"Oh, I hate it when you do that," she said. Before he could respond, she told him to turn right. Ace wheeled the car around the corner, then stabilized it as they found themselves on a rather narrow residential street with a lot of two and three story apartment buildings. Ace shot another angry look toward Penny as they proceeded down the block, so he didn't notice that the dark blue sedan that had been following them went straight. But the gray laundry truck that had also been behind them, made the right turn also. And there was a very huge-looking man at the wheel.

* * *

"Hirum," Penny said, lifting her arms to give the elderly man in front of them a hug. They had parked in front of a modest bungalow sandwiched between two apartment buildings. The name above the mailbox said A.F. North, but Penny had just shaken her head when Ace had pointed at it. Moments later, when the grizzled old face appeared at the door, Ace immediately recognized the old man, even though it had been some time since they'd met. He was rather tall, but somewhat stooped, with a full head of wavy gray hair, wire rim glasses, and a craggy face. His thin upper body was swathed in a worn red cardigan sweater.

After finishing their embrace, Hirum Heath stepped back and extended his hand toward the interior of his house.

"Welcome to my humble abode," he said.

"Hirum, this is Ace Assante," Penny said.

"Yeah, I remember him," Hirum said, shaking Ace's hand warmly. "You're a lawyer, right? You two made quite a nice looking couple, too, as I recall."

Ace flushed, and Penny mumbled, "Yes, at one time we did."

Hirum took the hint and, after they'd sat down on the sofa in his living room, he asked them if they'd like some coffee or tea.

"Actually," Penny said, "Ace has to get to the opera tonight, and I'm racing a deadline. "She smiled and looked over at the photograph of a woman's face encased in an ornate frame sitting on a near-by coffee table. "By the way, where's Louise?"

Hirum's face seemed to tighten.

"I sent her to her sister's in Union City, New Jersey," he said, lowering himself into a chair across from her. "When all that gangster stuff started happening with Johnny Apollo. I got worried that they'd start looking for me again."

"That's one of the things I wanted to talk to you about," Penny said. "You've heard about the recent murders of Judge Taylor, Vito Giretti, and Lou Stoner then?"

"Sure," Hirum said. "Just because I dropped out of sight, doesn't mean that I stopped reading the papers." He smiled at her avuncularly. "Especially your columns."

"Thanks, Hirum," Penny said, reaching forward and squeezing his arm.

"You know then," Ace said, "that each of the three victims was found with a playing card in his hand?"

"The ace-of-spades," Hirum said, nodding slowly. "That was Johnny Apollo's trademark. As soon as I read that, I figured it was someone out for vengeance because of his execution. I sent Louise away and crawled back into hiding."

"You went into hiding before?" Ace asked.

"Sure," Hirum said. "Right after poor old Bobby Grell was killed while he was being guarded by a group of coppers in that hotel. I received a dead mackerel in a package on my doorstep the next day. That's when I knew they had someone on the inside. . . In the police department or the district attorney's office. Maybe even higher."

"You suspected internal corruption?" Ace said.

"Sure," Hirum said. "How else could they have gotten to Grell while he was still being held in protective custody. It was just lucky that Judge Taylor let his testimony stand as part of the record."

"Hirum decided that he might be next," Penny said, looking toward Ace. "He just sort of retired after that."

The old man smiled.

"In body, but not in spirit," he said.

"Weren't you still afraid they'd come after you?" Ace said.

"Not for myself," Hirum said. "But that note on the mackerel was addressed to my wife." His mouth drew up into a tight line. "I called Apollo's lawyer Sorakas the same day. Told him that I'd left several sealed copies of a letter identifying the inside members of Apollo's organization in the legitimate positions with certain individuals who had instructions to give the letters to the authorities should anything happen to either of us. I also told him that I was retiring as a reporter effective immediately."

"Did Sorakas go for it?" Ace asked.

Hirum smiled weakly, then said, "I'm still here, aren't I?" He gave a phlegmy sounding laugh, which started him coughing. It took him about half a minute to compose himself. "He seemed satisfied. We moved out here to Queens, and started going by the name of Mr. and Mrs. North." Hirum smiled. "Like the radio show. Penny and poor old Lou, God rest his soul, were about the only two who actually knew where we went."

"So did you have any ideas as to who might be involved on the inside?" Penny asked.

Hirum shook his head slowly.

"Well, I had some suspicions," he said.

Suddenly the door bell rang. Ace's brow furrowed and he gripped his sword cane tightly.

"Expecting someone?" he asked.

"No, I'm not," Hirum said, getting up and moving to the windows. He moved one of the lace curtains and peered out. Then he let it fall back in place. "It's just a laundry truck in front." he said, ambling toward the door. "Probably something that Louise set up for me while she was going to be away. "He grinned as he twisted the door knob, but for some reason the hairs on the back of Ace's neck were beginning to stand up. A second later he knew why, as Hirum was pushed back into the room, and the huge figure of Luca, with Silky right behind him, stepped into the room. Both of them were holding large frame revolvers.

"Good evening, folks," Silky said, grinning wickedly. "We're all going for a nice little ride."

* * *

It was barely nine-thirty when Deagan inserted his pass key into the special lock that controlled Doc's express elevator to his headquarters. Stepping inside, Deagan waved fractionally at the large globe on the ceiling of the car, figuring that Doc was probably watching the ascent on the video monitor upstairs. But upon arriving about 90 seconds later, Deagan was surprised to find the office section empty. Wandering around, he explored the laboratory and gymnasium areas first, then went through the library, kitchen, and finally Doc's living quarters. He was set to explore the secretarial office section on the floor below when he heard the single pinging sound that indicated that the elevator had been summoned from the lobby. Going to video monitor, Deagan switched it on and saw Doc step inside the elevator car carrying a large canvas bag slung over his left shoulder. Knowing Doc's tremendous strength, Deagan figured the bag might contain anything from a body to an engine block. Seconds later, when Doc stepped out and greeted him, Deagan knew it was the former.

"I hadn't expected you until 2300 hours, Thomas," Doc said, his voice showing no strain from the squirming burden on his shoulder.

"Ahhh . . . after Polly and me ate she told me she was really bushed and had to get up real early tomorrow, so I just took her home," Deagan said. He pointed to the bag. "Who you got there?"

Doc continued to walk past him toward the lab.

"A special delivery, courtesy of The Wraith," Doc said over his shoulder.

"The Wraith?" Deagan said, following. "What's he doing involved in this?"

"Actually he isn't," Doc said. "Knowing that his knowledge and under-world contacts eclipsed our own, I simply contacted him and requested that he deliver a suitable subject for interrogation."

Deagan raised his eyebrows in approval. Even though the Wraith operated outside the law, he and Doc had worked together busting up a criminal gang a few months back.

Doc set the body down on one of the stainless steel tables in his lab area and removed the bag, except for the portion over the man's head. Deagan could see that The Wraith had done an exceptionally thorough job in securing the man's arms and legs. And from the muffled cries, he assumed the gag had been applied with equal aplomb. Doc went to the refrigerator and removed an oval bottle and a syringe. After inverting the bottle, he sunk the needle into the rubber surface and drew back the plunger.

"Prepare his arm, Thomas," Doc said, setting the syringe down on a sterile tray while he replaced the bottle in the refrigerator. Deagan rolled the man's shirt sleeve up on his right arm and twisted a rubber hose around the lower biceps area. Doc moved over to the table and quickly jabbed the end of the syringe into the now bulging vein. After a moment the man's struggling ceased, and Doc completely removed the canvas bag.

"What did you give him?" Deagan asked. "That truth serum stuff?"

"Sodium pentathol," Doc said. "It should make him more susceptible to the hypnosis procedure. "After checking the dilation of the man's pupils, he removed a pen-light from his vest and held it a few inches in front of the man's eyes. Doc's voice soothingly spoke to the man, telling him in reassuring tones that he was feeling very sleepy, and after counting backwards from five, the only sound that he would hear, the only thing that would matter, would be the sound of Doc's voice. "Do you understand?" Doc asked.

"Yes," the man said, and began his backward count.

"What is your name?" Doc asked.

"Willard Clayton," the man said.

"What was your connection to Johnny Apollo?"

"I ran his place, the Coco Banana Club," Clayton said. His voice was clear, yet distant. As if he were speaking while his attention was focused looking down a long tunnel.

"When is the last time you saw Apollo?" Doc asked.

"I seen him last night," Clayton said.

Deagan and Doc looked at each other in amazement.

"How is that possible?" Doc asked. "Apollo was executed over a month ago."

"I thought so too," Clayton continued in his dreamy tone. "We all did, and we went to that meeting because we thought that the committee was gonna decide who was gonna take over. . . But it turns out the boss wasn't dead after all."

"Explain that," Doc said.

"There was this doctor. . . Some kind of foreigner scientist," Clayton said. His face contorted now as he spoke, as if remembering some unpleasant sight. "He told us that he'd put the boss's brain in this gorilla." He paused and his breathing became somewhat labored. Deagan's brow was furrowed in amazement, but Doc's expression hadn't changed.

"Continue," Doc said.

"Well, at first I didn't believe it," Clayton said, his voice evening out somewhat. "Then I saw it with my own eyes. This gorilla writing on a chalkboard, and knowing things that only the boss coulda known." His expression suddenly went from one of child-like wonder to a desperate grimace. "Vito. . ."

"Are you referring to Vito Geretti?" Doc said. Clayton's head bobbled.

"He was there also?" Doc asked.

"Yes," Clayton said.

"Tell us what happened next."

"Vito was arguing with Silky over not wanting to take orders from a monkey," Clayton said. "Then the next thing I know, the gorilla pulls out this forty-five and shoots him."

Deagan's jaw dropped upon hearing this. He stared intently at Doc, who still looked impassive.

"What happened then?" Doc asked.

"The gorilla handed Silky one of his cards, the ace of spades, and Silky put it in Vito's hand," Clayton said. His face contorted again. "That's when we knew it was really him. It had to be him. . ."Clayton's voice trailed off.

Doc inquired where this had happened, and Clayton recited an address of a house in Brooklyn. Doc then instructed the man to rest, and that he would not hear anything until Doc returned. He motioned for Deagan to step away from the table and they made their way out of earshot.

"Doc, this is unbelievable," Deagan said, his gestures animated with excitement. "I saw this movie a couple of years ago that was just like this. This scientist transplanted this executed convict's brain into this gorilla's body, and then the gorilla started remembering that he was framed, see, and he went around bumping off the guys that set him up."

Doc frowned slightly. As a scientist, he knew that such a brain transplantation was preposterous. Yet this man was clearly under the influence of the sodium pentathol. It was perplexing.

"Well, Doc," Deagan asked. "Do you think that's what that guy, Dr. Essence, did?"

Doc did not reply. He stepped back over to the supine form of Clayton and spoke again.

"Willard Clayton, what crimes have you committed for which you have not been caught?"

Clayton licked his lips lethargically, then began reciting a list of acts ranging in seriousness from theft, to extortion, to murder. Doc centered on his most recent murder, and then gave the man some cogent instructions.

"After I count to ten, you will be wide awake, but you will not recall any the events that occurred here tonight," he said. "Nor will you remember the incident when Vito Giretti was killed. When anyone asks you to recite the events concerning the homicide which you have just described to me, you will find it impossible to tell them anything but the truth. This will occur no matter who asks you these questions, or where you are. Do you understand?"

"Yes," Clayton said.

Doc turned to Deagan and motioned him away again.

"Call the police and tell them that we have a confessed murderer here who wishes to turn himself in," Doc said. "Then take him down to the lobby. I have to review the information that Polly obtained from the newspaper morgue as well as some computer findings."

Deagan nodded and went to the next room to use the phone, wondering why Doc had deleted the mention of the gorilla from Clayton's memory. Then it dawned on him: If Clayton repeated that, the cops would probably think he was nuttier than a fruitcake.

Approximately ten minutes later Deagan received a call from the doorman that the police had arrived. After taking the now babbling gangster down to the lobby, Deagan went back up to the 86th floor with a wide smile on his face. The expression on the two copper's faces had been priceless. But when the elevator doors popped open, Deagan was greeted by a grim looking Doc Atlas, who was strapping his specially-equipped pistol belt around his waist. He nodded toward the desk where several weapons and two army field radios lay.

"Polly called a few minutes ago," Doc said. "It seems that a woman named Lola called her to inquire about Ace not showing up to take her to the opera." His eyes looked intense as he added, "I then called Penny's apartment. There was no answer. She's not at the newspaper office either."

"You think they're in trouble then?" Deagan asked, moving toward the desk and picking up a 12 gauge shotgun with a twenty round ammo drum.

"I'm afraid that seems to be the case," Doc said, heading for the elevator. "Come on, Thomas. There's not a minute to lose."

* * *

Penny, Ace and Hirum all sat on the floor in the middle of the sparsely furnished room, their hands on their heads. The big hoodlum Luca held a forty-five automatic loosely in his grip as he smoked a cigarette. His eyes kept sweeping over Penny, but every time Ace made the slightest movement, Luca's grip on the weapon tightened.

"Can't you at least let her put her arms down?" Ace said, nodding toward Penny.

Luca smiled, showing his bad teeth.

"She looks good that way," he said.

The hoodlum's callous attitude toward granting them even a modicum of comfort made Ace all the more certain that they meant to kill them. If only he'd been able to notify Doc somehow. . . But they'd taken them directly to the laundry truck from Hirum's house, and with one of the hoods driving the Cadillac, Ace couldn't get near it to activate the secret emergency beacon on the floorboard. But they were obviously keeping them alive for the moment, which meant that they wanted something. The question was what? And could they stay alive long enough to effect an escape?

The door opened up and Silky came in, handing a glass with some amber liquid in it to Luca. The bigger man accepted it in one of his massive hands and brought it up to his lips. He took a sip, then smiled as the liquor burned its way down his esophagus.

"Hey, doll, maybe later you and me can have a drink together, huh?" he said huskily.

"I doubt it," Penny said. Her arms felt ready to fall off, but she stared back at the big hoodlum with as much defiance as she could muster.

Luca laughed heartily, then turned to Silky.

"She's got some fire, that one," he said, taking another sip from the glass. "I wonder if the boss will let me have some fun with her later?"

Silky shrugged, as his eyes also roamed hungrily over Penny's form.

"I wouldn't think about hurting any of us unless you want to tangle with Doc Atlas. He knows how to deal with bottom feeders like you," Ace said, hoping to get a chance for a dive at the gun if the crook moved closer.

"Shaddup," Luca said, rising. He started to move toward Ace, holding the forty-five up, but Silky stopped him.

"Don't," Silky said. "The boss'll be here any minute."

"What the hell's taking so long?" Luca said, glancing malevolently at Ace, then returning to his chair.

"They were at one of them fund raisers," Silky said, sticking a cigarette between his lips and lighting it. "Them politicians gotta show their faces to bring in the dough."

"The inside man," Hirum whispered to Penny.

"No whispering," Luca said.

The noise of some voices drifted into the room from the hallway. Silky blew out a cloud of smoke and smiled.

"That sounds like them now," he said as he left. Luca took a large swallow from the glass and tossed it in the corner. Ace's eyes followed it to see where it landed.

"Go on, try for it, pretty boy," Luca said, raising the automatic again. When Ace didn't move the big hoodlum grinned widely.

The door swung open and Silky came in and said, "The boss says to put 'em in the room with Samson."

Luca's smile faded slightly and he seemed to shudder involuntarily.

"Well get that cretin Essence and his monkey man," Luca said. "I ain't going in there by myself."

He ordered Penny, Ace, and Hirum to get to their feet. Ace had a little trouble with his leg, since they'd confiscated his cane, so Penny helped him.

"Gotta have a woman help ya, huh?" Silky said.

Ace made a mental note to set the crook on the seat of his pants the first chance he got. They were marched down a hallway and into a stairway that led to the basement. The musty odor in the air soon gave way to another, more foul stench. Silky unlocked a heavy wooden door and swung it open. He roughly pushed Ace, who stumbled, and then Penny, followed by Hirum. The room was dark and Ace's hands felt the rough texture of the concrete floor. The smell was more pungent now, and suddenly a low rumbling growl could be heard. Bright lights came on, almost blinding them momentarily, then they saw a huge metal cage at the far end of the room. Inside of it sat an enormous gorilla wearing a metal apparatus on its head. The huge beast eyed them warily as he rolled to his feet with an effortless grace and gripped the thick steel bars with hands the size of baseball mitts. Piles of hay and discarded fruits were strewn over the floor of the cage, as well as obvious patches of gorilla spoor.

"Move over there," Luca said, directing them closer to the door of the cage. They reluctantly complied. The closer they got, the more overpowering the stench became. At their movements the ape opened his mouth and emitted another growling sound, then pounded his fists on his chest.

"Oh my God," said Penny. "Is he going to attack?"

Ace stared back at the beast grimly, knowing that no man would have a chance against such a monster.

The door swung open farther and two more people stepped in. Ace and Penny stared in disbelief as Congressman Roscoe Kelly entered looking quite dapper in a black tuxedo. Next to Kelly was the same blond woman with whom he'd been dancing at the mayor's charity ball. Penny stared at her, them the realization hit her like a runaway train.

"It's you!" she said. "You're the same one who was at the mayor's charity ball."

Zelda smiled and reached up, pulling off her blond wig, them fluffed out her mane of bright red hair. With each movement, her large breasts seemed ready to spill out of the low-cut lavender evening gown that she wore.

"I didn't think you'd recognize me without my veil," she said. A wicked-looking smile spread over her face. "But then again, when I'm dressed to kill, most people don't notice my face too much." She turned to Silky and said, "Where's Essence?"

"I am right here," a voice said. The small, bearded man came in the room, followed by one of the strangest looking creatures that Penny had ever seen. The man was wearing only a tight black swimming suit, and his body was virtually devoid of hair, including his scalp, which was covered with a dark stubble. He walked with a cat-like grace, and his extremely long arms reached almost to his knees. The exaggerated length of his extremities was matched only by the grotesqueness of his features. Obviously, he was afflicted with some form of acromegaly.

"Well, get your beast out here," Zelda said. "We've got to get some information, and I'm in a hurry. You know I hate the smell down here."

Essence nodded to the acromegalic and said, "Zorran, go open zee cage."

Zorran nodded and picked up a hefty looking bundle of apples and bananas. He moved over to the large cage and shoved several of the fruits through the bars. The big gorilla's mouth opened in a squeal of what could have been fear or pleasure. Tentatively, the ape reached for one of the apples as Zorran unlocked the heavy padlock that secured the door and swung it open. Zorran moved away slowly as the monster ape eyed him, then the now open cage door. He bit into an apple, chewed, then threw the remainder to the floor.

"This is the way it is, old man," Zelda said, accepting a cigarette from Silky. "We know you've got some letters with names and details about our organization. We want them back tonight, otherwise. . ."

"If I tell you will you let us go?" Hirum asked, fear causing his voice to quiver like a tuning fork.

"Sure we will," Zelda said, smiling.

"You have our word," Silky added.

"Don't listen to them, Hirum," Ace said. "As soon as they have what they want, they'll kill us for sure."

Hirum cast a fearful look at him, then at Penny. "What should I do then?" he asked.

"Hey, you," Zelda yelled "Quit putting ideas into his head. Tell us what we want to know now, you old goat, or I'll turn our hairy friend loose on you." She nodded toward Essence who took a metallic box about the size of a cigarette pack out of his pocket. His fingers grasped a silver disk on one end of it and pulled, extending an antenna. Essence held the box outward and pressed a button with his thumb. Seconds later the gorilla stopped perusing the pile of fruit and jumped, as if hit by an electric shock. The massive animal got to his feet and opened his mouth with a heavy roar.

"Darling, I'm not so sure this is a good idea," Congressman Kelly said, tentatively placing his hand on Zelda's arm. "After all, they are friends of Atlas's-"

"Shut up, you big idiot," she spat at him. "What do you think, I'm gonna let everything that I've worked for go down the drain because you have a weak stomach?" She gave him a hard shove. "Go on, get outta here. I'll call you when it's over."

His head down, Kelly left the room. Zelda turned to Luca. "Go put a couple of the boys at the front and back just in case. And keep an eye on the congressman too."

She smirked as Luca said, "I'll just point him toward the bar."

Essence moved closer to the cage, pressing the buttons on the metal box. With each compression of his finger, the big ape seemed to recoil in pain, then become more enraged. The beast quickly moved out of the cage area and stood in the center of the room.

"Who should we have him go after first?" Zelda said, her lips curling over her teeth. "Any volunteers?"

"At least let her go," Ace said, nodding at Penny. "She's not part of this."

"Oh, a hero," Zelda said, "How chivalrous. Do her first, Professor."

Essence cocked his head and pressed the button again. The huge gorilla lurched forward toward the three cowering humans.

Penny's scream seemed to reverberate through the room, coupled with Zelda's husky laughter.

* * *

"How can you be sure that this is the house where they're at, Doc?" Deagan asked as he drove slowly by the large mansion using the hand brake to slow the vehicle so as not to illuminate the car's stoplights. Lights twinkled behind the glass of the windows, but the expansive yard area was extremely dark.

"I can only hope that it is, Thomas," Doc said. "Besides being the address mentioned by the hypnotized subject, the shipping manifests that I reviewed, along with the records of deliveries of huge quantities of fruits and vegetables, suggests that they're housing some type of a large herbivore here."

"A large herbivore, huh?" Deagan said. "But I thought you didn't buy that stuff about the gorilla?"

"This is a very convoluted affair," Doc said, raising a pair of special night-vision binoculars to his eyes. "Suffice to say that not all is as it appears to be. "He scanned the yard area and then said, "Penelope and Ace are most probably in there. The Cadillac is parked by the side of the house in the shadow of those trees."

"Okay," Deagan said. "What's our plan?"

Doc considered this for a moment, then said, "Drop me off here. I'll work my way around the back. There appear to be at least two sentries stationed at the front of the house. When I'm in position, I'll need you to create a diversion while I effect entry to the rear."

"Gotcha, Doc," Deagan said, patting the barrel of the automatic shotgun on the seat beside him. As the car slowed Doc opened the door and stood on the running board: Deagan coasted around the dark corner and said, "Good luck." But Doc had already silently vanished. Swinging the Packard around, Deagan cut off the lights then pulled up to access the terrain of the expansive front yard. He pulled the second pair of night-vision binoculars up to his eyes and scanned the area. There was a long driveway that wound through a thatch of trees. The drive formed a circular path around a fountain in front of the main entrance. Several wide pillars sat imposingly on either side of the front door. Mad Dog could see two figures milling about in front of the place. They didn't appear too alert, and that would be to his advantage. Suddenly a flood of memories came rushing back to him of covert operations in the European Theater during the war. . . Of Doc and him leading a platoon of men through bomb-scarred cities. But this was Brooklyn, not the European Theater of Operations, and it was just the two of them. Yet Deagan knew in his heart that he couldn't ask for a better man to trust in an operation like this than Doc.

"Thomas," Doc's voice came over the radio. "I'm in position. Are you ready to proceed, over?"

"Roger wilco, Doc," Mad Dog said, formulating his plan as he set the radio down. "Get ready, 'cause here I come."

Deagan knew that there was no time for a long silent approach, so he opted for the element of shock and surprise. He set the Packard into gear and floored the accelerator, sending the big dark vehicle shooting across the street and up the long drive. The night-vision glasses had given him a clear idea of the roadway, so he kept the lights off until he roared past the fountain, then he pulled the switch back and punched the bright-lights button. The two hoodlums by the front door were hustling to get their guns out when Deagan spun the wheel and accelerated, expertly swinging the big car into a partial sideways spin, causing the right side wheels to flair outward toward the house. At the same time he popped open the driver's side door and jammed on the brakes. As the vehicle lurched to a stop, Mad Dog swung the barrel of the shotgun across the hood and fired a blast over the heads of the two men.

"Drop 'em or die, grease balls," he yelled, leveling the weapon so that they were looking down the large bore. But before the surprised hoodlums could comply, a third one wheeled from behind one of the pillars and started firing a Thomson submachine-gun. Deagan crouched down with the aplomb of a professional soldier as the bullets tore into the side of the Packard. The other two hoodlums were firing now too, and Mad Dog could hear the plunking sound of the rounds striking the metal. The fiery blast from the machine-gun seemed to leap out at least a foot.

I sure hope this is a big enough diversion for ya, Doc, Deagan thought as he raised the shotgun over the hood and returned fire. He moved to the rear of the car, stuck the gun around, and got a clear sight picture of one of the hoods with a pistol.

The blast from the shotgun literally knocked the man off his feet. Stunned, the other two began to whirl, but Mad Dog already was swinging the barrel toward the second exposed killer. He fired just as the guy with the Thompson brought the machine gun around, spraying the rear fenders and sending a shower of shattered glass over Deagan's head and shoulders. Mad Dog ducked down for a split second, then brought the shotgun to bear again. Having been highly trained on the use and firing patterns of the Thompson, Deagan knew that after the first few seconds of concentrated automatic fire, the recoil of the weapon had a tendency to raise the muzzle slightly. Unless the user was experienced enough to anticipate this and compensate. This one wasn't, and Deagan's blast took out his legs. He tried to continue firing, but Mad Dog elevated the barrel, placing the next round directly in center mass.

"Guess you stayed home during the war, huh?" Deagan said as he kicked the Thompson out of the dead man's stiff fingers.

* * *

Just as the gorilla moved toward them, Ace had stepped in front of Penny. The big beast stopped momentarily, then, after a prodding from the professor, leaped forward and struck Ace with a horrific blow, knocking him into the wall. Assante seemed to crumple to the floor and lay still. Then the sudden sounds of gunfire erupted. The beast paused again, as Penny screamed.

"What the hell's going on out there?" Zelda said.

"I dunno," said Silky.

"Doc Atlas is here, you creeps," Penny yelled. "Now you'd better call off your monkey or there'll be hell to pay."

Dr. Essence looked with uncertainty toward Zelda who said, "What are you waiting for? The boys can handle it. Find out where that damn letter's at."

Dr. Essence's tongue flicked out over his lips and he again pressed the button on the transmitter. Ace, who had appeared to be unconscious, rolled over and groaned.

"No, wait," Hirum yelled, folding his arms across his face. "I'll tell you! I'll tell you! Just call him off."

"Spill it then!" Zelda said, her voice a bellicose growl.

"There really were no letters," Hirum said in a quavering voice. "I just told that to Sorakas so he would stop looking for me."

"Wrong answer, buster," Zelda said. Then to the professor, "Do it."

Dr, Essence held up the transmitter, seeming to prod the gorilla toward Penny. Suddenly Ace was on his knees, his arm cocked back like Joe DiMaggio. He let fly an apple that the gorilla had discarded. The hard piece of fruit struck Essence in the left eye socket, causing the little bearded man to recoil in pain and surprise. As he did this, his grip on the transmitter loosened, and Ace was darting across the floor in front of the big ape to wrest the black transmitter from the professor's hand. Silky began to move forward at that moment, but Ace had the transmitter and knocked Essence to the floor.

"Get him, you idiot," Zelda yelled.

Silky and Ace became locked in a fierce struggle and twisted together. The grotesque Zorran rushed forward also and began pounding Ace with blows to the back. In desperation Ace tossed the transmitter away from him. It bounced once, twice, then skidded near the open door of the cage. Essence, who had gotten to his feet, quickly skittered across the floor like a rat going for a piece of cheese and grabbed the transmitter. Standing, he emitted a staccato-sounding little laugh. But he stopped abruptly when the huge black hands abruptly seized him around the throat.

* * *

Doc had managed to subdue the two rear guards rather quickly. Both men had been standing together smoking when the gunfire erupted in the front of the house. Doc then stepped around and hurled in quick succession two large rocks which he had obtained from the shrubbery. Both hoodlums were silently rendered unconscious in a matter of seconds. After securing both men with some special wire snares that he carried in his utility belt, Doc stealthily moved inside. His goal was to find Penny and Ace as soon as possible. He would deal with the rest of the gang when he was sure they were safe.

But as he turned the corner after entering the kitchen, Doc came face-to-face with another gangster, this one already raising his pistol. Having little choice, Doc's hand blurred as it pulled his knife from the sheath on his boot and sent it hurting toward his foe with an incredibly accurate underhand throw. The blade sunk into the man's abdomen, right below the rib cage. He did a little stutter-step forward, then collapsed.

Doc moved forward to remove the blade, but as he was bending over the prone man, Doc heard the ominous sound of the hammer of a weapon being pulled back. Whirling as he picked up the dead gangster, Doc pulled the limp body up in front of him just as Luca's forty-five went off. The bullet almost penetrated the dead man's body, for Doc saw a sudden crimson blur on the back of the man's white shirt. Using the momentum of his swing, Doc hurled the body at the big gangster then followed it by executing a powerful springing leap.

Luca brushed away the flying body, but wasn't prepared as the golden avenger crashed into him. Doc's hands closed over Luca's wrist and weapon, stripping it from his grasp. But the wily gangster, veteran of a score of prison yard fights, twisted and the big fingers of his left hand clutched over Doc's face, banging his head into the wall.

Stunned, Doc lost the forty-five, and Luca leaned forward, pinning Doc to the wall. With his superior size and weight Luca held Doc there and began a series of looping punches into Doc's gut. But suddenly Luca felt himself being turned, and Doc's left arm was curled around the bigger man's neck, cutting off his air supply. Luca reared back, slamming Doc into the wall again, but instead of breaking the choke-hold, this seemed to enable Doc to snare Luca's legs in some sort of hold. Luca felt as if he'd been grabbed by a python, each breath becoming harder and harder to catch. Seconds later, the blackness overwhelmed him.

The shotgun roared again from the front part of the house, then Deagan appeared at the opening in the hallway in time to see Doc rise from the unconscious form of Luca. Doc bent and quickly secured the big hoodlums hands behind his back with one of the wire cuffs. Then he picked up Luca and slapped him several times. The big man seemed to snap awake, struggle, then set his face into a sneer.

"Where are the hostages?" Doc asked.

"Go to hell," Luca said.

"Tell us now, unless you want to lose your head," Deagan said, moving forward and jamming the circular end of the shotgun's barrel against Luca's cheek. Something in Mad Dog's expression told Luca that another sarcastic answer would not be advisable.

"The basement," Luca said.

"How many of your compatriots are with them?" Doc asked.

"Huh?" Luca said.

"How many of you creeps are down there?" Deagan roared, twisting the shotgun so that it left a quarter-sized impression in Luca's face.

"Silky and the boss," Luca said quickly. "The professor, and his assistant. Kelly. . ."

"Roscoe Kelly?" Doc asked. "Is he behind this?"

"Not hardly, Doc," Deagan said. "I found him cowering behind the bar with a bottle in the other room and knocked him silly."

Doc heard Penny's scream and dropped Luca. He and Deagan rushed down to the stairway going to the basement. Pausing, Doc indicated that he would go first, and with a tremendous leap, jumped nimbly downward, bypassing the entire stairway. As he landed he immediately sprang toward the heavy wooden door as Deagan rushed down, brandishing the shotgun.

Doc pulled open the door in time to see a remarkable scene. A huge black gorilla with a silver mane stood at the opening to a large steel-barred cage. Two bodies lay on the floor. One, crushed almost beyond recognition, was Dr. Essence. The other was a semi-nude man with grotesquely malformed limbs. Ace stood holding a small black box with a extended silver antenna, and Zelda stood near Penny and Hirum in one corner. Between Ace and the gorilla, Silky Moran puffed on all fours, twin trickles of blood dripping from his mouth and nose.

As Doc entered, Ace used the transmitter to force the ape back in its cage, then walked somewhat unsteadily to slam the door shut.

"It appears that all is complete here," Doc said as he and Deagan stepped inside the room.

"Not quite," Penny said, turning and balling up her right fist. She twisted and let go with a haymaker that caught Zelda flush on the side of the jaw.

The voluptuous redhead fell in a twisted heap on the floor.

"Jeese, Penny, that was a great right cross," Deagan said, moving forward. "I didn't know you could punch like that."

"Yeah," she said, "but I think I broke my hand." She flexed her fingers gingerly. "Anyway, you should've seen Ace," she said, pointing to the still incapacitated Silky. Penny smiled as she moved over to Assante and placed her hands on his arm. "He literally saved our lives." She brushed away some errant strands of dark hair from Ace's forehead, then leaned forward and kissed him gently on the cheek.

"Aww, shucks, ma'am," Ace said, mimicking a western drawl. "It weren't nothin'."

After directing Deagan to go upstairs to summon the police, Doc moved over and secured the lock on the cage door, then immediately began inspecting the transmitting device that Ace handed him. After a few minutes of careful inspection of both the device and the gorilla, Doc nodded slightly.

"That metal apparatus on the animal's head must have received electrically transmitted shocks that prodded the ape to do the evil bidding of man," Doc said.

"So that explains why Judge Taylor and poor Lou were so terribly beaten," Penny said.

"But this seems like a very elaborate ruse to go through," Ace said. "Why get the gorilla in the first place?"

"Hey, look at me," a somewhat subdued voice interjected from the doorway. They turned to see the head of a gorilla, replete with a matching metal crown to the other ape's, on top of Deagan's body. He moved forward and danced around, mimicking an ape, then he paused and pulled off the head. Ace seemed to collapse with laughter.

"I found a whole gorilla costume in the other room when I was looking for the phone," Deagan said. "The rest of it didn't look like it would fit me, but the head part slid on all right."

"My guess is that it was specially made for him," Doc said, pointing to the inert form of Zorran.

"I'll bet this explains who shot Vito and started this gorilla killer thing," Deagan said.

Penny and Ace looked confused.

"One of the stories that Polly found in the newspaper morgue," Doc said, "was that of a circus gorilla named Samson and his handler who disappeared several months ago while in this area. A charlatan European physician, named Hugo Liechtenstein, who worked with the circus, also disappeared." His amber eyes calmly surveyed the room.

"Why, Zelda had ties to the circus life," Hirum said. "She used to be a fortune teller before she met up with Johnny Apollo."

"That explains how and why these stooges were approached by the villains to help perpetuate this elaborate scheme," Doc said, pointing toward the crushed figures of Zorran and the doctor. "A plan designed to prey upon the superstitious nature of the feeble and susceptible criminal mind, in order to assume control over the fallen mantle of Johnny Apollo's underworld empire."

"Hey, slow down, guys," Penny said. "I'm having trouble following all of this."

"Oh, we'll explain it all to you so you can write another one of those pulp novels about it," Deagan said. "As long as you don't mention me putting on this ape-head, all right? I don't want to end up looking like the monkey's uncle again."

Ace, who was still in the throes of laughter, paused long enough to breathlessly say, "Talk about type-casting. . ."

Deagan frowned.

"Well, I will be glad to write it up for the paper and tell what heroes you all were," Penny said. "That is if Hirum won't mind me sharing his by-line. "She turned and smiled at the elderly man who had been standing quietly to one side.

"You want me to write your column with you?" he asked.

She nodded. "I wouldn't have it any other way," she said. A single tear wound its way down the old man's cheek.

Deagan moved over and glanced at the big gorilla who had reposed himself in the farthest reaches of the cage and was staring warily at the assortment of humans around him.

"Hey, Doc," Mad Dog asked. "What's gonna happen to him?"

Doc turned.

"His misdeeds were precipitated by evil men, Thomas," Doc said. "I'll have him shipped to a zoo where the metallic apparatus can be removed, and he can live out his days in peace."

"So you never really bought that stuff the one gangster told us about the gorilla shooting Vito and having Apollo's brain, huh?" Deagan asked.

"Having Apollo's brain?" Penny said incredulously.

"Yeah, it was just like that movie, *The Monster and the Girl*," Deagan said. "This mad scientist transplanted this convict's brain into the body of a gorilla. . ."

"I still haven't figured out what on earth you two are talking about," Penny said.

"It was a ruse that Zelda and friends came up with to prey upon the ignorance of their companions in crime," Doc said. "Vito was obviously shot by that man who was impersonating a gorilla." He gestured at the acromegalic. "Again, it is a plot so fantastic, it would even seem dubious in one of Penelope's fantasy novels."

"Except the part about Mad Dog wearing the gorilla head," Ace said, his face still flushed. "By the way," he added, gesturing at the gorilla. "Are you two related?"

"Seems to me you're forgetting who got here in time to save your bacon, flyboy. And you know, you could be replaced by a monkey yourself," Deagan said with a grin. Then, leaning close to Doc, he asked. "So what do you think? Would it ever really be possible to transplant somebody's else's brain into another person's body?"

"Even if it were, Thomas," Doc said. "I doubt that man is ready, at this point in our evolution, to make an attempt to play God." He gazed over at the crushed form of Essence, then to the huge, almost majestic looking gorilla who was busily picking through the pile of fruit. "But it never ceases to amaze me the lengths to which some men will go to invent new ways for perpetrating evil upon their fellow men." Doc slowly shook his head.

"Yeah," Mad Dog said, glancing over at Zelda, who was now managing to assume a sitting position. "And some women, too."

THE END

Arctic Terror IV

December 13th, 1953
The Far Northwest
Territories Near
The North Pole

IT SCREAMED OVER the horizon with a winding moan, lighting the darkened sky, changing night into day, and leaving a turbulent roar in its wake. The vibration was severe. Like a thousand thunders, Nat Kallipik thought, as the frigid water slapped suddenly out of the hole he'd cut in the pack ice. The ground rumbled again and his team of dogs cried and yelped like frightened puppies. Nat's dark eyes traced the source of the disturbance, fixing it with seemingly meaningless landmarks on the bleak tundra. It couldn't be more than ten miles away, to the northeast.

The rumbling stopped and Nat began immediately to shoulder his rifle and pick up his hunting gear. His brother Oingoot, who had cut his hole about fifty yards away, called to him in their native Inuit.

"An airplane, do you think?"

"I don't know, but we'd better check," Nat called back. "Someone may be out there."

Oingoot studied the vestiges of the strange orange glow that was still faintly visible on the horizon, and he felt a shiver move up his spine.

"Something is out there, all right," he muttered to himself as began to collect his own gear.

Thirty-Six Hours Later
19,000 Feet, Somewhere Above The Arctic

Doc Atlas took a sip from the steaming cup as he made a slight adjustment to the defrosting unit on the left propeller system of his massive DC-3 cargo plane, the *Athena*. He checked his wristwatch and the compass reading, then estimated their progress against the stiff head wind. He turned to "Ace" Assante whose eyes were busily scanning the instruments on his side of the cockpit.

"We should be there in another hour, Ace," Doc said, stripping off his head-set and getting out of the pilot's seat. As he stood, the immense proportions of his upper body seemed to fill the small area, but even dressed in his heavy parka, the powerful symmetry of his limbs was evident.

"I'm going to see if the others want some coffee," he said, grabbing the oversized thermos.

"Right, Doc," Ace said with a grin, his lean handsome face a dead ringer for Errol Flynn's. "We're sure making better time than Peary did."

Doc showed no emotion as he slipped through the curtain separating the cockpit from the body of the airplane. Its concave walls were covered with netting and straps to secure the sleeping compartments and equipment to the sides. He moved down the corridor holding the thermos until he came to a group of people huddled around a large wooden crate. Three tin cups had been secured to the top of the crate by several strips of heavy masking tape. The one in the middle held several coins. On the left side of the crate a man, who was short but powerfully built, was hunched over rearranging a poker-hand of cards. The hood of his parka was hanging in back of his unkempt mane of coarse reddish hair. A meager amount of coins sat in his cup. Opposite him sat a stunningly beautiful woman, also in a sleek parka, staring intently at her array of cards. Her face brightened considerably as Doc approached, and she brushed some of her black hair away from her face. The cup in front of her was overflowing with money. Several young soldiers, all in regulation cold-weather gear, were gathered on either side of the crate, ostensibly watching the poker game, but most of their eyes kept straying to the woman.

"I thought you might want some coffee," Doc said holding out the thermos.

"Thanks," Penelope Cartier said. She closed her cards together and reached for a new cup.

"She don't need no extra edge, Doc," the man said. "She's just about cleaned us out. I'm the last one, and I consider myself a poker-playing expert."

"Perhaps you should consider another game, Thomas," Doc said. "Like chess."

"I ain't even got enough left to consider checkers," Thomas "Mad Dog" Deagan said. He tossed the few remaining coins into the center cup and said, "Okay, Penny, I'll raise you ten."

Penny smiled, deposited her dime, and dropped another nickel into the cup. Doc allowed himself a brief smile as he poured some coffee into the plastic cup and handed it to her. She squeezed his hand with a knowing intimacy as she accepted the coffee.

"We'll be there in less than an hour," Doc said, filling a second cup and handing it to Mad Dog.

"Another hour?" Deagan said. "Swell, that'll give me a chance to get even."

"Optimist," Penny smiled, taking a sip. "Just be glad this isn't strip poker. You'd all be frozen stiff by now."

An embarrassed laugh sputtered from a few of the young soldiers. Deagan grinned as he plunked another nickel into the pot. Doc held up the thermos, but he had no takers among the enlisted men.

"Is Lieutenant Sinclair awake?" Doc asked.

"Yes, sir," one of the young soldiers said. "He's in the rear of the hold by the dogs, sir."

Doc nodded his thanks and made his way to the rear of the cargo hold. Several more GIs were sleeping, strapped into folding cots that were suspended from the walls on the plane. Two teams of Alaskan Huskies, secured in kennel-cages howled and barked as Doc strode by. Beyond the cages Doc saw Sinclair standing against the wall wiping the slide of a Government Model forty-five, a cigarette smoldering between his lips.

"Lieutenant," Doc said. "I thought you might like some coffee."

Sinclair stood and released the slide of the pistol slowly, snapping on the safety before inserting the clip and replacing it in his holster. He held out his plastic cup and Doc poured some of the hot liquid into it. Sinclair balanced himself, with one hand, holding the cup and the cigarette in the other. "Thanks, Major Atlas," Sinclair said.

Doc smiled slightly.

"I'm not a major any more, Lieutenant," he said. "That was a while ago."

"Yes," Sinclair said. His eyes narrowing grimly. "Another war ago now, right? But I made a phone call to D.C. and checked your service record when I heard you'd volunteered to fly us up here. I haven't had the time to say so, but I'm mighty glad to have you along. Although I'm not so sure about some of the other members of your crew." He cast a somewhat scornful glance down the hold at Deagan, who howled in exhilaration as the game finally turned in his favor. "A retired Lieutenant Colonel playing cards with enlisted men . . ." Sinclair let his voice trail off in disgust.

"I'm sure if you check the service record of Thomas Deagan you'll find it replete with accomplishment. More than a match for mine." Doc turned and glanced at the card players. "Don't mistake his empathy for the common man for a lack of sophistication. Many men have made the mistake of underestimating him, to their lasting chagrin."

"No offense intended," Sinclair said quickly. "I know he's your good friend and associate. And, as I mentioned, I'm very grateful for your assistance."

"We were glad to oblige," Doc said. "Especially since the Air Force had no transport planes at the base that could beat the approaching storm front."

"Speaking of which, how soon before we arrive at the research base?"

Doc glanced at his watch. "It should be within the hour."

"Then I'd better show you this," Sinclair said. He went to a haversack stowed against the wall and withdrew a locked diplomatic pouch. Withdrawing his dog tag chain and slipping it off, he gripped a key that was secured on it. Sinclair inserted the key into the lock and slid back the heavy metal zipper. "Having checked your record, I know you still have a very high security clearance," he said. "So I regret not showing this to you earlier, but I had my orders." He handed a folder to Doc. It was marked TOP SECRET across the flap in bold black letters. "I'm afraid that this was no ordinary plane crash," Sinclair said in a low whisper. "The word is some

Eskimos found some sort of wreckage and brought it to the research base. There's an international group of scientists there. They radioed that it's the possible remains of Flying Saucer."

Doc's amber eyes narrowed as he opened the cover of the folder. It read:

14 DEC '53, two Eskimos brought wreckage to Research Station Zulu from unknown crash site located approximately 90 degrees north. Wreckage described as possible space-like craft displaying undetermined technology. Professor Smithfield (USA) at research base requests immediate transference of wreckage to secure area. Other members at base are Professors Trudeau (Canada), Hoeton (USA), Carrington (Great Britain), and Stevens (USA). Proceed to base immediately and secure wreckage for earliest possible transport to Anchorage. Expedite and use caution. Soviet ship reported to be in the area.

"That last sentence is particularly troubling," Sinclair said.

Doc nodded and looked up. "I thought that the Government discontinued all Unidentified Flying Object investigations in 1949 after the Roswell, New Mexico, incident."

"Officially we have," Sinclair answered. "But we can't afford not to check something like this out. Especially if the Russians are involved. They've been all over the Pole since the end of the fighting in Korea." Sinclair ran his fingers through his lank blond hair, then sighed. His face looked almost boyish. "So you can see, Major, the urgency of the situation. If this is some sort of advanced alien technology, it can't be allowed to fall into Communist hands."

"Do you have reason to believe that the Russians also know about this?" Doc asked.

"One of our listening posts in Japan intercepted a partial transmission about investigating some sort of *paketa*," Sinclair said. "That's Russian for rocket. The storm front made it impossible to monitor the entire transmission clearly, but we have to go on the assumption that they know and are headed there also."

"Perhaps it's one of their SS-6 rockets," Doc said. "They are trying to develop an intercontinental ballistic missile."

"Doubtful," Sinclair said. "Our intelligence sources haven't reported any launches recently. Besides the range of the SS-6 is substantially less than one thousand miles, and this is a lot farther from any of their launch sites. No, it has to be something from space. There's no other explanation." Sinclair's lips drew into a thin line. "There's more. My verbal orders are to secure the spacecraft at all costs. Under no circumstances am I to let it fall into enemy hands." He took one last puff on his cigarette and then extinguished it in the coffee with an angry sounding hiss. "I'm to destroy it if necessary."

Doc glanced over a schematic drawing of the research base, then flipped the folder closed and handed it back to Sinclair.

"I'm going to assemble my people for a briefing," Doc told him. "I suggest you do the same with your men."

"Wait," Sinclair said, grabbing Doc's massive forearm. "Is that wise? I mean, Deagan and Assante are both WW II heroes, but they're civilians now. And Miss Cartier is . . ." The eyes of the two men met. Sinclair looked away and added, "a reporter."

Doc's amber eyes narrowed and Sinclair quickly withdrew his hand from Doc's arm.

"Lieutenant, I trust all the members of my group implicitly, including Miss Cartier. We've been through many adverse times together." Doc's voice became low and forceful as he added, "And I suggest again that you brief your own personnel, unless you're in the habit of sending men into dangerous situations without letting them know all of the facts."

Sinclair pursed his lips and nodded. Turning slightly he called for his men to assemble in the rear of the plane. They quickly dropped their cards and stood up, shuffling toward their Lieutenant in the cargo hold. Doc moved to the side to let them pass, then started back to the front. He paused by the now empty area where the crate had held the card players. The deck was back in the box and the cups with the change were no longer in evidence.

"I take it the game over, Thomas?" Doc asked moving farther forward toward the cockpit.

"Yeah, she took all our dough, and then some." He was crammed next to Penny in the small aisle next to the curtain that housed the pilots' compartment.

Doc pulled the curtain back, exposing Ace's shoulders and the instrument panel.

"I have something to tell you regarding this mission," Doc said. He gave them a brief summary of the secret correspondence involving the mysterious wreckage.

A simpering grin stretching across Deagan's rugged features. "Hey, Doc, you know what? This kinda reminds me of a monster movie that I took Polly to a couple of years back. It was called *The Thing*, and it was set in the North Pole, too."

"You mean, 'at the North Pole'," Assante said caustically, looking up from the instrument panel of the cockpit. Through the windows the clouds below them had begun to swirl and darken slightly. "I just wonder what this wreckage really is. There's got to be a logical explanation."

"In that movie *The Thing* was this guy from outer space," Deagan continued. "And he was a real tough son-of-a-gun, too."

"Well, this is real life," Assante said, his tone still sarcastic. "Not some B-movie about Martians and U.F.O.'s."

"You don't believe in U.F.O.'s?" Deagan said, a wry grin creeping over his lips. "Why not? What's wrong with ya?"

"Nothing's wrong with *me*," Ace shot back. "It's just that a fine legal mind like mine, being honed to razor-sharpness, requires proof, before jumping to some improbable conclusion."

"I ain't jumping to nothing," Deagan said. "It's just that you don't keep an open mind about things."

"As I remember it," Ace countered, "you were all set to draw some similar, unsubstantiated, wild conclusions when we were involved in that Roswell incident."

"That was different," Deagan growled. "And listen, wise guy, lots of people have seen U.F.O.'s, right Doc?"

Doc Atlas didn't answer. He'd learned long ago not to get between Mad Dog and Ace during their constant, but good-natured bickering.

Penny placed a well-manicured hand on Deagan's arm. "Well, all I want to know is how soon I'll be able to call in my story. This could win me another Pulitzer."

"Oh, come on," Ace said, turning his attention back to the controls momentarily. "It's probably some old airplane wreckage that nobody's identified yet. For all we know it could even be a hoax perpetrated by those Eskimos."

"It'll still make a great story, if I write it correctly," Penny said, her blue eyes widened and she held up her hands to frame an imaginary headline. "A race against the Commies at the top of the world to investigate some strange phenomenon."

"Hey, that almost sounds like one of them pulp novels you write about Doc's adventures," Deagan said. "The ones where you use different names for us, but I always end up looking like some monkey's uncle."

"Now *that* does sound distinctly plausibile," Ace said, looking back at Deagan with a wide grin.

Approximately Fifty-One Minutes Later

"Research Base Zulu, this is *Athena-one,*" Doc said into the radio mike. "Do you read? Over."

The distant sounding reply came after several attempts.

"*Athena-one,* this is Zulu," a British-sounding voice said. "We read you. What is your estimated time of arrival? Over."

"We should be there within fifteen minutes," Doc replied. "But we need you to send us a constant radio signal. We are past magnetic north. Over."

"Roger, *Athena,*" the voice said. "I'll leave this key open. I say, isn't the *Athena* Doc Atlas's plane? Over."

"Roger, Zulu," Doc said. "This is he. Over."

After a pause, the voice said, "I'll be looking forward to meeting you, Doctor Atlas. Very much. Zulu out."

"Looks like your fame has spread to the far reaches of the earth, Doc," Ace said.

Doc nodded. The many accolades bestowed upon him by the countless organizations and governments mattered little to him. Independently wealthy due to his father's prolific career as an inventor, Doc's whole life had been designed with one overriding purpose: To combat evil. Not only was he a world-renown scientist and physician, but Dr. Michael G. Atlas was also a world-class athlete, capable of breaking many Olympic records. However, his adventures had taken center stage in his life, and he frequently allowed others to take the credit for many of his accomplishments, just as he preferred to be called simply Doc by his friends and associates.

He watched as the frequency indicator needle homed in on the radio signal from the research base. Doc went back and told everyone to fasten their seatbelts as they would be landing very shortly. Penny asked if she could come to the cockpit to snap a photo of the landing site.

Doc shook his head. "You should be securely fastened."

"How about if I sit on your lap and you let Ace land the plane," she said coyly. "I mean, it's not every day a girl gets to snap a picture of the North Pole."

Doc compromised, agreeing that she could snap one picture as they circled the landing strip, but then she would have to secure herself in the navigator's seat behind the pilots' compartment. Penny's eyes widened in excitement. Suddenly the radio cracked with the same British-sounding voice as before, only this time it was infused with panic.

"*Athena-one,* this is Zulu! What is your location? What is your location?" The transmission was more of a scream than a question.

"We're approximately twelve minutes away, Zulu. Over."

"For God's sake, man, hurry," the voice said. "We're under attack. Do you have soldiers on board?"

"We do, Zulu," Doc said, trying to speak in a calm voice.

"How many?"

Doc ignored the question. "Who is attacking you, Zulu? Over."

"How many soldiers are coming?" A distant scream punctuated the transmission.

"Who is attacking you, Zulu?" Ace asked. "Are they Russians?"

"Russians?" the voice yelled. "No. My God, it's some sort of monster. Some sort of . . . Thing. I can't say just what it is, but for God's sake, man, hurry. Please hurry."

The transmission faded to static, and then ceased. Doc did not attempt to contact the research base again. He told Ace to monitor the radio signal, and went back to notify Lieutenant Sinclair of this latest development.

"I knew it," Sinclair said. "It's got to be those damn Russians. They must have beat us there."

"The eastern storm front would make that dubious," Doc said. "And we specifically asked him if the attackers were Russians. He replied in the negative."

Sinclair's brow furrowed. "Did he say who they were?"

"He referred to the attacker as some 'monster' or 'thing'."

"What the hell does that mean?" Sinclair asked. "Do you suppose it could be some sort of a . . ."

His voice trailed off.

"I think." Doc said, "we had better be prepared to enter a hostile situation when we land. What type of weapons do you have?"

"Carbines and side arms mostly," Sinclair said. "Nothing heavy. We're an advanced reconnaissance force. But we do have a fifty-caliber and a good supply of ammunition."

"Do you have any explosives?" Doc asked.

"We've got about twenty grenades, and some thermal bombs," Sinclair said, looking at Doc. "As I mentioned, my orders were specific."

Doc nodded. "I have a small assortment of handguns for my crew, too. We'll be taking a pass-over in about five minutes, then land. You'd better prepare your men to clear the facility as soon as we've touched down."

Sinclair nodded. Doc went back to the front and found Penny briefing Deagan on what she'd heard.

"Hell, Doc," Mad Dog said. "This is really weird. It's just like that movie I was telling you about. A man from Mars . . . Jeese."

"Get sidearms for yourself, Ace, and me from the storage compartment, Thomas," Doc said. "Then get strapped in for the landing."

"Too bad I can't parachute in," Deagan said. "I'd take care of that Martian all by my lonesome."

"What about a gun for me?" Penny asked.

"You won't need one if you stay in the plane," Doc answered.

"Oh, swell," she said, placing her hands on her hips. "Suppose some Russians storm the plane while I'm waiting for you guys to finish your man's work? What am I supposed to do then? Show 'em my legs?"

"Hey, that'd work on me," Deagan said, grinning as he spun the combination lock on the weapon-storage compartment.

Doc looked at Penny momentarily, then said, "Thomas, see if you can also find a suitable weapon for Penelope." He turned and pushed through the curtain separating the cockpit from the rest of the plane.

"Any further transmissions?" Doc asked Ace.

Assante shook his head. He was scanning the area through the windshield intently as he cut the defrosting units of the propellers to increase the RPMs. The *Athena* slowly descended, going through a wispy layer of clouds. The ground below them became visible with a sudden abruptness: a vast white canopy, incredibly flat and desolate. Doc checked the wind direction and velocity, then scanned the terrain for a suitable landing strip. Several small dots, resembling toothpick houses in snow, sprang into view. The research base was composed of several long buildings, sturdily constructed of heavy, weather-resistant timber. The buildings formed an elongated Y-shape. A large structure, disconnected from the other buildings by about twenty feet, was to the immediate right. An observation tower, a high metal antenna, and a rotating radar dish sat in between.

"That building over there is the garage and storage facility for their equipment," Doc said. "Sinclair had a schematic of the facility in his packet. The laboratory is on the left upper end of the Y. On the opposite end is a greenhouse. The radio room is at the base. The infirmary, mess hall, and living quarters in between."

After completing their approaching circle into the wind, they began the final descent. Doc advised the others over the speaker system that they were touching down. The big plane had been equipped with skis to facilitate the ice landing. Doc set it down as smoothly as if they were tobogganing down a hill. The *Athena* coasted to a stop perhaps fifty feet from the nearest building.

"Atlas," Sinclair called from the rear cargo door. "I'm sending a squad of five men to clear the first section. We'll signal when it's secure for you to move up."

They watched as the men disembarked, jumping from the open cargo door and rushing about ten feet before dropping to their stomachs, their rifles extended. Cautiously two men rose and quickly moved to the corner of the first structure. The squad leader shouted a command and the others moved up under cover of the first two.

"They look pretty damn good, don't they?" Deagan said proudly. "Them guys are Rangers. Soldiers trained to fight anywhere, anytime, anyway. I helped start that specialized unit during the War. Helped train 'em, too."

"Well, let's hope that fact doesn't impinge on their fighting ability," Assante said with a smirk.

"Not if the guys that taught these kids remembered what I taught them," Deagan said.

Sinclair's second squad moved to the perimeter of the building, with the Lieutenant bringing up the rear. They trained their rifles on the storage facility. Sinclair's voice boomed out of the radio speaker.

"Atlas, they've found several civilian casualties in there. You're a doctor, aren't you? Can you come over at once?"

"Roger," Doc replied. "I'm on the way."

Doc unsnapped the bolts securing the cockpit emergency hatch and dropped to the ground. The hard-packed snow crunched under his boots as he ran toward the facility with such speed that he seemed to be a tan streak to Penny and the others watching from the plane. As he approached the two soldiers covering the storage facility, Doc paused, removed his forty-five, and racked a round into the chamber.

"It's dark in there, sir," one of the soldiers said, handing Doc a flashlight. "Lights are out."

Doc nodded a "thanks" and switched on the flashlight, keeping it in his left hand and the forty-five in his right. He pushed open the heavy wooden door and stepped inside, his feet making creaking sounds as he traveled over the thick wooden planking that served as the floor.

Inside the facility Doc saw that it was a series of connected rooms, each furnished in a utilitarian sort of way, fashioned from heavy beams of wood. His flashlight swept over chairs and tables along each side and an oil-burning heating unit in the center of each room, its long metal stovepipe extending up through the ceiling. Windows afforded a minimum of light, except in the hallways, which were totally black. The next rooms were obviously dormitories, and the mess hall was beyond that. One solider was crouching at the juncture of the extending corridors. He flashed his light twice and pointed the beam to the right.

"They're down there, sir," he said.

Doc nodded and moved cautiously down the hall. He entered an infirmary where a man lay on his side in a puddle of blood. Large gashes had torn his throat open and the dark crimson flow had begun to coagulate. Doc stopped and felt the man's neck for a carotid pulse. Feeling none, he quickly advanced, pausing only to pick up a nearby first-aid kit marked with a large red cross. Sinclair and two other men stood just beyond the infirmary kneeling over another prone and bloodied man.

"This one's still alive," Sinclair said. "The generator room's down there. We're working on getting it started again."

Doc knelt next to the injured man. He appeared to be in his late thirties, bearded, with pepper-colored hair. Deep gashes ran from the top of his head to just above his ear. The wounds did not appear to be life threatening, although they were bleeding copiously. They heard a metallic sputtering sound from down the hall and the saucer-sized overhead lights flickered, then came on.

Doc placed a large compress on top of the man's head and tapped his face gently. With a rasping cough, the man's eyes suddenly snapped open and he immediately tried to get up.

"Stay down," Doc said. "You're safe. We're with you. Can you tell us what happened?"

"Did you find it?" the man asked in a terror-filled voice.

"Find what?" Doc asked.

"I. . .I'm not sure," the man said. His voice had the same British accent that Doc had heard earlier on the radio. "I'm Professor Jerome Carrington." He stared at Doc momentarily. "Are you Atlas?"

"I am. Can you tell us more about who attacked you?"

"Sir!" one of the soldiers called from down the hall. "Sergeant Dwyer's found something in the other section. You'd better take a look."

"Wait here," Doc said, standing. "Your wounds don't appear serious. We'll be back momentarily."

"No," Carrington screamed. "Don't leave me alone. Please. It may still be lurking in here."

"What the hell are you talking about?" Sinclair said.

"Whatever it was it was huge and incredibly powerful," Carrington said. "And it moved with incredible speed. Like some sort of shadow. First, the generator shut off, and then the lights went out. Suddenly this . . . monster was upon us, glowing in the darkness. It hit me on the head, knocking me across the room. Its hands were like huge claws. That's the last thing I remember until you woke me up."

Doc lifted Carrington to his feet and helped him walk down to the juncture where the other soldier stood. As they stepped over the corpse in the infirmary section, Carrington gasped.

"My God," he said. "Poor Harold."

Deagan and Assante came running up, each holding a forty-five locked and cocked.

"Where's Penny?" Doc asked.

"We left her guarding the *Athena*," Deagan said. "We wasn't about to let the chance to get into a good scrap go by. Ace was so excited he even forgot to bring his sword cane."

Assante grinned in spite of himself.

"Deagan leaned close to Doc and whispered, "I gave her that little .22 derringer for protection. She's keeping it in her mitten."

"Ace, you stay here with Professor Carrington," Doc directed. "Thomas, I may need your first aid expertise in the other section."

Deagan nodded. Although not a doctor, his extensive military career had placed him in the vicinity of many bloody battlefield situations, and he was very adept at administering life-saving first aid. They followed Sinclair down the other hallway. The first room was a laboratory. One soldier knelt over the body of a severely wounded man who was thrashing about. Doc immediately went to the man and directed Deagan to hold him down. Blood poured from a large gash on the man's throat. Several other puncture wounds were evident on his chest. Foaming blood bubbled from one of them.

"He has a thoracic injury," Doc said, sifting through the first-aid kit. "I need to find something to seal the wound site." Unable to find what he needed, Doc glanced around. Several small, clear plastic bags had been knocked from one of the counters. Doc grabbed one and ripped open the man's shirt. Fending off the man's bloody hands, Doc attempted to seal the wounds by holding the plastic over the punctures, but the man continued to squirm about.

"He's going into shock," Doc said quickly. Then, to the man, "Don't move. We're trying to help you. I'm a doctor."

The man's eyes widened and he seemed to see Doc for the first time. His mouth opened and he tried to speak, but it was obvious his larynx had been badly damaged by the vicious attack.

"Don't try to talk," Doc said. He glanced down at the blood pooling under the plastic, then felt the man's abdomen. Doc peeled back the edge of the bag, allowing a minute amount of air to escape from the wound site, then quickly covered it again.

"We can't let the pressure in the chest build up too much or his lung will collapse," Doc said. "We've got to move him to the infirmary immediately."

Hearing this, the man shook his head and reached a bloody hand toward Doc's head. Instinctively Doc pulled back, and the hand instead snared the hood of Deagan's parka. Pulling hard, the man managed to jerk Mad Dog's head downward, while at the same time expelling words with a gasping desperation. Deagan's powerful fingers curled around the bloody hand and disengaged it from his parka.

"Comprendez-vous?" The man's desperate eyes seemed to search Deagan's face for an indication that he'd understood.

"What did he say?" Sinclair asked.

"I don't know," Deagan said. "I sounded like Spanish or French or something. Sorts like 'Ken say. Lou Jose eh ken se.' Or something like that."

Doc leaned his head down and asked the man to repeat what he'd said, but as he tried, the words turned into a frothy death gurgle. His eyes rolled up into sightlessness, and the heaving of his chest ceased with a low rattle.

"He's gone," Doc said.

From the next room another voice called nervously: "Lieutenant Sinclair! Lieutenant Sinclair!"

Gently setting the dead man's head down on the floor, Doc rose and followed Sinclair and Deagan into the next room. It was a large greenhouse full of rows of various kinds of plants. A row of colorful flowers, petunias, daffodils, and tulips all sat in bright repose under some high-powered lights attached to a low-hanging beam. Farther down, connected to the same beam as the lights, Doc could see the bound feet of two men. Stepping around the base of the plant containers, they saw that the men had been suspended upside down from the beam, their arms dangling lifelessly toward the floor. Each man's throat had been slashed and a large bucket was under each, catching the draining blood. One soldier, a buck sergeant, stood next to the dangling bodies, his rifle held at port-arms. The second was hunched in a corner vomiting.

"Damn, will you look at that," Sinclair said. "What the hell kind of monster are we dealing with?"

"I found 'em just like that, Lieutenant," the buck sergeant said. He was tall and rangy, and had a smug look on his face as he shot a glance at his still nauseous partner. "I could tell they was dead, so I figured to leave 'em till you got a look-see. Want me to cut 'em down now?"

"Yes, Sergeant Dwyer," Sinclair muttered. He looked at the vomiting soldier. "Private Potter, square yourself away."

"Wait," Doc said, moving toward the bodies. "These men are obviously beyond help, so I would like to make a thorough examination of the scene before it's disturbed."

Deagan moved to Private Potter's side and patted him gently on the back. "Take it easy, son," he said. "The first time's always the hardest."

After agreeing not to disturb the suspended bodies, Sinclair dispatched the rest of his men to check around the perimeter of the base. Before they could move in to clear the large adjacent storage facility, Professor Carrington warned them off.

"The craft's in there," he said. "And it would be prudent to stay away from it in the meantime. It's highly radioactive."

They found no recent tracks in the hard packed snow around the storage building, as well as no indications that any of the doors had been recently opened. After setting up the fifty-caliber machine gun and placing several strategic mines around the perimeter of the base, they felt reasonably secure. Doc told Deagan to escort Penny in from the plane. As soon as she entered the facility, she began scribbling notes and snapping pictures. She let the bulky camera dangle from a nylon strap placed around her neck and followed Doc's every move as he brought Professor

Carrington into the infirmary and stitched up the gashes on the scientist's head and neck. While he was being attended to, Carrington gave them an account of the attack.

"As I said before, the lights went out." His voice sounded nervous and dry. "This was not an uncommon occurrence, so I went on to re-set the generator. Suddenly, this huge, glowing—thing, for lack of a better term, seemed to come out of nowhere and knocked me across the room. Harold Stevens ran toward the infirmary screaming, with the thing in close pursuit. That's the last I remember. I must have blacked out." Carrington sighed. "I suppose that I'm lucky that you arrived when you did. You must have frightened it off. Otherwise, I'd probably have met the same fate as my colleagues."

"Hold still, Professor," Doc said. "You still have some injuries that have to be attended to."

Carrington's face shook visibly and he closed his eyes.

"If only I'd been able to do something," he said. "But, we never imagined that anything like this would happen."

"Who could?" Penny said, quickly scribbling some notes on her pad. "When can I get a couple of pictures of the craft?"

Carrington frown and looked at her. "As I said, it's radioactive. It would be rather dangerous to get too close at this point, without the proper protective equipment."

"What about the Eskimos who brought it here?" Doc asked. "Did they exhibit any symptoms of radiation sickness?"

"They were given new clothing, and advised to destroy anything that came in direct contact with the craft," Carrington said. "But they are a very stubborn people, ignorant in many way to the modern world. I can only hope that they followed our advice."

Sergeant Dwyer entered the infirmary and went to the space heater. Warming himself, he told Lieutenant Sinclair that the patrol had found some tracks leading away from the base, but they stopped after approximately one hundred yards.

"What, did the wind cover them?" Sinclair asked.

"No, sir," Dwyer said. "They just kinda stopped. I guess it could have been the wind blowing over them, but it's getting kind of dark out there now and it's hard to tell."

"Yes," Carrington said. "This time of year the darkness is practically constant. We have only a few hours of daylight."

"You mean it's just like they say?" Deagan asked. "The nights really are six months long?"

Carrington allowed himself a weak laugh.

"Yes, it seems like that at times," he said. "In the spring it's just the opposite. Almost continuous daylight."

"Do you feel strong enough to show us the craft, Professor?" Sinclair asked.

Carrington got to his feet somewhat unsteadily, then nodded. Doc had applied a gauze bandage, giving the professor's head a turban-like appearance. He moved to one of the shelves and removed a box-shaped Geiger counter. "As long as we take this," he said, "and don't directly touch the craft, you should be able to snap a few photos, Miss Cartier, although I'm not at all sure of the effect the radioactivity will have on your film. In any case, we'll obviously have to limit our exposure in terms of time and distance."

"Swell," Penny said. "I can see that Pulitzer Prize getting closer all the time."

A frigid blast hit them as soon as they opened the door. They left the main facility, following Carrington's lead. He grabbed a horizontally suspended line extending from the building they had just left and ventured into the white void. Together, they made their way across the frozen expanse toward the storage unit

"There's a network of these static-lines strung between all the buildings," Carrington said. "They help guide you around in the low visibility. If this storm picks up, you could stumble away and not be found."

The wind continued to howl around them, obscuring the large building in front of them with a blinding white haze. It gradually became visible as they drew closer.

"Damn snow's moving in," Deagan said. "Pretty soon it'll be unbearable out here."

"Even for a missing link," Ace said, his teeth chattering so hard that his words were barely understandable.

Deagan seemed ready to respond, but then pulled his scarf across his exposed face. They walked with hunched-over steps leaning forward until the edge of the storage facility blocked some of the wind.

Carrington stopped.

"Prepare yourselves for a glimpse into the future," he said, his breath crystallizing as it left his lips. Another hard blast blew the fur lining of his parka as they made their way the twenty yards or so to the storage facility. When they got to the main doors, Carrington held up his hand to halt the procession. Doc, Penny, Ace, Deagan, and Sinclair all stopped.

"Again, I must warn you," Carrington said. "Do not under any circumstances, step into the doorway. Once I open it, stand off to the side to minimize your exposure to any ion particles."

In addition to the strong wind, the needle-like snow was smacking their faces. It had rapidly begun to darken and Deagan looked around warily. "Like I said, that storm must be right on top of us."

"You're right. We'd better make this quick," Carrington said. "These arctic storms can strike with a sudden and deadly viciousness." He moved to the large door and lifted the heavy board securing it in place. He pulled on the door, swinging it outward. The accompanying creak floated and died in the wind. Carrington stepped quickly away from the opening. Again he held up his palm and, with his other hand, held the Geiger counter in the open space of the doorway. The instrument emitted an electronic squeal and the monitor-needle shot to the upper part of the gauge.

Inside, perhaps fifty feet away, they could see the twisted metal of some sort of craft in the darkened area. No lights were necessary because the entire wreckage seemed illuminated with a strange yellowish glow. A metallic sphere, perhaps ten feet in diameter with spike-like antennas, resting atop the long metallic shafts that had been blackened by some tremendous heat. But everything was significantly overshadowed by the luminescence and the unnatural eeriness of the glow.

"Well I'll be a monkey's uncle," Deagan said, his jaw gaping.

"Ah, you've finally admitted what the rest of us only suspected all this time," Ace said. The group laughed at his quip, but more out of nervous tension than agreement with the bickering humor.

Penny reached around with the camera and snapped a picture, the flash's pop echoing hollowly in the ambient darkness.

Carrington pointed to the Geiger counter letting the squeal remind all of them of the brevity he'd urged.

"I'm afraid I must close this now," he said, pushing the door toward the adjacent jamb. "As I told you, it's too dangerous to attempt to examine the wreckage without protective equipment."

"I'm surprised you didn't request some when you radioed the base in Alaska," Doc said.

Carrington raised his eyebrows, then sighed. "Yes, a costly oversight."

As the professor was replacing the board that held the door in place Sinclair asked, "Aren't you going to secure that any better?"

"With what?" Carrington's bitter laugh was almost lost in the wind. "And whom do you expect to come steal it on a night like this?"

They gripped the static line that had been strung between the storage building and the other structures. Already poor visibility and the sharp wind made travel dubious. Doc tugged on Deagan's sleeve and slowed his pace, drawing them back from the others momentarily.

"Thomas, as clearly as you can recall, repeat exactly what that dying man said to you earlier," Doc whispered.

Deagan considered the request, scrunched up his face, then repeated the words, sounding them out phonetically.

"I dunno, Doc," he said. "That's the best I can do. Like I said, it musta been French. That guy was the Canadian, right? He musta been from Montreal."

Doc nodded. Jean Claude Trudeau, the man they spoke of, had been a world-renowned chemist and botanist. According to the dossier provided by Sinclair, Trudeau had been in the arctic experimenting with chemical fertilizers in sub-zero temperatures. Carrington had haltingly identified the bodies in the greenhouse as the two American scientists Ronald Smithfield and Jacob Hoeton.

"Did you know them guys, Doc?" Deagan asked as they were approaching the yellow lights of the main building. "From any scientific conventions, or anything?"

Doc shook his head.

"Regrettably, Thomas I haven't been able to attend as many of the scientific conventions that I would have liked in the last few years." He fell silent, and his mouth drew into a grim line as they walked the few remaining steps to the structure. Carrington graciously held the door open for them.

Forty Minutes Later ... Main Facility Building

"Dammit, Lieutenant, it's gotta be twenty-five below out there," Sergeant Dwyer said, his face contorting angrily. "We were just out there walking those damn sled dogs."

"I gave you an order, soldier," Sinclair said. "Two-man, roving patrols around the perimeter. Follow those static lines. You'll be relieved in two hours." He stared at the enlisted man intently, until the other buckled and transferred his gaze to the floor. "Communicate by these walkie-talkies. They're set to the radio frequency in here." Sinclair pointed to the base radio. "And keep your eyes open for anything suspicious. Call in every fifteen minutes."

"Suspicious?" Private Potter, the second man designated for guard duty, said. "Who's gonna try to sneak up on us in this kind of weather?" He pointed to the window, which showed the bleak arctic night and the whistling howl of the storm.

"Maybe some Russians who are a lot tougher than you," Sinclair snapped. "Or maybe even the thing that attacked the base earlier."

"What are our orders if we see it, sir?" Dwyer asked.

"Standard orders. Challenge anyone . . ." Sinclair paused, "or anything, that approaches. If they do not acknowledge, treat them as hostile."

The two men moved reluctantly to the door, shouldering their weapons and adjusting their cold weather gear. Dwyer shot a resentful look over his shoulder at the lieutenant, but left without saying anything. Sinclair shook his head in disgust. "These young troops today . . ." he said, letting his voice trail off.

"Oh, I don't know," Deagan said. "I always had the most respect for my commanding officers when they weren't afraid to get their hands dirty."

"Meaning what?" Sinclair asked.

"Meaning that if you want to motivate your men, ya gotta learn how to lead 'em," Deagan shot back. "If you expect them to be out there in the cold, they should know that you're gonna be right in there with 'em. You coulda walked with them part of the way for the first patrol."

"Oh, swell." The heavy lilt of sarcasm tinctured Sinclair's voice. "That makes perfect sense. Send the general into the battle to get killed on the front lines instead of being able to direct his troops. What ragtag army did you serve in, Mr. Deagan?"

"That's Colonel Deagan to you, pup, and we ain't talking battles, and we sure as hell ain't talking generals." Mad Dog's voice became a harsh growl. "We're talking a patrol, which you're supposed to be leading, at the top of the world. You're supposed to leading by example, by the way."

"You got a problem with my leadership, Mister?"

"I told you, it's 'Colonel'," Deagan said.

"You don't deserve that title," Sinclair said, his lips twisting downward.

"Listen, bub, I earned it while you were still in diapers."

Sinclair made a scoffing sound. Professor Carrington stood up, walked over to Deagan, and said, "You don't deserve to be treated like that, chap." He looked at Sinclair, who glared back.

Deagan's expression hardened, but a quick glance from Doc seemed to make it soften slightly. Mad Dog took a deep breath and held up his hands, palms outward.

"Look, my point is, it just don't make good sense to spread out a small patrol like this in hostile terrain, where they're not gonna be able to see anything, anyhow." He continued talking using his hands for emphasis. "It'd make more sense to set up posts at all the strategic points inside the compound and kill all the lights."

Sinclair blew out another derisive breath. "And this coming from a former officer who loses all his money playing cards with enlisted men. That doesn't fit with my definition of a leader."

"Maybe you and I ought to have a little talk about leadership sometime," Deagan said, his anger obviously building again. "Look me up when this is over with."

"That's the spirit," Carrington said, his voice rising gleefully.

"And I don't have to take that from some washed up old has-been who's forgotten what it means to be an officer," Sinclair spat.

"Coming from a butter-bean second-looie," Deagan said, his voice a low growl, "I'll take that as a compliment."

"Why you—" Sinclair rushed forward, trying to grab the shorter man by the neck. Deagan side-stepped nimbly and pushed the lieutenant into a wall. Mad Dog's immense hands drew into fists the size of grapefruits.

"Come on, pretty boy," he said. "I'd like to see what you got before I bust you up."

"Jolly good show," Carrington yelled from the side. "Show him what you're made of, Yank."

Sinclair began to move toward him when Doc Atlas stepped between the men. He cast a reproachful glance at Deagan, who immediately lowered his fists. Turning, Doc addressed both combatants.

"Gentlemen, it seems the enemy is already among us. It would behoove all of us to remain calm and concentrate our efforts on the tasks at hand."

Deagan shook his head. "Yeah, you're right, Doc. I blew my top and I shouldn't have." He extended a big palm toward the lieutenant. "Sorry, Sinclair, I guess I ain't never been much good at being cooped up waiting."

Sinclair stared at Deagan's massive palm, then reluctantly shook it.

Doc turned and stared at Professor Carrington. "And I'm surprised at you, as well. Your comments helped escalate the situation."

Carrington nodded and his gaze fell to the floor. "You're absolutely right. I should've shown more circumspection. Gentlemen, my apologies to all."

Sinclair nodded and moved across the room and began to take a cigarette from his pack. He stuck it between his lips, took out his lighter, then his head jerked. "Did you hear something?"

Doc nodded and went to the radio. "Dwyer, do you have traffic? Over."

A static-laden scream was the only reply. It sent all three men scrambling for their parkas and weapons. Doc had his on and was already out the door as Deagan and Sinclair were fumbling with theirs. Sinclair shouted for several of the other soldiers to suit-up.

"And somebody man the damn radio!" he screamed as he exited.

The mixture of snow and wind made visibility possible for only a few feet. They grabbed the suspended static lines and were able to follow the tracks that had been made by the two departing sentries. The footprints went off on an oblique angle around the storage facility. The sudden sound of automatic gunfire, punctuated by a scream, pierced the turbulent night. Moving toward the sound, Doc rounded the corner of the building and found Potter unconscious in the snow, blood seeping from large tears across his face and back. Dwyer lay ten feet beyond him, face down in the snow, a bloody halo surrounding his head. The large board used to secure the storage facility door was next to his unmoving form. Both of their rifles, as well as the radio, were missing. Glancing around but seeing no one, Doc scanned the tracks in the snow. Large footprints seemed to lead off into the distance, but the blowing wind made it impossible to see how far they went. Picking up one man under each arm, Doc turned and met the others as he headed back toward the main base buildings.

"What happened?" Sinclair asked, looking at the two inert men Doc was carrying. The wind tore his words away, and the relentless snow was already caking up on his eyelashes.

"Both sentries were attacked," Doc said. "Come on, we've got to get these men inside right away."

Another burst of staccato gunfire erupted. Deagan and Sinclair rushed back to the corner of the building then stopped abruptly. Some fifty feet beyond them, the dark forms of two more GIs lay bloodied in the snow. More screams, followed by more gunshots sent them edging forward. Two soldiers were firing their carbines at a huge, glowing figure. It was clear by the jumping snow that most of their rounds were missing the mark. The creature occasionally jerked as a round hit, but it seemed mostly unaffected by the fusillade. At the top of a snow bank the figure turned, showing a hideously sinister face and hands like massive spiked claws. It appeared to be clad in some sort of dark uniform, but the eerie yellow glow made it somewhat indistinct. Under each of its arms it carried the rifles of the fallen GIs. Then suddenly it vanished.

"Come on!" Deagan shouted. "Let's go after it."

"Cease fire!" Sinclair screamed. "Cease fire!"

But the two soldiers ignored him, continuing to empty their magazines, despite the thing's abrupt disappearance.

Sinclair and Deagan worked their way to the forward position, with Deagan arriving there first. He placed his hands on the shoulders of each of the two men firing and leaned down.

"It's okay," he said, his voice almost gentle, yet still harsh enough to be heard. "You guys can stop firing now."

Inside The Infirmary

Doc worked quickly on the four casualties, setting up I.V.s on two of them. But Sergeant Dwyer's skull had been crushed, so it was estimated that he had died almost immediately. One of the other soldiers was also dead on arrival with a broken neck. And the third had lost a significant amount of blood from a severed artery and had slipped into a coma. Doc was able to stabilize him. Of the four of them, Private Potter was the least injured with a broken collarbone and numerous lacerations.

Sinclair watched intently, suddenly seeming to fall apart at the sight of the dead men.

"You were right," he said to Deagan. His voice sounded brittle. "I sent those men out to die."

"Your first fire-fight?" Deagan asked.

Sinclair's mouth puckered and he nodded.

"Don't feel bad," Deagan said. "I threw up after mine."

"Private Potter has regained consciousness," Doc said, leaning over to inject some painkiller into the I.V. line. "Can you tell us what happened, private?"

"It was unreal," Potter said, his voice trembling. "One minute we were walking along, complaining about the lieutenant, then all at once it was. . . It was on top of us." He closed his eyes and a solitary tear wormed its way down his cheek. "Like it came outta nowhere. All bright and glowing and . . ."

Penny, who'd been helping Doc tend to the injured, reached over and patted Potter's hand. The young soldier began sobbing softly.

Professor Carrington gave Doc's shoulder a nudge. "It was the same for me. The creature seemed to just suddenly appear. How could something so large move so quickly?"

Doc ignored the question and turned to Mad Dog. "Thomas, were you able to follow the tracks?"

"Nope. We went over to that place where we seen him, but couldn't find nothing. Like he just plain vanished into thin air."

Even Ace, who normally wouldn't let an opportunity to chide Deagan about losing a trail, remained silent.

"He's reduced our force by a third," Sinclair said, cupping his face in his hands. "My first chance at command and it's been a disaster."

"What did I tell you about that negative thinking?" Deagan said. "Ain't you ever read Norman Vincent Peale?" He draped his long arm over the taller man's shoulders. "Casualties happen in combat. Come on, let's you and me set up check points inside the facility. We're just pulling back our perimeter, that's all."

Penny smiled at Doc after watching the two unlikely companions leave the infirmary. "Hard to believe that just a little while ago those two were at each other's throats, isn't it?" she said.

"Thomas is a man of tremendous compassion," Doc said, checking the flow meter on the I.V. line. "And the lieutenant carries a heavy burden."

"Nonetheless," Professor Carrington said, lighting up his pipe and taking between puffs. "I think this points out that we are dealing with a being of startlingly high intelligence." He removed the pipe from his mouth, gesturing as if the stem were a pointer. "For instance, it knew enough to strike at Dwyer, the sergeant, first, dealing him a mortal blow. And it also realized what the radio was, and that the rifles were weapons—- a potential threat. It's obvious that it can move among us with impunity."

"Maybe not," Ace said, coming in and shaking the hood of his heavy parka. "I just went back to that place where we thought we saw it. I couldn't find any tracks, but there was no point of reference with the snow being so fresh. No blood or anything either."

"Then perhaps," Carrington said, "we are going about this in the wrong manner."

"Exactly what is your point, Professor?" Penny asked.

"That perhaps we should make an attempt to communicate." He replaced the pipe in his mouth. "Instead of shooting at it, which is obviously having little effect."

"It doesn't seem to be giving us much choice about that," Ace said.

"Dr. Atlas," Professor Carrington said, exhaling a cloudy breath. "You're a man of science. What do you think?"

"I think," Doc answered, "that perhaps we shouldn't underestimate it, nor should we jump to any unsubstantiated conclusions."

The others seemed to be confused by his remark.

Doc turned to Ace. "Let's wrap these two corpses and put them with the rest of the bodies in the greenhouse."

Ace nodded grimly.

"I'll give you two a hand," Carrington said.

Hours Later ... Caught In A Void Of Perpetual Darkness

A silent calm eventually settled over the compound after the sentries were posted. As the shock of the sudden attack wore off, a wave of fatigue seemed to sweep over the party. Doc suggested they all try to get some much-needed rest lest their overall alertness be dissipated. They found the empty sleeping quarters all too inviting, and as the lights were extinguished, most of them were asleep within minutes. After he was certain that each of the others was slumbering, Doc slowly unzipped the sleeping bag and withdrew his legs. In the bunk next to him, Penny's breathing was sonorous. Mad Dog snored loudly a few feet away, and the other reposing bodies breathed with the regularity of deep sleep. Doc retrieved his boots and parka and carefully carried them silently out of the room. In the hallway he paused to slip on the boots, but still kept the parka slung over his arm. He moved down the hallway, stepping gingerly around one of the slumbering GIs. Doc paused to shake him awake, not wanting to get inadvertently fired upon should the soldier awake on his own.

"What? Who goes there?" the young soldier blurted out groggily. Then, upon seeing it was Doc, said, "Oh, I'm sorry, sir. Guess I dozed off for a minute."

"That's all right," Doc told him. "We're all exhausted."

Moving down the hallway to the laboratory, Doc pushed open the door and took out his pencil-sized flashlight. Scanning the counters he saw the Geiger counter and retrieved it. Doc switched it on, turning down the volume on the speaker, and watched the indicator needle as he passed his radium watch dial under the cathode. No sound was emitting from the machine. Replacing the instrument on the counter, he turned and went to the window. Outside the darkness remained imposing, the lonely and foreboding howl of the storm still whistling past the structure. But the faint yellowish glow through the window of the storage building reassured him that the mysterious craft was still in there.

Doc moved silently out of the lab and back into the hallway. When he passed the sentry the youth was wide-awake this time.

"Sir," the young soldier asked, "you aren't going to tell Lieutenant Sinclair that I was dozing, are you?"

"If you don't tell, I surely won't," Doc said, smiling pleasantly. "However, I am going out to check those dogs and my plane. Don't worry if I'm gone a while."

Arctic Dawn ... Hours Later

Penny stirred awake and saw the slight vestiges of sunlight filtering in through the still curtained window giving her an indication of the time. She glanced at her watch, which said six-thirty-five. She wiggled out of her thermal sleeping bag and managed to shuffle over to the latrine relieve herself. When she placed her feet on the cold planks of the floor and began slipping into her boots, she noticed something else. Doc's boots were gone.

It wasn't until she'd gone to the washroom and freshened up that she encountered Deagan and Assante.

Deagan was frying a skillet full of eggs over one of the stoked-up heating stoves. Ace held up a metallic pot and smiled.

"Coffee?" he asked. "I have to hand it to our friend here. All those years living in a tent have convinced him that he knows the rudiments of cooking."

Deagan snorted as he kept stirring the eggs. "You think you can do any better, shyster?"

Penny smiled at the interchange, then grew serious. "Have either of you seen Doc?"

"No," Deagan said, his brow furrowing. "I figured he was still sleeping."

"Doc sleeps less than any man I've ever known," Ace said, the concern evident on his face as well. He got to his feet. "I'd better have a look around."

"I'm coming with you," Penny said.

It wasn't until they'd made a quick run-through the facility that they traced down the night-sentry. Waking the kid from a sound sleep, they listened to his earlier encounter with Doc. It became clear that Doc had not returned from checking the plane.

"But he said it might take some time," the soldier said.

Deagan and Ace glanced at each other and immediately began getting dressed in their parkas. After they'd thoroughly searched the *Athena* to no avail, they came trudging back across the frozen expanse. The wind had died down, but the fresh snow from the night's storm had obliterated any vestiges of footprints. Everyone was up now and gathered together.

"Like I told you, the major said he was going to check on the sled dogs and the plane," the young sentry repeated. "He told me not to worry if he was gone a while."

"And you didn't think to check on him?" Ace snapped. "Or wake one of us up so we could?"

Deagan blew out a laborious breath. "Look, we all know Doc can take care of himself. Let's not let our imaginations run wild."

"But with all the unusual events of the last few hours," Carrington said, lighting his pipe, "it might be prudent to be concerned."

"The only thing to do is to form a search party and go look for him," Ace said.

"Spread us out even more thinly?" Sinclair said harshly. "No, the sensible thing to do is to load that damn wreckage into the plane, radioactive or not, and fly the rest of us the hell out of here."

"And leave Doc alone here to deal with that thing?" Penny said. "Un-un, buster. Not on your life."

Sinclair's nostrils flared, but he said nothing.

"Mr. Assante is right, Lieutenant," Professor Carrington said. "The storm seems to have abated, and I know from experience that our daylight hours are precious few. Surely a party of few can't hurt. It's easy to get lost out there because everything looks the same. There aren't any landmarks. You have a team of sled dogs, don't you?"

"You know how to use a sled, Deagan?" Sinclair asked.

Mad Dog grinned. "Hell, I grew up reading Jack London stories."

"Just make sure you keep your portable radios tuned to the proper frequency to find your way back," Ace said. "Remember, your compass will be useless out there."

Deagan nodded grimly, then put a hand on Penny's shoulder. "Don't worry, if Doc's out there, we ain't coming back without him."

After hooking up the dog sleds, it was decided that Deagan would take two men with him and head due east. Three other soldiers would go west on the other sled. After an hour they would circle around and loop back in the opposite direction. If either party got in trouble or sighted Doc, they were to fire three shots. Ace, being the only other person capable of flying the *Athena,* would remain with Penny, Sinclair, Carrington, and the wounded soldiers. The one remaining healthy GI was assigned to monitor the radio. The others were posted as guards at either end of the corridors. As they departed Carrington turned to Penny and Ace.

"I'm certain they'll find him," he said.

Penny closed her eyes and shivered, holding back the tears.

Fifty Minutes Later ...

Professor Carrington moved carefully down the hallway, holding the two steaming cups of coffee out in front of him. Glancing quickly over his shoulder and seeing no one, he turned and went into the radio room. The soldier at the table jumped up nervously and Carrington laughed.

"A little jumpy, are we...Murphy?" Carrington said, straining to read the young soldier's name tag.

"Yes, sir," Murphy said. "And if I don't mind saying so, sir, ain't I got a right to be?"

Carrington laughed again and held out the cup.

"Here, I thought you could use this," he said. "The others are all in the mess hall."

"Thanks," the soldier said, reaching for the cup.

"Murphy. That's a good Irish name, isn't it?" Carrington asked, his voice becoming imbued with the inflections of thick brogue.

"Yes, sir," Murphy said. He took the cup from the professor's hand with a grin. "You Irish too, sir? I thought you were a Brit?" He raised the cup to his lips and took a cautious sip. It was scalding hot.

"Irish? No," Carrington said almost absently. "No, I'm not." Before Murphy could react any further to what was said, the bearded man threw the contents of his cup into the young soldier's eyes. Recoiling, shaking his head, Murphy had barely enough time to gasp before the long blade was thrust up under his rib cage severing his aorta. He tried to scream, but his throat was clutched in a steel-like grasp. Meekly, he emitted a pitiful moan as he slumped to the floor.

Carrington went to the entrance and quickly checked the hallway. Satisfied at seeing no one, he gently closed the door and wiped off the blade of the knife on the supine man's pantleg. He replaced it in a sheath under his lab coat, then began stripping Murphy of his weapons. Tucking Murphy's sidearm in his belt, he checked to make sure that the weapon was properly concealed, then turned to the radio adjusting the frequency. Moments later he left the radio room and began walking leisurely down the hall softly whistling.

Death In The Mess Hall ...

"It looks like the storm has completely cleared," Sinclair said, staring out the window of the mess hall. "Assuming they're back before it gets dark, how long before we'll be able to take off?"

"I'm not flying that thing in the *Athena* if it's radioactive," Assante said. He placed a cigarette between his lips and flicked his lighter.

"And we're not leaving without Doc," Penny said emphatically.

"Damn civilians," Sinclair said. "Don't you two realize that something like this transcends all of us? Major Atlas would be the first to agree with me. Can't you see the big picture?"

"Why don't you talk about the big picture to those GI's who had to watch the A-bomb test on Bikini Island in forty-seven," Ace said. "Doc and I helped evacuate some of the injured to Guam after the blast. A lot of them will never be the same, and who knows how we'll all be affected twenty years from now."

Sinclair snorted.

"I thought that you, a former officer, would understand. You think I liked sending those men off to die?" His head canted with a questioning look. "Did you hear that?"

Ace went to the window, swiveling his head too.

"If I didn't know better," he said, "I'd say there was another plane coming in for a landing on the other side of the compound."

The drone of the motors became more distinct. They moved from one window to the next, finally seeing the large cargo plane dip through the clouds and begin its circling descent toward the base.

"You have any binoculars?" Sinclair said, his voice quivering.

"I don't need any to see that it's a Russian plane," Ace said quickly, managing to discern the red star on the plane's side. "How soon are our reinforcements arriving?"

"Unfortunately, not soon enough, Mr. Assante," a voice said from just outside the door. It was a strange voice, devoid of inflection or accent, but yet strangely familiar. "Now, I'll thank you all to lay your weapons on the table there, it you please."

Professor Carrington entered the mess hail, the forty-five caliber Government Model 1911 extended out in front of him.

"Carrington? What?" Sinclair said.

"No, not Carrington," the bearded man said with his flat, toneless voice. "I am Colonel Mikhail Markov, MVD." He allowed himself a slight smile. "Ah, Ministry for Soviet State Security."

"Soviet?" Sinclair said incredulously. "You're a damn Communist spy?"

A cruel smile became more pronounced on the bearded man's lips.

"Not a spy, Lieutenant. A soldier, much like yourself, only highly trained and educated in the ways of western decadence." The smile vanished quickly. "And now, the guns. Put them on the table, or I will be forced to shoot you. Ah, your weapon too, Miss Cartier. The small caliber pistol in your mitten." He gestured with the auto pistol.

"You're bluffing," Ace said desperately. "You won't shoot us. If you did, the other GIs would be in here in a second."

"They will be of little concern soon enough," Markov said.

"Then what about that thing that's creeping around?" Sinclair asked. "We can't afford to let political rivalries interfere with what we've discovered here."

Markov chuckled softly.

"You pathetic Americans," he said. "Always trying to hide your fear and incompetence by delving into religious mythology instead of true science. Afraid of facing certain truths. I harbor no such fear." The corners of his mouth twisted downward suddenly and he raised the pistol. The sound of the shot echoed on the large room, and Sinclair bent over suddenly holding his abdomen. The young lieutenant stumbled back a step, then he crumpled to the floor, a red puddle seeping out from beneath him.

Ace glanced at the door, then back to Markov, who still stood there smiling.

"One of the reasons that I have allowed this little game to continue, was that I was interested in meeting the famous hero of the West, Doc Atlas. The tales of his incredible feats are the stuff of legend." He moved forward and placed the barrel of the forty-five against Penny's temple. "You see, we in the Soviet Union have been experimenting. Developing men of similar qualities." He reached across the table and pulled Penny's mitten next to him, then dumped out the derringer. "I am one such man. Mentally, I am more than the equal of Doc Atlas."

He grabbed Penny's head with his left hand. The right still held the big pistol close to her temple. "Now, your gun, Mr. Assante," Markov said, allowing the barrel to bump against Penny's head with mild force. "I will not hesitate to shoot the female." He watched Ace's reaction, seeming to relish the agony.

Ace stood and began to reach for his sidearm, but the Russian grunted. Ace froze and Markov released Penny and slapped Ace's hand away from his holster and removed the gun himself. Markov stepped back and withdrew a long cord from the pocket of his lab coat. "Turn around and place your hands behind you."

Ace cast another furtive glance at the door and Markov chuckled again. "Do you think I would he so remiss as to not anticipate a rear attack by the pawns before I captured their queen?" He smiled wickedly. "I'm afraid your much vaunted Rangers were no match for my counterpart." He looped the rope around Ace's hands and pulled it taunt. "Sergei," he called out.

Through the door of the mess hall stepped a huge man almost seven feet tall clad in a dark, futuristic uniform. Reaching quickly toward his head, he stripped off the hideous mask that he was wearing, revealing the prominent facial bones of an acromegalic. His hands, which he held in front of him like the claws of a great bear, were as large as gallon milk bottles. Each one was covered with a tight-fitting leather glove, the back of which had razor-like spikes projecting over the knuckles. With lips curled back in something akin to a smile, he exposed rows of fang-like teeth, reinforced by stainless steel, as his great mouth opened. His glazed eyes displayed something more closely akin to an animal cunning than a look of intelligence.

"As I told you, we have been experimenting with genetic enhancements," Markov said, looping the rope around Penny's wrists. "While my development has been chiefly in the area of cerebral developments, Sergei's were of a physiological nature."

"So he's the *thing* we saw," Penny said, trying to pull her hands out of the rope. Markov gave her a backhanded slap across the face.

"Do not try to do that again," he said.

A needle-like trickle of blood seeped down the comer of her chin.

Suddenly, the sounds of explosions followed by bursts of machine gun and rifle fire erupted from outside the windows. Markov smiled.

"Ah, at this moment the *Spetsnaz* troops that just landed are dispatching Mr. Deagan and the rest of your over-rated Rangers. Soon, they will be loading the wreckage of the *sputnik* in our cargo plane."

"So that's what this was all about," Ace said, trying desperately to keep the Russian talking until he could figure out a counter move. "You were just stalling us until the eastern storm front cleared and your own troops could fly here."

"Ingenious, wasn't it?" Markov said. "But since I intend on taking both of you back to the Soviet Union with me, as prisoners of war, you'll have plenty of time to appreciate the Russian penchant for planning, as well as the masterful achievements of Soviet science."

"The Soviet Union?" Penny's face turned pale. "You can't. We're not military. We're civilians."

"Who know far too much," Markov said. "But do not despair. Once we have cleared your minds of all useful information, a beautiful woman such as yourself will not be lacking for male companionship." He leered at her salaciously. "You will bring a good price in one of our labor camps in Siberia."

She spit at him, and Markov backhanded her face again.

"You dirty son of a—" Ace shouted jumping up and trying to bowl the Russian over with his shoulder. Without the use of his arms, he was an easy target. Markov smashed his fist into Ace's jaw. Assante fell onto the table, his mouth welling with blood. He sat up and spat out a crimson mist, and was just about to try and muster enough strength for another charge at the Russian, when Markov brought the heavy pistol down repeatedly on Ace's head. Assante slumped forward, dark blood streaming from several large gashes.

"No, please," Penny cried. "Don't hit him any more. Stop it!"

Despite her pleading Markov raised the pistol again and was set to deliver still yet another crushing blow to the unconscious man. Then suddenly his eyes widened. Across the room, by the far wall, stood Doc Atlas. Markov raised the pistol and began rapidly firing. Doc merely smiled as the bullets seemed to pass right through him. The slide on the forty-five locked back with a snap, and Doc seemed to evaporate into thin air. Markov swore and whirled toward the door in time to see the real Doc Atlas barreling through, driving the monstrous Sergei off his feet. Doc continued forward, plowing into Markov. As the bearded Communist was knocked to the floor, the sound of explosions and automatic weapon fire resounded from outside the structure. Doc grabbed Markov's head and smashed it into the heavy wooden table with terrific force. He reached over and partially untied Penny's bonds, but Sergei had regained his feet and immediately lumbered toward Doc.

The malformed giant's first blow landed with cat-like quickness, stunning Doc and sending him to one knee, a bloody gash torn across the back of his parka. Sergei whirled and delivered a hooking kick, which caught Doc in the side. One of the massive hands captured the golden avenger's face and literally tossed Atlas over the tabletop. With ursine power, Sergei swept the furniture out of his way and strode forward, the spikes dangling like claws from the tight gloves. For such a big man, the giant seemed to move with uncanny grace and fluidity, like some large, feral animal.

Doc attempted to roll away from the larger man's grasp, but the big Russian clasped Doc's left arm. With a deft twist, Sergei spun and flipped Doc with a judo throw. His mouth opened in a hideous smile, and he followed up with another kick, the oversized boot colliding with Doc's face.

Reeling, Doc staggered backward, blinking to try and clear his head. Sergei raised a spiked glove and aimed for Doc's throat. But at the last moment Doc managed to block the giant's punch, using the big man's momentum to push him into a wall.

The spikes sunk into the wall, and before the Russian could turn, Doc delivered a solid one-two punch to the massive back. The giant grunted slightly, the gaping mouth twisting downward in a scowl of pain. Doc stepped back and delivered a powerful jumping-kick of his own, then grabbed a chair and smashed it over the Sergei's upraised arms. The giant sagged to the floor briefly, leaving the broken razor-spikes in the wall. He rose slowly, but then bared his steel teeth in a fearsome snarl and charged. Doc sidestepped and delivered a blow to the solar plexus, followed by a whistling hook to the jaw. The giant tumbled again, but, at the last moment, managed to snare Doc's arm.

Using his superior weight, Sergei dropped to the floor, dragging Doc down with him. The huge head snapped downward, the steel fangs ripping at Doc's sleeve, tearing through the parka and drawing blood. Swinging his legs upward, Doc caught the large head in a scissor-like grasp.

The giant immediately released his grip on Doc in an attempt to free his head, but Doc arched his body and twisted his foe over on his side. Getting to his feet first, Doc moved in and delivered a furious combination of punches. Sergei seemed to shake them off and seized Doc's throat. Realizing that he had to break the iron grip or be asphyxiated, Doc Atlas raised his fists and pounded at the Russian's arms. But the forearms were like tree branches and seemed unaffected. Black dots began to swarm in front of Doc's eyes. Gasping, he managed to snap his foot upward into the giant's groin. The monster expelled a foul breath, and his grip weakened slightly. Doc repeated the kick more forcefully.

Sergei crouched and moved in closer, seeking to maintain his hold while eliminating Doc's range of kicking motion. At that moment Doc sent his stiffened fingers into the looming throat, tearing and ripping at the delicate cartilage that was lodged there. The Russian's big hands left Doc's neck and went to his own. Emitting an almost pathetic gurgling the giant stepped in a ludicrous little circle, before collapsing in a heap. Doc staggered against the wall, his breath coming in heavy rasps.

Movement flickered in the corner of Doc's eye, and he looked across the room in time to see Markov snapping a fresh magazine into the forty-five. The Communist extended his arm, aiming the pistol directly at Doc.

"Now, you die, American dog," he said, his crimson teeth glaring through his soiled beard.

Doc stiffened, expecting the bullet to pierce his chest.

But the report that sounded was off to the side. Markov's head jerked slightly, and the extended gun slowly lowered. The bearded lips twisted into something almost resembling a smile, then he collapsed, a round hole in his left temple. As the Russian fell, Doc saw Penny holding the derringer. Stumbling slightly, Doc moved across the room and kicked the gun from the Communist's numb fingers.

"Is he dead?" Penny asked haltingly. Her face was chalk white.

Doc stooped to check him, then nodded.

"Good," she said.

Six Hours Later ... In The Air Over The Arctic

Despite Ace's mild concussion, and the turban-like bandage that covered his formidable collection of stitches, he said that he felt fully capable of flying the *Athena* while Doc checked on his patients. Peeling back the curtain, Doc went to the various stretchers on which Lieutenant Sinclair, Private Potter, and the other wounded GI were strapped. Doc checked the life-giving plasma I.V. line to the Lieutenant, then took the man's pulse.

"How are you feeling, Lieutenant?' he asked.

I'm very glad to be alive," Sinclair said, a weak smile stretching over his haggard face. "Never been shot before. It hurts."

"Hopefully, you won't make a habit of it," Doc said. Several of the young soldiers sitting around their squad leader laughed. Doc moved farther toward the rear and found Penny busily scribbling in her notebook. He moved close to her and clasped her arm.

"And how are you?" he asked softly.

"I'll survive," she said, then shuddered.

He reached out and placed a hand on her shoulder. "It's all right. Sometimes we have to kill."

A tear wound its way down her cheek, and she looked up at him. "I really didn't have a choice, did I?"

Doc shook his head.

Deagan, who'd been staring at the twisted metal of the wreckage farther back in the cargo hold, clucked loudly.

"Man, did we kick those Commie's butts, or didn't we?" he said grinning. "I ain't set up an ambush like that since the Philippines. But after you intercepted us, how'd you know they'd be coming, Doc?"

Doc moved to him. "Actually, you can take credit for that, Thomas."

"Me? Ya gotta be kiddin', right?"

Doc shook his head. "My first clue that something wasn't right was the dying message that the French-Canadian scientist gave you," he said. "He said 'Le chose est quinze,' or 'The thing is fifteen.' Remember, he was a man of science, and he saw his murderer standing undetected among us. Fifteen is the atomic number for phosphorous. Trudeau obviously knew that the real Professor Carrington had been killed, and wanted to tell us that Markov had used the phosphorus from the greenhouse to give the wreckage, as well as the monster, the eerie yellowish glow. He must have known he didn't have time for a detailed warning, so he put it in the form of a cryptic message."

"I woulda never figured that one out," Deagan said, rubbing his chin.

Doc regarded his friend for a moment. "When Markov finally let us view the wreckage, claiming it was radioactive to keep us from examining it, I suspected that it had been covered with some foreign substance." He moved forward and ran his handkerchief over the smooth metal, then held it up for the others to see. It was covered with a fine chalky powder. "I subsequently checked the reliability of the Geiger counter with the radium dial of my watch. After verifying it was a fake, I was certain that Carrington had concocted the elaborate subterfuge to delay us, while awaiting the arrival of the contingent of Russian troops. He and Sergei must have been flown here by jet, knowing the larger, slower cargo plane would never have been able to fly in that eastern storm front."

"So it was a Russian rocket the whole time," Penny said. "Not a space ship. What was it that he called it? A *sputnik*?"

"That means traveler in Russian," Doc said. "The wreckage is actually one of their SS-6 rockets with an experimental navigational device."

"But how did it end up all the way up here at the North Pole?" Deagan asked.

"I've been thinking about that," Doc said. "The Soviets, under the direction of an unidentified master designer, have been trying to develop intercontinental ballistic missiles. The range of such rockets is thought to be much less than one thousand miles."

"And we're a long way from Siberia," Deagan said.

"Exactly," Doc continued. "Which makes me think that they fired this rocket upward, toward space instead of in the usual trajectory."

"But why?" Penny asked.

"Are you at all familiar with the writings of Englishman Arthur C. Clarke?" Doc asked. Penny shook her head. "A number of years ago Clarke wrote an article theorizing that if a rocket could be launched from earth with enough thrust to escape the gravitational pull, it would reach a plateau above the atmosphere and orbit the earth."

"That sounds preposterous, doesn't it?" Penny said.

"No, I do not disagree," Doc said, patting the side of the wreckage. "I believe that this craft achieved such an orbit. A polar orbit, and re-entered the atmosphere near the crash site."

"Wow," said Deagan. "I guess them space movies ain't so far-fetched after all."

"This is going to make a great story," Penny said.

Doc shook his head.

"I'm not sure that would be such a good idea at this point," he said. "With all the turmoil in the country today, would it really be wise to let something like this out? In any case, we've been assisting the military on this matter. They will have a say in this, I'm sure."

"I'm afraid it's a matter of national security, Miss Cartier," Sinclair said, struggling to push himself up on one arm.

"Can't I even use the part about you using the holograph to save us?" Penny said.

"Yeah, how'd you know about that, Doc?" Deagan asked.

"I suspected as much when the rifle bullets had no effect on the monster during the first attack. It was fortuitous that I found their projection device hidden near this." He patted the side of the Soviet *sputnik*.

"A thing from another world," Deagan said, smacking himself on the side of the head. "I oughta had more sense than to buy into that crap."

"We should remember that the worst monsters are always human, Thomas," Doc said. He turned to Penny. "I would rather you concentrated your story on the heroic efforts of Lieutenant Sinclair, his brave troops, and the invaluable assistance of Thomas 'Mad Dog' Deagan."

"Heroic efforts on *my* part?" Sinclair said. His jaw sagged down.

"Sure," Deagan said. "After all, we was just setting up that ambush of that Commie cargo plane on your orders, Lieutenant. Hell, all you guys will probably get some ribbons outta this one." His face split in a huge grin.

"I just feel fortunate to be alive," Sinclair said. "And to have served with men like all of you. And you also, ma'am," he added, looking at Penny. He held his hand out toward Deagan, who grasped it and shook it warmly.

"Well, all I know," Penny said, flipping her notebook closed with an emphatic snap, "is that I've got to get to someplace with a hot bath pretty soon. I haven't washed my hair in almost forty-eight hours. Plus, I don't want my legs to end up looking like Mad Dog's."

"Hey, what's the matter with my legs?" Deagan asked in mock indignation.

"They're hairy, for one thing," Penny shot back with a smile.

"Well, how the hell would you know?" he said.

"Simple," she said. "I've seen them."

"Oh yeah? When?"

"At the beach last year. Remember? You, Polly, Doc, and me at Coney Island. You wore swimming trunks. Remember?"

"Is that who that was?" Ace said, pulling back the curtain by the cockpit. "I thought it was Polly's pet chimpanzee."

Deagan snorted. "That's enough, shyster. Just fly the damn plane."

"I put it on auto-pilot so I could watch you make a fool out of yourself," Ace said, grinning wickedly. "Again."

Doc turned and began to work his way back toward the cockpit, the shadow of a smile tracing its way across his even features. Despite the adventure, it was getting back to business as usual again.

THE END

The Satan Plague

June 3, 1951
Somewhere near Bear Mountain State Park,
New York

AFTER HAVING LOADED the final canvas-wrapped carcass into the back of the ambulance, West stripped off his rubber gloves and used a handkerchief to wipe his face. Moving over toward the corner of the brick building, he unbuttoned the fly of his pants and paused to urinate. Then he moved with a weary trepidation back to the vehicle. Inside, he checked the tops of the two five-gallon geri-cans and momentarily pondered pouring a little bit of the gasoline on a rag to hold under his nose. Anything to deaden the overwhelming odor that continually wafted from the canvas containers.

Starting it up, he snapped on the headlights and drove into the macadamized roadway that swung sinuously around the camp, past the metal corrugation of the Quonset huts and along the high cyclone and concertina wire covered fence. He drove down toward the entrance, coming to a stop in front of the long metallic arm of the barricade, and watched as the door to the small cubicle inside the fence-line opened leisurely.

"So you taking this load of stinkers over, West?" the burly man at the gate asked. He was dressed in a military field uniform but it was devoid of patches or insignias. The rifle in his hand was an M-l Carbine.

"Yeah, gives me the creeps, too," West said. "They sure we're safe handling these bodies?"

The gate guard raised his eyebrows and started to lean toward the window. He recoiled and held his nose. "As long as the smell don't kill ya." He laughed and when West didn't show amusement, the guard added, "Relax. They assured us that these suckers ain't contagious as long as they're dead, remember?"

West shoved the olive drab military ambulance into gear and drove through as the gate guard raised the barrier. West relaxed slightly as he saw it lowering behind him in the side-vision mirror, and he settled in for what he hoped would be a quick run.

Haven't driven so many dead bodies around since the war, he thought. It wasn't until after he'd rounded the first curve that he heard the stirring behind him and slowed down.

"What the hell?" he muttered as he turned. But it was too late. The thin man had twisted the wire around West's throat and began bearing down. West struggled furiously for a few moments, but the other man dropped to the floor, bringing the hapless driver with him. A few seconds more and the thrashing ceased. The ambulance rolled to a stop, the engine choking and sputtering out from being left in gear. It was several seconds before the thin man could gather enough strength to rise up and get behind the wheel. His foot pressed against the starter button and the engine came to life once more. But just the exertions of the last few minutes had been draining to him. A spasm shook him and he began to cough. It was a moist-sounding cough, and when he spat out the window he was sure it was bloody. But this only seemed to fill him with more resolve.

I have to get to New York, he thought. Find Doc Atlas before it's too late.

Then another spasm shook him and he realized it was probably already too late for him. But the others, he thought shoving the gearshift into first and easing out the clutch. Got to make it for the sake of the others. And all the others to come.

* * *

New York City
Just outside of the Empire State Building

Thomas "Mad Dog" Deagan held the end of the car-lighter to his cigar and took copious puffs while they waited, the big Chrysler idling at the curb. He was a short but broad-shouldered man in his early forties, with coarse reddish colored hair and a face somewhat flattened and misshapen by one too many a boxing bout. His hands were huge, and the long cigar looked almost tiny as he held it between his fingers. "What I don't understand, shyster, is what's the big deal?" he said. "So Doc gets called in front of this committee and says he's not a Communist. Everybody knows he ain't. What're you so damn worried about?"

Edward "Ace" Assante glanced around, wanting to see if the arrival of Doc Atlas at the vehicle was at all imminent. "What I'm worried about, you knucklehead, is this modern- day inquisition." He was slightly younger than Deagan and nicely dressed in a tailored blue suit. His dark hair was swept back from his forehead and the neatly trimmed mustache made him a dead ringer for a younger version of Errol Flynn. "But I suppose any allusion to history is wasted on the likes of you."

"Ha," Deagan said, blowing a prodigious cloud of smoke toward Assante. "Remember a couple of years ago when Bogey came to D.C. and spoke out against the hearings? Then he changed his mind 'cause he saw they were a good thing. Hell, even J. Edgar Hoover's in favor of 'em. And you can't ask for much more integrity than that."

"It used to appall me that the mentality of this country today would allow somebody like this McCarthy character to rise so quickly," Assante said, taking a cigarette out of his pack. "But a ten-minutes with you and I understand it completely."

"Ah, you just don't like Tailgunner Joe cause you're a Democrat," Deagan said. "He ain't so bad, and I'll go with a fellow vet anytime."

"Hey, guys, how about saving the argument until after the hearings, okay?" The speaker was a stunningly beautiful woman. Her jet-black hair was exquisitely coifed so that it graced her flawless features. She was seated in the back seat area impatiently glancing out the window. "What time does our train leave?"

"Oh, Penny, you can't possibly agree with this ignorant ex-dogface, can you?" Ace asked.

"That's ex-Lt. Colonel dogface to you, fly-boy," Deagan said, blowing more smoke toward Ace. "Remember , you were only a captain."

Penelope Cartier knew better than to get in the middle of one of their constant, but good-natured arguments. Deagan and Ace were actually the best of friends, but arguing for them was a way of life.

"You can read my story on it when my article comes out in tomorrow's edition," she said, taking out her own cigarettes. "And, Mad Dog, how about cracking that window some more and blowing more of the smoke from that El Ropo outside."

"Perhaps it would be prudent for everyone to extinguish his smoking materials," a serene but powerful looking man said as he suddenly appeared next to the window. He pulled open the rear door and slid inside. "The breeze will not adequately supply quality breathing air."

The man had a golden mane of hair that was combed back from his forehead and intense eyes that were just a tad darker than amber. Moments after he settled into the seat next to Penny, he appeared to go deeply into thought, his strong chin resting on a large, but perfectly formed hand, as he gazed out the window.

"Sure, Doc," Deagan said, quickly tossing his cigar out of the car. "Didn't mean to bother ya. We all know how you feel about smoking."

Assante immediately crushed his cigarette out in the ashtray, and Penny quickly slipped hers back into her pack. They rode the rest of the way in silence.

* * *

United States Congress, House of Representatives, Committee Room A
Washington D.C.

As the towering figure of Doc Atlas strode into the hearing room accompanied by his attorney, Edward "Ace" Assante, a hush seemed to sweep over the crowd of congressmen, senators, and reporters. For a moment the only sound that could be heard was the soft whirring of the television and newsreel cameras. Large sets of extremely bright lights had been positioned at each corner, making it difficult to see the outer aspects of the huge hearing room. Ace and Doc took their seats at the rectangular wooden table in the center of the hall. Two bulbous microphones protruded from the middle of the table. In front of them, on a raised platform behind more microphones, sat the committee. At the podium in the center the senator from Wisconsin seemed to beam down at them with relish. Suddenly, a hint of a scowl drew down the corners of the senator's mouth, and, as his head canted back, the lighting highlighted the shiny parts of his scalp. His head looked the size of a basketball. "Please state your name for the record and spell your last name," the clerk said.

"My name is Michael G. Atlas," Doc said. He spelled out the letters and the clerk administered the oath that what he was going to tell was the whole truth, and nothing but the truth, so help him God.

"Doctor Michael G. Atlas," Senator Joseph McCarthy said slowly. He drew out the last name, then one side of his mouth twisted up into a smile. "That's an interesting name for a real living, breathing, American hero, isn't it?" This time he stressed the word "American." Doc said nothing. Ace was frantically trying to read McCarthy, attempting to figure out where this meandering was leading. He'd already advised Doc not to answer anything, explaining that he should use his Fifth Amendment rights.

"But I have nothing to hide," Doc had told him. Now Ace wondered if that was the case, why they'd been called here in the first place. He knew that Doc was no Communist, but he also knew that they wouldn't be sitting in the hot seat unless this demagogue, McCarthy thought he could benefit in some way.

What's his damn trump card? Ace thought.

"Funny thing about names," the senator said. He paused and took a drink of water. The man was sweating profusely, and large wet spots were starting to soak through the underarms of his suit jacket. "Especially Americanized names."

Suddenly a page came up to McCarthy and whispered something in his ear. The senator's eyebrows raised momentarily, then he leaned forward and said into the microphone, "It seems we have to take an emergency recess. Dr. Atlas, I'm told you have an urgent phone call waiting."

He pointed toward the door as he got up. Immediately the room came alive with reporters shoving microphones at Doc and Ace as they made their way down the corridor. Doc seemed oblivious to all the questions, and Ace just kept repeating that they had no comment to make. Off to one side, Penny and Mad Dog stood watching. Every time a reporter shoved a microphone at Doc, Deagan smacked his big fist into his palm.

"Man, you reporters can really be obnoxious," he said. "You ain't never like that, are you Penny?"

"Only in special cases," she said, looking in the opposite direction. "And with special people. Come on." She brushed in front of him, going away from the crowd following Doc and Ace. Deagan glanced after her, then followed. Senator McCarthy was ducking out a side door, and Penny was right behind him. "Senator, Penelope Cartier with the *New York Times.* May I speak to you for a moment?"

McCarthy's big head swiveled toward her. Upon seeing that she was a beautiful woman, he paused and smiled.

"Miss Cartier," he said, drawing out the pronunciation of her name. "Welcome to Washington. Enjoying your stay here?"

"Actually, I'm on assignment," Penny said, showing her teeth in a dazzling smile. "But I would enjoy it a lot more if you gave me an indication of why you summoned Doc Atlas here. Do you really suspect that he's a Communist?"

McCarthy smiled. "Why don't you come by my office and I'll show you my list of two hundred and ten card-carrying Communists who work for the State Department."

"I thought it was only two hundred-five?" she said, still smiling alluringly.

"Perhaps I've found a few more," he said. Then his face twisted into a frown. "Your boyfriend Atlas has been known to work for the government upon occasion, hasn't he?"

Penny's smile faded. Her relationship with Doc, while not a secret, was hardly common knowledge either. For this man to know that, he'd obviously done his homework.

"So you're implying that Doc Atlas is a Communist?" she said. "Do you have evidence of such a claim?"

His grin turned malevolent. "I imply nothing. I merely state the facts. And I have nothing more to say. You want to know anything, you can wait for the hearings to resume."

"Hey, Joe," Mad Dog said extending his big palm out toward the senator. "I'm Lt. Colonel Thomas E. Deagan, retired. I served with Doc during the War, and I can vouch for him. Totally. After all, we're all vets, ain't we? You were a gyrene, right?" McCarthy stared at Mad Dog's big hand in front of him, but made no move to shake it. The cords in his rather corpulent neck stood out and his voice trembled up the scale with a light quaver. "Both of you leave me alone!" he shouted. He turned to go, then paused, pointing his finger at them and said, "And you can tell Atlas not to send any more flunkies around to try to intimidate or threaten me. The truth will come out." As they watched him storm off down the hall, Penny and Mad Dog exchanged worried looks.

"There goes trouble," Deagan said.

* * *

When they met up, Deagan tried to read Doc's usual inscrutable expression for any signs of anxiety, but if any were present they didn't manifest themselves outwardly. Doc asked him to arrange for the military car that General Happy Jack Harding had loaned them to take them to the train station. "We've been summoned back to New York at Governor Dewey's request," Doc said. "It seems they have a strange case with which they need my assistance. We have exactly fifteen minutes before the next express train leaves."

"But what about the hearings?" Penny asked.

"The hearings will have to wait," Doc said.

"But don't you want to clear your name?" she asked. "Get this situation resolved?"

"There is nothing to resolve," he said, and held open the door for her.

* * *

The train rumbled slightly as it began its departure from the station. They watched through the window as the sight of the people on the platform gave way to a section of darkness before they passed through into the brightness of the sunshine. After riding part of the way in silence, Deagan was the first to speak.

"I don't know," he said. "There's something about that McCarthy. I mean, I tried to talk to him vet-to-vet, but he wouldn't even listen to me. Something's weird about that guy."

"For once we agree," Assante said. "The man's a demagogue, so intoxicated with his own sense of power that he doesn't care whom he hurts." Ace turned to Deagan and pointed emphatically. "Now do you see why I'm so against these damn hearings?"

Deagan said nothing, but nodded slightly.

"Finally!" Ace said. "Some common sense has finally seeped into that thick skull of yours." He waited, but when Deagan continued to stare out the window in silence, Assante slumped back in his seat as well.

"Why do you think McCarthy made such a point over your name, darling?" Penny said to Doc.

Doc, who had also been staring out the window, turned to her. "Men like McCarthy, as Ace suggested, are transparent in their desires," he said. "But not in their schemes."

"But what's so significant about the name Michael Atlas?" she asked. "Wasn't that your father's given name too?"

"Actually, no," Doc said. "My father changed our family name when he came to this country. My real name is Michail Gabriel Atlanski. That is what my mother originally put on my birth certificate. My father had it changed a year later."

"What? Is that Polish," Penny asked.

A slight smile crept over Doc's lips. It was tinged with a bit of irony. "No, it's Russian," he said.

"Oh my God," Penny said. Deagan and Assante looked equally stunned. "You're Russian?"

"Actually," Doc said, "my parents were born in the Ukraine."

"Which is part of the good old Soviet Union," Deagan said. His face looked ashen.

"This'll play right into that madman McCarthy's hands," Ace said. "Look at what he did to poor, old Senator Tydings with that phony photo of him and Stalin together."

The group sat stone-faced for a moment, then Deagan began patting his pockets. "Come on, Ace," he said. "I need some cigars. Let's take a walk to the club car."

Ace nodded and rose, grabbing his ebony cane for support on the swaying train. His right knee had been ripped up on his last bombing mission over Berlin. The unlikely pair shuffled down the corridor and Deagan slid open the door separating the interior from the exit/entrance ports. He paused, looking out the big window, and took out a cigar and his Zippo Storm King. Placing the cigar in his mouth, he flipped open the lighter and spun the wheel, holding it toward Ace. Assante held his cigarette into the flame and nodded a thanks. Deagan bit off the end of the cigar and spat it on the floor.

"So," he said, rotating the tip of the cigar in the flame, "How bad does it look for Doc?"

"It's a veritable catch eighteen," Assante said.

"Huh?"

"Oh, that was this expression we used to use when we were flying bombing missions," Ace said. "They started out by telling you that you only had to fly so many missions, amass so many points, before you'd be eligible to be shipped home. Then when you got to that number, they'd always add a few more. They kept coming up with these additional rules for amassing the points. We called them 'catches.' It allowed them to keep changing the rules to extend your run. So we came up with the term catch eighteen. One of the bombardiers in my company said he was going to write a book about it someday."

"Heads I win, tails you lose, eh?" Deagan looked grim. "So what's in store for Doc?"

Assante sighed. "The problem with these hearings, given the hysterical mood the country's in right now, is that they lend themselves to innuendo. Doc will have to plead the Fifth Amendment to any and all questions; otherwise, McCarthy will drag in this business about him being Ukrainian and link it to the Russians and use it to ruin him."

"But won't it look like he's hiding something if he pleads the Fifth?" Deagan asked.

"It doesn't matter. No matter what he does, McCarthy will find some stooge to testify at the hearings to impeach Doc," Assante said. "To say he has ties to the Soviets." He blew some smoke out his nostrils. "By the time we can investigate that person's statements and prove them false, the damage will already have been done."

"And that's the catch-eighteen," Deagan said, blowing out a cloud of smoke.

"You catch on fast for an infantryman," Ace said with a slight smile. But Deagan did not grin. Instead he puffed on the cigar for a few moments more, then looked at Assante.

"Doc's the finest man I've ever known," he said.

Assante nodded in agreement. "He saved my life."

"So we can't afford to let that happen, Ace," Deagan said. "We gotta do something. We have a promise to keep."

The smile faded from Assante's lips, and he let more smoke trail out of his nostrils as he nodded again, slowly.

* * *

New York City
Grand Central Station

Deagan was the first off the train and managed to secure a cab for them. As they proceeded at Doc's direction to the city morgue, Ace told them to drop him at the Federal Building. "I've got to go over some case law and transcripts of other hearings," he said, pausing to smile at Doc and Penny as he got out. "Got to get ready for round two." When his gaze got to Deagan his lips tightened into a thin line and he nodded. Deagan nodded back fractionally.

At the morgue Doc was met by two physicians from the Cornor's office. Both men looked grim, standing there in their scrubs. One of them, Dr. Ruskin, shook Doc's hand. "I'm concerned about what we might have," he said. "I appreciate you coming, Doctor. Perhaps with your extensive experience you might better be able to judge exactly what we were dealing with."

Ruskin led Doc into the examining room. Inside, he removed his jacket and shirt and slipped into a scrub top and apron. "You might want to put these on," Ruskin said, holding out a surgical mask and rubber gloves. Doc's amber eyes swept the other man's worried face as he pulled on the gloves.

Inside the refrigerated room eight nude bodies lay on stainless steel tables. They all looked shrunken and were speckled with purplish blotches. Dried blood stained the areas around their faces, necks and buttock. Two had been separated from the others and lay on a table next to the autopsy area.

"These are the last ones we did," Ruskin said. "I estimate that they've both been dead about twelve hours now. They were apparently the last ones to die. He was driving the ambulance when it crashed into the first floor of the Empire State Building." He pointed to the corpse on the right. "His apparent cause of death was hemorrhagic, just like the others. This one, however, shows no signs of the disease." Ruskin pointed to the neck of the body on the left. "Death was caused by strangulation. He was also wearing some sort of military- style uniform."

"And the others?" Doc asked.

"Naked. They were stored in the compartments, contained in body bags. They all show the same symptoms."

Doc put on a pair of protective glasses and gripped both sides of the incision, peeling apart the chest cavity of the dead man on the right. The man's internal organs lay in a bloody syrup practically unrecognizable.

"We tried to preserve them as best we could," Ruskin said. "All his organs seem to have . . . liquefied. It's the same in the others, but to a greater degree. I've never seen anything quite like it."

"Are you certain this man died only twelve hours ago?" Doc asked. "From the look of his liver and intestines he's been dead for several days."

"Yes, we noticed the sloughing of the intestines too," Ruskin said. "It's more pronounced in the other corpses. From the skin hemorrhaging and the orificial bleeding, we first assumed that it was bubonic plague, put no traces of Pasteurella Pestis could be found."

"I've never seen such rapid deterioration," Doc said. "I'll need to take some tissue samples back to my laboratory."

"Of course. We've already prepared some."

"You said that the rest of them were unclothed?" Doc asked. "From where were they being transported?"

"That's unknown," Ruskin said, handing Doc a set of syringes and test tubes. "It was a military ambulance, but we've been unable to trace its origin or destination."

"And this driver," Doc said, indicating the body on the table. "Did he have any identification?"

"None. Just some scraps of paper in his pockets and . . ." Doc looked at him.

"He'd written something in his own blood on the windshield," Ruskin said, handing Doc a black-and-white photograph. "An apparent death threat against you. That's another reason we felt it prudent to notify you.

Since your headquarters is in the same building that he crashed into."

The picture of the windshield showed *DOC ATLAS KILL*— written in a frantic scrawl. Doc showed no reaction to this. He merely scanned the body closer, passing his gloved fingers carefully over the man's forearm.

"It was apparently written with the man's own blood," Ruskin said.

"Have his fingerprints been sent to the FBI for identification purposes?" he asked.

Ruskin replied that they had.

Doc rotated the dead man's arm. "This appears to be a military tattoo."

"Yes. We sent a photo of it, along with the fingerprints, by special courier several hours ago."

"I'll need to examine their clothing," Doc said. "And any miscellaneous papers they had on them."

Ruskin indicated two paper bags under the table. Doc quickly and silently went through the contents. Then he said, "I'm finished here."

After taking extra care in cleaning up and ordering that the bodies be kept in a quarantined area, Doc met Penny and Deagan in the waiting room. Two men in suits were seated beside them.

Deagan jumped up as Doc entered and grinned. "Find anything out, Doc?" he asked.

Doc Atlas ignored the question, as was his custom in front of strangers. Realizing this, Deagan said, "Oh, Doc, it's okay. These guys are G-Men."

"Actually, we're Military Intelligence," one of the men said, standing. He looked to be in his mid-twenties, with a medium build and a somewhat pudgy-looking face. This was made more noticeable by his rather high forehead where the recession of his blond hair had already begun. "Frank Killjoy, Doctor Atlas. It's a pleasure to meet you. This is my partner Roy Otto." The second man, who was dark complexioned and smaller than Killjoy, bobbed his head. He had a long nose and a well-clipped mustache.

As Doc shook hands with both men, Deagan clapped Killjoy roughly on the back. "I was telling them that I spent a good deal of time in military intelligence until Pearl Harbor. Then I transferred back into the infantry. I told him it's too bad that his name wasn't Killroy, Doc. Then it woulda been plastered over half of Europe in the last war."

"That's the story of my life," Killjoy said. "Always missing greatness by a hair. Anyway, we found that the ambulance had been reported stolen from Camp Humphreys, upstate. We'd like to assist in the investigation."

"Thomas," Doc said. "It's imperative that we get this man identified as soon as possible. His prints have been sent in, but call and tell them to narrow their search to the records of men who served in the Hundred and First Cavalry Group."

Deagan nodded, then paused. "Hey, Doc, we were attached TDY to the one-oh-one during that Von Strohm thing, weren't we?"

Atlas nodded, then said, "I have to do some tests on these tissue samples in my laboratory. It should take me a few hours. I want you to check at this address regarding the man who was killed." He handed Deagan a slip of paper. "Dr. Ruskin can supply you with a picture. See if you can locate any information on him."

"This flophouse is in the bowery," Deagan said, looking at the address. "I'd better drop you off at home first, Penny."

"Not on your life," she said, glancing over his shoulder. "There's a story in all this. I can smell it."

"Very well, but meet me back at headquarters no later than six," Doc said. "I'll be busy in my laboratory. We have much to discuss, and time is of the essence."

"Say, wed like to tag along to that hotel," Killjoy said. "Probably be a good idea to have several of us going down to that area." He crammed his hat on his head. "If you don't mind, that is."

"Not at all," Deagan said. "The more the merrier."

"Great," Killjoy said, smiling. His teeth were small and slanted inward. "Say, can we ride together? We took a cab over here."

"Thomas, go pick up the LaSalle," Doc said. "The four of you will be more comfortable in it. I'll make my own way to headquarters." He turned and began walking down the hallway toward the door. Deagan ran to catch up to him.

"So what kind of case we working on here, Doc?" Deagan asked, leaning close.

Doc's lips tightened into a grim line. "Something very sinister, Thomas."

* * *

The bowery flophouse was a run-down hotel that had seen its heyday many decades before. Several unshaven men in worn looking suits sat in the lobby, and the desk area was enclosed by a wire barricade that ran from the counter to the ceiling. Behind it sat a grotesquely obese man eating a bag of potato chips and reading a girlie magazine. He ran his tongue over his teeth as Deagan, Penny, and the two G-men walked up. "Yeah, whatcha want?" the clerk said.

"Not too friendly is he?" Penny said.

"Let me handle this," Deagan answered. He turned to the clerk. "Say, mack, we'd like to know about a guy that was staying here. About five-ten, maybe one-sixty. In his thirties. Had a military tattoo right here." He pointed to his forearm.

"What's his name?"

Deagan smiled. "I used to know him as Joe, but that mighta been a nickname. I got a picture." He held up the morgue shot and the clerk's eyes narrowed.

"What the hell happened to him?" He stuffed some more potato chips into his mouth.

"He died," Deagan said. "Recognize him?"

The clerk's dark eyes narrowed as he glanced at Deagan for a moment. "You — ain't from the cops, are ya? Not with a skirt with ya."

Mad Dog looked at Penny, then turned back to the clerk. "You're right, I ain't a cop," he said. His big fingers traced the edge of the wire cage. "Now I hate to repeat myself, pal. So tell me about the guy in the picture."

"Ahh, go scratch yourself. I don't gotta tell you nothing, if I don't want to." He shoved another handful of potato chips into his mouth, then his eyes narrowed shrewdly. "But, on the other hand, maybe I *could* remember something if you made it worth my while." He rubbed his greasy index finger and thumb together.

Deagan smiled, then nodded slowly. He reached in his pants and took out his wallet, removing a dollar bill. The clerk's eyes lit up. But as he reached for it, Deagan pulled it back.

"Un-un, you first," he said.

"His name was Douglas Astor," the clerk said. "He stayed up in room five fifty-six." He shoveled more chips into his mouth.

"When's the last time you seen him?" Deagan asked.

The clerk's sloping shoulders shrugged. "He left about two weeks ago, with the rest of the them fellas that signed up for the special work."

"What special work?" Deagan asked. "Where'd they go?"

The clerk shook his head. "Upstate some place. There was these guys that came by, left one of these fliers asking if anybody was interested in doing some kinda special work. Pay was decent, and they guaranteed the men room and board. Even paid for their rooms here till the end of the month." He tilted the bag up, pouring the remaining crumbs into his mouth.

"How about we look through his room?" Deagan asked, holding the dollar near the opening in the cage for the man to take.

"Maybe for about twenty more of these," the clerk said with a laugh, quickly grabbing the bill. But Deagan's powerful fingers caught the man's wrist and bent back his hand. The big clerk tumbled forward, squealing in pain.

"Lemme go, mister. Lemme go," he said. "I told you what you wanted."

"Yeah, you did," Deagan said. "But you forgot something."

"No I didn't." The clerk grunted in pain.

"You forgot to give me that pass key."

The clerk fumbled around with a ring of keys on his belt, then shoved them through the opening.

"Which one is it?" Deagan asked, still bending the fat wrist farther back. The clerk sorted out one key with the pudgy fingers of his left hand. Deagan nodded, then released him after saying, "Thanks."

"You ain't got no right to go pushing me around like that," the clerk shouted, rubbing his wrist and staring at them through the wire cage.

"Consider it a lesson on the seven deadly sins," Deagan said, grinning as he tossed the keys in the air and caught them again. "You obviously didn't learn the one about gluttony, so I figured to give you a little help with greed."

Searching the room yielded nothing. In fact, it was obvious from talking to a few of the residents there that the clerk had sub-rented the rooms that had already been paid for by the men offering the special work detail. Several men, perhaps as many as fifteen, had signed up to go. None had returned as yet.

"Where's their stuff?" Penny asked.

One of the bums led them to a large storage closet and pointed. Deagan gave the man a dollar and used the ring of keys to open the door. Fifteen duffel bags had been stacked haphazardly in the space. Deagan sorted through them until he found *DOUGLAS ASTOR* stenciled on one of them. He opened it and dumped out the contents. Except for some clothes and several sets of old shoes, the only other item of interest was a small metal box. Inside, Deagan found a folded, yellowed newspaper clipping. Carefully, he opened it and was surprised to see a picture of Doc, dressed in his military uniform, staring back at him under the headline: *MAJOR ATLAS LEADS IOIST CAV IN RAID ON NAZI CASTLE.*

"I remember this mission," Deagan said. "I told Doc we was assigned to one-oh-one for TDY."

"Looks like we've got our victim identified," Killjoy said. "Roy," he said to his partner, "why don't you call in and see if there's any updates on that other stuff."

His long-nosed partner nodded and went down the stairs. Deagan, Penny, and Killjoy sorted through the rest of the bags, jotting down whatever information they could find.

Most of the bags contained worn, aromatic clothing, but very little in the way of personal papers. They had six more names when Otto came shuffling back up the stairs.

"They got a lead on who stole that ambulance, Frank," he said. "We got to run up to Camp Humphreys right away."

"You're both welcome to come along," Killjoy said, turning to Deagan. "I got a feeling this all ties together somehow."

"I'd say you're right about that, mack," Deagan said.

* * *

Deagan took the LaSalle through its paces as he drove out of the city and north on Route 9 toward the upstate location of Camp Humphreys. The sleek looking Cadillac seemed to hum as it reached cruising speed on the highway. After they'd crossed the Hudson River wooded areas quickly replaced buildings and towns as they neared Bear Mountain State Park. Killjoy sat up front beside Deagan, while Penny and the rat-faced Roy Otto sat in back. Penny was busily writing notes on her steno pad. She looked up and tapped Deagan on the shoulder. "Hey, what time is it?" she said.

Deagan glanced at his watch and said, "Four-thirty. Why?"

"Didn't Doc say to meet him back a HQ by six?"

"Yeah, he did," Deagan said. "But he'll understand since we're following a hot tip."

"You can call him from the fort if you like," Killjoy said.

"Yeah, thanks," Deagan said with a grin. "Say, I been meaning to ask. How come you guys are assigned stateside when there's a war going on?"

Killjoy lifted his eyebrows nonchalantly. "It ain't a war. It's a police action."

"Come on," Deagan said. "I'm serious."

Killroy looked at him for a moment. "Well, actually it's because of these hearings in Washington. The House UnAmerican Activities Committee."

"Huh?" Mad Dog said. "I thought the FBI would be handling them kind of things?"

"Actually," Killjoy said slowly. "We're sort of attached to a special unit that assists the Bureau."

"We report directly to J. Edgar himself," Roy said from the back seat. "We belong to a very special branch."

Deagan caught Penny's smirk in the mirror.

"You know," Deagan said, "I used to think that these hearings were a good thing, with the reds having the bomb now and all. But what I can't understand is why they'd want to subpoena a man like Doc. Did I tell you guys that me and him served together in the last war?"

"Yeah. Several times," Killjoy said, glancing out the window.

"I knew his dad, too," Deagan said. He paused and squinted. "Hey, looks like something up ahead."

Perhaps a hundred yards ahead, two cars sat facing each other blocking both lanes.

"It must be an accident," Killjoy said. "Pullover there, I'll see if anybody's hurt."

Deagan slowed to a stop and the G-men jumped out. As they ran up toward the two cars, Deagan stared at the scene. "Maybe I'd better go help too," he said, starting to get out. But suddenly an olive drab half-ton truck pulled out from the thick shrubbery on the side of the road and blocked the LaSalle to the rear.

"What the hell?" Deagan muttered as he glanced in the rear-vision mirror. He looked ahead and saw Killjoy and his partner standing with their hands on their heads, men in military field uniforms pointing weapons at them.

"Damn! It's an ambush, Penny!" Deagan yelled. He was attempting to jam the LaSalle into gear when a group of men, led by an extremely large blond man, suddenly surrounded their car. The leader pointed a Carbine in Deagan's face and said with a thick German accent, "Get out of da car."

"We'd better do what he says, Tom," Penny said. One of the other men pulled open the rear door and pointed a rifle at her as well.

"Get out of da car. NOW!" the big man shouted. He was huge and had a thick, powerful build.

"Ah, keep yer pants on, Fritz," Deagan said, reaching down with his foot to press a button on the floor near the pedals.

The big man ripped open the door and grabbed Deagan's arm, pulling him onto the road in one smooth motion. Deagan replied with a looping punch, which the blond man slipped with the aplomb of an experienced fighter. He brought the butt of the rifle down on Deagan's head, sending him to his knees. He struggled for consciousness, but the big German sent the stock crashing down again. The last sound Mad Dog heard as the blackness swept over him was Penny's scream.

* * *

Doc's Laboratory
New York City

After several hours of painstaking, uninterrupted work, Doc had finally isolated the microbe. It was smaller than any known bacterium, so he had quickly eliminated any suspicion that it may have been a new form of bubonic plague. That meant it was some form of unknown virus. After pausing to review the latest texts on genetic recombination by Delbruck and Hershey, which dealt with the different strains of bacteriophages infecting the same cell, Doc placed a newly cultured slide into his prototypical electron microscope. A microbe appeared on the screen invading the host cell, first by penetrating the wall, and then sending in its own genetic material to take over the metabolic activity to reproduce itself. The host cell soon began producing replicants, and the virus then moved on to the next cell at an incredible rate.

Doc adjusted the power after transferring some of the solution on a separate slide. The image of the killer virus took shape on the screen: a polyhedrally-shaped head, housing the genetic core and a long twisting tail made of protein.

It was *filo* virus—Latin for thread. He'd read about them, but this was the first time he'd ever seen one. The tail cut through the host's cell wall and, one by one, the host's body began to replicate the virus, destroying the cell in the process. When enough critical cells died, so did the host. The perfect killing machine. But ironically, without the host, the virus could not reproduce. Thus, when the host perished, the virus had killed itself, or rather put itself into a state of limbo until the arrival of the next host.

Doc stared grimly at the screen with grudging admiration of the angular symmetry of the microbe's powerful architecture. If this were spread aerially, he thought, it could decimate the entire city in a matter of days.

* * *

Ace paid the cabbie and headed for the main entrance of the Empire State Building. His knee felt stiff and he leaned on his cane as he moved, his walk seeming to echo the frustration that he was feeling after searching through the congressional transcripts. Deagan's words, that it was up to them to do something, kept ringing in his ears. But after spending the day searching for some legal footing, he'd been unable to find anything.

"Good evening, Mr. Assante," O'Bannion the doorman said to him. "Give my regards to Dr. Atlas when you see him."

Ace nodded wearily. As he went to the private express elevator that went directly up to Doc's floor, three men in suits approached him. One held out a wallet with a card encased in plastic, a gold badge on the opposite flap.

"Edward Assante?" the man said. "We're with the FBI."

Ace used his passkey to activate the elevator. The doors opened. "What can I do for you?" he asked wearily.

"You're the attorney representing Dr. Michael G. Atlas?"

Ace nodded.

"We have a warrant to search the offices and headquarters of Doc Atlas," the man said. "Under the Subversive Activities Act. "

"I'd be very interested in reviewing that document," Ace said.

"We'll give you that opportunity," said another of the men, holding up a briefcase. They stepped into the elevator car with Ace and he placed his key in the slot. The car rushed upward at an incredible rate of speed.

"Damn, what a ride," one of the men said.

"You'll experience it again on the way down after this ridiculous exercise is over," Ace said. "This is outrageous. What is it that you hope to find?"

As the elevator doors opened at Doc's floor, the man with the briefcase stepped out and began to open it. Ace's attention was momentarily diverted and the man standing directly behind him swung a blackjack against Ace's right ear. Assante staggered forward, his hat falling from his head. The man with the sap followed, crisscrossing the heavy leather over Ace's left ear. He slumped to the floor.

The man holding the briefcase pulled out a Mauser with a rifle stock. He pointed to the glass door that said simply, *DR. MICHAEL G. ATLAS* in gold embossed letters. The second man, who was also now holding a gun, went to the door and twisted the knob. The door swung open.

"Harry, you stay with that one," the man with the Mauser said. "Come on, Burt."

Burt nodded and the two men entered the waiting room of Doc Atlas Headquarters. A large stainless steel desk was in the middle of the room, and several comfortable looking chairs sat on either side of the entrance. Solid wooden doors were on either wall. The two men exchanged glances.

"Which way you think is the lab?" Burt said.

"Let's try 'em both while we still got the element of surprise," the one holding the Mauser said. "You take that one."

Burt moved to the door on the left, but as he reached for the knob he heard a wispy sound and then thud. Doc Atlas, who had wedged himself near the ceiling by extending his body between the doorframe and the perpendicular wall, had suddenly jumped down in back of the intruder. Burt attempted to turn, bringing his gun hand around, but Doc's left arm whipped outward, the edge of his palm catching the man's wrist. Doc's right hand slammed with tremendous force into the man's gut. The air went out of him with a whoosh.

Whirling, Doc twisted Burt in front of him as the Mauser exploded. The bullets ripped into Burt's body as Doc's hand closed over the dying man's pistol. The man with the Mauser continued to fire, but as the rounds strayed upward toward Doc's head, the golden avenger sighted Burt's pistol and squeezed the trigger.

The bullet caught the second assailant between the eyes and he was dead before he hit the floor. Doc strode over toward him, then suddenly looked to his right to see the third man, Harry, pointing a forty-five semi-automatic at him. Harry's finger tightened on the trigger, but he abruptly jerked forward, his mouth twisting into a brutal grimace, a metallic point extending from the center of his chest. As he twisted to the floor Doc saw a bloodied Ace Assante standing there, the bottom half of his sword cane in his hand.

Doc rushed forward and kicked the pistol away from the dead man's fingers.

"Ace, are you all right?" he asked, immediately fingering the bloody welts on Assante's head.

"You tell me, Doc."

After a few moments of examination, Doc said, "Your injuries appear to be superficial in nature. Contusions and lacerations to the scalp." He shone a penlight into Ace's eyes. "Any blurred vision?"

"Only when I laugh at my own stupidity." Ace grinned. "These idiots claimed to be FBI, but I should've known it didn't smell right. I figured you'd see us coming up on the elevator camera monitor anyway."

Doc nodded. "Come on, I'll clean and dress those wounds. Do you feel well enough to accompany me?"

"Where to?"

"I'm afraid Penelope and Thomas are in grave danger," Doc said. "I received the emergency beacon broadcast from the LaSalle."

"If Tom and Penny are in trouble," Ace said, "Let's not wait."

* * *

When Deagan's eyes flickered open he saw Penny's face looking down at him, then her bare shoulders, and he realized his head was lying on her lap. He tried to get up and felt the searing pain sweep through his head and he recoiled.

It was then that he realized that he was clad only in his underwear.

"Be careful, Tom," Penny said. "I was worried about you. Your head took an awful bang."

"What? Where the hell are we?" He looked at her and saw that she only had on her brasserie and underpants. Ordinarily, such a sight would have delighted him, but this time it only filled him with trepidation. It meant that whoever had captured them was serious. And experienced at handling prisoners. He got to his feet and took a few steps, looking down at his bare feet.

"They took our clothes," she said. "Put us in this room. I haven't seen Killjoy or Otto since they brought us here."

"Where's this?" Mad Dog asked. He surveyed the windowless room with the solid metal door.

"It looks like some sort of military compound," Penny said. "I couldn't see too much on the way because they kept us in that truck, but when we got out it looked like some sort of camp."

"Can't be Camp Humphreys," Deagan said. "More likely it's some isolated training facility or something." The floor was slick tile, the walls cinder block. He moved to the door and ran his fingers over it. "No hinges on this side. Door's solid metal. Deadbolt-lock. Looks like we're trapped here till the cavalry arrives." He managed a weak grin.

The door suddenly opened and the big blond man stood there with two assistants in fatigue uniforms devoid of insignias.

"Well, lookie what we got here," Deagan said. "Fritz and his toy soldiers."

"*Komm hier,*" the big man said. One of the assistants pointed a pistol at Deagan. "Girl too."

"We'd better do as they say, Tom," Penny said, standing and crossing her arms to conceal her breasts as much as possible. The eyes of the two assistants were glued to her, but the big man kept his focused on Deagan. They all went down a hallway and into a room. The long, vertical blinds were still open and the view through the windows told Deagan that they were at least three stories up. He saw two men in lab coats standing near some long tables that contained a cluster of bottles, test tubes, and beakers. The bluish flame from a Bunsen burner slowly heated some sphere-like flask, which in turn was being titrated into a complex construction of tubes. Several stainless steel tables sat off in one corner with metal manacles dangling from the sides.

"Bring them over here, Hans," one of the men said. He was bald and short in stature. The gold rimmed glasses and wrinkles gave his face a sinister cast. His voice had a foreign sound to it.

"Professor Dortchmann, we need to discuss this," the other man said in a voice distinctly American. He was taller than Dortchmann and several years younger. His thick glasses were encased in tortoise shell frames, and his black hair was flecked with gray. The man's face looked taught and pinched.

"What is to discuss?" Dortchmann said. He turned and uttered something in German to Hans, who prodded Deagan with a pistol.

Mad Dog reluctantly hopped on the steel table and Hans immediately fastened the manacles around his wrists and ankles. Then they escorted Penny to the adjacent table and secured her in similar fashion. Dortchmann looked at her with approval. "It's too bad we have run out of other test subjects," he said. "This one would serve a useful purpose otherwise."

"Doctor," the second scientist said. "I must strongly protest this."

Dortchmann turned to him and laughed.

"You Americans, so squeamish when it suits your purpose," he said. "If only you'd waited until we had the British on their knees before you'd entered the war. Then you would have had no base from which to launch your invasion of the Fatherland. We would be *your* masters now."

"Now see here," the other man said.

"No, Dr. Cobb," Dortchmann said, pointing at him. "*You* see here. We are so close now to perfecting the serum, we can not be deterred by your vagaries."

"But doing experiments on bowery bums is one thing," Cobb said, lowering his voice to a harsh whisper. "These people are—"

"These people are the final documentation for my greatest achievement," Dortchmann shouted. "Your government did not take pains to bring us here so we could debate about trivialities. Not with the hoards of barbarian Russians and Chinese poised at your gates. Imagine, a way to conquer the most powerful armies without even firing a shot. The Satan Plague . . . The country that perfects it first will rule the world."

Cobb cast a quick glance toward Penny and Mad Dog, then looked away.

"I thought you would see it my way," Dortchmann said, smiling triumphantly. "Now prepare the prescribed dosage."

He walked across the room and rubbed his hands over Deagan's muscular arms and legs. "This man is very strong. It will be interesting to see how long it takes before he dies."

Mad Dog glanced quickly at Penny, who had a look of abject horror on her face.

"Listen," Deagan said. "You'll never get away with this. You ever hear of Doc Atlas? Well, we're good friends of his. Anything happens to either of us, he'll track your dirty Nazi hide to the ends of the earth. . . "

Dortchmann chuckled softly.

"Good. Maintain your fighting spirit, " he said. "You will need it over the course of the next few hours. And as for your much vaunted Doc Atlas, I'm sure if he were not already dead, Hans would enjoy the challenge of destroying such an overrated American legend."

Hans, who had been standing near-by, smiled broadly and said, "Ya."

* * *

New York City
Near the Hudson River

The lengthening shadows of dusk were descending by the time Doc and Ace got to the private hanger on the small airfield that housed several of Doc's planes. He also had a big warehouse situated on the Hudson River, giving him the option of leaving the city by air or water. Doc told Ace to do a pre-flight inspection of the Pegasus IV, his single-engine Navion Rangemaster. The plane sat five and was ideal for short excursions over the countryside.

Doc slipped inside a locker room adjacent to the hanger area. When he emerged, he was wearing a black nylon jump suit and had a military-style utility belt strapped to his waist.

He chambered a round in his Government Model Colt Forty-five, snapped on the safety, and inserted another round into the magazine.

"I guess we're expecting more trouble, right, Doc?" Ace asked, watching him.

Doc ignored the question. He grabbed a parachute and began checking the rigging. When Ace had completed his checklist, Doc hoisted the parachute and set it inside the plane's cabin. After pressing the button to raise the enormous overhead door at the far end of the expansive hanger, Doc scanned the rapidly darkening sky, and went back inside the locker room. He came out with two black plastic helmets. On the front of each was a cumbersome looking set of goggles.

"We may need these," Doc said, handing one of the helmets to Ace. "It'll be completely dark by the time we reach our target area."

"And where's that?"

"The beacon signal is coming from the north," Doc said. They both entered the plane and taxied it into position on the runway. Doc pressed a radio transmitter that closed the doors of the hanger. As they approached the end of the runway, with the tree line looming beyond it, the engine sputtered slightly then caught as they rose into the open air.

"No problem taking off into that wind, but I hope we don't have to fight it all the way north," Ace said with a grin.

But Doc wasn't smiling. His features were as implacable as always, but Ace sensed his mood and said nothing else.

*   *   *

The beacon signal was strongest over a heavily wooded area near Bear Mountain State Park. Despite the growing darkness, Doc and Ace could make out a small road leading into a thatch of trees. As the Pegasus looped over it, a small compound became visible.

"Do a wide arc and circle back at 13,000 feet," Doc said as he began strapping on his parachute.

"Doc, you're not going to try a jump into that, are you?" Ace said, scanning the dense underbrush. "Not with wind like this."

"I should be all right," Doc said. "Regardless, we haven't time for an alternative plan. Penelope and Thomas are in extreme danger at this very moment."

Ace sighed and banked left, beginning the arc.

"As soon as I've exited, contact the State Police for assistance, then make your way back," Doc said. He went to the side door and twisted the handle.

"I will, Doc," Ace said, mustering a smile. "And I'll be back. Even if I have to land this crate on the highway and taxi back." He gave Doc the thumbs-up gesture. Doc nodded and pulled the door open.

Snapping the goggles in place, Atlas jumped out of the door. He sailed downward controlling his descent by angling his body against various wind currents. With his special night vision goggles in place, he could scan the dense terrain below. He checked his altimeter: 2500 feet. Doc straightened out and soared further, estimating that he'd have perhaps 60 to 90 seconds before he'd have to open his chute. That would be cutting it close, but he didn't want to alert anyone on the ground who may have heard the plane of his imminent arrival. Twisting slightly, he angled off toward the compound. Lights were visible in some of the buildings acting like landing signals for him.

He let himself free-fall until 1300 feet, which was about as close as he dared, then he pulled the rip cord. The chute popped open above him and he glanced upward scanning its square shape. It was made of black silk, so as to be practically indiscernible from the ground. Doc's special glasses allowed him to verify that the panels had opened correctly. He felt the drag as he floated, wishing that he could have simply flown down at the free-fall speed. Maybe someday, he thought as he steered toward the small open expanse in the forest. At 500 feet he checked the layout of the compound, memorizing it. Several Quonset huts of varying sizes surrounded a larger, four-story brick structure. A sturdy cyclone fence topped by concertina wire wound around the perimeter, the only access point being a front gate.

Doc adjusted the toggles to steer himself toward the large building. Perhaps if he could land on top of it, he could remain undetected. Suddenly something red flashed from an area near the tree-line below. At first Doc thought it was a muzzle flash, but quickly realized it wasn't. The dot flashed again, and Doc could see two figures. Sentries smoking . . . a sure sign of a poorly protected perimeter. Hopefully the rest of the night crew would be equally lax.

Suddenly a burst of wind tore Doc away from his targeted landing zone. He pulled quickly at the toggles, trying to compensate, but he was too close to the trees. Glancing below him he saw the branches reaching up for him like fingers of a savage mob. His boots brushed the first small tendrils, followed by the solid, heavier resistance. Doc locked his legs together and brought his arms up over his face.

* * *

Dortchmann had donned rubber gloves and a surgical mask, but his sinister little eyes still stared ominously from behind his glasses. Deagan strained at the manacles, the muscles in his arms tensing like steel cables. The Nazi smiled at this and snorted out a quick, harsh laugh. Dr. Cobb came in with two capped syringes on a tray. He, too, was clad in surgical clothing. Behind his glasses his eyes peeped out nervously over his mask.

"You son of a . . ." Deagan started to say. "At least let her go." He nodded his head at Penny. "She don't have nothing to do with any of this."

"Ah, such chivalry," Dortchmann said. "But if you would know the truth, I haven't really had the opportunity recently to experiment on many women. At least not in this country. I'm sure this will prove . . . enlightening."

Deagan thrashed and strained at the bonds, but they held fast. Dortchmann grabbed one of the syringes and went to Deagan, who continued to squirm.

"Hans," Dortchmann said.

The big German came over and gripped Mad Dog's arm, crouching over it for leverage. Dortchmann instructed Dr. Cobb to tie a rubber hose around Deagan's upper arm, but the American hesitiated.

"Come, come, *herr doktor*," Dortchmann said. "This is no time to lose your nerve. We are so close."

"Don't do it, mack!" Deagan shouted. "Don't listen to this Nazi butcher." He struggled against the powerful Hans, but was unable to move his arm.

Dammit, this guy's strong, Mad Dog thought. Maybe even stronger than Doc.

Cobb reluctantly tied the band around Deagan's arm. Dortchmann indicated Penny by a toss of his head. Cobb started to speak, but Dortchmann cut him off with an explosive German phrase.

Despite Penny's protestations, Cobb's gloved fingers wrapped around the delicate-looking skin of her upper arm and wound the brown ligature in place.

"Doc Atlas will get you for this, you bastards," she spat.

"Hey, I'm begging ya, do what you want to me, but leave her out of it," Deagan said. He glanced up into Hans grinning face, then down to his forearm on which the veins were beginning to stand out.

"Record that I'm administering two mililiters of solution into test subject one at," Dortchmann glanced at the clock on the wall, "nine-oh-five, P.M." Cobb made the notation on the chart without looking up. Deagan felt the pinch of the needle as it sank into his vein. Dortchmann dropped the syringe on the tray and stepped around to Penny. Hans released Deagan's arm and followed. His big hands explored Penny's body roughly before gripping her right arm.

"Get your filthy hands off her," Deagan spat.

"You would do well to save your strength," Dortchmann said. "You may prolong your life by several hours."

"I'll live long enough to see you die, Nazi," Deagan growled.

"I sincerely doubt it," Dortchmann said with a laugh. He turned to Penny and patted her forearm. "You are an exceptionally beautiful woman," he said, picking up the second syringe. "I truly regret this, but it is just another of the many sacrifices I have made in the name of science."

Penny's eyes widened as she saw the end of the needle plunge into her arm. She managed enough pluck to spit into big Hans' face. He wiped at his cheek briefly, then slammed the edge of his hand across her temple. The last thing she remembered before passing out was a flash of him staring down at her, his grimace showing the millimeter gap between his front teeth.

* * *

"I think it came from over here," one of the guards said. He shone a flashlight over in the direction of the tree line.

"Ah, I didn't hear nothing," the second man said. "He paused and slung his rifle over his shoulder and took out another cigarette. Canting his head to light it, he had just snapped his lighter closed when the huge shadow seemed to leap out of the darkness at him.

"What? Hans?" the sentry said in the second before Doc's fist smashed into the man's gut. He doubled over, and Doc followed through with a quick chop to the throat.

The first sentry heard his partner's grunt and whirled, seeing only Doc's gloved fist milliseconds before impact. Stunned the man reeled backward, attempting to bring up his rifle. But before he could raise the rifle, it was ripped from his hands. An arm encircled the man's throat and then he was conscious only of Doc's voice whispering in his ear.

"If you want to live, tell me the truth," Doc said. "Where are the people who were captured earlier?"

"The ones in the LaSalle?" the man said, his words strained by Doc's powerful grip. "They're in the main building." He pointed at the three story lighted structure. "There."

"Where at in the building?"

"I dunno," the man said. He felt the iron grip tighten around his neck and quickly added, "Probably up in the lab. They take everybody to the lab eventually. There's a big holding pen on the second floor, and the lab's upstairs."

After inquiring as to the whereabouts and number of the rest of the guard staff, Doc increased the pressure on the man's carotid arteries, causing unconsciousness in a matter of seconds.

* * *

Dortchmann packed his pipe while Cobb nervously puffed on a cigarette. The enormous Hans sat impassively, watching Penny and Deagan. Dortchmann flicked his cylindrical lighter and held it over the bowl of his pipe. "Do you want to retire for the night, Doctor?" His tone was imbued with a condescending amusement.

Pursing his lips, Cobb stared at him, then shook his head.

"If my calculations are correct, it will be approximately forty minutes before the initial symptoms appear," Dortchmann said.

He strolled over to Penny, who had since regained consciousness, and fondled her breast casually through the fabric of her brassiere.

"You will soon be developing a general weakness along with a sudden headache which will increase in severity, my dear," he said. "Ah, but excuse me, you probably already have one of those because of Hans." He chuckled showing yellowed, corroded teeth. In German he said, "You must be more careful with our guinea pigs. We no longer have the luxury of the *Judisches*."

Hans smirked.

"What did you say?" Cobb asked.

Dortchmann smiled benevolently. "Nothing important, *herr* doctor. Nothing important."

Cobb stubbed out his cigarette angrily and started to speak. A sudden roar of noise, followed by an orange flash, lit up the western windows.

Doc, thought Deagan. It's gotta be Doc.

Hans rose and immediately adjusted the long vertical blinds, peering cautiously out a corner of the glass.

"An explosion of a truck in the main yard," he said. "Check with the guards," Dortchmann said.

The big man nodded and strode to the door.

"This is it for you, Nazi," Deagan said. "Your ticket's punched now. Doc Atlas is here."

Dortchmann reached into the pocket of his lab coat and removed a small Luger pistol. He walked over to Deagan and shoved the barrel against Mad Dog's nose.

"Do you have something more to say?" Dortchmann asked. "Perhaps you'd like to beg for your life?"

"Go ahead and pull that trigger, Fritz, cause I'd see you in hell first," Deagan sneered.

Dortchmann pressed the gun harder into Deagan's face, then withdrew it.

"This pistol was given to me by an SS officer who used it to exterminate *Judisches* after they were of no further use in the camps." He glared at Deagan, then said, "I'm sorely tempted to use it on you, but my experiment must take precedence for now. Besides, you imbecile, but I shall enjoy watching you die slowly." The Nazi smiled. "How is it you Americans say it? By centimeters?" He turned away and went to the windows.

"We use inches in this country, Nazi," Deagan said.

Dortchmann smirked. "By inches, then."

Deagan managed a quick glance at Penny and winked. "Don't worry, kid," he said. "Doc's here now."

She tried bravely to speak, but no sound came out. Her eyes returned to the purplish blot in the crease of her arm.

Oh please, please, God, don't let it be too late for us, she thought. Please, please, please.

Dortchmann approached the window and glanced out at the orange glow of the fiery truck. Something seemed wrong with the scene. They had at least half a dozen guards on night watch, but he saw no one around the burning vehicle. Just as he turned to speak to Cobb, a figure seemed to hurl through the windows above him. Dortchmann immediately leveled the Luger and began firing. Penny recoiled in horror as she saw the bullets striking the figure who was now half-hanging inside, his arms seeming to flail between the heavy vertical blinds, dancing against the shards of glass. Deagan glanced over there, too, ready to call a belated warning to the figure he at first thought must be Doc. Then he saw the hair was dark instead of light.

Across the room at the other set of windows a gloved fist smashed through the pane above the locking mechanism, and as the window slid open at an oblique angle, Doc Atlas nimbly slipped between the space, the end of a rope still in his left hand. Doc jerked the rope once more as he dropped silently to the floor and the figure caught in the glass jerked upward, like a drunken marionette. Dortchmann continued to fire until the ejection port clicked upward on the Luger, signaling that it was empty. Turning suddenly, the Nazi caught sight of Doc running at him from across the room. Struggling vainly, Dortchmann's finger clawed in the pocket of his lab coat for the second magazine.

He had it inserted when Doc seized him and, using the momentum from his run, spun the Nazi toward the table cluttered with test tubes.

Realizing he had misjudged the man's weight, Doc saw Dortchman fly over the tabletop, knocking the glass network into disarray. The beaker that had been heating over the Bunsen burner shattered, covering Dortchmann with the hot liquid. He screamed as the Bunsen burner fell on its side, igniting a pool of liquid from one of the dark beakers. The flame twisted like a serpent over the tabletop, and exploded into a fireball when it reached Dortchmann's lab coat. Screaming incomprehensibly he began running around the room, then veered for the door, almost totally engulfed in flames. He tried to open the door, then flung himself against the wall several times before collapsing in a blazing heap. The fire seemed to wind from the table top and suddenly the vertical blinds were ablaze.

Doc moved to the tables with Penny and Deagan.

"I knew you'd come," Mad Dog said with a wide grin. "Who"s your stand-in?" He nodded toward the dangling figure hanging partially through the window. His arm caught against the confining shackle as he tried to rise up.

"One of the sentries," Doc said. "His neck was broken earlier in a struggle." Doc reached over and caressed Penny's face briefly, then put both his hands on the manacle on Deagan's right wrist. The muscles seemed almost ready to rip through his shirt as he strained. His mouth twisted into an uncharacteristic grimace, and the chain securing the shackle broke free. Deagan reached across and was pulling on his left wrist.

"I'll give you a hand with this one," Mad Dog said. "We'd better hurry before this whole place goes up. Gimme your gun and I'll cover you."

"I lost it when I unexpectedly hit some trees during my jump," Doc said. He began to grasp the second manacle when a dark figure hurled through the doorway at incredible speed and knocked the golden avenger to the floor.

"Hans!" Deagan said. He reached over with his free hand and tried to smack the Nazi, but the other man merely swatted the blow away.

But the split second was all Doc needed to recover his footing. He settled into a fighting crouch as Hans rushed forward. Doc landed a two-punch combination, but the powerful German managed to grab him in a bear-hug. They went to the floor, Han's arms still squeezing Atlas.

"Doc, stay on your feet," Deagan shouted. "He out weighs ya. He'll use his weight to smother you."

The two men struggled viciously, Doc attempting to break the hold by pounding his fists into Hans's sides. Finally, with a grimace, Doc reached up and placed his own hands over the big German's. All movement seemed to stop. Doc's face darkened a shade, and suddenly he was free, holding his opponent's wrists. Rolling away Doc tried to get to his feet, but the wily Hans managed to execute a foot sweep, which dropped Doc on his side. The two big men scurried for position on their knees.

Penny felt a hand on her arm and glanced away from the struggle to see Dr. Cobb fumbling with some keys by her wrist.

"What are you doing?" she demanded.

"We've got to get out of here. There's benzene and other solvents in those dark bottles," he said, nodding his head toward the cluster of broken glass. "When the flames reach the storage cabinets, the whole lab will explode." After inserting a key into the manacle securing her left wrist, he reached across and unlocked her right one. Then he went to her feet. Penny sat up abruptly and grabbed the keys from the fumbling professor. "Give me those," she said. She unlocked the shackles around her ankles and swung her legs down.

"Please," Cobb said, " I was only trying to help."

"You've already helped enough," Penny said derisively.

She went to Deagan's side and began unlocking his bonds. There was a sudden crash as the heavy blinds fell to the floor in a burning pile. Grayish smoke was beginning to fill the room. Deagan freed himself and sat up.

Both Doc and Hans were on their feet now, arms locked together like two wrestlers, each slamming the other's body into whatever solid object he could. Doc made his move first, pulling low for a split second, then jamming his foot into the big German's stomach. Hans flew over as Doc dropped on his back and executed a perfect judo throw. Rolling to his feet, Doc was on Hans quickly, securing the bigger man's neck in a strangle-hold. A few rasping breaths seemed to escape as the Nazi struggled to break Doc's grip. The smoke had thickened noticeably as the death struggle continued. Flames traveled up the window

FAUROTE '98

frames to the ceiling, crackling over the sound of shattering glass. Hans plunged several elbow blows back into Doc's abdomen, then delivered a crushing groin blow. Stunned, Doc lost his grip on the choke-hold, and watched the powerful German slip away. Marshaling all his strength, Doc leaped and delivered a lunging kick, which sent Hans sailing over one of the lab tables. He rose unsteadily seconds later the muscles of his back seeming ready to burst through the dark fabric of his sweater. His head lolled over to one side, and he glanced at Atlas with half- closed eyes. A garbled utterance bubbled from his throat, exposing a protruding wedge of rounded glass when he turned to face them. His legs twisted underneath him as he fell. Deagan grabbed Cobb and called to Doc, "Come on. It's getting too bad in here."

The smoke suddenly strangled away their breath as they moved toward the door. Doc seemed to recover quickly, but the others were hacking and coughing as they went. Suddenly the door opened and Killjoy was there.

"Atlas, this way," he shouted.

They made for the door, the smoke trailing after them like wispy tendrils. Killjoy let the door slam behind them and started down the stairs. "Come on," he said. "This place is gonna blow. I've got a truck waiting to take us out of here."

Breathing was easier in the stairwell as they went down. The cool night air rushed over them, and they fell to their knees, coughing and vomiting. Doc urged them onward, away from the building, picking up Penny and carrying her along. Behind them the night sky exploded into yellow flames as the percussive wave of the laboratory explosion rippled over them. Turning, they watched as the building imploded, the walls crumbling inward upon themselves. Deagan still had one of his big hands rolled around the collar of Cobb's lab coat. After a few moments, they recovered enough to stand erect, and Doc immediately stripped off his shirt and handed it to Penny, who was standing there with her arms crossed in front of her breasts. Doc motioned to Deagan and Mad Dog grabbed Cobb's head and forcibly averted his eyes as Penny slipped into the garment. She still looked terrified.

"Doc, this S.O.B. and that damn Nazi injected me and Penny with something," Deagan said.

Doc's face showed a look of frozen horror.

"No, wait—" Cobb said.

Deagan tightened his grip and raised his arm, forcing Cobb on his tiptoes.

"You'd better come up with something to undo what you did," Deagan growled, "Or I'll snap your neck like a twig."

"Please," Cobb said. His voice was a whimper.

Penny turned to Doc. "Darling, there's an antidote, isn't there?"

Doc reached over and seized Cobb by the throat, pulling their faces inches apart. The Golden Avenger looked ready to tear the man limb from limb.

"Stop. Wait," Cobb muttered. "They weren't injected with the virus. I substituted distilled water in the syringes. I intended to release them later, and help them escape."

"You'd better be telling the truth," Doc said, releasing his grip. The way he'd said it told Cobb that he was a dead man if he was lying.

"Believe me," he said, "they would already be experiencing the first phase of debilitating weakness if they'd been injected with the virus."

"I don't feel weak at all," Deagan said. He grabbed Cobb by the collar and lifted him off his feet. "See?"

"I swear to you, my word as a scientist," Cobb said.

"Some scientist," Deagan said. "Playing patty-cake with a Nazi war criminal. How'd that guy get in this country anyway?"

"That's a good question," Killjoy said. "And I'll sure get to the bottom of it when I get Dr. Cobb back to Washington."

Killjoy's partner, Ray Otto, opened the door of a near-by truck and asked if they were ready to leave.

"We'd better make tracks," Killjoy said. "No telling how many more bogey men will come out of the woodwork."

"I believe I've subdued all the guards," Doc said. "There were only half a dozen or so."

The front gate banged open and several black and white Fords came in, oscillating red lights on their roofs.

"This is the State Police," an amplified voice said from one of the squads. "Put up your hands. You are surrounded."

"That should be Ace," Doc said.

"You know, for once I'm kinda glad to see that shyster making one of his grand-stand entrances," Deagan said with a grin.

"I'll take Dr. Cobb into custody now," Killjoy said, reaching for the scientist while holding out a pair of handcuffs.

"I think not," Doc said. He quickly stepped forward and twisted Killjoy's arm behind his back. "Thomas!" Doc said, nodding toward Otto.

Deagan leaped forward and floored Otto with a quick overhand right.

"What the hell is this, Atlas?" Killjoy said. "We're both on the same side."

"Whatever side you're actually on is dubious," Doc said, snapping the handcuffs over Killjoy's wrists. "As is your association with the government."

"What are you talking about?" Killjoy said. "Didn't I just help to save your lives?"

"Hardly," Doc said, pulling a large Colt, semi-automatic forty-five caliber pistol from a holster on Killjoy's belt. He strode over and frisked the unconscious Otto, removing a pistol from his pants as well. "I was initially suspicious of your convenient appearance at the morgue, especially in view of the somewhat cryptic message that the dying man attempted to scrawl on the windshield in his own blood. The police perceived it as a threat against me, but I believe the man was actually trying to warn me, by writing your name." Doc snapped a second pair of handcuffs over Otto's wrists. "Then when your confederates arrived to attack me at my headquarters, I knew for certain. And you undoubtedly orchestrated the capture of my friends also. No one else could have known our involvement or locations. You obviously weren't in captivity here."

"Hey," Deagan said. "I was wondering how they knew exactly where to ambush us." He moved forward to Killjoy, doubling up his huge fists. "Why I oughta give you a knuckle sandwich."

"What you ought to do is get some pants on," Ace said, peering from around the front of the truck. "Before somebody mistakes you for a striped-ass ape that escaped from the zoo."

Deagan grinned. "Good to see you too, shyster."

"Are we really all right?" Penny asked, massaging the center of her arm. "I mean as far as the injection?"

"I'll do blood tests as soon as we're back at headquarters to be sure," Doc said patting her on the shoulder.

"I swear, you're not infected," Cobb said. His gaze went to the ground. "In the beginning I justified it as serving my country . . . Serving the greater good. But then I realized that we'd lost all that along the way. When you two were captured, I just couldn't let that madman kill you."

"Was he really a Nazi?" Penny asked.

Cobb nodded.

"But how *did* he get in this country?" she said.

"Cobb, you fool," Killjoy said. "Keep your damn mouth shut."

"It was a deal we made with the devil," Cobb said. "Their freedom in exchange for them completing the experiments they were working on at the end of the war. They were so advanced. At first it seemed a small price to pay. Only now I realize that my soul went with it."

* * *

Senator Joseph McCarthy's mouth twisted into a dark line on his rotund face as he scowled at them momentarily before stepping out of the hallway and slamming the door. Deagan and Assante exchanged knowing smiles and shook hands. Then they ambled back to where Doc and Penny stood.

"Well, it's official," Ace said, clapping his hands together. "They're quietly dropping Doc's subpoena to testify before the committee."

"Great," Penny said, smiling. "I'm impressed. How'd you manage that?"

"Actually," Ace said, "the credit goes to Mad Dog here. He made a few well placed phone calls to some military friends and we found out that Tailgunner Joe isn't all he claims to be."

"That S.O.B. never flew no combat missions like he says he did," Deagan said. "He was a damn intelligence officer."

"Obviously an oxymoron when it comes to McCarthy," Ace said. "Anyway, rather than face questions about why he purported to be something he's not, we persuaded him it would be in all our best interests to drop the whole matter of Doc's Russian-Ukrainian heritage."

"Ace deserves most of the credit," Deagan said, patting Assante on the back. "You shoulda seen him talking up a storm. If my fat's ever in the fire, he's one guy that I want on my side."

"True, but it's nice of you to finally admit it, old man," Ace said, polishing his nails on his lapel.

"Hey, don't get a swelled head about it now," Deagan said. "Remember how many times, if it wasn't for me, you'd still be flapping in the breeze."

"The only breeze I'm feeling right now is coming from your big mouth," Ace retorted.

"Boys, please," Penny said. "I know things are back to normal, but I do need to get to a phone and call in this story that I stayed up all night working on." She held up her hands framing imaginary headlines. "Nazi War Criminals in Government Germ Warfare Plot."

"Should be some story, all right," Deagan said. "One that we both got a lot closer than I woulda liked, too."

"I'll say," Penny added. Then, turning to Doc, "So did you ever find out if there was an antidote?"

Doc shook his head. "I'm afraid there is no antidote. If Cobb hadn't substituted the distilled water for the virus, you both would have perished. Hopefully, the knowledge of such a deadly microbe as a weapon perished with Dortchmann."

"Yeah, but what about Cobb?" Deagan asked. "What'll happen to him?"

"He's in good hands," a voice said.

They turned suddenly to see Killjoy walking up to them with a triumphant smirk on his face.

"What *you* doin' here?" Deagan demanded. He moved forward, his big fists clenched, but Doc held him back with a hand to the chest.

"Good to see you all looking so well," Killjoy said. "And as for what I'm doing here, I work here."

"Not for the FBI you don't," Ace said. "We checked."

"Yeah, but I'm still a G-man. I had to pass myself off as F.B.I. since we usually only operate outside the U.S. Too bad you didn't check with the new company on the block. We're calling it the CIA." Killjoy stood back and beamed. "That stands for the Central Intelligence Agency. Of course, like I said, it's fairly new, but we've got a lot of influence."

"We'll see how much influence you have when I blow the lid off this Nazi war criminal thing," Penny said. "You'll be lucky if they don't tar and feather you."

Killjoy smiled again, shaking his head. "Actually, the director's already made a call to your editor, as well as the stockholders of the corporation that owns your newspaper. The whole story's been killed. Deader than a doornail, or, should I say, someone who was injected with the Satan Plague?"

"What?" Penny said. "You can't do that."

"Oh, but we can," Killjoy said. He removed a small card from his wallet and handed it to her. It said that he had authority to take control of the situation in the interest of national security. "I'm thinking of having a couple thousand of these printed up," he said with a grin.

"National security," Penny said, reading from the card. "I wonder how many times that little catch phrase is going to be used to step all over the First Amendment." Then, turning to the others, "We aren't going to let him get away with this, are we?"

"Perhaps it would be better to let the matter drop," Ace said.

"Yeah, considering we don't want to be back in front of some damn committee," Deagan chimmed in, turning toward her and silently mouthing, "For Doc's sake."

Penny read his lips, then drew her own mouth into a tight line. "Oh you guys are a bunch of . . . Killjoys." She turned to sneer at the CIA man. "Anyway, I'll just get Dr. Cobb to back me up. He seemed ready to spill the beans."

Killjoy's smile tightened into a thin crease. He sighed and shook his head slightly.

"I'm afraid he won't be available. Ever." He held out a folded newspaper, his index finger tapping a page two, column three story as Penny took it.

"Leading government scientist commits suicide," she said, reading from the heading. "When did this happen?"

"Last night," Killjoy said. "Seems the good doctor just couldn't live with himself." He turned and said over his shoulder, "See ya around, Atlanski." He walked about thirty feet down the hall then turned, leaning his back against the wall, and looked back at them with a smirk.

Penny's mouth drew into an angry pout.

"He can't get away with this, can he?" she said.

Ace sighed. "I'm afraid he already has," he said. "With Dortchmann's body and all evidence of his work destroyed, and Cobb, our independent witness gone, they could easily deny their involvement in the entire matter."

"And him callin' Doc by his Russian name was a warning that he could leak that bit of info should we press it," Deagan whispered.

They looked to Doc who had stood there stoically throughout the entire conversation.

"Perhaps, given the climate of the country," Doc said, "and with the current hysteria sweeping away reason, we should put the matter to rest. Let's just hope that we've seen the last of the Satan Plague also." He looked at each of them, and let a rare smile creep across his features. "Why don't we do some sight seeing since we're here in the capitol." Reaching down he took Penny's hand, and they began a slow walk down the expansive hallway.

"So are you ready to stipulate that your precious army, led by your hero, General Dwight D. Eisenhower, really dropped the ball in allowing that Nazi to escape," Assante said.

"Ha!" Deagan laughed. "It was your buddy old Harry S. Truman that probably authorized the whole thing."

Doc and Penny simultaneously glanced over their shoulders at the bickering pair.

"Their mutual admiration society sure didn't last long, did it?" Penny said. "Now that the adventure is over, it's back to business as usual."

Doc smiled.

As they rounded a corner they passed Killjoy who was leaning forward cupping his hands around a cigarette.

"Hey, Ace," Deagan said, "did I tell you about the dream I had about being injected with that stuff?"

Ace shook his head.

"Well," Mad Dog continued, "I was alone in this room, see, and all of a sudden this guy came at me with a syringe, see? Ya following me?"

Ace grinned. "All the way, partner. What did you do then?"

"This!" Deagan's big right hand shot out in a quick hooking motion and collided with Killjoy's chin, sending the man down in a heap. As Penny and Doc walked by they saw the G-Man's eyes rolled back in his head.

"*Now*," Deagan said, turning around to face them with a sly smile, "it's back to business as usual."

Penny laughed. Assante smiled.

"Yes, Thomas," Doc said. "I believe it is."

THE END

ACKNOWLEDGMENTS

DOC ATLAS LIVES . . . and there are so many people I would like to thank, most specifically Ray Lovato, my best friend since we both ran up opposite sides of a dirt hill back when we were five and six. Our childhood was filled with imaginative adventures. Heroes who were larger than life, who lurked in the darkness, keeping the mean streets safe by their own methods, and offering some of the most unique array of characters ever created. The genesis of Doc Atlas and his companions came about as a pastiche of the heroes of the old pulps and manifested with several novella-length stories and a full blown novel, *Melody of Vengeance*. The stories appeared in small press magazines, most notably Gary Lovisi's *Gryphon Doubles* and especially *Double Danger Tales*, published by Tom and Ginger Johnson, who more than anyone helped keep the modern pulps alive in their fine small press magazines. I always dreamed that the Doc Atlas stories would have accompanying illustrations, just like the old pulps, and my heart-felt thanks also goes to the great Geof Darrow, fantastic Tim Farote, and marvelous Matthew Lovato, the wonderful artists who helped bring the characters to life. I would also like to thank Julie Hyzy, who always offered great critiques and suggestions on how to keep Doc Atlas

on the cutting edge. And I'm very happy that Ray shares co-author credit for this omnibus. It is as it should be, because his contributions to the plots, characters, and writing brought me back to those halcyon days of our youth when we proved a very redoubtable pair thwarting all the other kids in the neighborhood with our cleverness and creativity. Thanks, brother.

I have often been asked at sci-fi and pulp conventions if I plan to write another Doc Atlas novel, and I always say I haven't ruled it out. The characters from these stories are near and dear to my heart. Ray and I envisioned doing something a bit different from the original pulps by writing these with a "historical retrospective." Recreating the pulp era was fun, especially with the benefit of twenty-twenty hindsight as far as historical matters and events of that time period. It was an advantage that our predecessors in the golden age didn't have. Recreating the pulp era was fun, especially with the benefit of twenty-twenty hindsight as far as historical matters and events of that time period. It was an advantage that our predecessors in the golden age didn't have. So I hope you have enjoyed this journey back into the past. And remember . . .

Doc Atlas will return in . . .

Made in the USA
Charleston, SC
14 November 2011